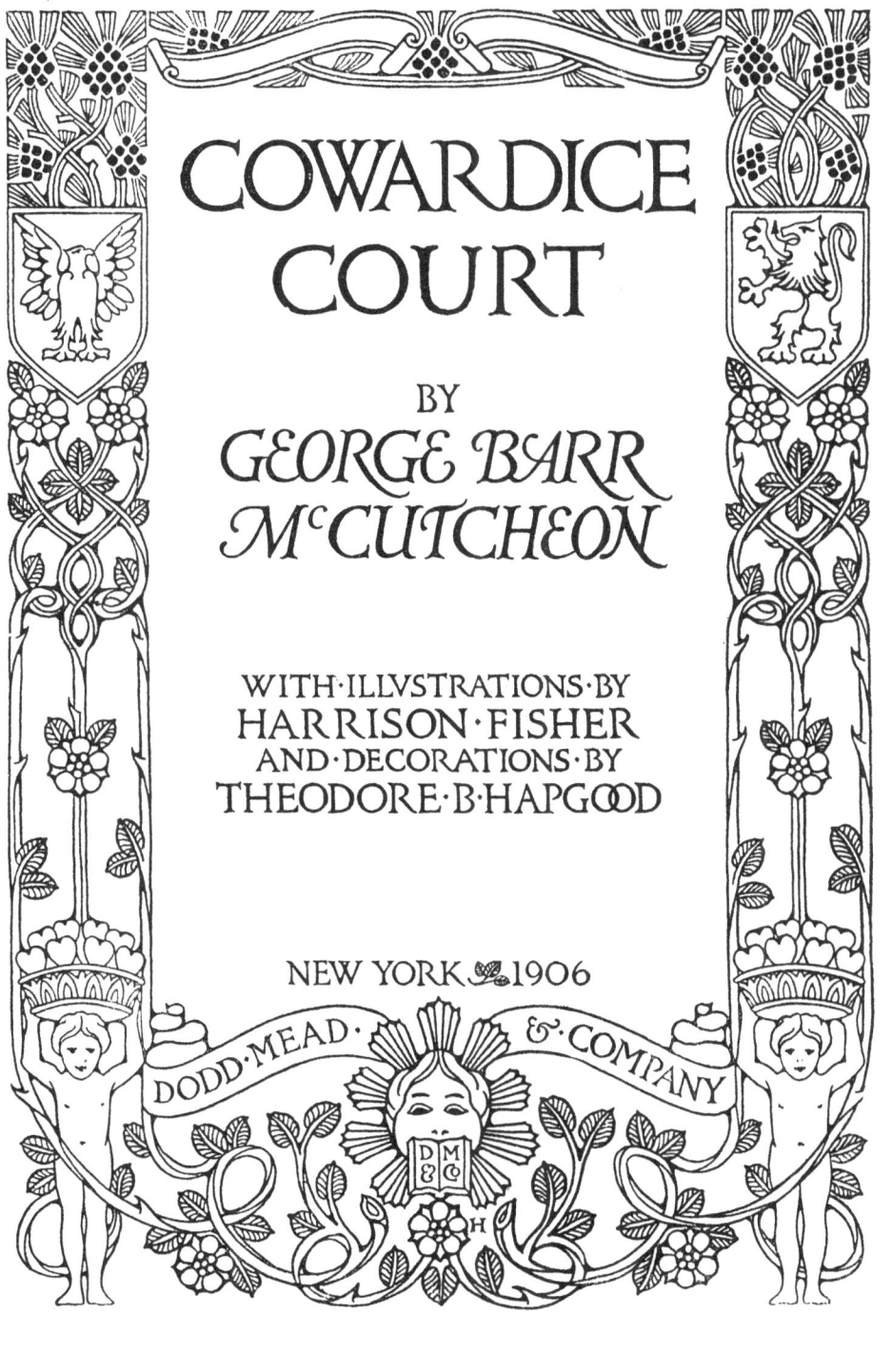

COWARDICE COURT

BY

GEORGE BARR McCUTCHEON

WITH·ILLVSTRATIONS·BY
HARRISON·FISHER
AND·DECORATIONS·BY
THEODORE·B·HAPGOOD

NEW YORK 1906

DODD·MEAD· & ·COMPANY

CONTENTS

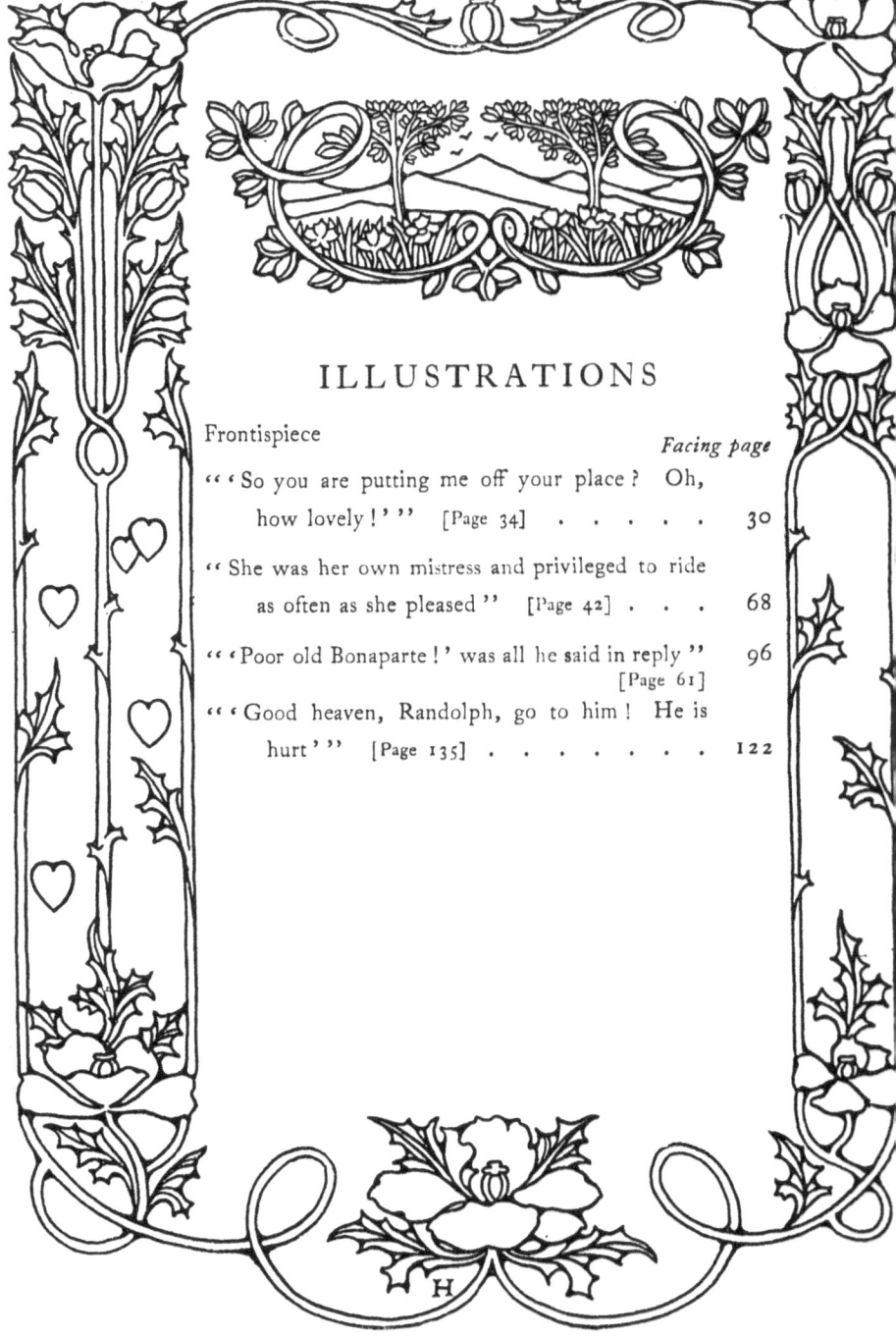

ILLUSTRATIONS

H

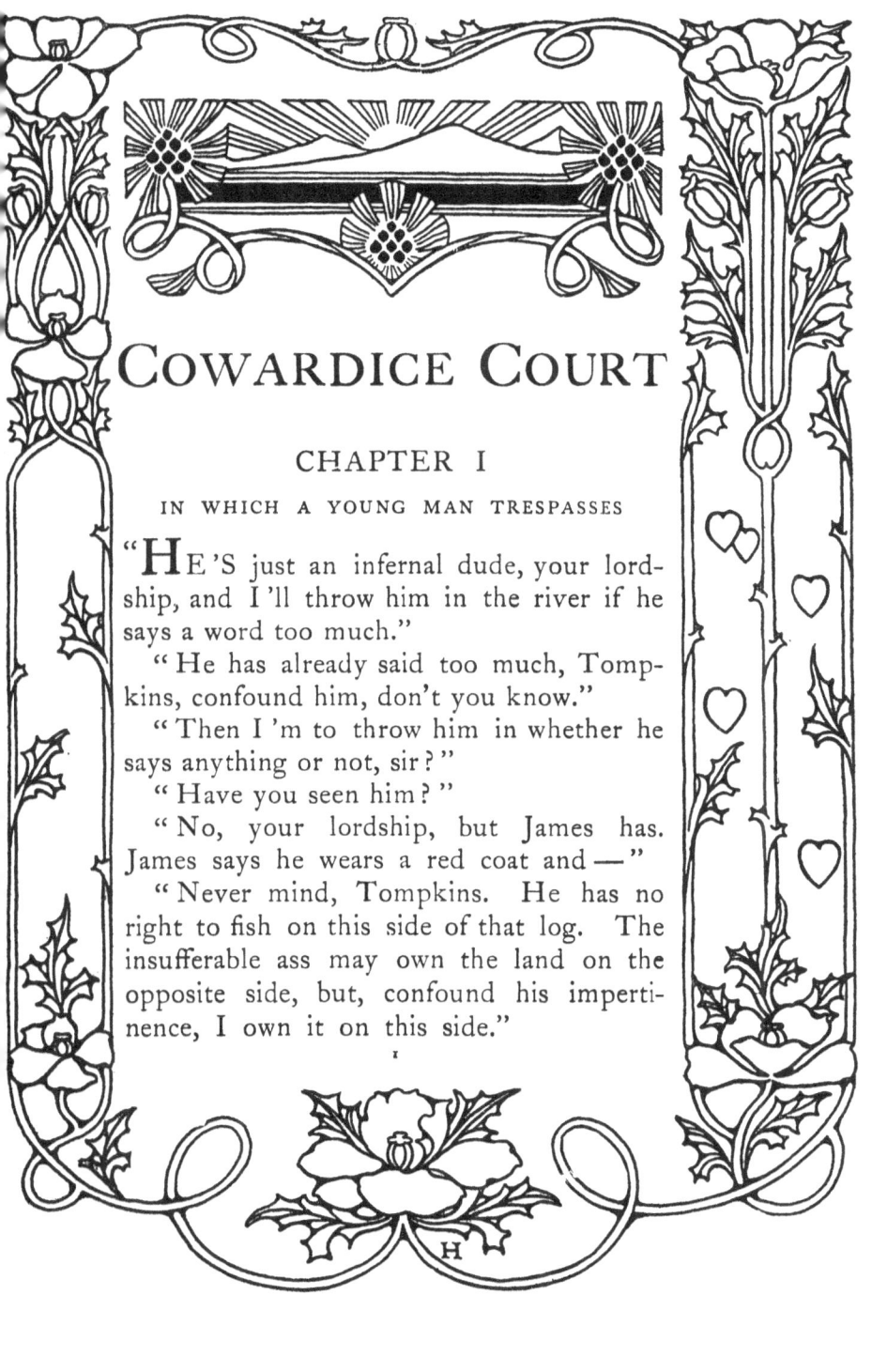

COWARDICE COURT

CHAPTER I

IN WHICH A YOUNG MAN TRESPASSES

"HE'S just an infernal dude, your lordship, and I'll throw him in the river if he says a word too much."

"He has already said too much, Tompkins, confound him, don't you know."

"Then I'm to throw him in whether he says anything or not, sir?"

"Have you seen him?"

"No, your lordship, but James has. James says he wears a red coat and—"

"Never mind, Tompkins. He has no right to fish on this side of that log. The insufferable ass may own the land on the opposite side, but, confound his impertinence, I own it on this side."

1

H

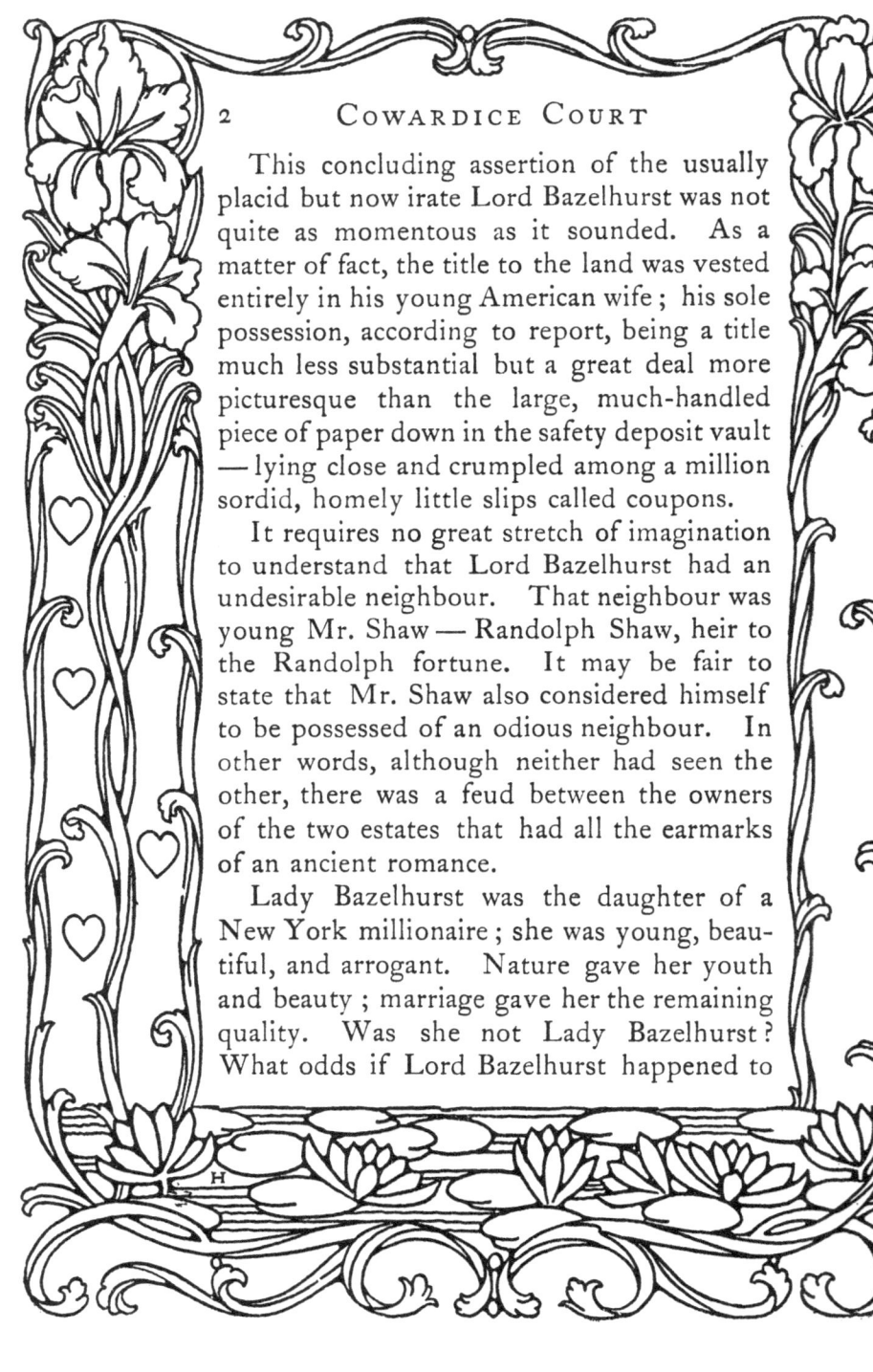

This concluding assertion of the usually placid but now irate Lord Bazelhurst was not quite as momentous as it sounded. As a matter of fact, the title to the land was vested entirely in his young American wife; his sole possession, according to report, being a title much less substantial but a great deal more picturesque than the large, much-handled piece of paper down in the safety deposit vault — lying close and crumpled among a million sordid, homely little slips called coupons.

It requires no great stretch of imagination to understand that Lord Bazelhurst had an undesirable neighbour. That neighbour was young Mr. Shaw — Randolph Shaw, heir to the Randolph fortune. It may be fair to state that Mr. Shaw also considered himself to be possessed of an odious neighbour. In other words, although neither had seen the other, there was a feud between the owners of the two estates that had all the earmarks of an ancient romance.

Lady Bazelhurst was the daughter of a New York millionaire; she was young, beautiful, and arrogant. Nature gave her youth and beauty; marriage gave her the remaining quality. Was she not Lady Bazelhurst? What odds if Lord Bazelhurst happened to

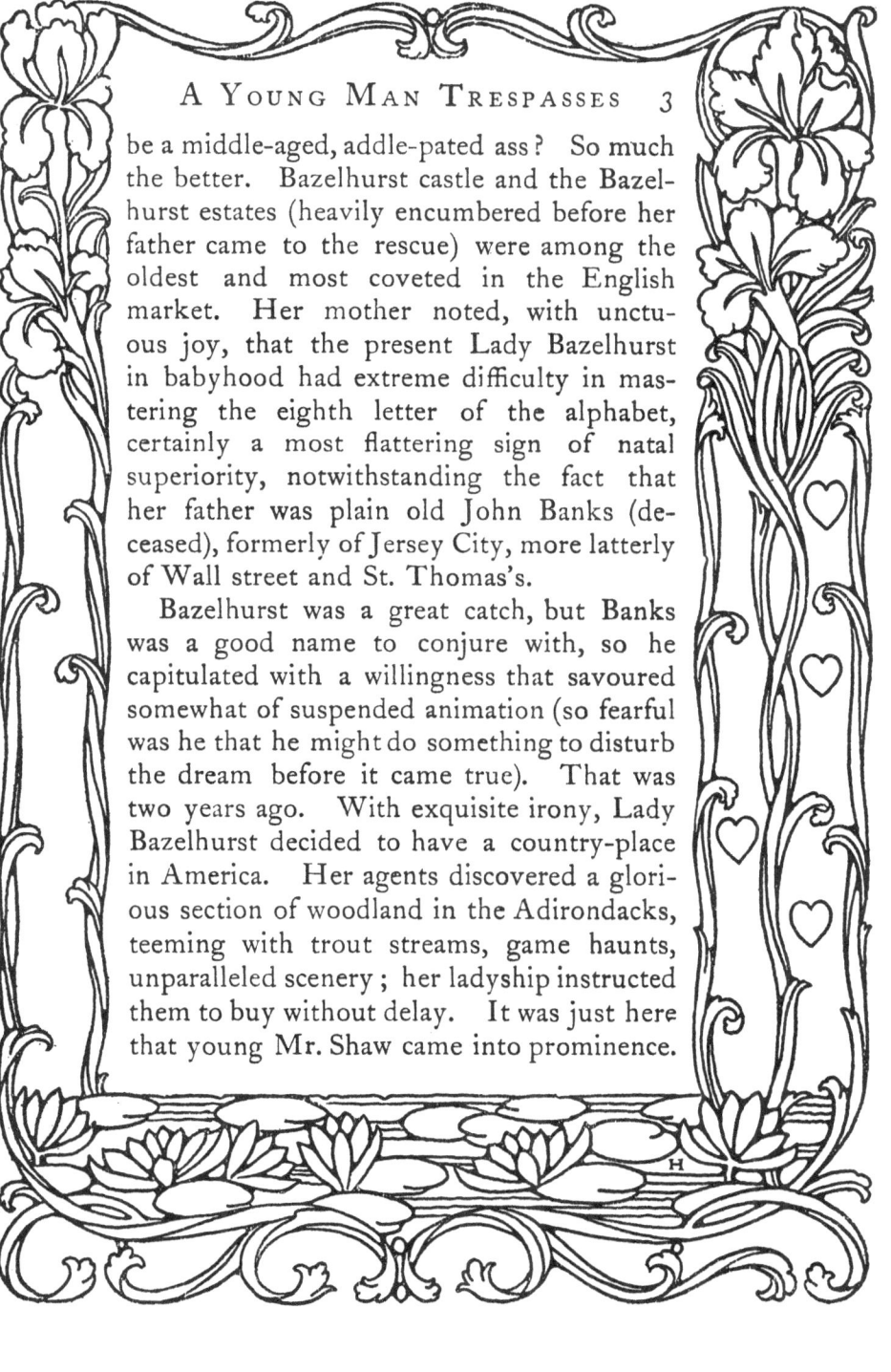

be a middle-aged, addle-pated ass? So much the better. Bazelhurst castle and the Bazelhurst estates (heavily encumbered before her father came to the rescue) were among the oldest and most coveted in the English market. Her mother noted, with unctuous joy, that the present Lady Bazelhurst in babyhood had extreme difficulty in mastering the eighth letter of the alphabet, certainly a most flattering sign of natal superiority, notwithstanding the fact that her father was plain old John Banks (deceased), formerly of Jersey City, more latterly of Wall street and St. Thomas's.

Bazelhurst was a great catch, but Banks was a good name to conjure with, so he capitulated with a willingness that savoured somewhat of suspended animation (so fearful was he that he might do something to disturb the dream before it came true). That was two years ago. With exquisite irony, Lady Bazelhurst decided to have a country-place in America. Her agents discovered a glorious section of woodland in the Adirondacks, teeming with trout streams, game haunts, unparalleled scenery; her ladyship instructed them to buy without delay. It was just here that young Mr. Shaw came into prominence.

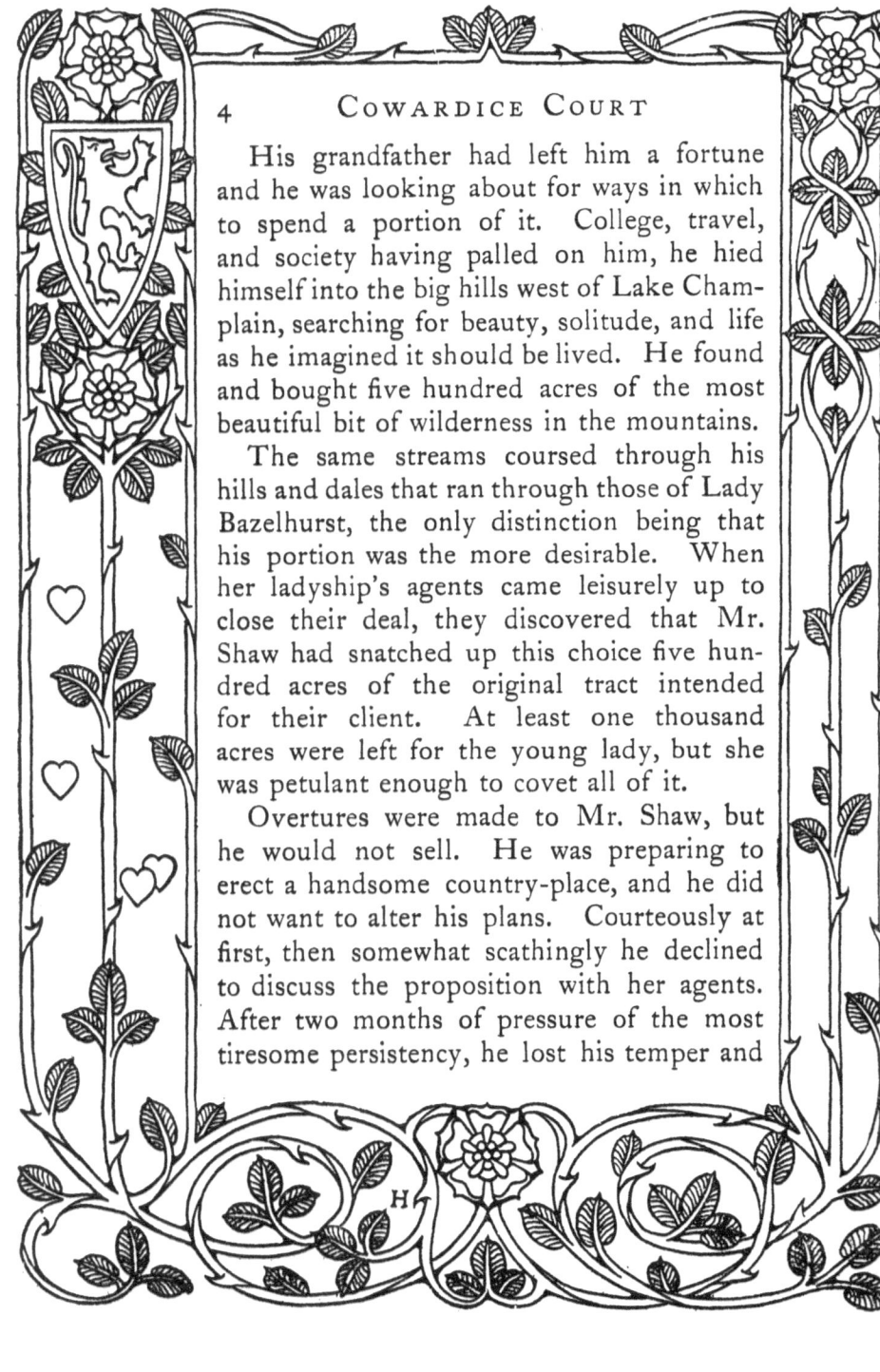

His grandfather had left him a fortune and he was looking about for ways in which to spend a portion of it. College, travel, and society having palled on him, he hied himself into the big hills west of Lake Champlain, searching for beauty, solitude, and life as he imagined it should be lived. He found and bought five hundred acres of the most beautiful bit of wilderness in the mountains.

The same streams coursed through his hills and dales that ran through those of Lady Bazelhurst, the only distinction being that his portion was the more desirable. When her ladyship's agents came leisurely up to close their deal, they discovered that Mr. Shaw had snatched up this choice five hundred acres of the original tract intended for their client. At least one thousand acres were left for the young lady, but she was petulant enough to covet all of it.

Overtures were made to Mr. Shaw, but he would not sell. He was preparing to erect a handsome country-place, and he did not want to alter his plans. Courteously at first, then somewhat scathingly he declined to discuss the proposition with her agents. After two months of pressure of the most tiresome persistency, he lost his temper and

sent a message to his inquisitors that suddenly terminated all negotiations. Afterwards, when he learned that their client was a
lady, he wrote a conditional note of apology,
but, if he expected a response, he was disappointed. A year went by, and now, with the
beginning of this narrative, two newly com-
pleted country homes glowered at each other
from separate hillsides, one envious and
spiteful, the other defiant and a bit satirical.

Bazelhurst Villa looks across the valley
and sees Shaw's Cottage commanding the
most beautiful view in the hills; the very
eaves of her ladyship's house seem to have
wrinkled into a constant scowl of annoyance.
Shaw's long, low cottage seems to smile back
with tantalizing security, serene in its more
lofty altitude, in its more gorgeous raiment
of nature. The brooks laugh with the glit-
ter of trout, the trees chuckle with the flight
of birds, the hillsides frolic in their abun-
dance of game, but the acres are growling like
dogs of war. "Love thy neighbour as thy-
self" is not printed on the boards that line
the borders of the two estates. In bold
black letters the sign-boards laconically say:
"No trespassing on these grounds. Keep
off!"

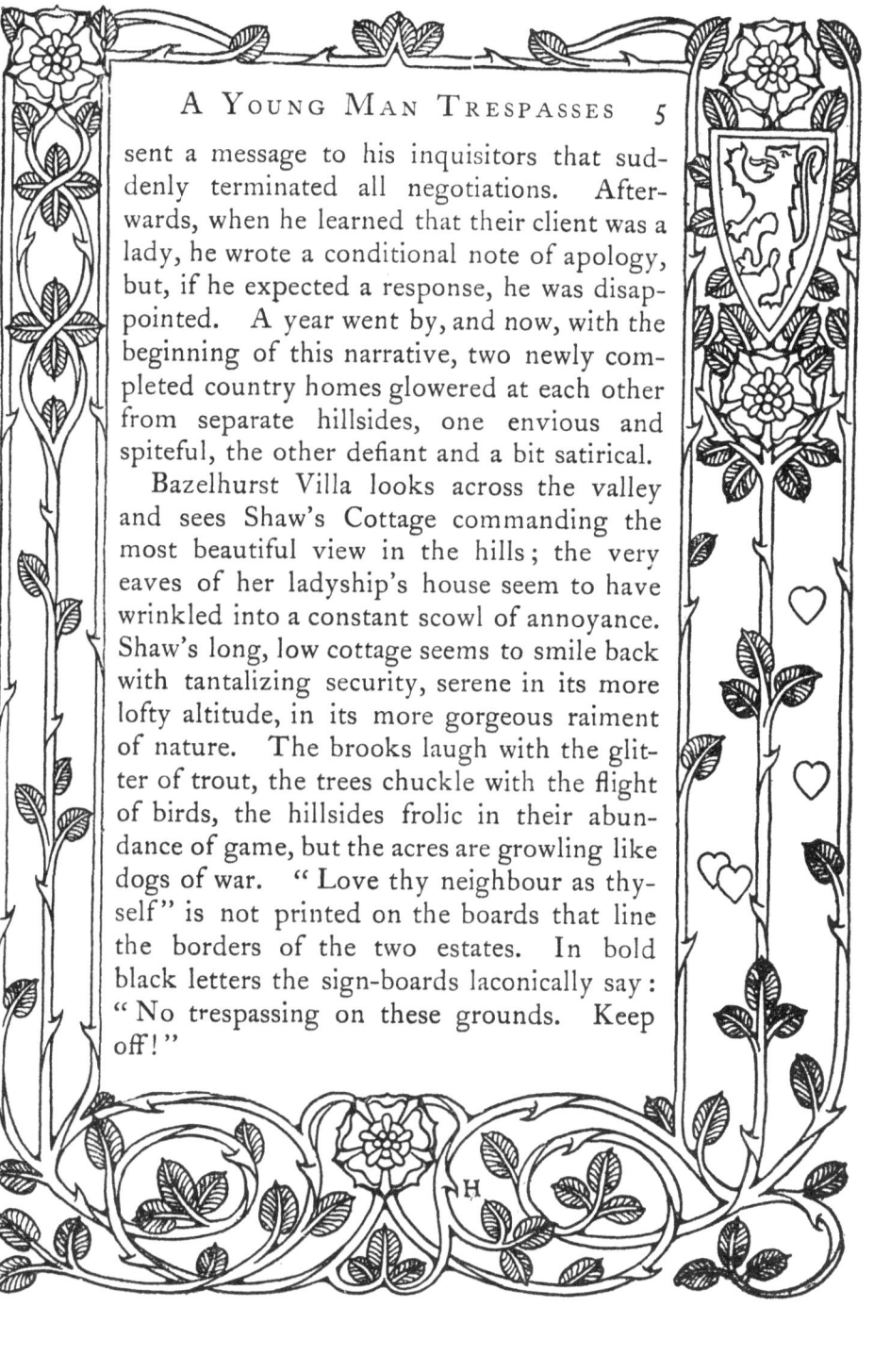

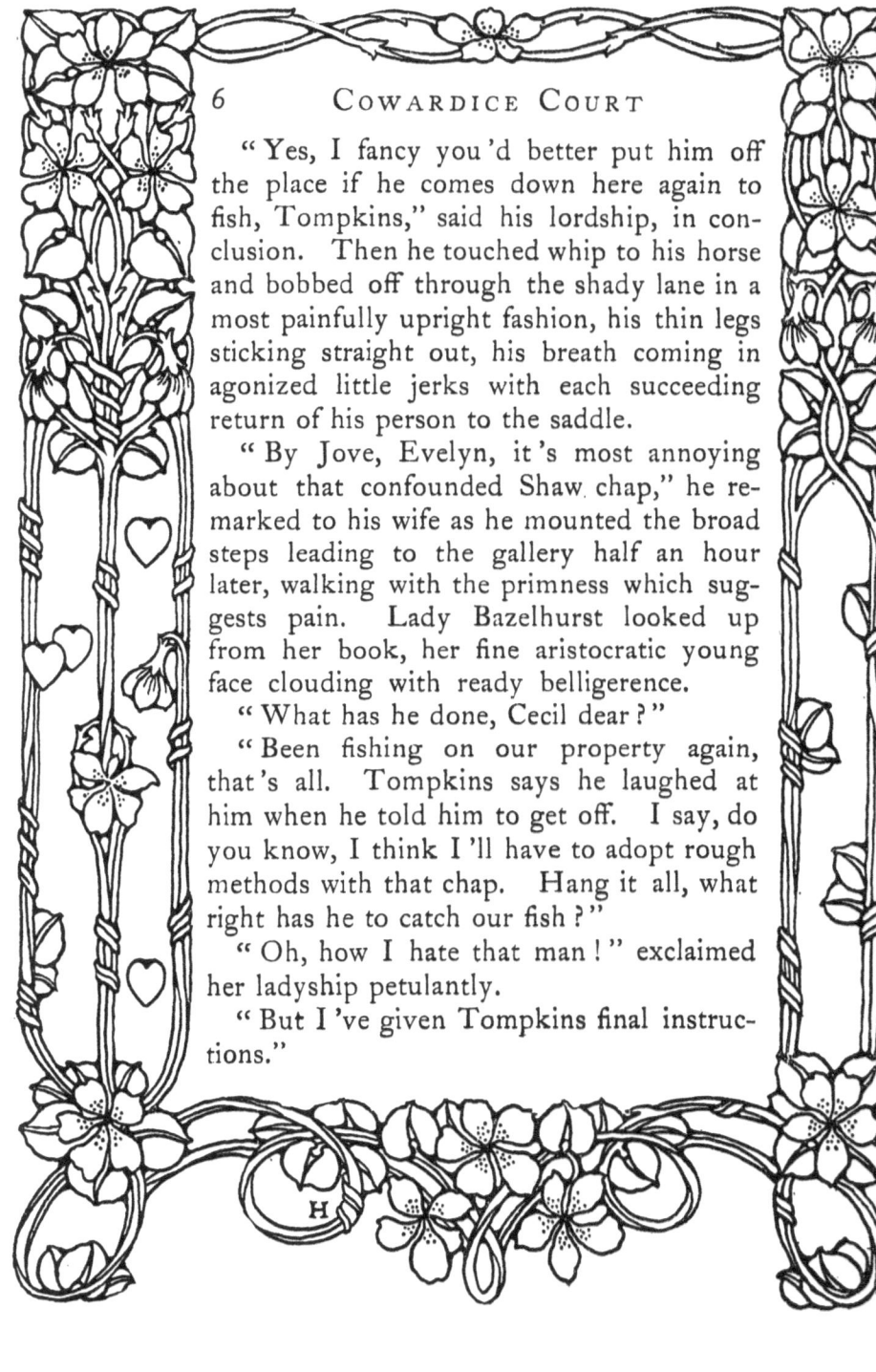

"Yes, I fancy you'd better put him off the place if he comes down here again to fish, Tompkins," said his lordship, in conclusion. Then he touched whip to his horse and bobbed off through the shady lane in a most painfully upright fashion, his thin legs sticking straight out, his breath coming in agonized little jerks with each succeeding return of his person to the saddle.

"By Jove, Evelyn, it's most annoying about that confounded Shaw chap," he remarked to his wife as he mounted the broad steps leading to the gallery half an hour later, walking with the primness which suggests pain. Lady Bazelhurst looked up from her book, her fine aristocratic young face clouding with ready belligerence.

"What has he done, Cecil dear?"

"Been fishing on our property again, that's all. Tompkins says he laughed at him when he told him to get off. I say, do you know, I think I'll have to adopt rough methods with that chap. Hang it all, what right has he to catch our fish?"

"Oh, how I hate that man!" exclaimed her ladyship petulantly.

"But I've given Tompkins final instructions."

"And what are they?"

"To throw him in the river next time."

"Oh, if he only *could!*" rapturously.

"*Could?* My dear, Tompkins is an American. He can handle these chaps in their own way. At any rate, I told Tompkins if his nerve failed him at the last minute to come and notify me. *I'll* attend to this confounded popinjay!"

"Good for you, Cecil!" called out another young woman from the broad hammock in which she had been dawdling with half-alert ears through the foregoing conversation. "Spoken like a true Briton. What is this popinjay like?"

"Hullo, sister. Hang it all, what's he like? He's like an ass, that's all. I've never seen him, but if I'm ever called upon to — but you don't care to listen to details. You remember the big log that lies out in the river up at the bend? Well, it marks the property line. One half of its stump belongs to the Shaw man, the other half to m— to us, Evelyn. He shan't fish below that log — no, sir!" His lordship glared fiercely through his monocle in the direction of the far-away log, his watery blue eyes blinking as malevolently as possible, his

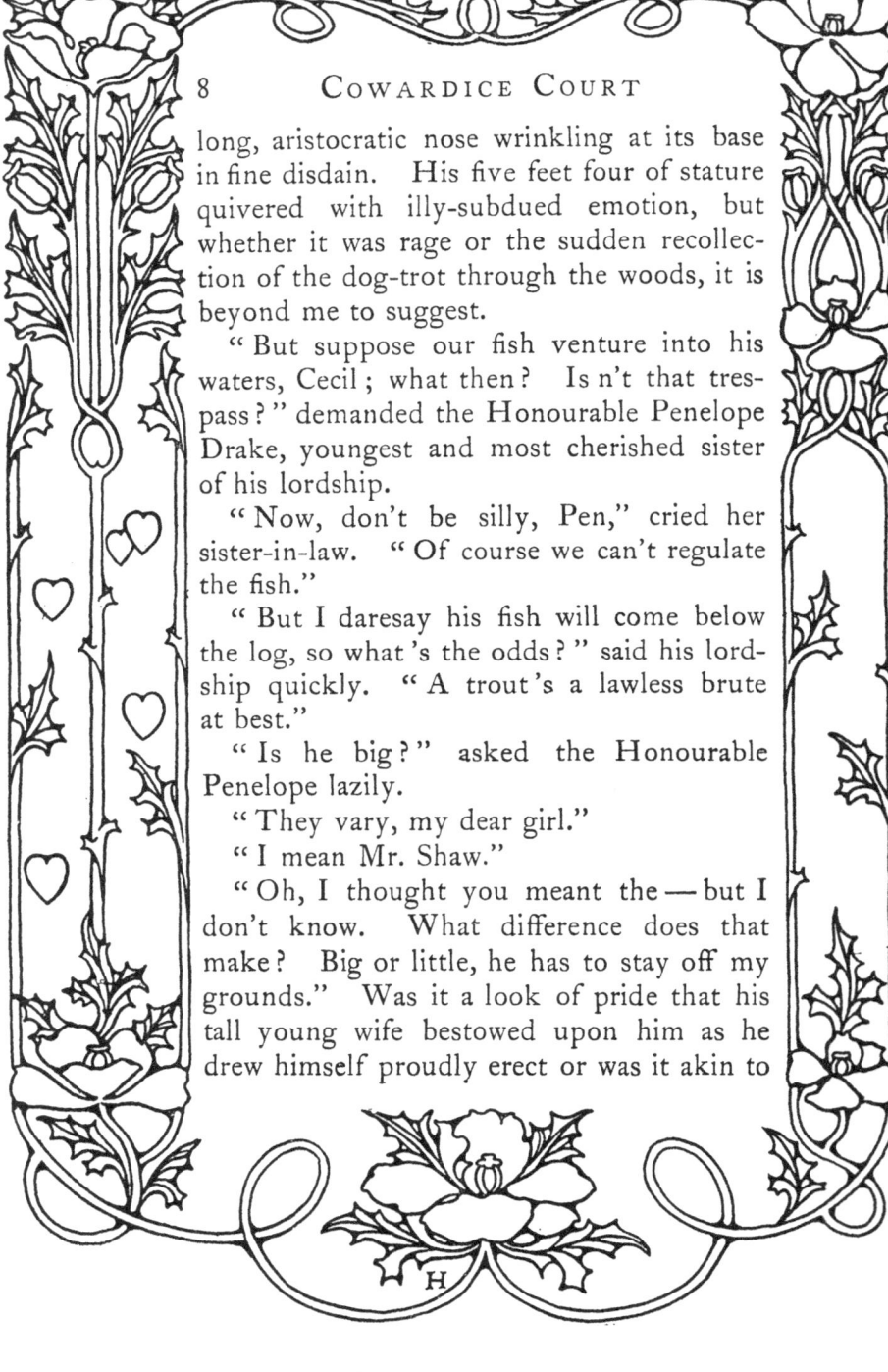

long, aristocratic nose wrinkling at its base in fine disdain. His five feet four of stature quivered with illy-subdued emotion, but whether it was rage or the sudden recollection of the dog-trot through the woods, it is beyond me to suggest.

"But suppose our fish venture into his waters, Cecil; what then? Isn't that trespass?" demanded the Honourable Penelope Drake, youngest and most cherished sister of his lordship.

"Now, don't be silly, Pen," cried her sister-in-law. "Of course we can't regulate the fish."

"But I daresay his fish will come below the log, so what's the odds?" said his lordship quickly. "A trout's a lawless brute at best."

"Is he big?" asked the Honourable Penelope lazily.

"They vary, my dear girl."

"I mean Mr. Shaw."

"Oh, I thought you meant the — but I don't know. What difference does that make? Big or little, he has to stay off my grounds." Was it a look of pride that his tall young wife bestowed upon him as he drew himself proudly erect or was it akin to

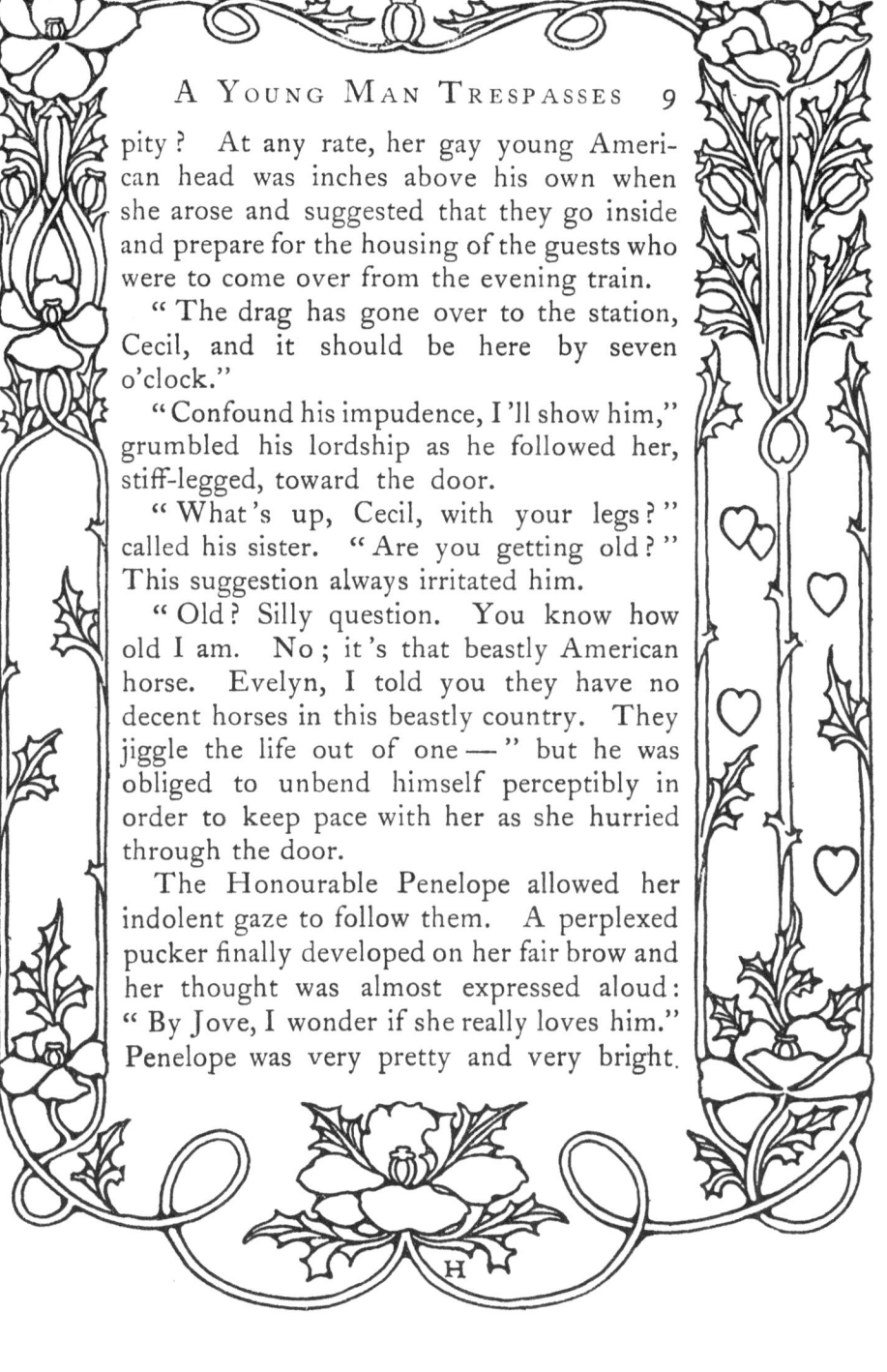

pity? At any rate, her gay young American head was inches above his own when she arose and suggested that they go inside and prepare for the housing of the guests who were to come over from the evening train.

"The drag has gone over to the station, Cecil, and it should be here by seven o'clock."

"Confound his impudence, I'll show him," grumbled his lordship as he followed her, stiff-legged, toward the door.

"What's up, Cecil, with your legs?" called his sister. "Are you getting old?" This suggestion always irritated him.

"Old? Silly question. You know how old I am. No; it's that beastly American horse. Evelyn, I told you they have no decent horses in this beastly country. They jiggle the life out of one—" but he was obliged to unbend himself perceptibly in order to keep pace with her as she hurried through the door.

The Honourable Penelope allowed her indolent gaze to follow them. A perplexed pucker finally developed on her fair brow and her thought was almost expressed aloud: "By Jove, I wonder if she really loves him." Penelope was very pretty and very bright.

H

She was visiting America for the first time and she was learning rapidly. " Cecil's a good sort, you know, even —" but she was loyal enough to send her thoughts into other channels.

Nightfall brought half a dozen guests to Bazelhurst Villa. They were fashionable to the point where ennui is the chief characteristic, and they came only for bridge and sleep. There was a duke among them and also a French count, besides the bored New Yorkers; they wanted brandy and soda as soon as they got into the house, and they went to bed early because it was so much easier to sleep lying down than sitting up.

All were up by noon the next day, more bored than ever, fondly praying that nothing might happen before bedtime. The duke was making desultory love to Mrs. De Peyton and Mrs. De Peyton was leading him aimlessly toward the shadier and more secluded nooks in the park surrounding the Villa. Penelope, fresh and full of the purpose of life, was off alone for a long stroll. By this means she avoided the attentions of the duke, who wanted to marry her; those of the count who also said he wanted to marry her but could n't because his wife would not consent; those of one New Yorker, who liked her because she was English; and the pallid chatter of the women who bored her with their conjugal cynicisms.

"What the deuce is this coming down the road?" queried the duke, returning from the secluded nook at luncheon time.

"Some one has been hurt," exclaimed his companion. Others were looking down the leafy road from the gallery.

"By Jove, it's Penelope, don't you know," ejaculated the duke, dropping his monocle and blinking his eye as if to rest it for the time being.

"But she's not hurt. She's helping to support one of those men."

"Hey!" shouted his lordship from the gallery, as Penelope and two dilapidated male companions abruptly started to cut across the park in the direction of the stables. "What's up?" Penelope waved her hand aimlessly, but did not change her course. Whereupon the entire house party sallied forth in more or less trepidation to intercept the strange party.

"Who are these men?" demanded Lady Bazelhurst, as they came up to the fast-breathing young Englishwoman.

"Don't bother me, please. We must get

him to bed at once. He 'll have pneumonia," replied Penelope.

Both men were dripping wet and the one in the middle limped painfully, probably because both eyes were swollen tight and his nose was bleeding. Penelope's face was beaming with excitement and interest.

"Who are you?" demanded his lordship, planting himself in front of the shivering twain.

"Tompkins," murmured the blind one feebly, tears starting from the blue slits and rolling down his cheeks.

"James, sir," answered the other, touching his damp forelock.

"Are they drunk?" asked Mrs. De Peyton, with fresh enthusiasm.

"No, they are not, poor fellows," cried Penelope. "They have taken nothing but water."

"By Jove, deuced clever that," drawled the duke. "Eh?" to the New Yorker.

"Deuced," from the Knickerbocker.

"Well, well, what 's it all about?" demanded Bazelhurst.

"Mr. Shaw, sir," said James.

"Good Lord, could n't you rescue him?" in horror.

"He rescued us, sir," mumbled Tompkins.

"You mean——"

"He throwed us in and then had to jump in and pull us out, sir. Beggin' your pardon, sir, but *damn* him!"

"And you did n't throw him in, after all? By Jove, extraordinary!"

"Do you mean to tell us that he threw you great hulking creatures into the river? Single-handed?" cried Lady Bazelhurst, aghast.

"He did, Evelyn," inserted Penelope. "I met them coming home, and poor Tompkins was out of his senses. I don't know how it happened, but——"

"It was this way, your ladyship," put in James, the groom. "Tompkins and me could see him from the point there, sir, afishin' below the log. So we says to each other 'Come on,' and up we went to where he was afishin'. Tompkins, bein' the game warden, says he to him 'Hi there!' He was plainly on our property, sir, afishin' from a boat for bass, sir. 'Hello, boys,' says he back to us. 'Get off our land,' says Tompkins. 'I am,' says he; 'it's water out here where I am.' Then——"

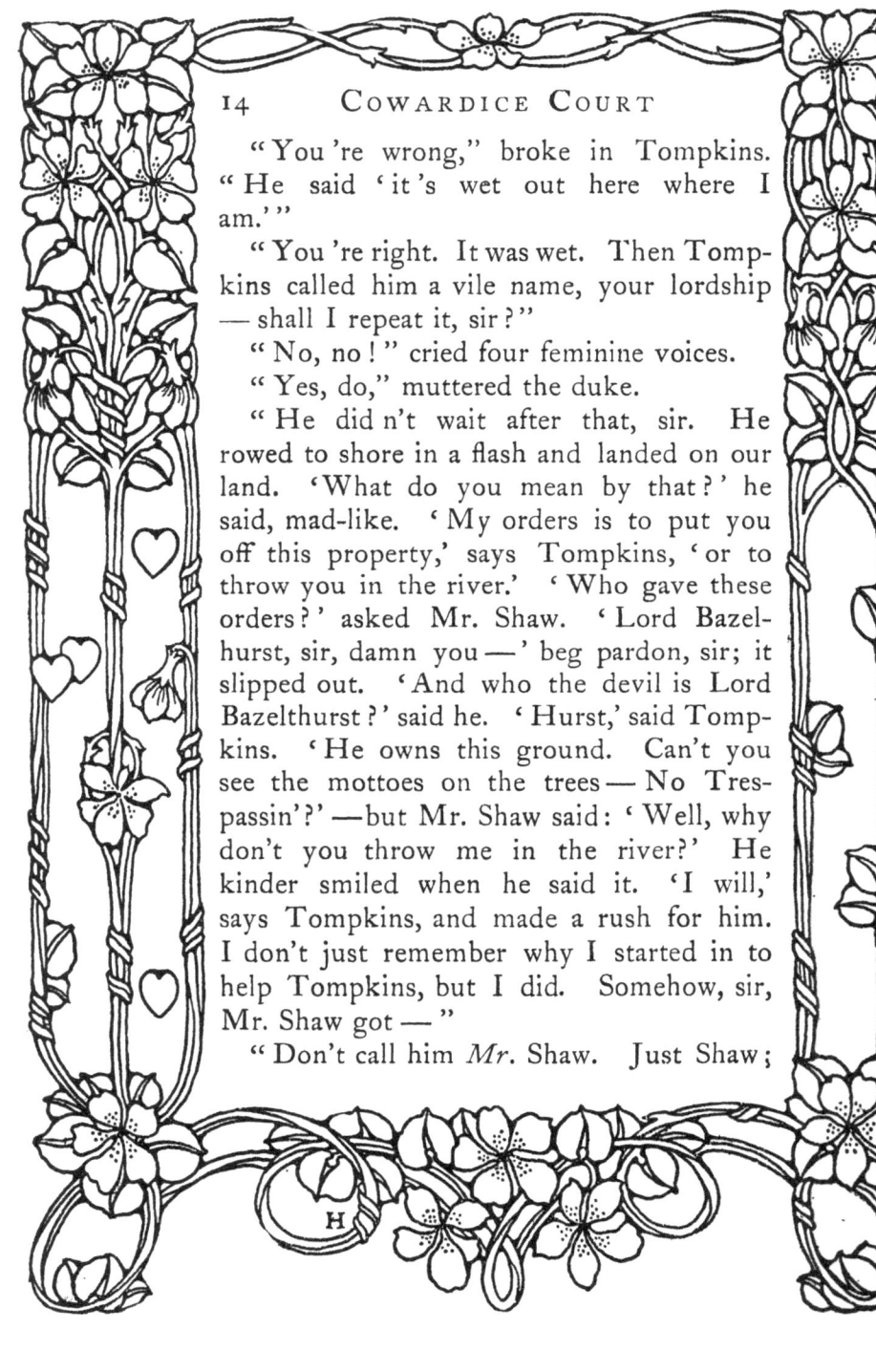

"You're wrong," broke in Tompkins.
"He said 'it's wet out here where I
am.'"

"You're right. It was wet. Then Tompkins called him a vile name, your lordship
— shall I repeat it, sir?"

"No, no!" cried four feminine voices.

"Yes, do," muttered the duke.

"He didn't wait after that, sir. He
rowed to shore in a flash and landed on our
land. 'What do you mean by that?' he
said, mad-like. 'My orders is to put you
off this property,' says Tompkins, 'or to
throw you in the river.' 'Who gave these
orders?' asked Mr. Shaw. 'Lord Bazelhurst, sir, damn you —' beg pardon, sir; it
slipped out. 'And who the devil is Lord
Bazelthurst?' said he. 'Hurst,' said Tompkins. 'He owns this ground. Can't you
see the mottoes on the trees — No Tres-
passin'?' —but Mr. Shaw said: 'Well, why
don't you throw me in the river?' He
kinder smiled when he said it. 'I will,'
says Tompkins, and made a rush for him.
I don't just remember why I started in to
help Tompkins, but I did. Somehow, sir,
Mr. Shaw got — "

"Don't call him *Mr.* Shaw. Just Shaw;

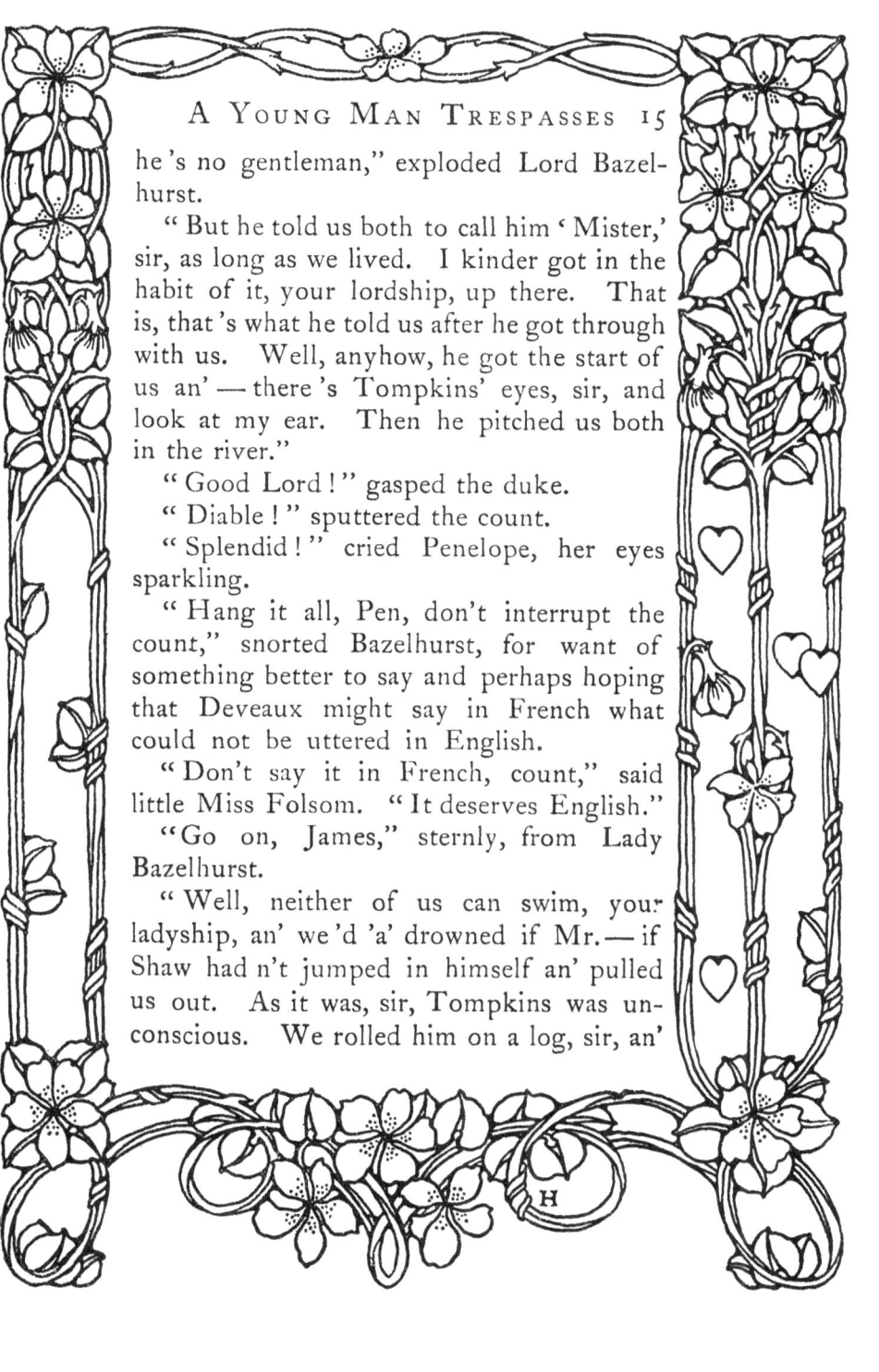

he's no gentleman," exploded Lord Bazelhurst.

"But he told us both to call him 'Mister,'
sir, as long as we lived. I kinder got in the
habit of it, your lordship, up there. That
is, that's what he told us after he got through
with us. Well, anyhow, he got the start of
us an' — there's Tompkins' eyes, sir, and
look at my ear. Then he pitched us both
in the river."

"Good Lord!" gasped the duke.

"Diable!" sputtered the count.

"Splendid!" cried Penelope, her eyes
sparkling.

"Hang it all, Pen, don't interrupt the
count," snorted Bazelhurst, for want of
something better to say and perhaps hoping
that Deveaux might say in French what
could not be uttered in English.

"Don't say it in French, count," said
little Miss Folsom. "It deserves English."

"Go on, James," sternly, from Lady
Bazelhurst.

"Well, neither of us can swim, your
ladyship, an' we'd 'a' drowned if Mr. — if
Shaw had n't jumped in himself an' pulled
us out. As it was, sir, Tompkins was unconscious. We rolled him on a log, sir, an'

got a keg of water out of him.   Then Mr.
— er — Shaw told us to go 'ome and get in
bed, sir."

"He sent a message to you, sir," added
Tompkins, shivering mightily.

"Well, I 'll have one for him, never fear,"
said his lordship, glancing about bravely.
"I won't permit any man to assault my servants and brutally maltreat them.   No, sir!
He shall hear from me — or my attorney."

"He told us to tell you, sir, that if he
ever caught anybody from this place on his
land he 'd serve him worse than he did us,"
said Tompkins.

"He says, 'I don't want no Bazelhursts
on my place,'" added James in finality.

"Go to bed, both of you!" roared his
lordship.

"Very good, sir," in unison.

"They can get to bed without your help,
I daresay, Pen," added his lordship causti-
cally, as she started away with them.   Penelope with a rare blush and — well, one party
went to luncheon while the other went to
bed.

"I should like to see this terrible Mr.
Shaw," observed Penelope at table.   "He 's
a sort of Jack-the-Giant-Killer, I fancy."

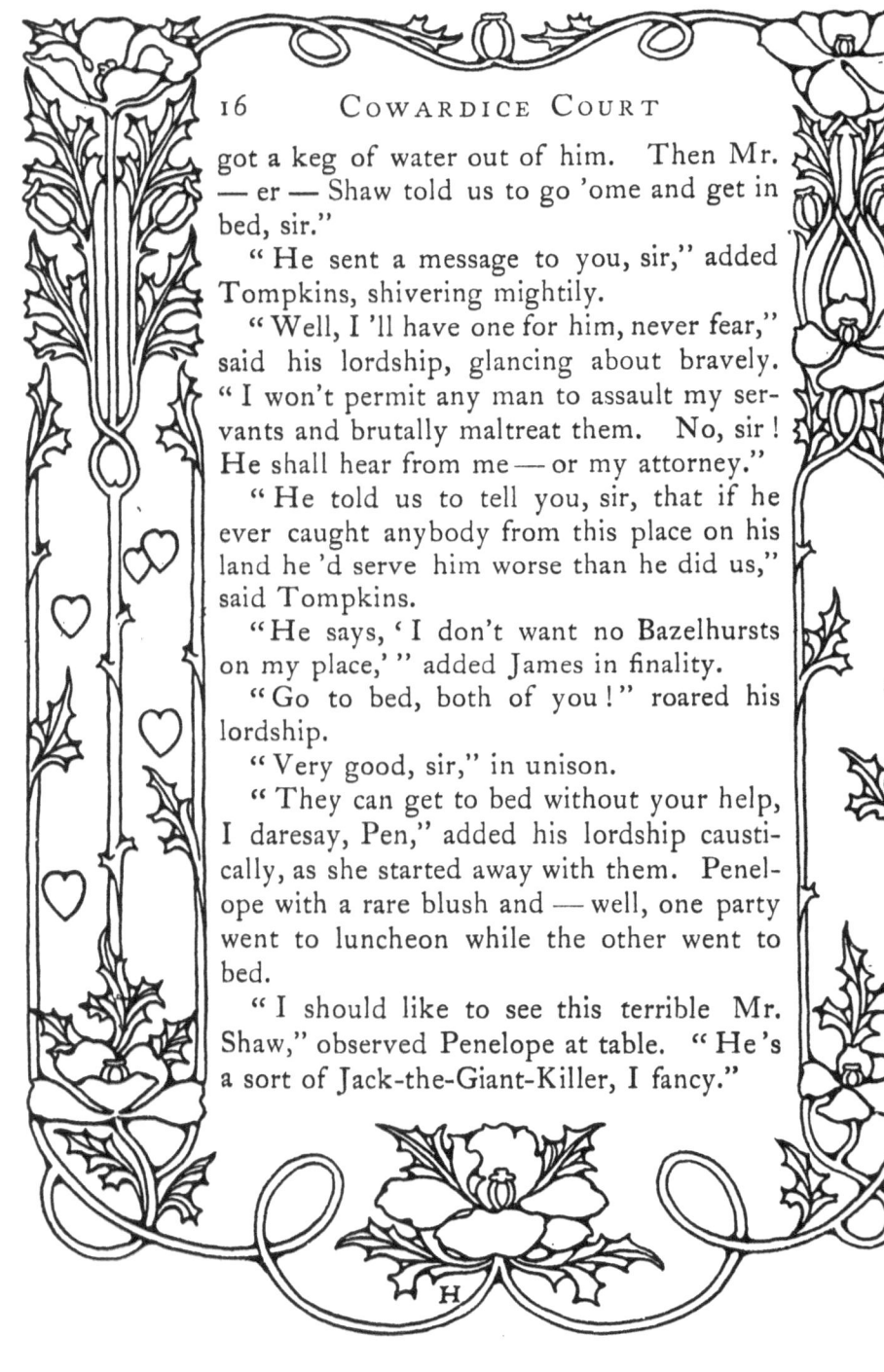

H

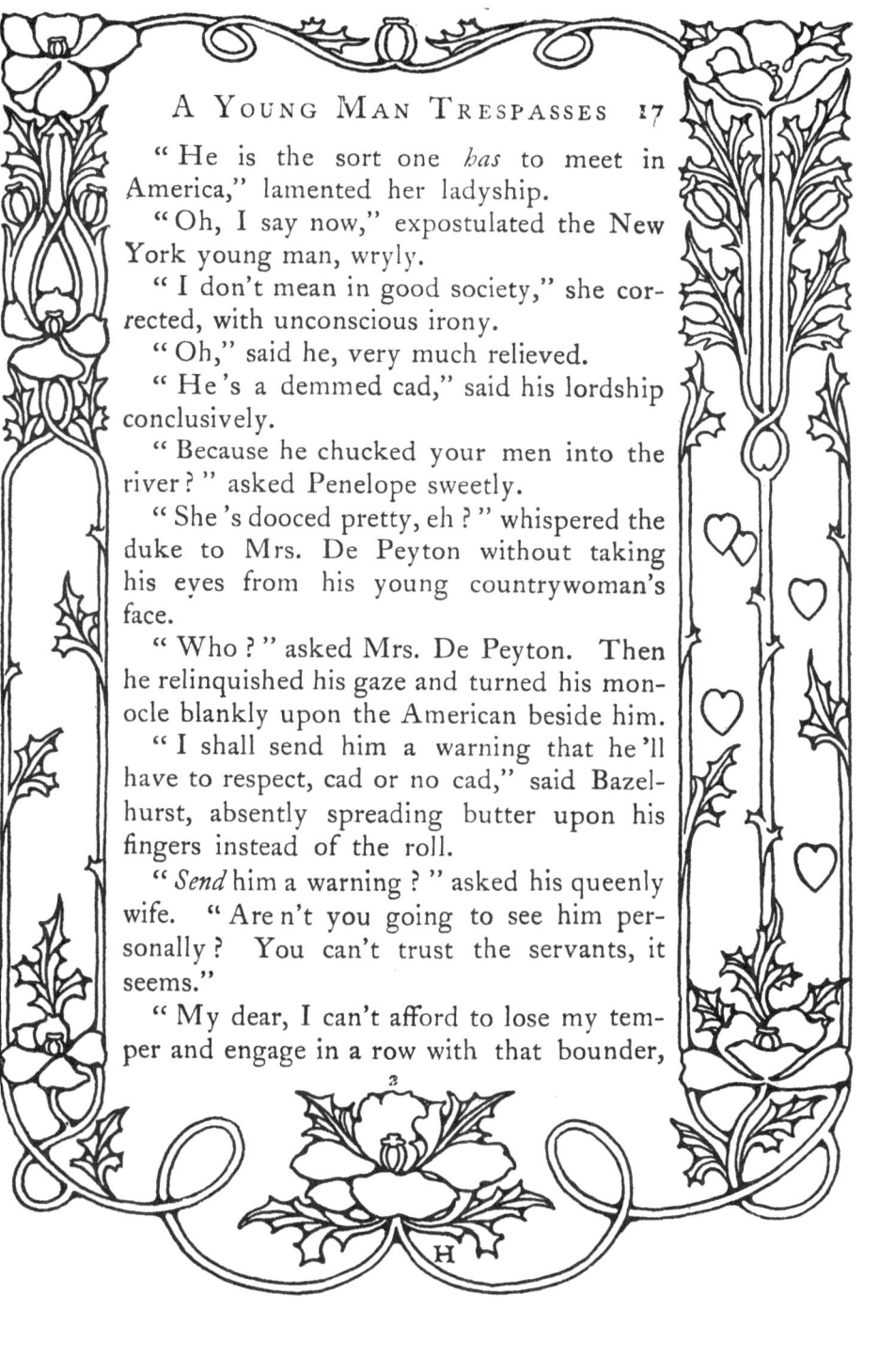

"He is the sort one *has* to meet in America," lamented her ladyship.

"Oh, I say now," expostulated the New York young man, wryly.

"I don't mean in good society," she corrected, with unconscious irony.

"Oh," said he, very much relieved.

"He's a demmed cad," said his lordship conclusively.

"Because he chucked your men into the river?" asked Penelope sweetly.

"She's dooced pretty, eh?" whispered the duke to Mrs. De Peyton without taking his eyes from his young countrywoman's face.

"Who?" asked Mrs. De Peyton. Then he relinquished his gaze and turned his monocle blankly upon the American beside him.

"I shall send him a warning that he'll have to respect, cad or no cad," said Bazelhurst, absently spreading butter upon his fingers instead of the roll.

"*Send* him a warning?" asked his queenly wife. "Aren't you going to see him personally? You can't trust the servants, it seems."

"My dear, I can't afford to lose my temper and engage in a row with that bounder,

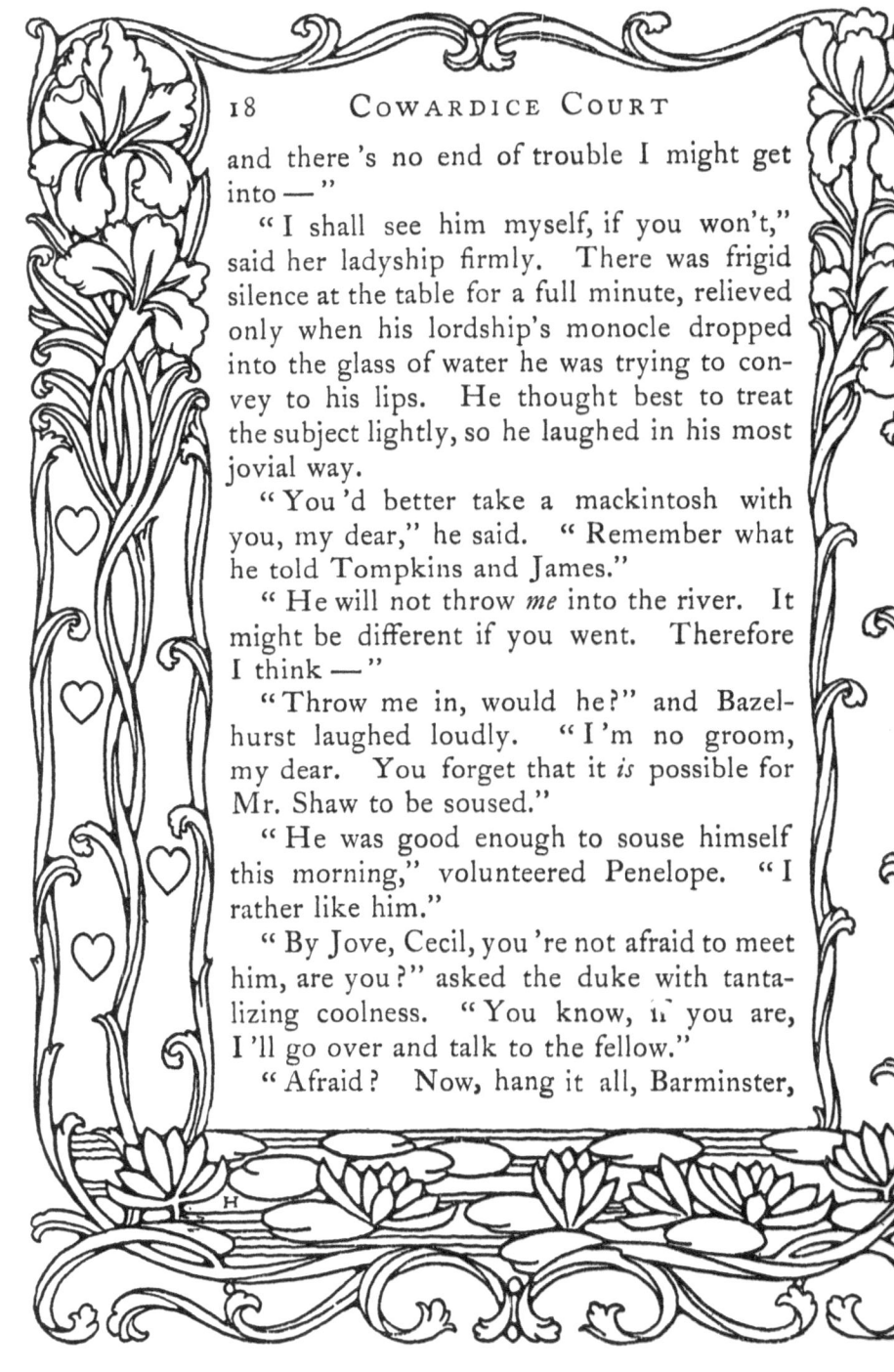

and there's no end of trouble I might get
into — "

"I shall see him myself, if you won't,"
said her ladyship firmly. There was frigid
silence at the table for a full minute, relieved
only when his lordship's monocle dropped
into the glass of water he was trying to con-
vey to his lips. He thought best to treat
the subject lightly, so he laughed in his most
jovial way.

"You'd better take a mackintosh with
you, my dear," he said. "Remember what
he told Tompkins and James."

"He will not throw *me* into the river. It
might be different if you went. Therefore
I think — "

"Throw me in, would he?" and Bazelhurst laughed loudly. "I'm no groom,
my dear. You forget that it *is* possible for
Mr. Shaw to be soused."

"He was good enough to souse himself
this morning," volunteered Penelope. "I
rather like him."

"By Jove, Cecil, you're not afraid to meet
him, are you?" asked the duke with tantalizing coolness. "You know, if you are,
I'll go over and talk to the fellow."

"Afraid? Now, hang it all, Barminster,

that's rather a shabby thing to suggest. You forget India."

"I'm trying to. Demmed miserable time I had out there. But this fellow fights. That's more than the beastly natives did when we were out there. Marching is n't fighting, you know."

"Confound it, you forget the time—"

"Mon Dieu, are we to compare ze Hindoo harem wiz ze American feest slugger?" cried the count, with a wry face.

"What's that?" demanded two noblemen in one voice. The count apologized for his English.

"No one but a coward would permit this disagreeable Shaw creature to run affairs in such a high-handed way," said her ladyship. "Of course Cecil is not a coward."

"Thank you, my dear. Never fear, ladies and gentlemen; I shall attend to this person. He won't soon forget what I have to say to him," promised Lord Bazelhurst, mentally estimating the number of brandies and soda it would require in preparation.

"This afternoon?" asked his wife, with cruel insistence.

"Yes, Evelyn—if I can find him."

And so it was that shortly after four

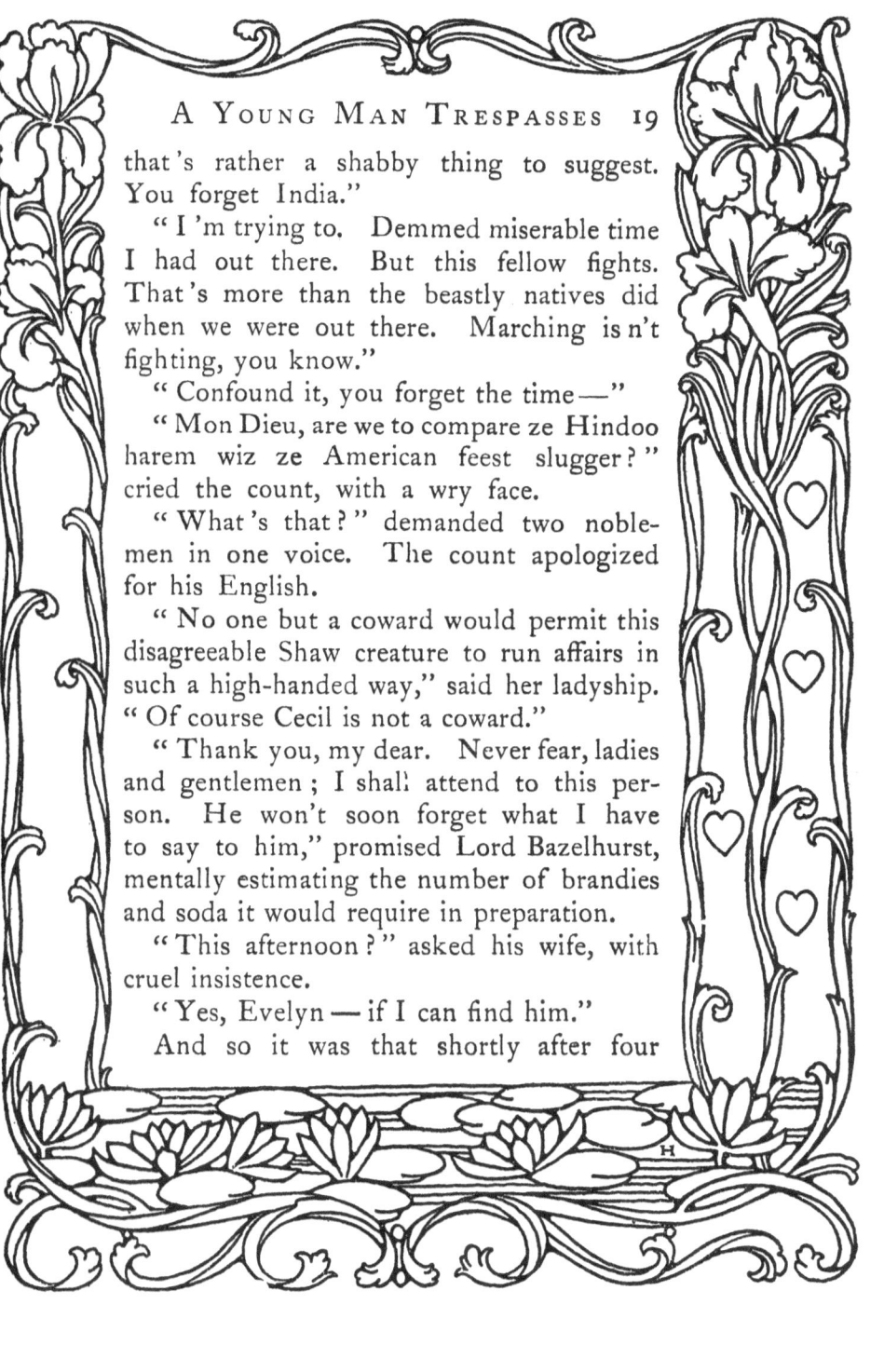

o'clock, Lord Bazelhurst, unattended at his own request, rode forth like a Lochinvar, his steed headed bravely toward Shaw's domain, his back facing his own home with a military indifference that won applause from the assembled house party.

"I'll face him alone," he had said, a trifle thickly, for some unknown reason, when the duke offered to accompany him. It also might have been noticed as he cantered down the drive that his legs did not stick out so stiffly, nor did his person bob so exactingly as on previous but peaceful expeditions.

In fact, he seemed a bit limp. But his face was set determinedly for the border line and Shaw.

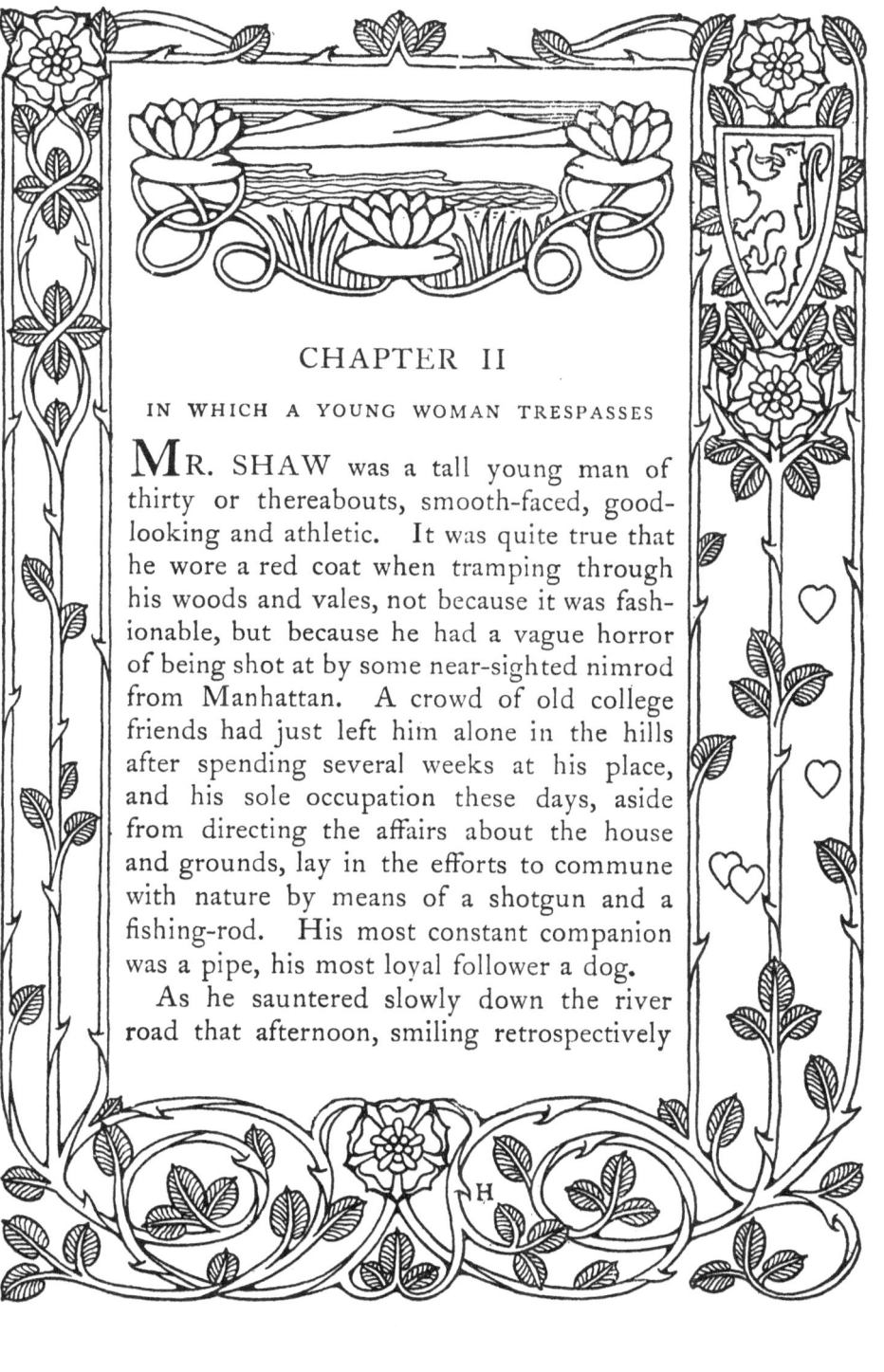

CHAPTER II

IN WHICH A YOUNG WOMAN TRESPASSES

MR. SHAW was a tall young man of thirty or thereabouts, smooth-faced, good-looking and athletic. It was quite true that he wore a red coat when tramping through his woods and vales, not because it was fashionable, but because he had a vague horror of being shot at by some near-sighted nimrod from Manhattan. A crowd of old college friends had just left him alone in the hills after spending several weeks at his place, and his sole occupation these days, aside from directing the affairs about the house and grounds, lay in the efforts to commune with nature by means of a shotgun and a fishing-rod. His most constant companion was a pipe, his most loyal follower a dog.

As he sauntered slowly down the river road that afternoon, smiling retrospectively

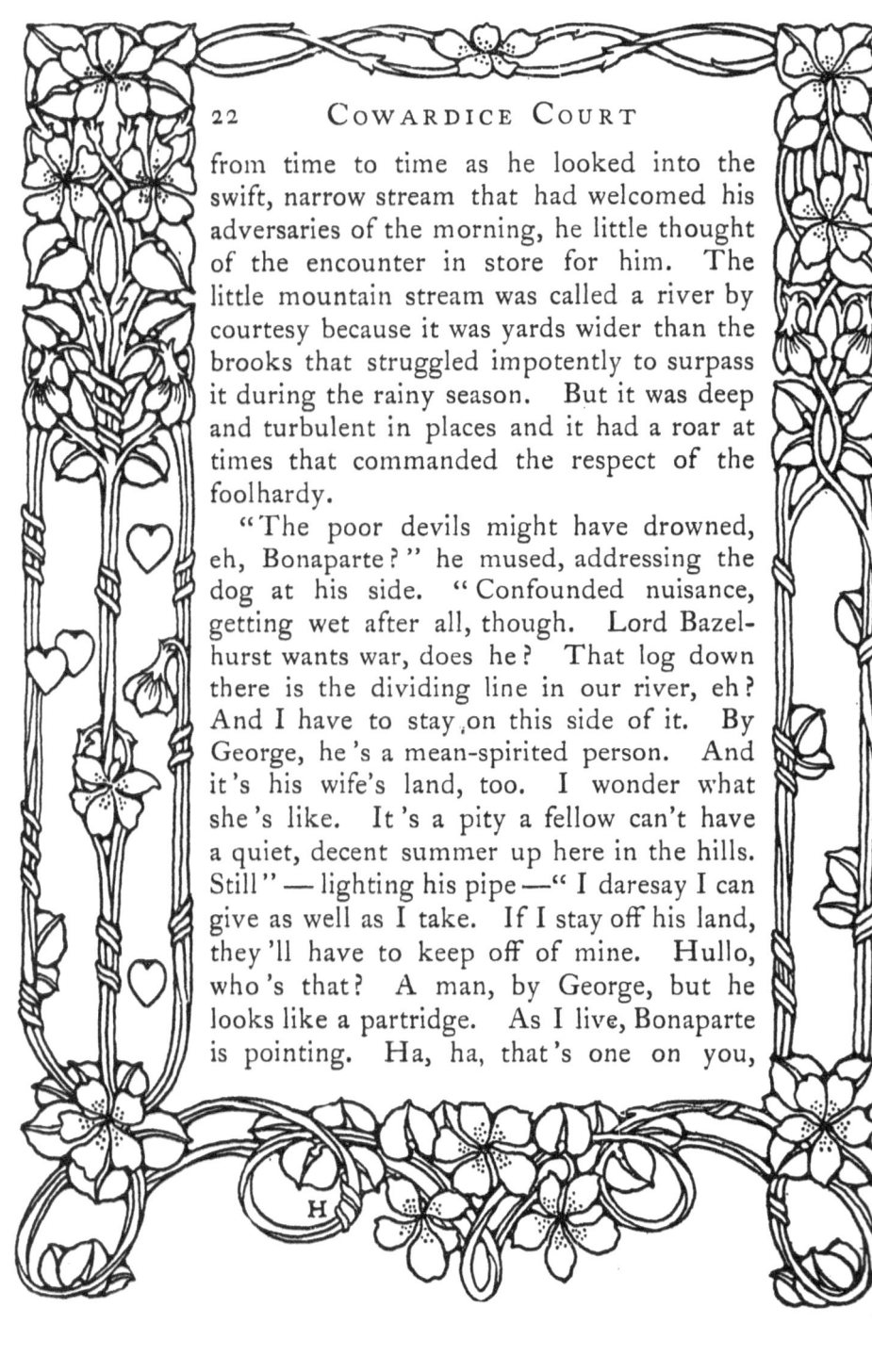

from time to time as he looked into the swift, narrow stream that had welcomed his adversaries of the morning, he little thought of the encounter in store for him. The little mountain stream was called a river by courtesy because it was yards wider than the brooks that struggled impotently to surpass it during the rainy season. But it was deep and turbulent in places and it had a roar at times that commanded the respect of the foolhardy.

"The poor devils might have drowned, eh, Bonaparte?" he mused, addressing the dog at his side. "Confounded nuisance, getting wet after all, though. Lord Bazel-hurst wants war, does he? That log down there is the dividing line in our river, eh? And I have to stay on this side of it. By George, he's a mean-spirited person. And it's his wife's land, too. I wonder what she's like. It's a pity a fellow can't have a quiet, decent summer up here in the hills. Still" — lighting his pipe —"I daresay I can give as well as I take. If I stay off his land, they'll have to keep off of mine. Hullo, who's that? A man, by George, but he looks like a partridge. As I live, Bonaparte is pointing. Ha, ha, that's one on you,

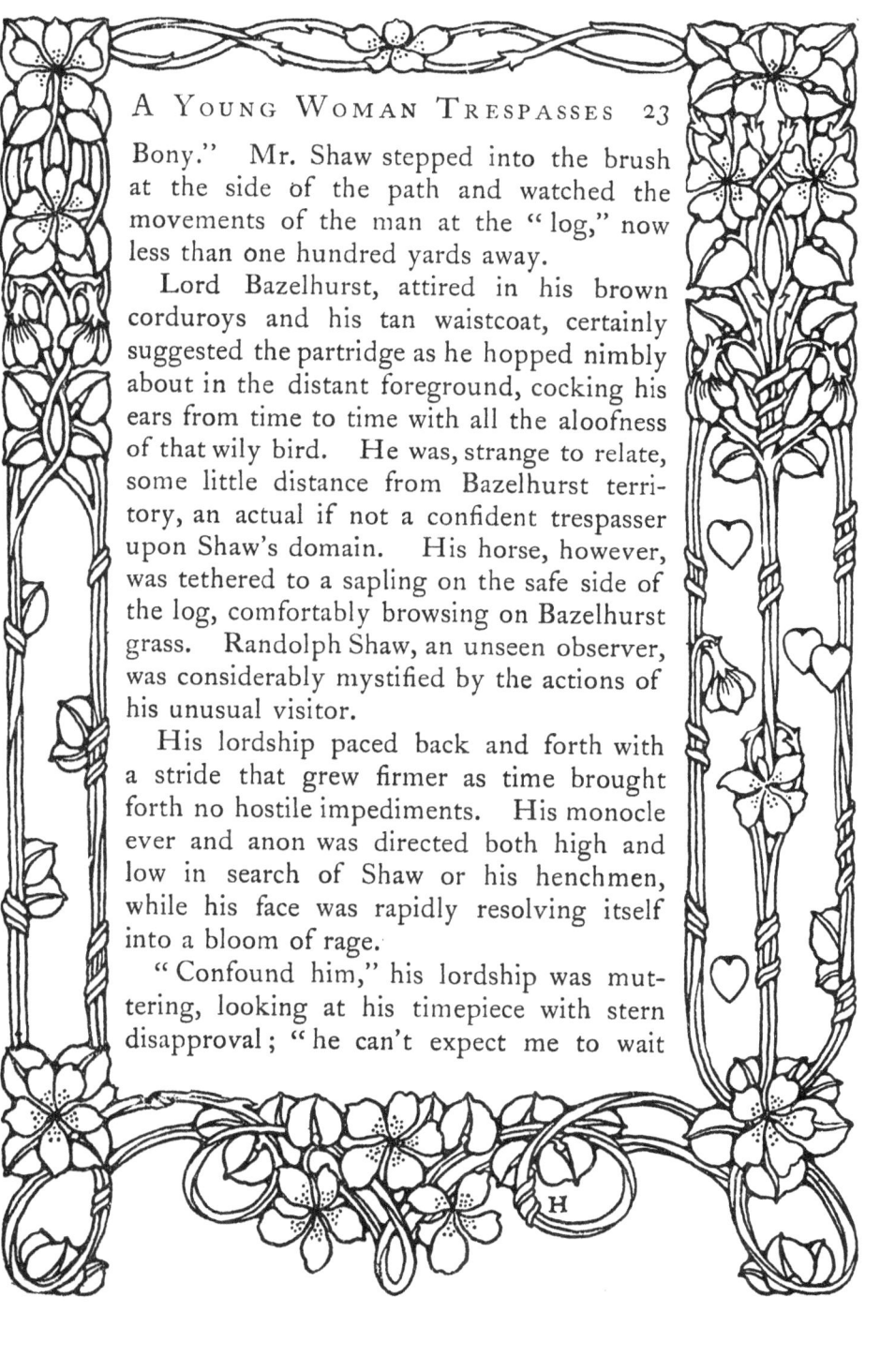

Bony." Mr. Shaw stepped into the brush at the side of the path and watched the movements of the man at the " log," now less than one hundred yards away.

Lord Bazelhurst, attired in his brown corduroys and his tan waistcoat, certainly suggested the partridge as he hopped nimbly about in the distant foreground, cocking his ears from time to time with all the aloofness of that wily bird. He was, strange to relate, some little distance from Bazelhurst territory, an actual if not a confident trespasser upon Shaw's domain. His horse, however, was tethered to a sapling on the safe side of the log, comfortably browsing on Bazelhurst grass. Randolph Shaw, an unseen observer, was considerably mystified by the actions of his unusual visitor.

His lordship paced back and forth with a stride that grew firmer as time brought forth no hostile impediments. His monocle ever and anon was directed both high and low in search of Shaw or his henchmen, while his face was rapidly resolving itself into a bloom of rage.

" Confound him," his lordship was muttering, looking at his timepiece with stern disapproval; " he can't expect me to wait

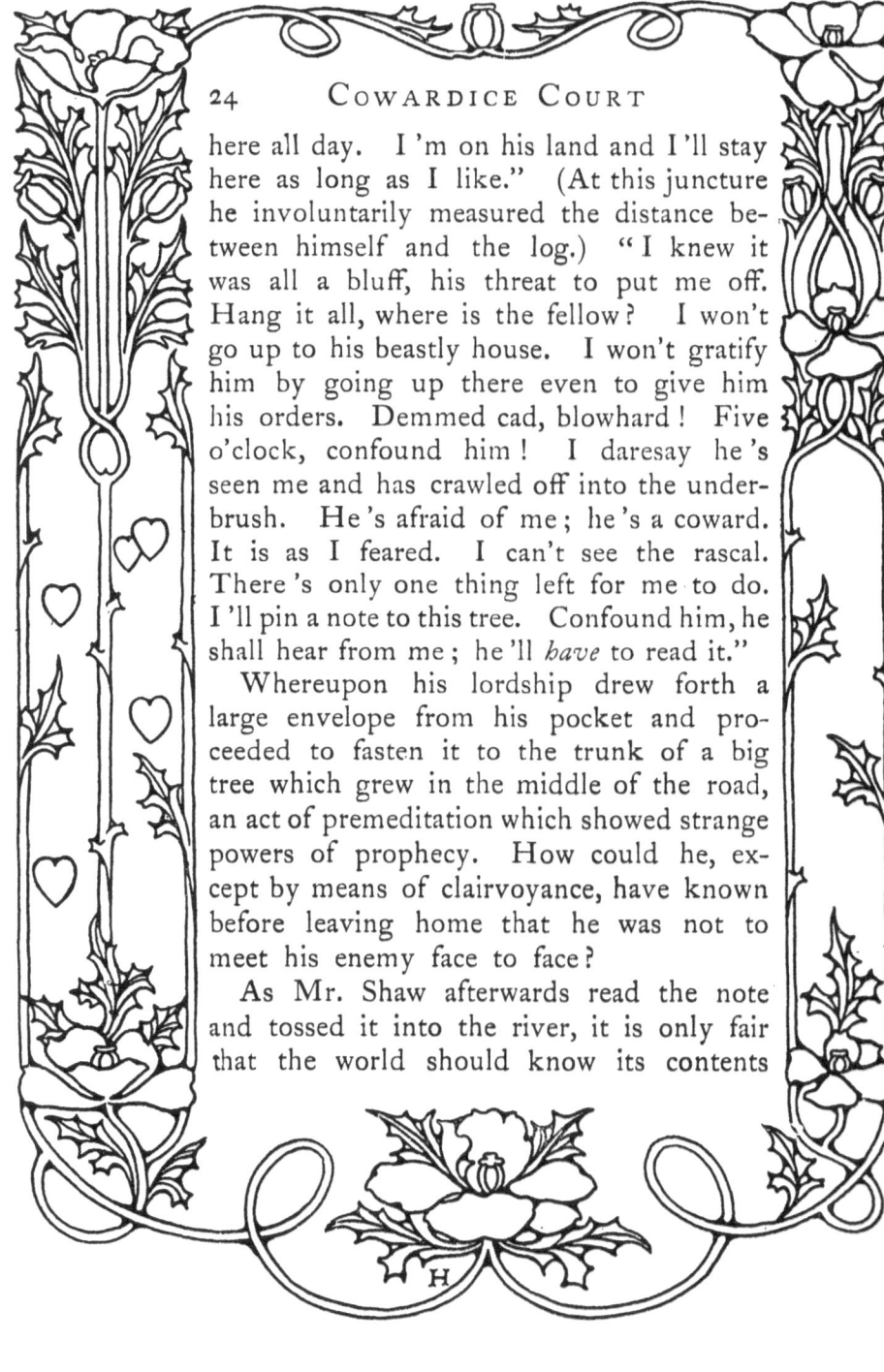

here all day. I'm on his land and I'll stay here as long as I like." (At this juncture he involuntarily measured the distance between himself and the log.) "I knew it was all a bluff, his threat to put me off. Hang it all, where is the fellow? I won't go up to his beastly house. I won't gratify him by going up there even to give him his orders. Demmed cad, blowhard! Five o'clock, confound him! I daresay he's seen me and has crawled off into the underbrush. He's afraid of me; he's a coward. It is as I feared. I can't see the rascal. There's only one thing left for me to do. I'll pin a note to this tree. Confound him, he shall hear from me; he'll *have* to read it."

Whereupon his lordship drew forth a large envelope from his pocket and proceeded to fasten it to the trunk of a big tree which grew in the middle of the road, an act of premeditation which showed strange powers of prophecy. How could he, except by means of clairvoyance, have known before leaving home that he was not to meet his enemy face to face?

As Mr. Shaw afterwards read the note and tossed it into the river, it is only fair that the world should know its contents

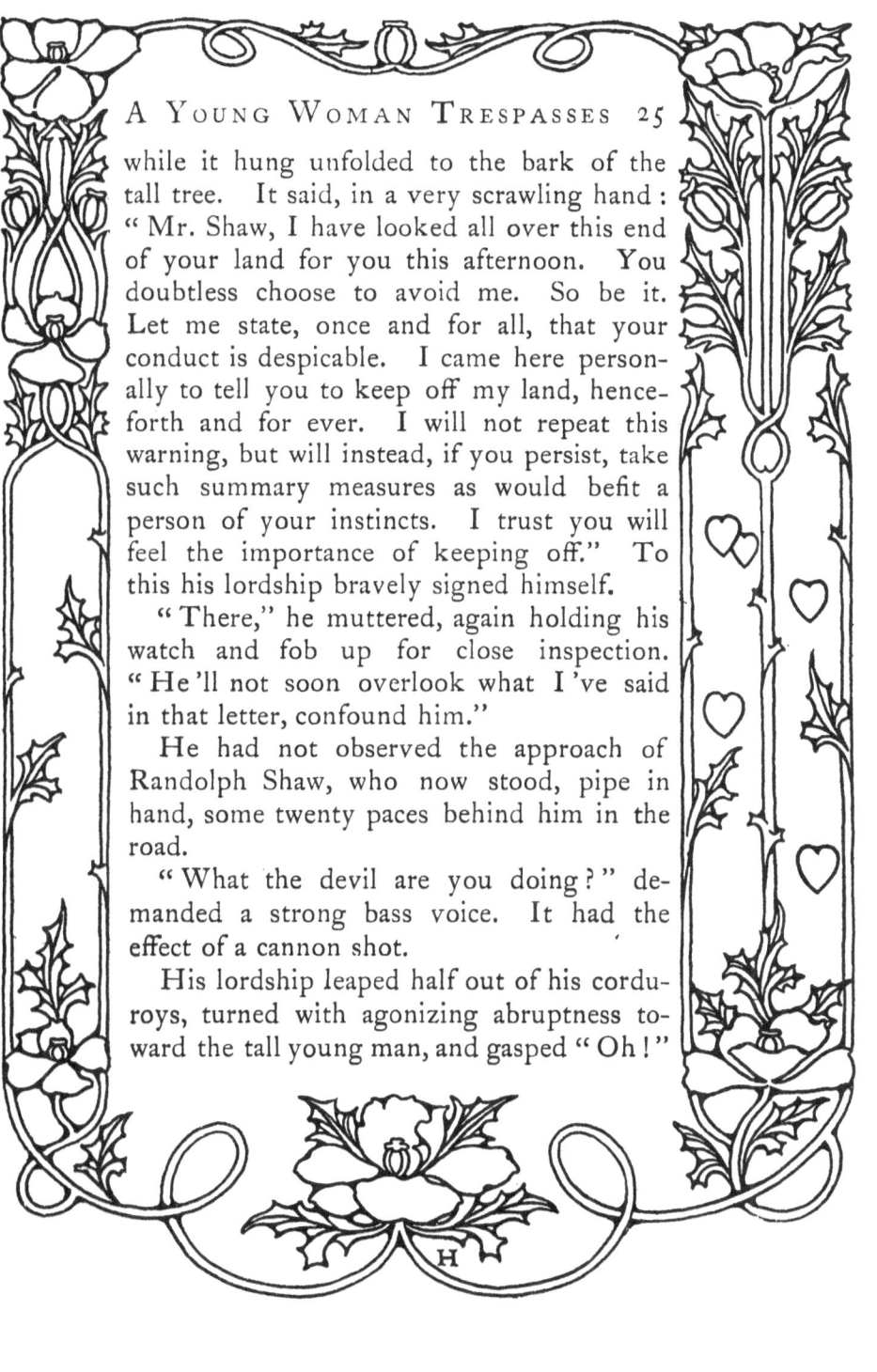

while it hung unfolded to the bark of the tall tree. It said, in a very scrawling hand: "Mr. Shaw, I have looked all over this end of your land for you this afternoon. You doubtless choose to avoid me. So be it. Let me state, once and for all, that your conduct is despicable. I came here personally to tell you to keep off my land, henceforth and for ever. I will not repeat this warning, but will instead, if you persist, take such summary measures as would befit a person of your instincts. I trust you will feel the importance of keeping off." To this his lordship bravely signed himself.

"There," he muttered, again holding his watch and fob up for close inspection. "He'll not soon overlook what I've said in that letter, confound him."

He had not observed the approach of Randolph Shaw, who now stood, pipe in hand, some twenty paces behind him in the road.

"What the devil are you doing?" demanded a strong bass voice. It had the effect of a cannon shot.

His lordship leaped half out of his corduroys, turned with agonizing abruptness toward the tall young man, and gasped "Oh!"

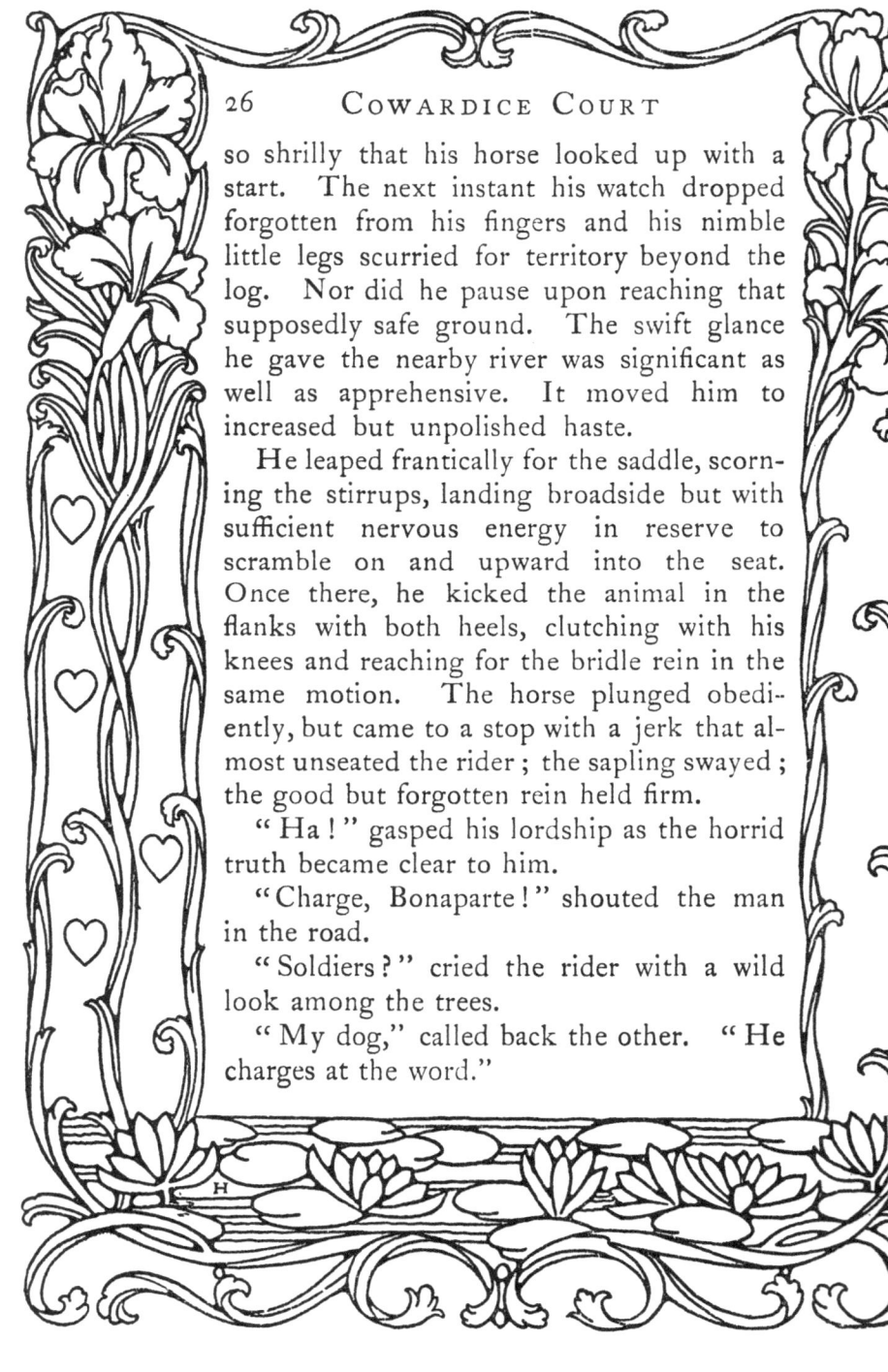

so shrilly that his horse looked up with a start. The next instant his watch dropped forgotten from his fingers and his nimble little legs scurried for territory beyond the log. Nor did he pause upon reaching that supposedly safe ground. The swift glance he gave the nearby river was significant as well as apprehensive. It moved him to increased but unpolished haste.

He leaped frantically for the saddle, scorning the stirrups, landing broadside but with sufficient nervous energy in reserve to scramble on and upward into the seat. Once there, he kicked the animal in the flanks with both heels, clutching with his knees and reaching for the bridle rein in the same motion. The horse plunged obediently, but came to a stop with a jerk that almost unseated the rider; the sapling swayed; the good but forgotten rein held firm.

"Ha!" gasped his lordship as the horrid truth became clear to him.

"Charge, Bonaparte!" shouted the man in the road.

"Soldiers?" cried the rider with a wild look among the trees.

"My dog," called back the other. "He charges at the word."

"Well, you know, I saw service in the army," apologized his lordship, with a pale smile. "Get ep!" to the horse.

"What's your hurry?" asked Shaw, grinning broadly as he came up to the log.

"Don't — don't you dare to step over that log," shouted Bazelhurst.

"All right. I see. But, after all, what's the rush?" The other was puzzled for the moment.

"I'm practising, sir," he said unsteadily. "How to mount on a run, demmit. Can't you see?"

"In case of fire, I imagine. Well, you made excellent time. By the way, what has this envelope to do with it?"

"Who are you, sir?"

"Shaw. And you?"

"You'll learn when you read that document. Take it home with you."

"Ah, yes, I see it's for me. Why don't you untie that hitch rein? And what the dickens do you mean by having a hitch rein, anyway? No rider —"

"Confound your impudence, sir, I did not come here to receive instructions from you, dem you," cried his lordship defiantly. He had succeeded at that moment in sur-

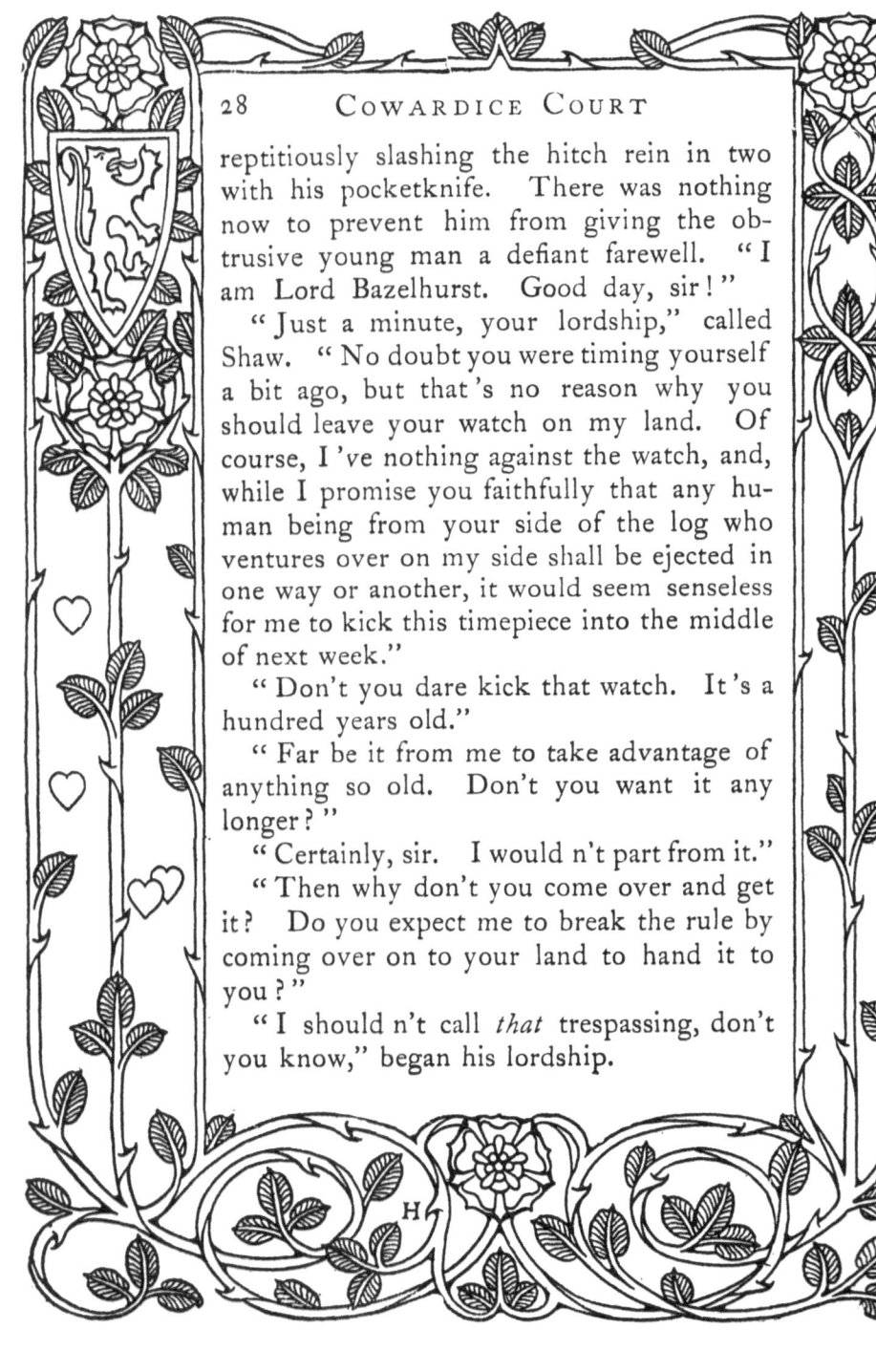

reptitiously slashing the hitch rein in two with his pocketknife.   There was nothing now to prevent him from giving the obtrusive young man a defiant farewell.   " I am Lord Bazelhurst.   Good day, sir ! "

" Just a minute, your lordship," called Shaw.   " No doubt you were timing yourself a bit ago, but that's no reason why you should leave your watch on my land.   Of course, I 've nothing against the watch, and, while I promise you faithfully that any human being from your side of the log who ventures over on my side shall be ejected in one way or another, it would seem senseless for me to kick this timepiece into the middle of next week."

" Don't you dare kick that watch.   It's a hundred years old."

" Far be it from me to take advantage of anything so old.   Don't you want it any longer ? "

" Certainly, sir.   I would n't part from it."

" Then why don't you come over and get it ?   Do you expect me to break the rule by coming over on to your land to hand it to you ? "

" I should n't call *that* trespassing, don't you know," began his lordship.

"Ah? Nevertheless, if you want this watch you 'll have to come over and get it."

"By Jove, now, that 's a demmed mean trick. I 'm mounted. Beastly annoying. I say, would you mind *tossing* it up to me?"

"I would n't touch it for ten dollars. By the way, I 'll just read this note of yours." Lord Bazelhurst nervously watched him as he read; his heart lightened perceptibly as he saw a good-humoured smile struggle to the tall young man's face. It was, however, with some misgiving that he studied the broad shoulders and powerful frame of the erstwhile poacher. "Very good of you, I 'm sure, to warn me."

"Good of me? It was imperative, let me tell you, sir. No man can abuse my servants and trample all over my land and disturb my fish —"

"Excuse me, but I have n't time to listen to all that. The note 's sufficient. You 've been practising the running mount until it. looks well nigh perfect to me, so I 'll tell you what I 'll do. I 'll step back thirty paces and then you come over and get the watch — if you 're not afraid of me — and I 'll promise —"

"Afraid? Demmit, sir, did n't I say I

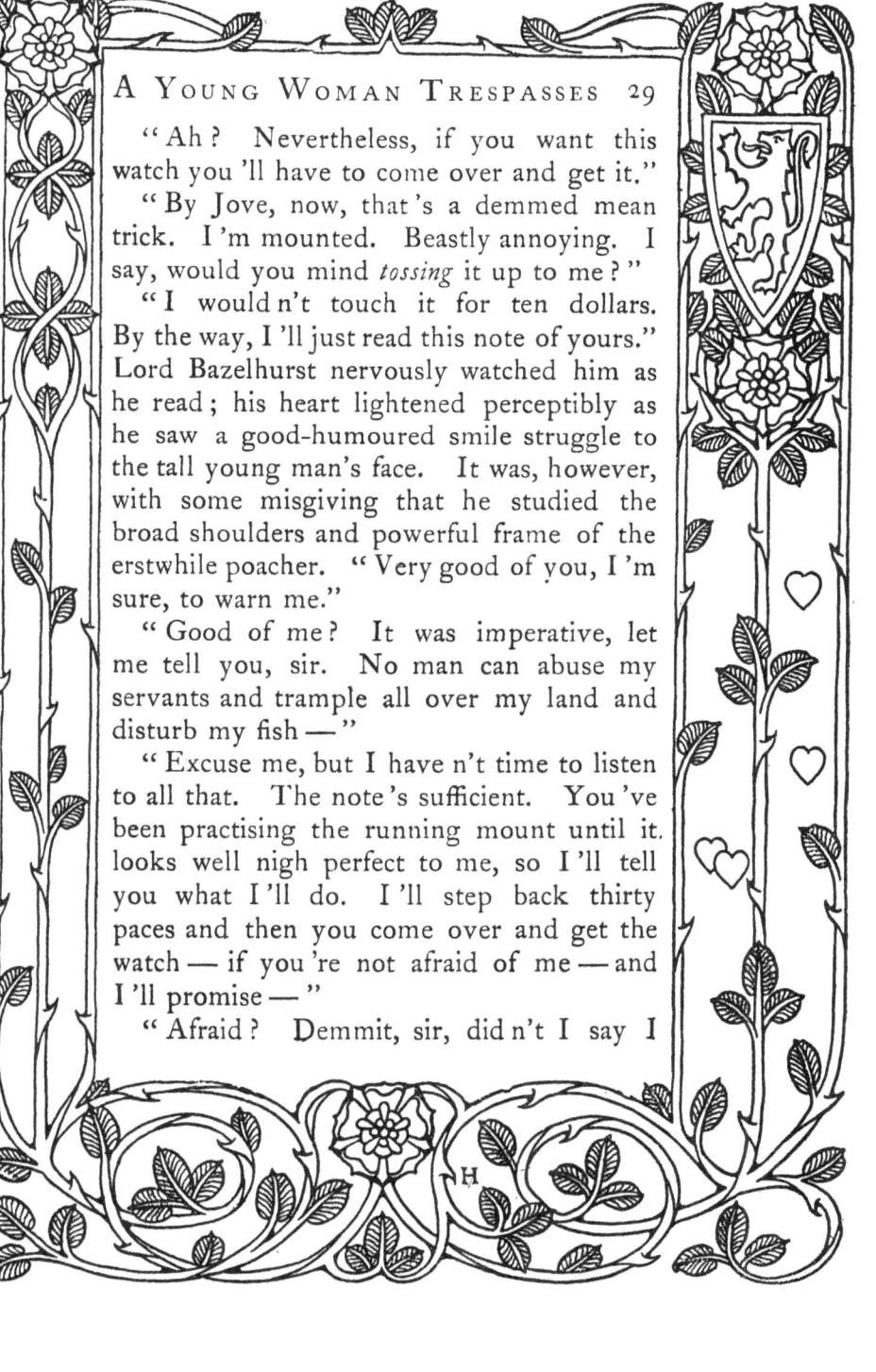

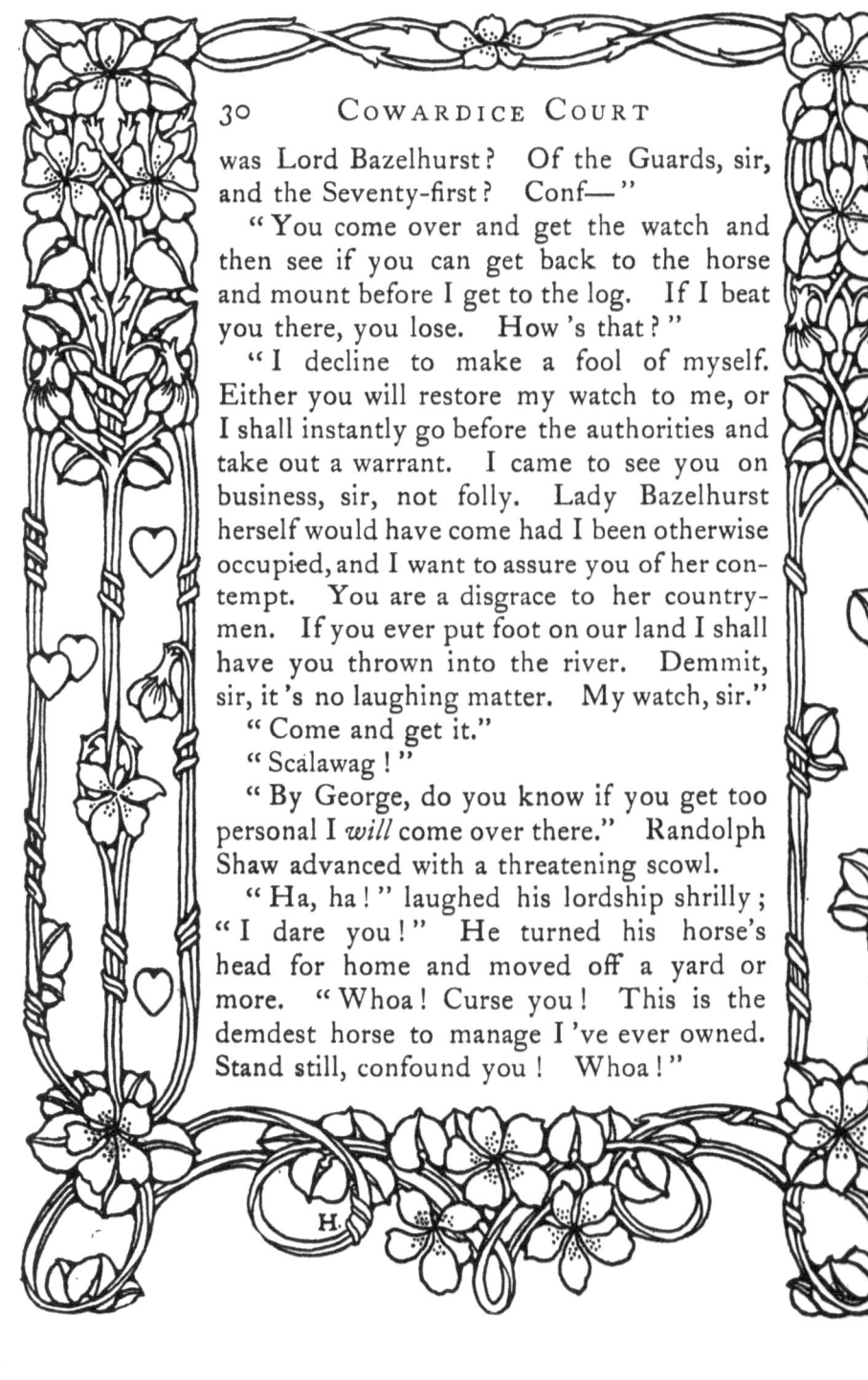

was Lord Bazelhurst?   Of the Guards, sir,
and the Seventy-first?   Conf—"

"You come over and get the watch and
then see if you can get back to the horse
and mount before I get to the log.   If I beat
you there, you lose.   How's that?"

"I decline to make a fool of myself.
Either you will restore my watch to me, or
I shall instantly go before the authorities and
take out a warrant.   I came to see you on
business, sir, not folly.   Lady Bazelhurst
herself would have come had I been otherwise
occupied, and I want to assure you of her con-
tempt.   You are a disgrace to her country-
men.   If you ever put foot on our land I shall
have you thrown into the river.   Demmit,
sir, it's no laughing matter.   My watch, sir."

"Come and get it."

"Scalawag!"

"By George, do you know if you get too
personal I *will* come over there."   Randolph
Shaw advanced with a threatening scowl.

"Ha, ha!" laughed his lordship shrilly;
"I dare you!"   He turned his horse's
head for home and moved off a yard or
more.   "Whoa! Curse you!   This is the
demdest horse to manage I've ever owned.
Stand still, confound you!   Whoa!"

" ' So you are putting me off your place ?   Oh, how lovely ! ' "

"He'll stand if you stop licking him."

"Halloa! Hey, Bazelhurst!" came a far distant voice. The adversaries glanced down the road and beheld two horsemen approaching from Bazelhurst Villa — the duke and the count.

"By Jove!" muttered his lordship, suddenly deciding that it would not be convenient for them to appear on the scene at its present stage. "My friends are calling me. Her ladyship doubtless is near at hand. She rides, you know — I mean dem you! Would n't have her see you for a fortune. Not another word, sir! You have my orders. Stay off or I'll — throw you off!" This last threat was almost shrieked and was plainly heard by the two horsemen.

"By Jove, he's facing the fellow," said the duke to the count.

"Ees eet Shaw? Parbleu!"

"I'll send some one for that watch. Don't you dare to touch it," said his lordship in tones barely audible. Then he loped off to meet his friends and turn them back before they came too close for comfort. Randolph Shaw laughed heartily as he watched the retreat. Seeing the newcomers halt and then turn abruptly back into their

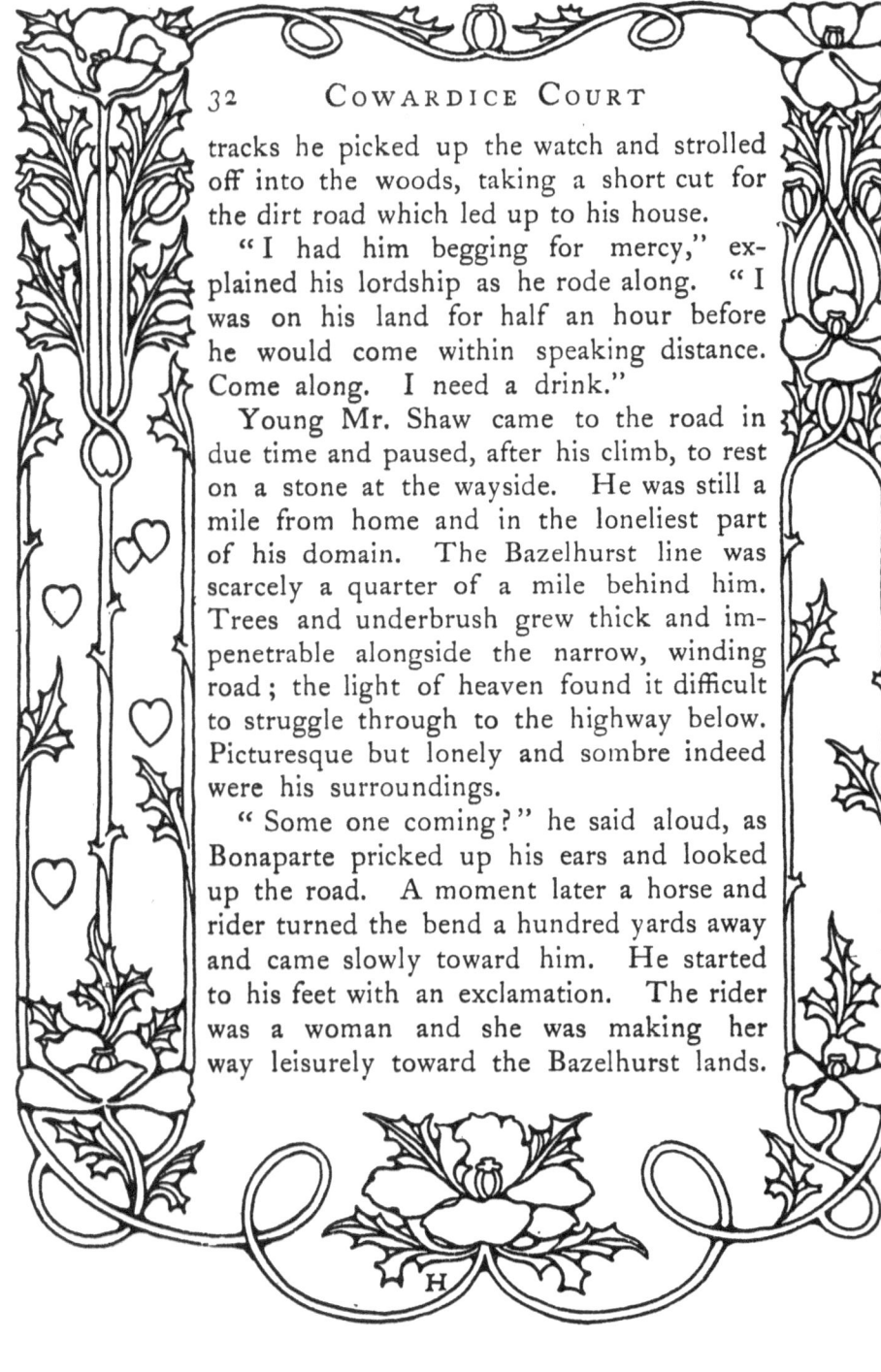

tracks he picked up the watch and strolled off into the woods, taking a short cut for the dirt road which led up to his house.

"I had him begging for mercy," explained his lordship as he rode along. "I was on his land for half an hour before he would come within speaking distance. Come along. I need a drink."

Young Mr. Shaw came to the road in due time and paused, after his climb, to rest on a stone at the wayside. He was still a mile from home and in the loneliest part of his domain. The Bazelhurst line was scarcely a quarter of a mile behind him. Trees and underbrush grew thick and impenetrable alongside the narrow, winding road; the light of heaven found it difficult to struggle through to the highway below. Picturesque but lonely and sombre indeed were his surroundings.

"Some one coming?" he said aloud, as Bonaparte pricked up his ears and looked up the road. A moment later a horse and rider turned the bend a hundred yards away and came slowly toward him. He started to his feet with an exclamation. The rider was a woman and she was making her way leisurely toward the Bazelhurst lands.

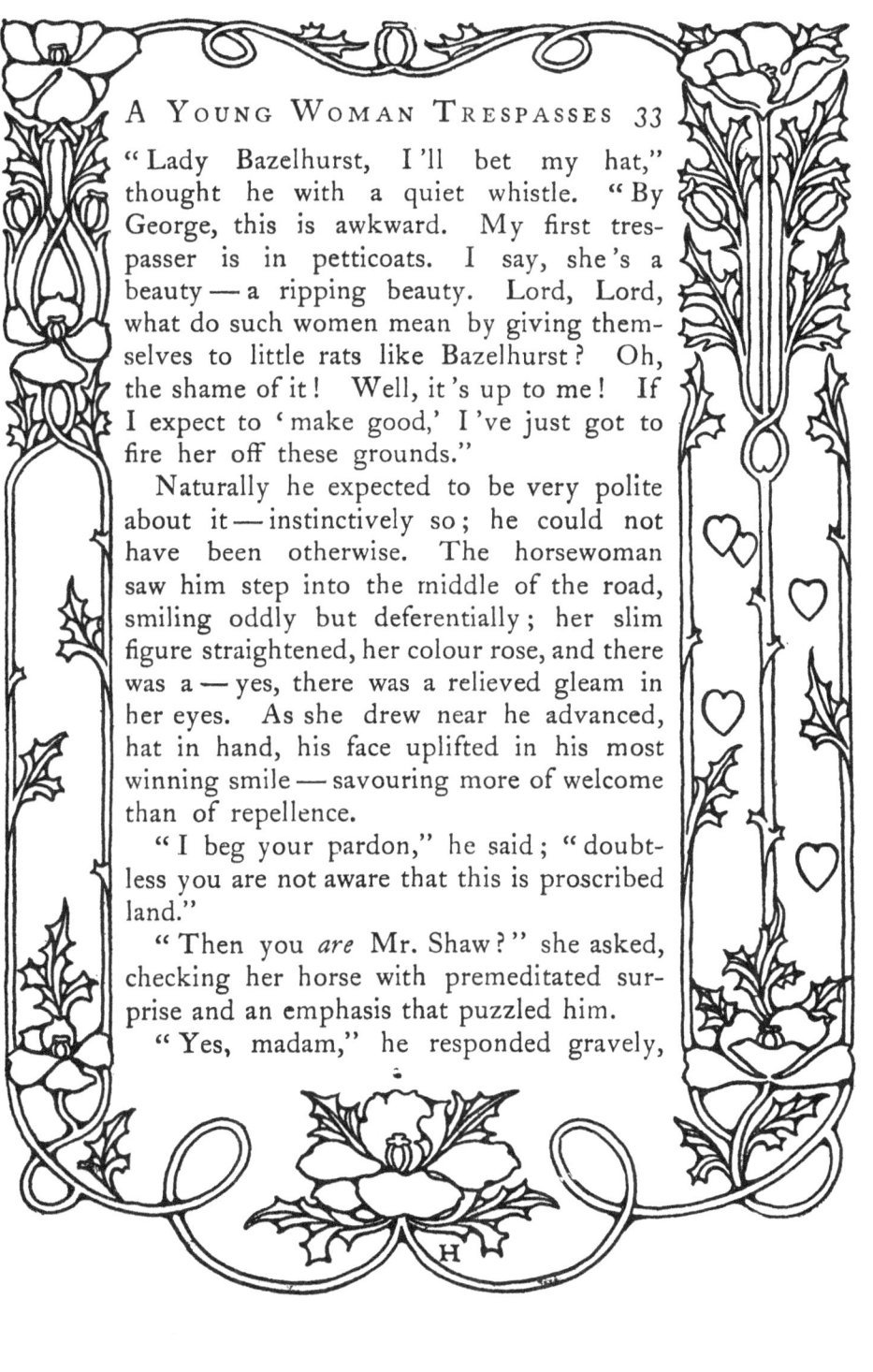

"Lady Bazelhurst, I'll bet my hat," thought he with a quiet whistle. "By George, this is awkward. My first trespasser is in petticoats. I say, she's a beauty — a ripping beauty. Lord, Lord, what do such women mean by giving themselves to little rats like Bazelhurst? Oh, the shame of it! Well, it's up to me! If I expect to 'make good,' I've just got to fire her off these grounds."

Naturally he expected to be very polite about it — instinctively so; he could not have been otherwise. The horsewoman saw him step into the middle of the road, smiling oddly but deferentially; her slim figure straightened, her colour rose, and there was a — yes, there was a relieved gleam in her eyes. As she drew near he advanced, hat in hand, his face uplifted in his most winning smile — savouring more of welcome than of repellence.

"I beg your pardon," he said; "doubtless you are not aware that this is proscribed land."

"Then you *are* Mr. Shaw?" she asked, checking her horse with premeditated surprise and an emphasis that puzzled him.

"Yes, madam," he responded gravely,

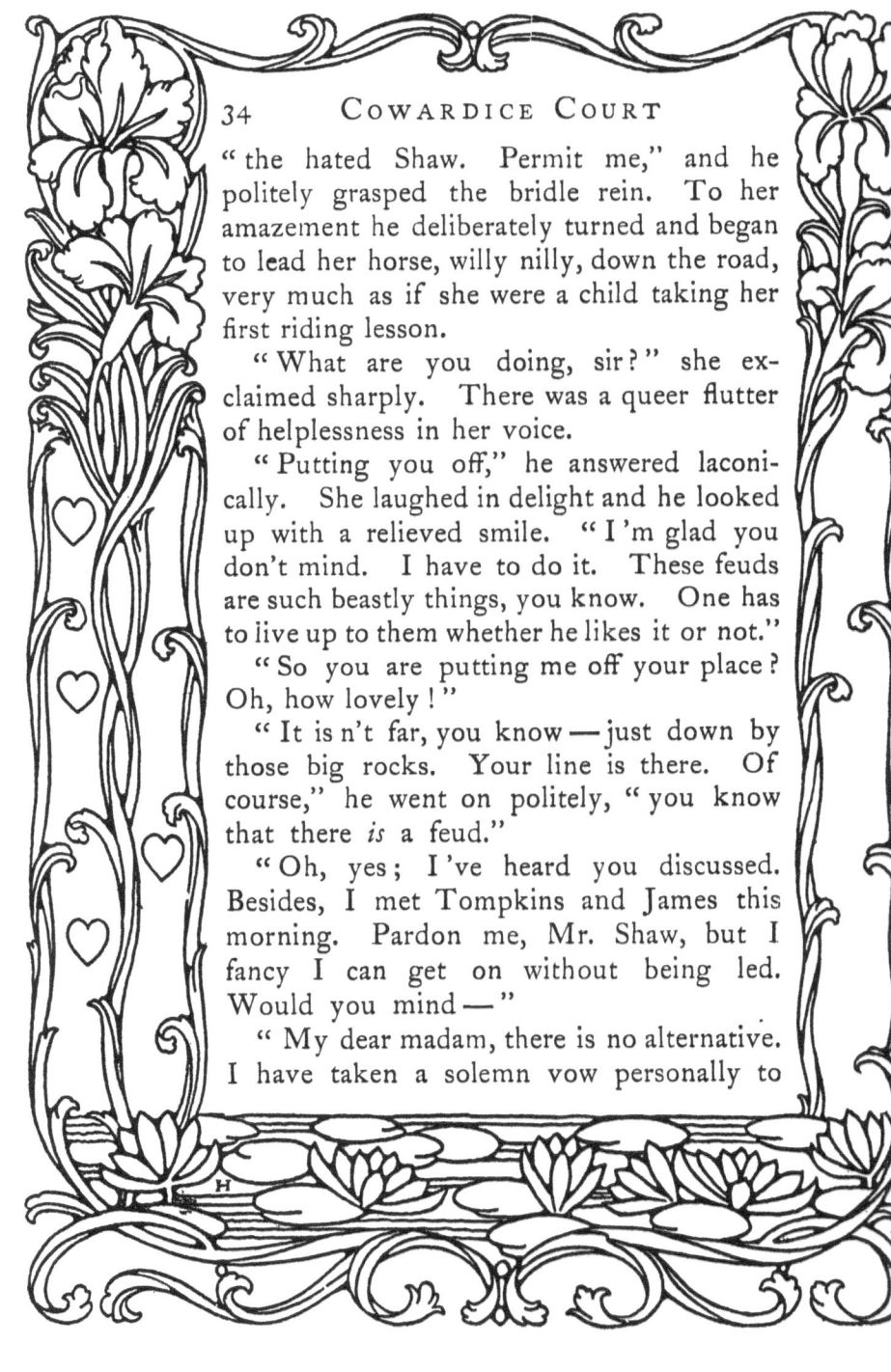

"the hated Shaw. Permit me," and he politely grasped the bridle rein. To her amazement he deliberately turned and began to lead her horse, willy nilly, down the road, very much as if she were a child taking her first riding lesson.

"What are you doing, sir?" she exclaimed sharply. There was a queer flutter of helplessness in her voice.

"Putting you off," he answered laconically. She laughed in delight and he looked up with a relieved smile. "I'm glad you don't mind. I have to do it. These feuds are such beastly things, you know. One has to live up to them whether he likes it or not."

"So you are putting me off your place? Oh, how lovely!"

"It isn't far, you know — just down by those big rocks. Your line is there. Of course," he went on politely, "you know that there *is* a feud."

"Oh, yes; I've heard you discussed. Besides, I met Tompkins and James this morning. Pardon me, Mr. Shaw, but I fancy I can get on without being led. Would you mind —"

"My dear madam, there is no alternative. I have taken a solemn vow personally to

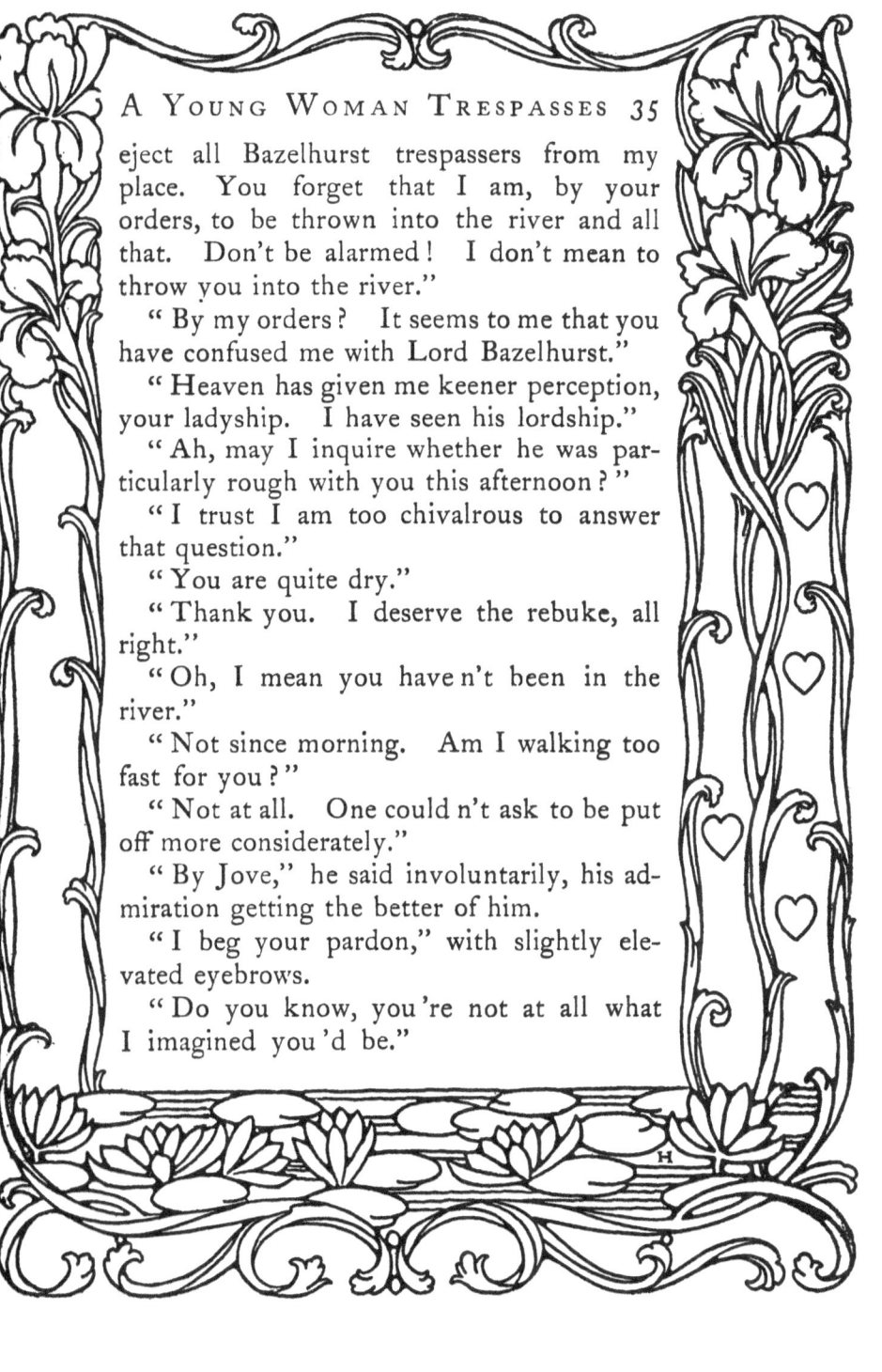

eject all Bazelhurst trespassers from my place. You forget that I am, by your orders, to be thrown into the river and all that. Don't be alarmed! I don't mean to throw you into the river."

" By my orders? It seems to me that you have confused me with Lord Bazelhurst."

" Heaven has given me keener perception, your ladyship. I have seen his lordship."

" Ah, may I inquire whether he was particularly rough with you this afternoon?"

" I trust I am too chivalrous to answer that question."

" You are quite dry."

" Thank you. I deserve the rebuke, all right."

" Oh, I mean you have n't been in the river."

" Not since morning. Am I walking too fast for you?"

" Not at all. One could n't ask to be put off more considerately."

" By Jove," he said involuntarily, his admiration getting the better of him.

" I beg your pardon," with slightly elevated eyebrows.

" Do you know, you 're not at all what I imagined you 'd be."

"Oh? And I fancy I'm not at all *whom* you imagined me to be."

"Heavens! Am I ejecting an innocent bystander? You *are* Lady Bazelhurst?"

"I am Penelope Drake. But"—she added quickly—"I *am* an enemy. I am Lord Bazelhurst's sister."

"You—you don't mean it?"

"Are you disappointed? I'm sorry."

"I am staggered and—a bit skeptical. There is no resemblance."

"I *am* a bit taller," she admitted carefully. "It isn't dreadfully immodest, is it, for one to hold converse with her captor? I am in your power, you see."

"On the contrary, it is quite the thing. The heroine always converses with the villain in books. She tells him what she thinks of him."

"But this isn't a book and I'm not a heroine. I am the adventuress. Will you permit me to explain my presence on your land?"

"No excuse is necessary. You were caught red-handed and you don't have to say anything to incriminate yourself further."

"But it is scarcely a hundred feet to our line. In a very few minutes I shall be

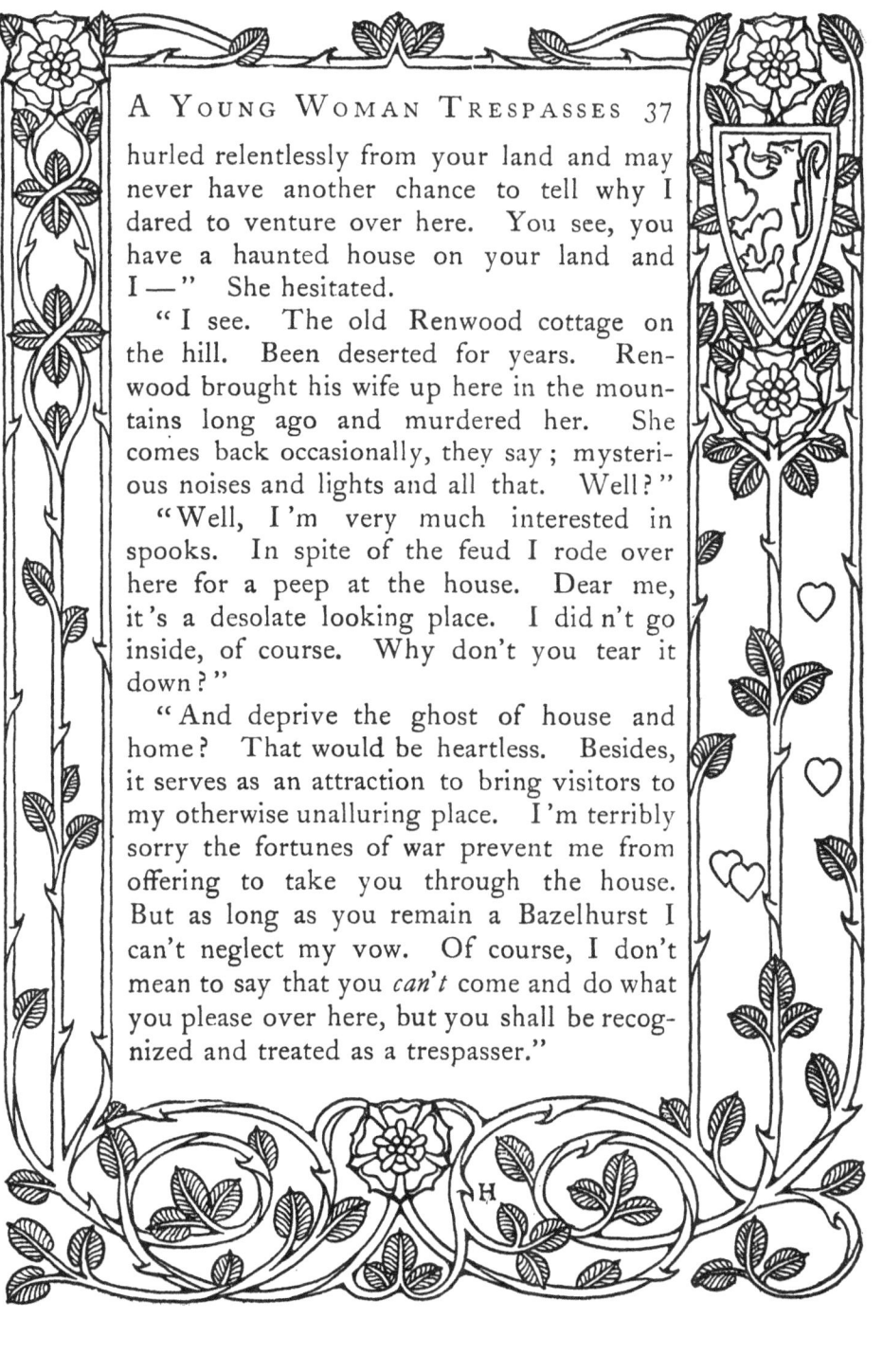

hurled relentlessly from your land and may never have another chance to tell why I dared to venture over here. You see, you have a haunted house on your land and I —" She hesitated.

"I see. The old Renwood cottage on the hill. Been deserted for years. Renwood brought his wife up here in the mountains long ago and murdered her. She comes back occasionally, they say; mysterious noises and lights and all that. Well?"

"Well, I'm very much interested in spooks. In spite of the feud I rode over here for a peep at the house. Dear me, it's a desolate looking place. I didn't go inside, of course. Why don't you tear it down?"

"And deprive the ghost of house and home? That would be heartless. Besides, it serves as an attraction to bring visitors to my otherwise unalluring place. I'm terribly sorry the fortunes of war prevent me from offering to take you through the house. But as long as you remain a Bazelhurst I can't neglect my vow. Of course, I don't mean to say that you *can't* come and do what you please over here, but you shall be recognized and treated as a trespasser."

" Oh, that's just splendid ! Perhaps I 'll
come to-morrow."

" I shall be obliged to escort you from the
grounds, you know."

" Yes, I know," she said agreeably. He
looked dazed and delighted. " Of course,
I shall come with stealth and darkly. Not
even my brother shall know of my plans."

" Certainly not," he said with alacrity.
(They were nearing the line.) " Depend on
me."

" Depend on you ? Your only duty is to
scare me off the place."

" That's what I mean. I 'll keep sharp
watch for you up at the haunted house."

" It 's more than a mile from the line,"
she advised him.

" Yes, I know," said he, with his friend-
liest smile. " Oh, by the way, would you
mind doing your brother a favour, Miss
Drake ? Give him this watch. He — er — he
must have dropped it while pursuing me."

" You *ran?* " she accepted the watch with
surprise and unbelief.

" Here is the line, Miss Drake," he
evaded. " Consider yourself ignominiously
ejected. Have I been unnecessarily rough
and expeditious ? "

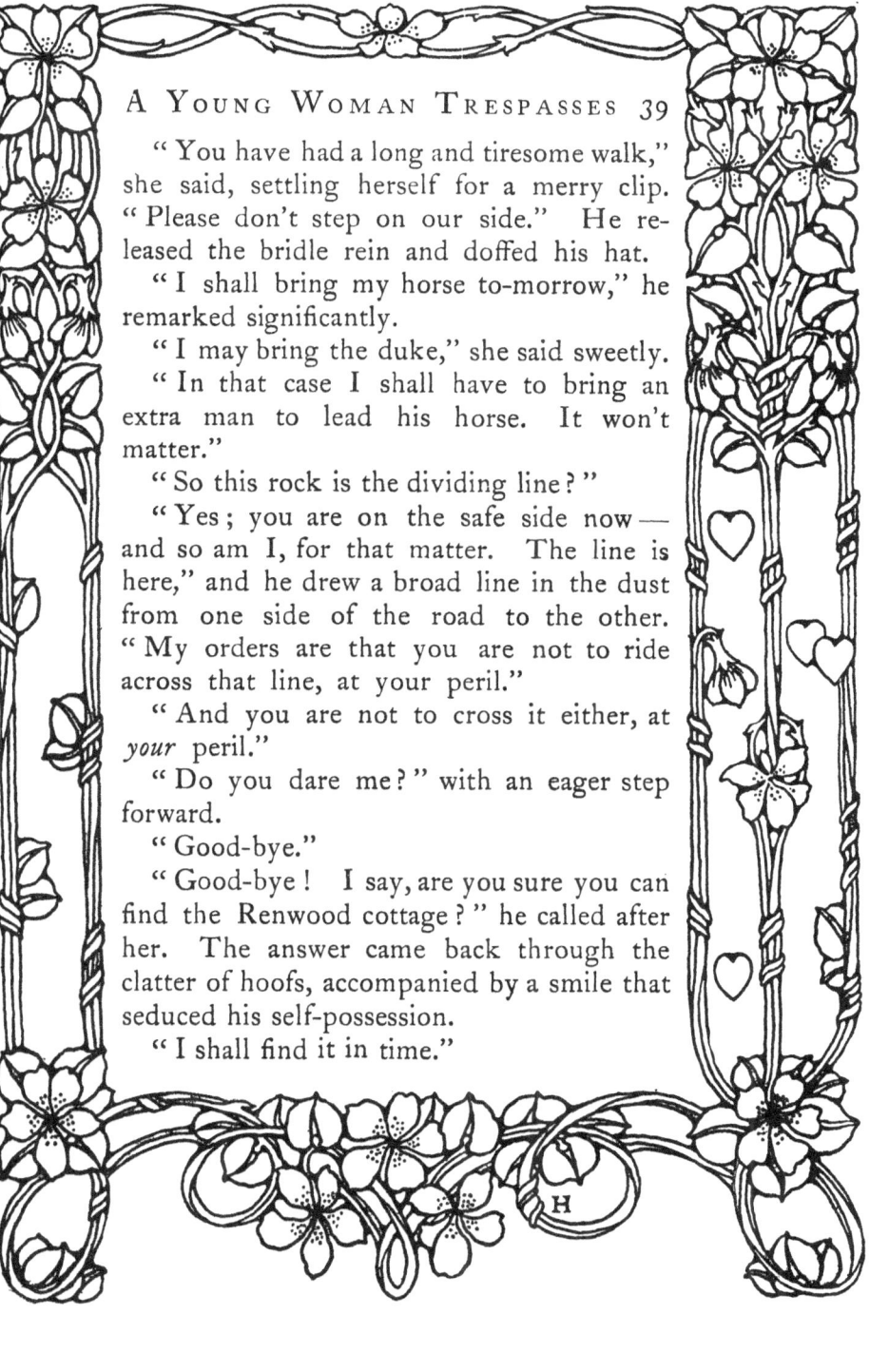

"You have had a long and tiresome walk," she said, settling herself for a merry clip. "Please don't step on our side." He released the bridle rein and doffed his hat.

"I shall bring my horse to-morrow," he remarked significantly.

"I may bring the duke," she said sweetly.

"In that case I shall have to bring an extra man to lead his horse. It won't matter."

"So this rock is the dividing line?"

"Yes; you are on the safe side now — and so am I, for that matter. The line is here," and he drew a broad line in the dust from one side of the road to the other. "My orders are that you are not to ride across that line, at your peril."

"And you are not to cross it either, at *your* peril."

"Do you dare me?" with an eager step forward.

"Good-bye."

"Good-bye! I say, are you sure you can find the Renwood cottage?" he called after her. The answer came back through the clatter of hoofs, accompanied by a smile that seduced his self-possession.

"I shall find it in time."

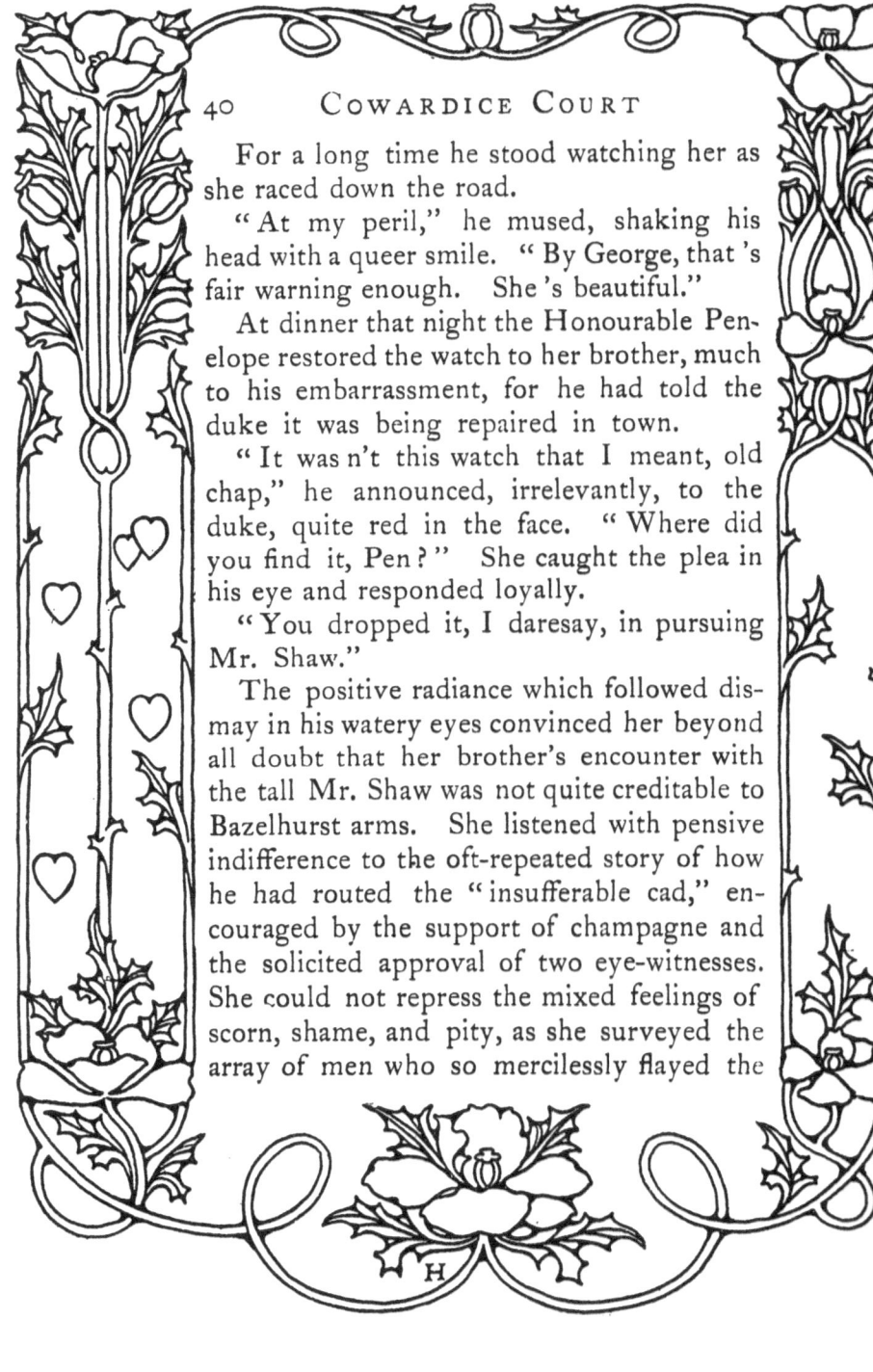

For a long time he stood watching her as
she raced down the road.

"At my peril," he mused, shaking his
head with a queer smile. "By George, that 's
fair warning enough. She 's beautiful."

At dinner that night the Honourable Penelope restored the watch to her brother, much
to his embarrassment, for he had told the
duke it was being repaired in town.

"It was n't this watch that I meant, old
chap," he announced, irrelevantly, to the
duke, quite red in the face. "Where did
you find it, Pen?" She caught the plea in
his eye and responded loyally.

"You dropped it, I daresay, in pursuing
Mr. Shaw."

The positive radiance which followed dismay in his watery eyes convinced her beyond
all doubt that her brother's encounter with
the tall Mr. Shaw was not quite creditable to
Bazelhurst arms. She listened with pensive
indifference to the oft-repeated story of how
he had routed the "insufferable cad," en-
couraged by the support of champagne and
the solicited approval of two eye-witnesses.
She could not repress the mixed feelings of
scorn, shame, and pity, as she surveyed the
array of men who so mercilessly flayed the

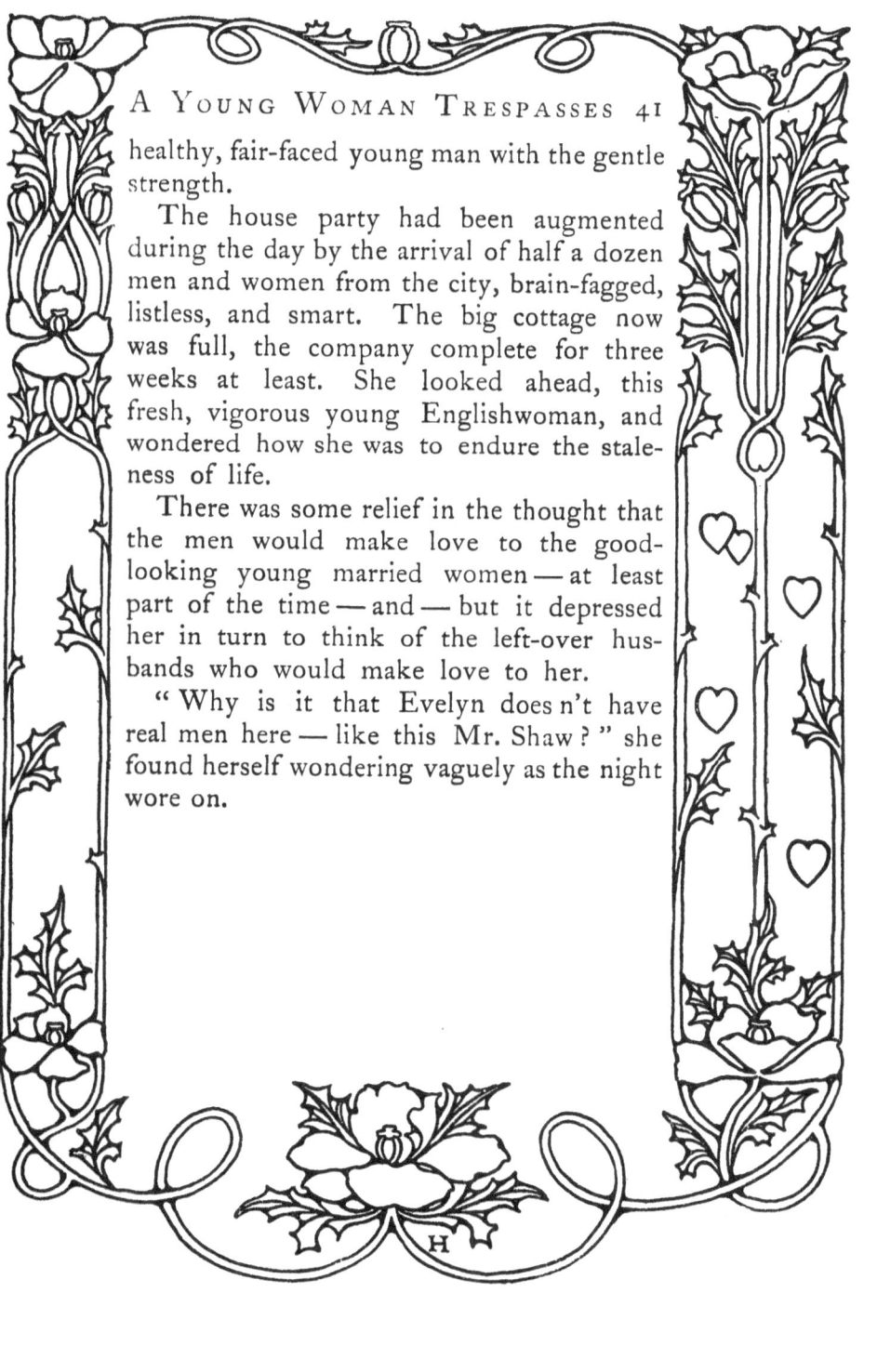

healthy, fair-faced young man with the gentle
strength.

The house party had been augmented
during the day by the arrival of half a dozen
men and women from the city, brain-fagged,
listless, and smart. The big cottage now
was full, the company complete for three
weeks at least. She looked ahead, this
fresh, vigorous young Englishwoman, and
wondered how she was to endure the stale-
ness of life.

There was some relief in the thought that
the men would make love to the good-
looking young married women — at least
part of the time — and — but it depressed
her in turn to think of the left-over hus-
bands who would make love to her.

"Why is it that Evelyn does n't have
real men here — like this Mr. Shaw?" she
found herself wondering vaguely as the night
wore on.

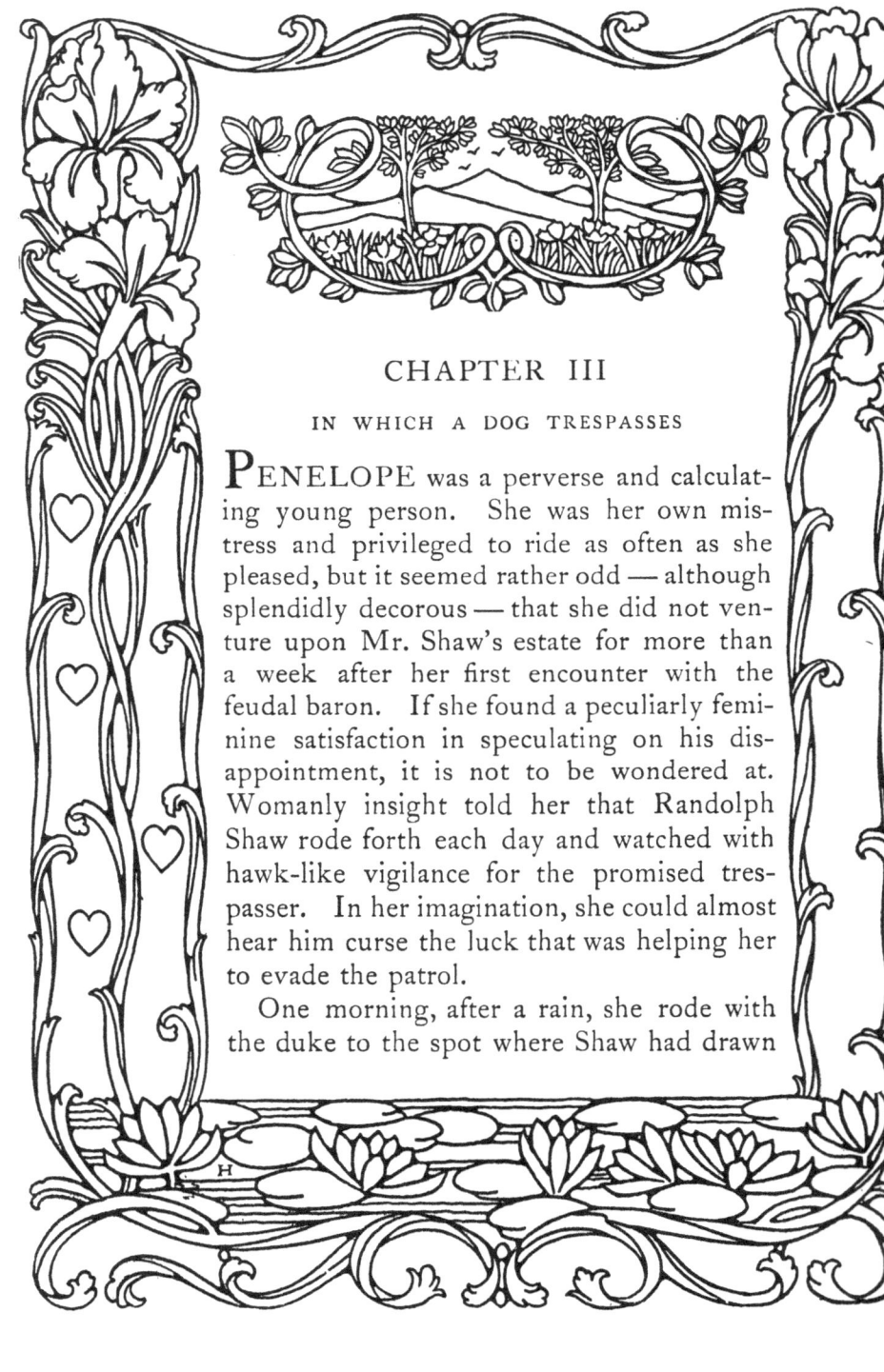

CHAPTER III

IN WHICH A DOG TRESPASSES

PENELOPE was a perverse and calculating young person. She was her own mistress and privileged to ride as often as she pleased, but it seemed rather odd — although splendidly decorous — that she did not venture upon Mr. Shaw's estate for more than a week after her first encounter with the feudal baron. If she found a peculiarly feminine satisfaction in speculating on his disappointment, it is not to be wondered at. Womanly insight told her that Randolph Shaw rode forth each day and watched with hawk-like vigilance for the promised trespasser. In her imagination, she could almost hear him curse the luck that was helping her to evade the patrol.

One morning, after a rain, she rode with the duke to the spot where Shaw had drawn

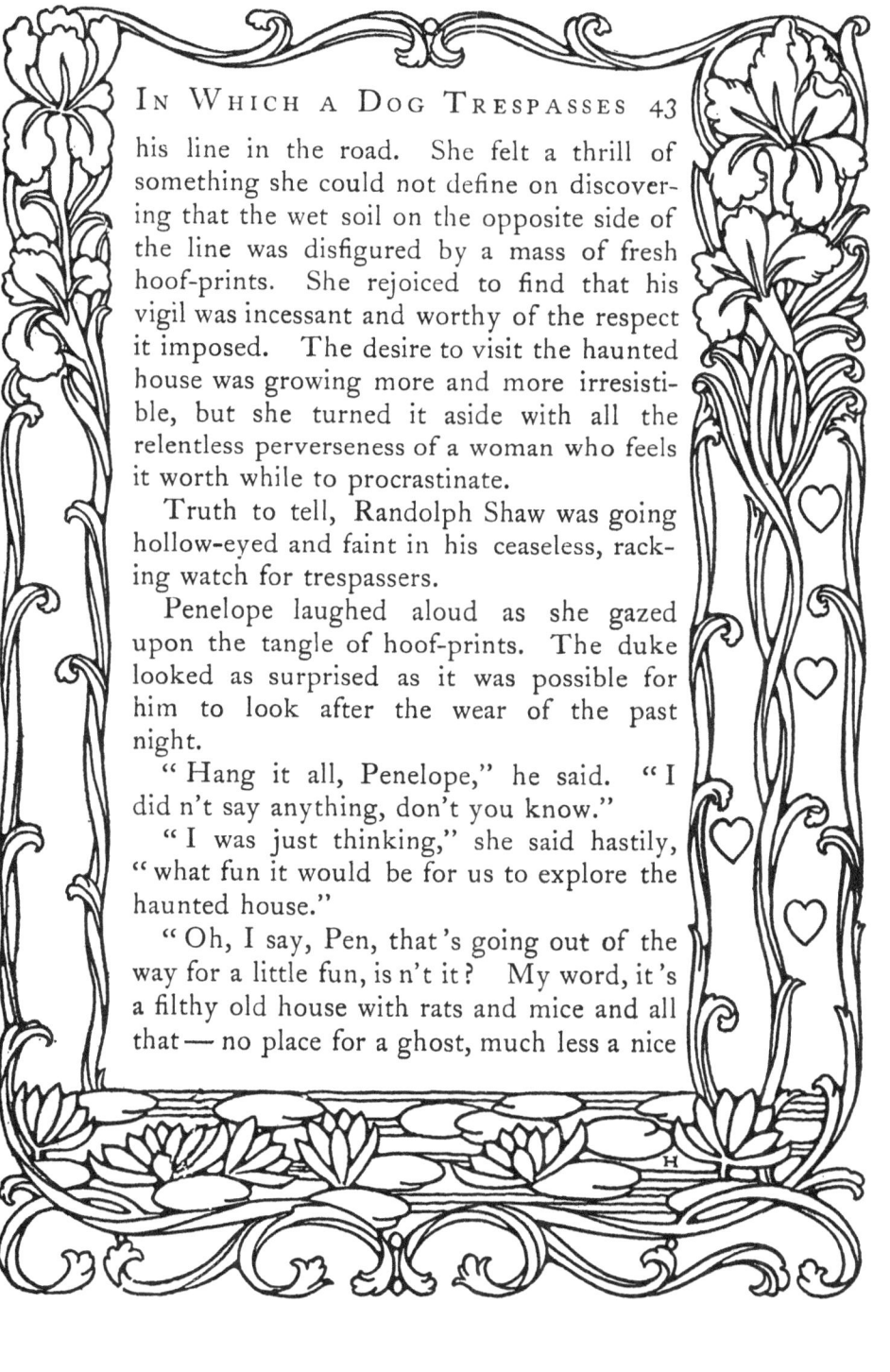

his line in the road. She felt a thrill of
something she could not define on discover-
ing that the wet soil on the opposite side of
the line was disfigured by a mass of fresh
hoof-prints. She rejoiced to find that his
vigil was incessant and worthy of the respect
it imposed. The desire to visit the haunted
house was growing more and more irresisti-
ble, but she turned it aside with all the
relentless perverseness of a woman who feels
it worth while to procrastinate.

Truth to tell, Randolph Shaw was going
hollow-eyed and faint in his ceaseless, rack-
ing watch for trespassers.

Penelope laughed aloud as she gazed
upon the tangle of hoof-prints. The duke
looked as surprised as it was possible for
him to look after the wear of the past
night.

"Hang it all, Penelope," he said. "I
did n't say anything, don't you know."

"I was just thinking," she said hastily,
"what fun it would be for us to explore the
haunted house."

"Oh, I say, Pen, that's going out of the
way for a little fun, is n't it? My word, it's
a filthy old house with rats and mice and all
that — no place for a ghost, much less a nice

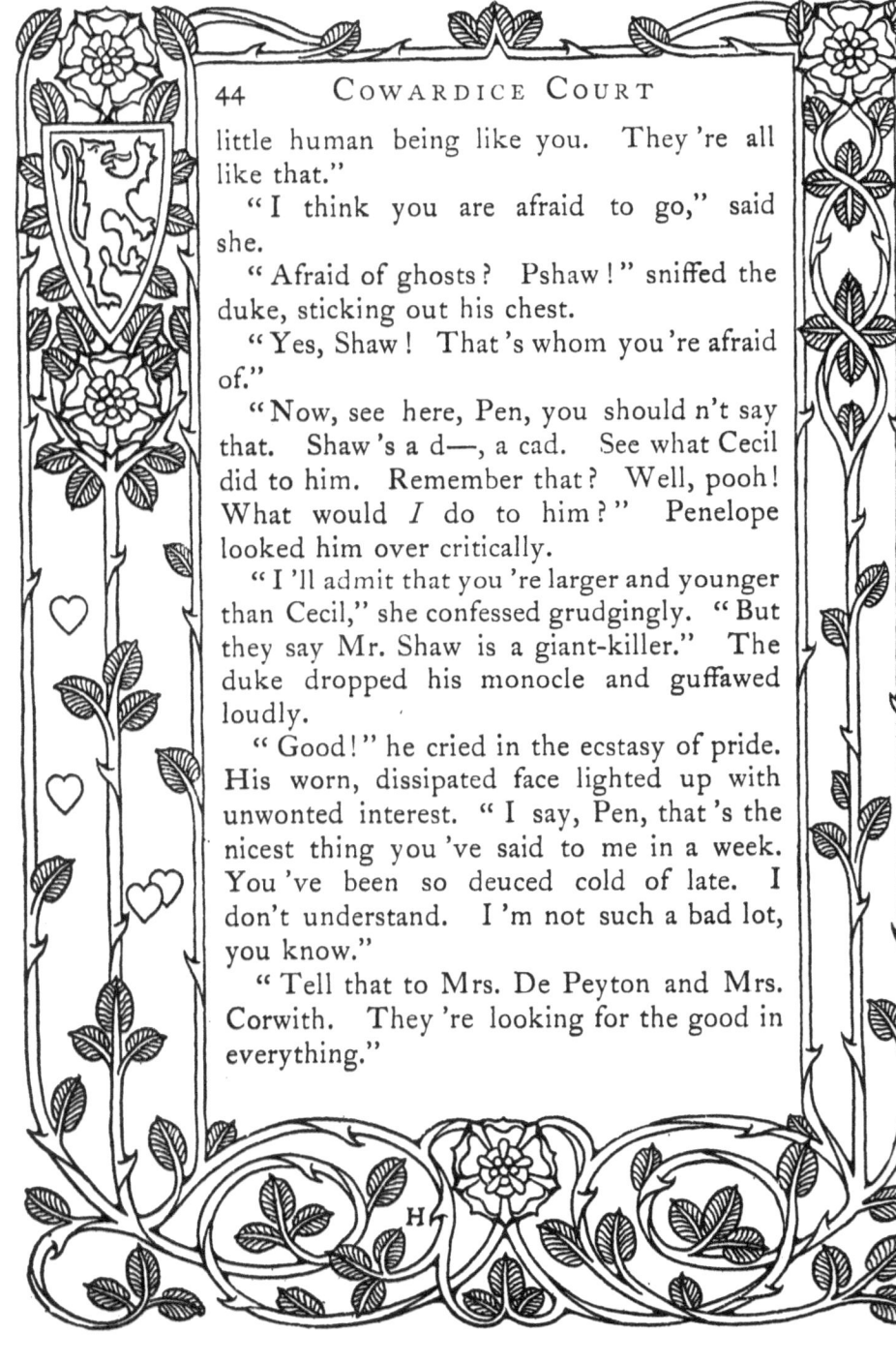

little human being like you. They're all like that."

"I think you are afraid to go," said she.

"Afraid of ghosts? Pshaw!" sniffed the duke, sticking out his chest.

"Yes, Shaw! That's whom you're afraid of."

"Now, see here, Pen, you shouldn't say that. Shaw's a d—, a cad. See what Cecil did to him. Remember that? Well, pooh! What would *I* do to him?" Penelope looked him over critically.

"I'll admit that you're larger and younger than Cecil," she confessed grudgingly. "But they say Mr. Shaw is a giant-killer." The duke dropped his monocle and guffawed loudly.

"Good!" he cried in the ecstasy of pride. His worn, dissipated face lighted up with unwonted interest. "I say, Pen, that's the nicest thing you've said to me in a week. You've been so deuced cold of late. I don't understand. I'm not such a bad lot, you know."

"Tell that to Mrs. De Peyton and Mrs. Corwith. They're looking for the good in everything."

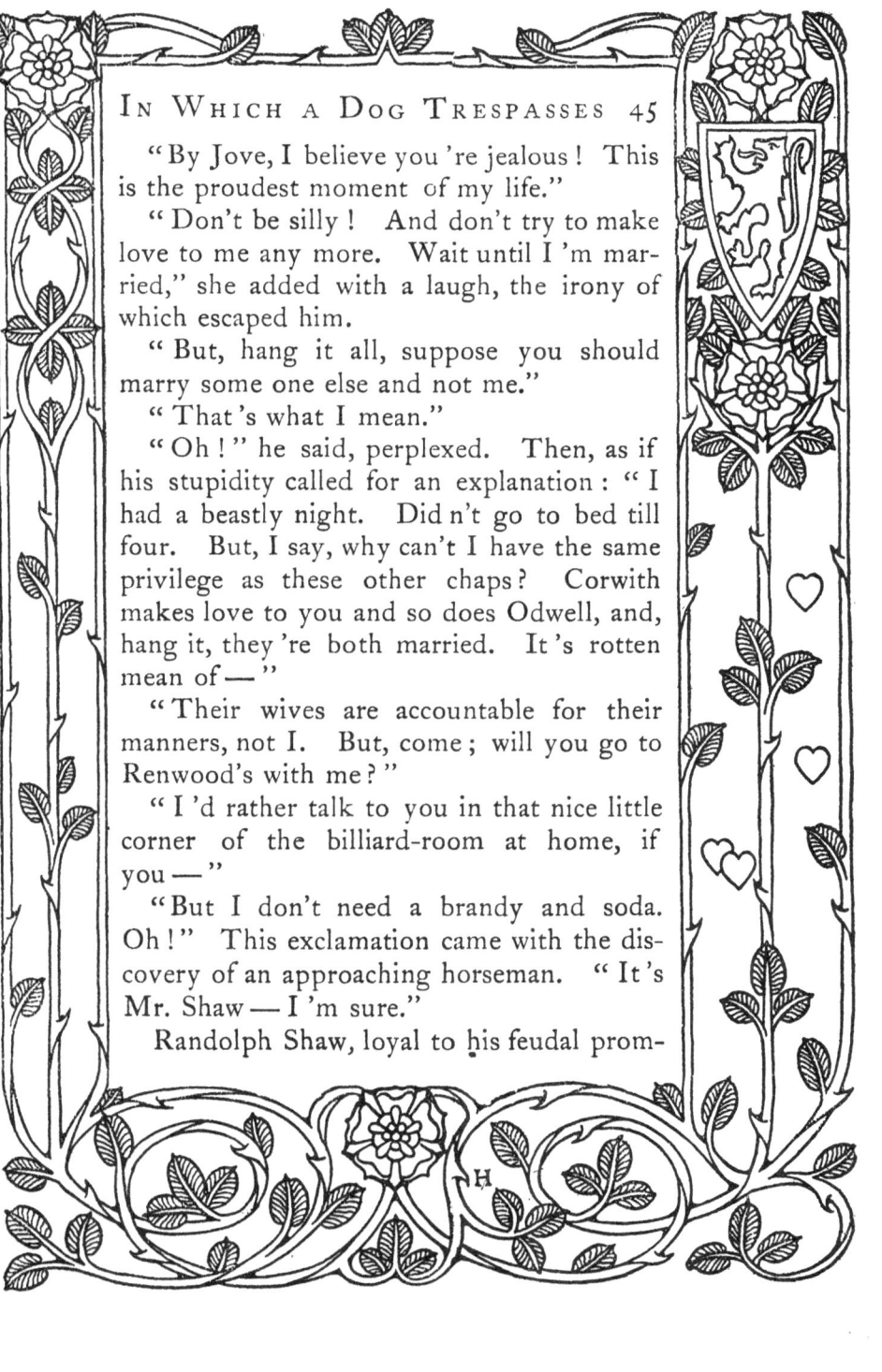

"By Jove, I believe you're jealous! This is the proudest moment of my life."

"Don't be silly! And don't try to make love to me any more. Wait until I'm married," she added with a laugh, the irony of which escaped him.

"But, hang it all, suppose you should marry some one else and not me."

"That's what I mean."

"Oh!" he said, perplexed. Then, as if his stupidity called for an explanation: "I had a beastly night. Didn't go to bed till four. But, I say, why can't I have the same privilege as these other chaps? Corwith makes love to you and so does Odwell, and, hang it, they're both married. It's rotten mean of —"

"Their wives are accountable for their manners, not I. But, come; will you go to Renwood's with me?"

"I'd rather talk to you in that nice little corner of the billiard-room at home, if you —"

"But I don't need a brandy and soda. Oh!" This exclamation came with the discovery of an approaching horseman. "It's Mr. Shaw — I'm sure."

Randolph Shaw, loyal to his feudal prom-

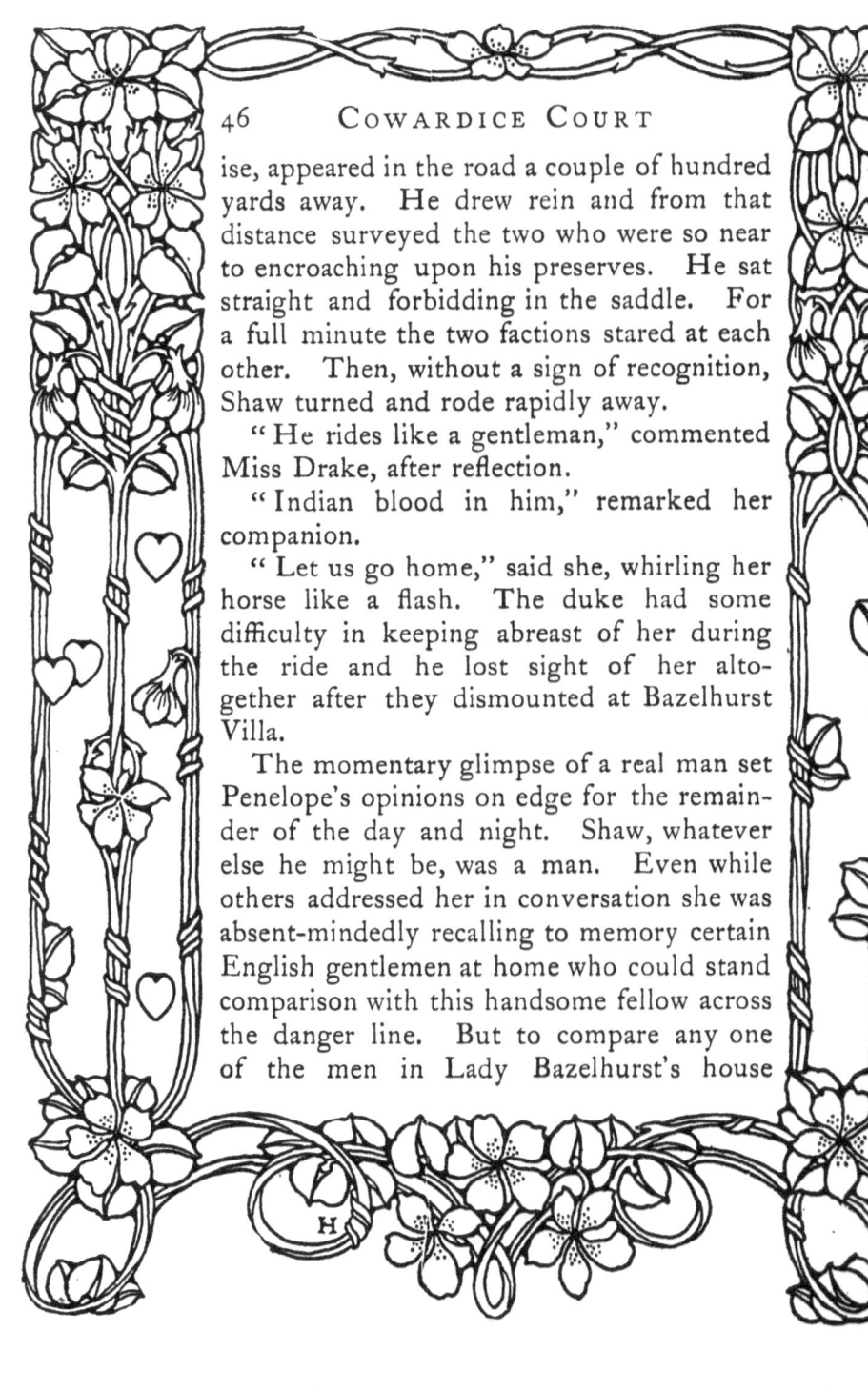

ise, appeared in the road a couple of hundred yards away. He drew rein and from that distance surveyed the two who were so near to encroaching upon his preserves. He sat straight and forbidding in the saddle. For a full minute the two factions stared at each other. Then, without a sign of recognition, Shaw turned and rode rapidly away.

"He rides like a gentleman," commented Miss Drake, after reflection.

"Indian blood in him," remarked her companion.

"Let us go home," said she, whirling her horse like a flash. The duke had some difficulty in keeping abreast of her during the ride and he lost sight of her altogether after they dismounted at Bazelhurst Villa.

The momentary glimpse of a real man set Penelope's opinions on edge for the remainder of the day and night. Shaw, whatever else he might be, was a man. Even while others addressed her in conversation she was absent-mindedly recalling to memory certain English gentlemen at home who could stand comparison with this handsome fellow across the danger line. But to compare any one of the men in Lady Bazelhurst's house

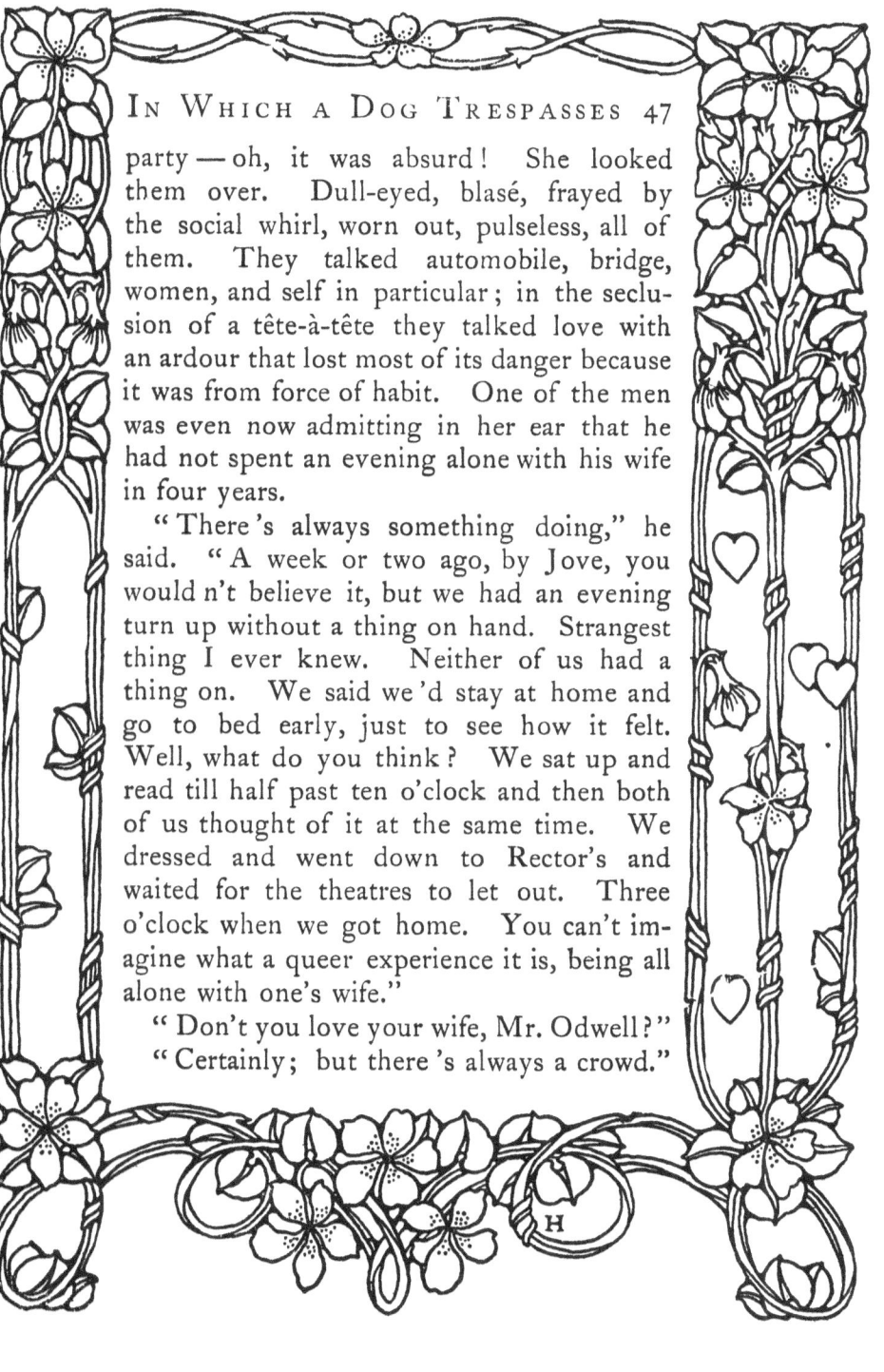

party — oh, it was absurd! She looked
them over. Dull-eyed, blasé, frayed by
the social whirl, worn out, pulseless, all of
them. They talked automobile, bridge,
women, and self in particular; in the seclu-
sion of a tête-à-tête they talked love with
an ardour that lost most of its danger because
it was from force of habit. One of the men
was even now admitting in her ear that he
had not spent an evening alone with his wife
in four years.

"There's always something doing," he
said. "A week or two ago, by Jove, you
would n't believe it, but we had an evening
turn up without a thing on hand. Strangest
thing I ever knew. Neither of us had a
thing on. We said we'd stay at home and
go to bed early, just to see how it felt.
Well, what do you think? We sat up and
read till half past ten o'clock and then both
of us thought of it at the same time. We
dressed and went down to Rector's and
waited for the theatres to let out. Three
o'clock when we got home. You can't imagine what a queer experience it is, being all
alone with one's wife."

"Don't you love your wife, Mr. Odwell?"

"Certainly; but there's always a crowd."

H

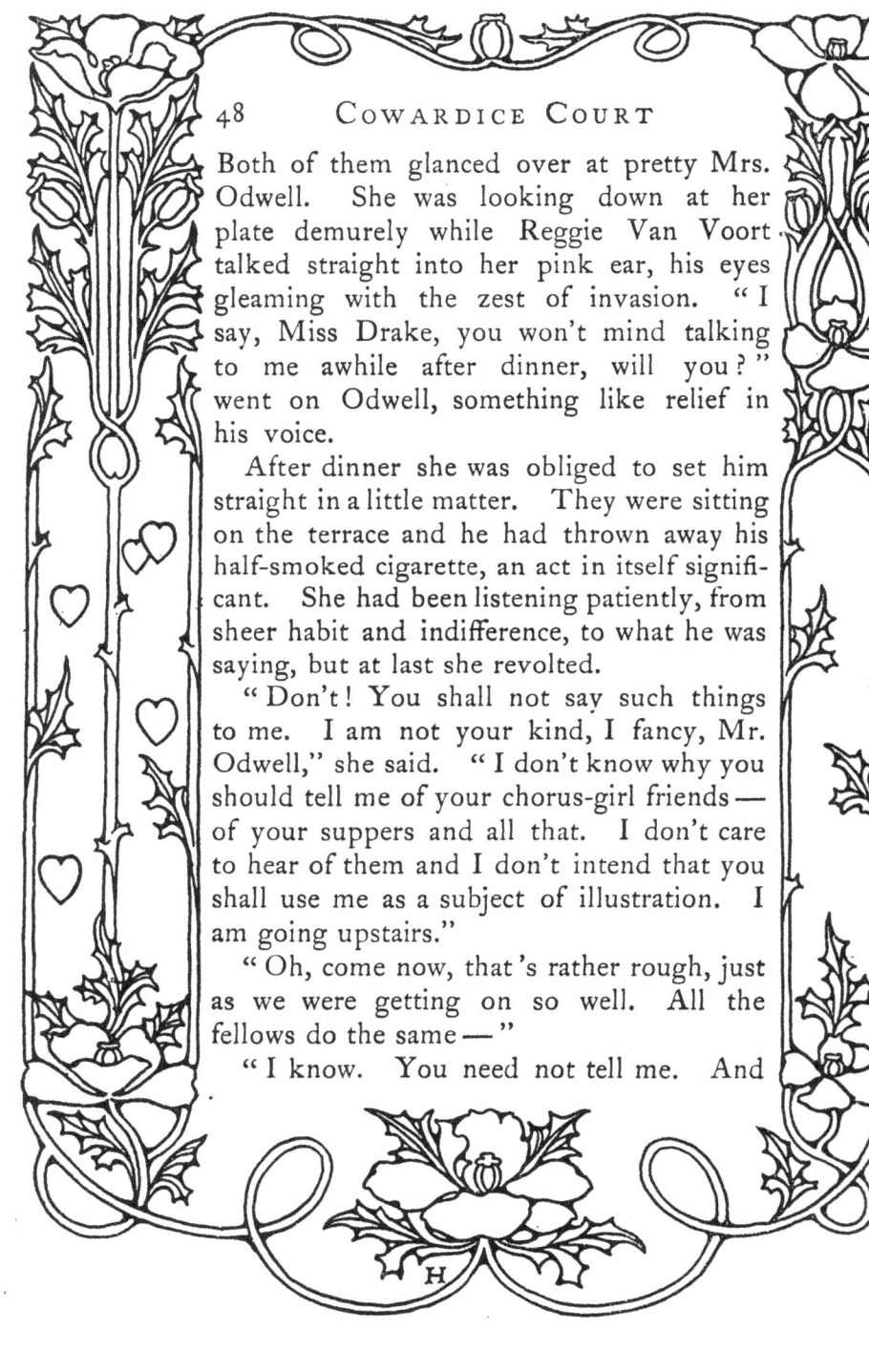

Both of them glanced over at pretty Mrs. Odwell. She was looking down at her plate demurely while Reggie Van Voort talked straight into her pink ear, his eyes gleaming with the zest of invasion. " I say, Miss Drake, you won't mind talking to me awhile after dinner, will you ? " went on Odwell, something like relief in his voice.

After dinner she was obliged to set him straight in a little matter. They were sitting on the terrace and he had thrown away his half-smoked cigarette, an act in itself significant. She had been listening patiently, from sheer habit and indifference, to what he was saying, but at last she revolted.

" Don't! You shall not say such things to me. I am not your kind, I fancy, Mr. Odwell," she said. " I don't know why you should tell me of your chorus-girl friends — of your suppers and all that. I don't care to hear of them and I don't intend that you shall use me as a subject of illustration. I am going upstairs."

" Oh, come now, that 's rather rough, just as we were getting on so well. All the fellows do the same — "

" I know. You need not tell me. And

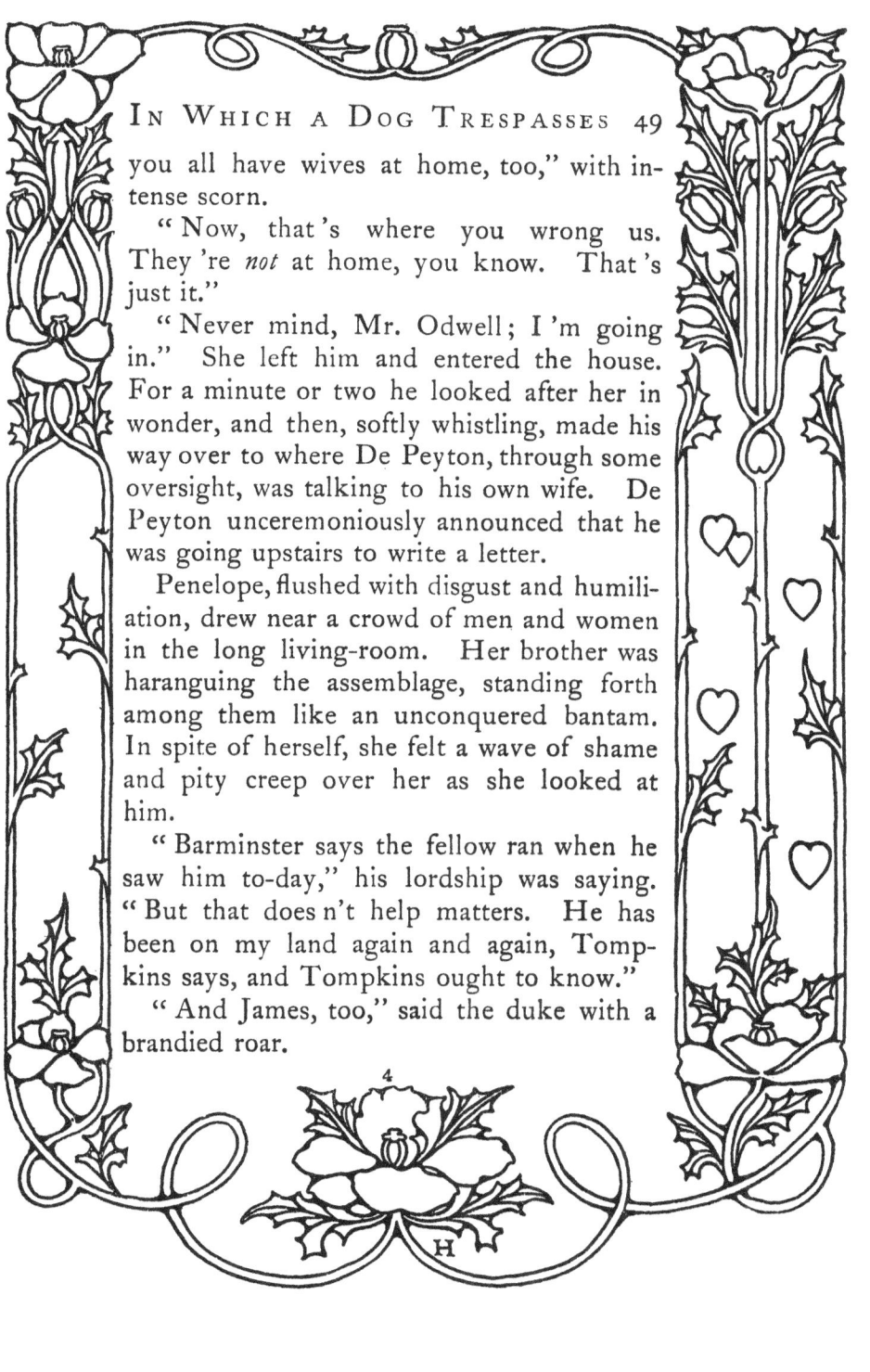

you all have wives at home, too," with intense scorn.

"Now, that's where you wrong us. They're *not* at home, you know. That's just it."

"Never mind, Mr. Odwell; I'm going in." She left him and entered the house. For a minute or two he looked after her in wonder, and then, softly whistling, made his way over to where De Peyton, through some oversight, was talking to his own wife. De Peyton unceremoniously announced that he was going upstairs to write a letter.

Penelope, flushed with disgust and humiliation, drew near a crowd of men and women in the long living-room. Her brother was haranguing the assemblage, standing forth among them like an unconquered bantam. In spite of herself, she felt a wave of shame and pity creep over her as she looked at him.

"Barminster says the fellow ran when he saw him to-day," his lordship was saying. "But that doesn't help matters. He has been on my land again and again, Tompkins says, and Tompkins ought to know."

"And James, too," said the duke with a brandied roar.

4

H

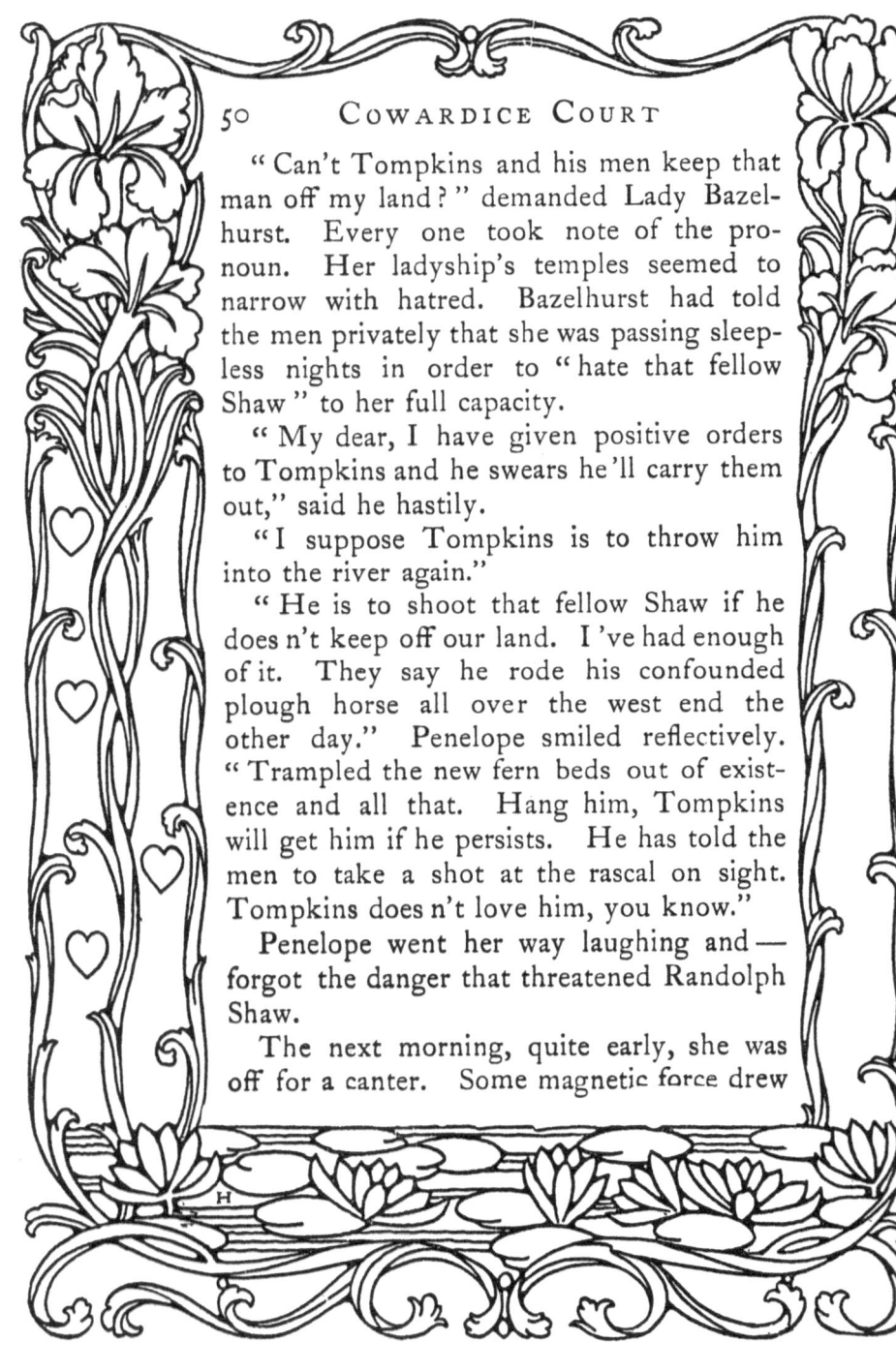

" Can't Tompkins and his men keep that man off my land ? " demanded Lady Bazelhurst. Every one took note of the pronoun. Her ladyship's temples seemed to narrow with hatred. Bazelhurst had told the men privately that she was passing sleepless nights in order to " hate that fellow Shaw " to her full capacity.

" My dear, I have given positive orders to Tompkins and he swears he'll carry them out," said he hastily.

"I suppose Tompkins is to throw him into the river again."

" He is to shoot that fellow Shaw if he does n't keep off our land. I 've had enough of it. They say he rode his confounded plough horse all over the west end the other day." Penelope smiled reflectively. " Trampled the new fern beds out of existence and all that. Hang him, Tompkins will get him if he persists. He has told the men to take a shot at the rascal on sight. Tompkins does n't love him, you know."

Penelope went her way laughing and — forgot the danger that threatened Randolph Shaw.

The next morning, quite early, she was off for a canter. Some magnetic force drew

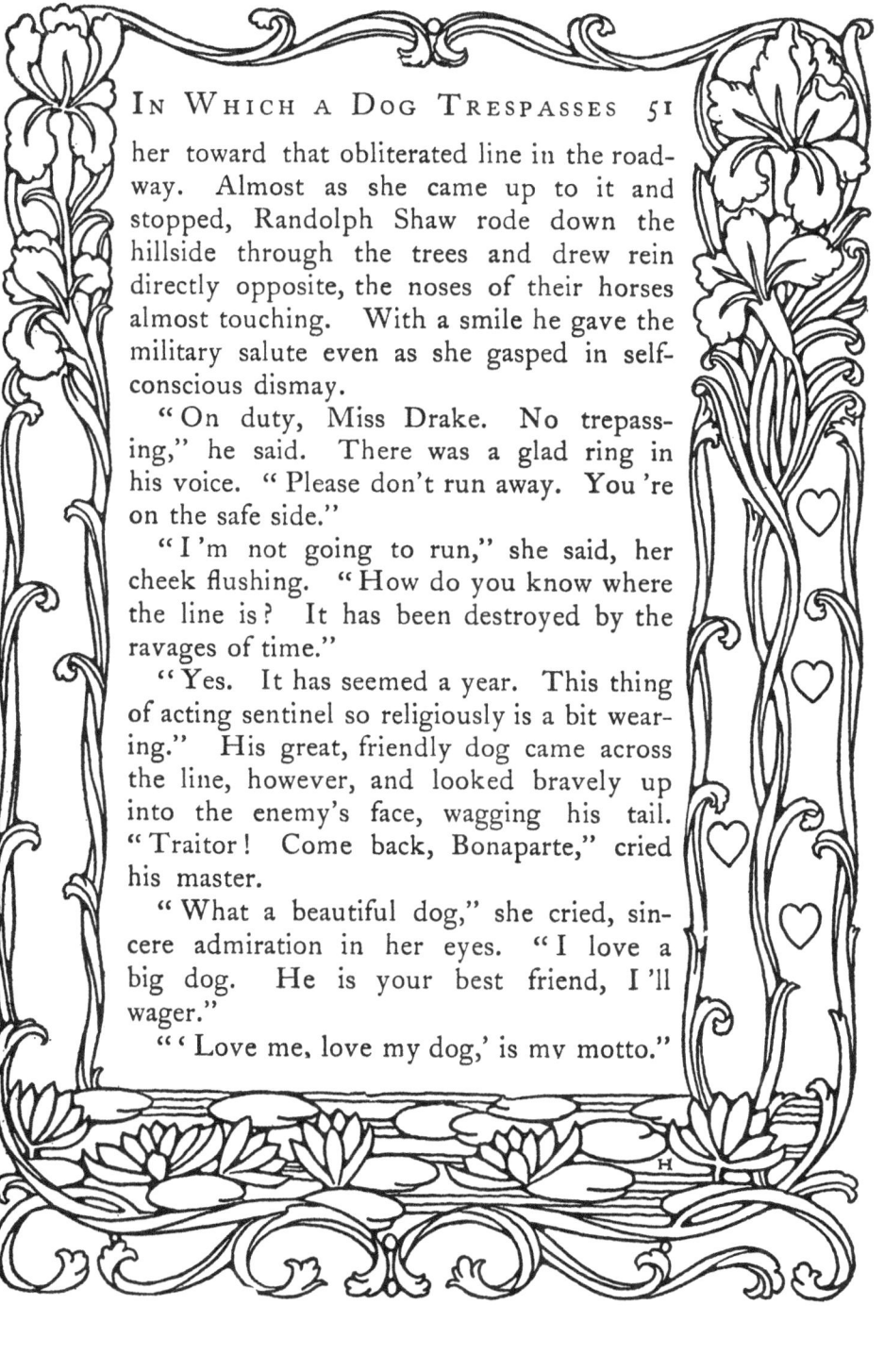

her toward that obliterated line in the roadway. Almost as she came up to it and
stopped, Randolph Shaw rode down the
hillside through the trees and drew rein
directly opposite, the noses of their horses
almost touching. With a smile he gave the
military salute even as she gasped in self-
conscious dismay.

"On duty, Miss Drake. No trepass-
ing," he said. There was a glad ring in
his voice. "Please don't run away. You're
on the safe side."

"I'm not going to run," she said, her
cheek flushing. "How do you know where
the line is? It has been destroyed by the
ravages of time."

"Yes. It has seemed a year. This thing
of acting sentinel so religiously is a bit wear-
ing." His great, friendly dog came across
the line, however, and looked bravely up
into the enemy's face, wagging his tail.
"Traitor! Come back, Bonaparte," cried
his master.

"What a beautiful dog," she cried, sin-
cere admiration in her eyes. "I love a
big dog. He is your best friend, I'll
wager."

"'Love me, love my dog,' is my motto."

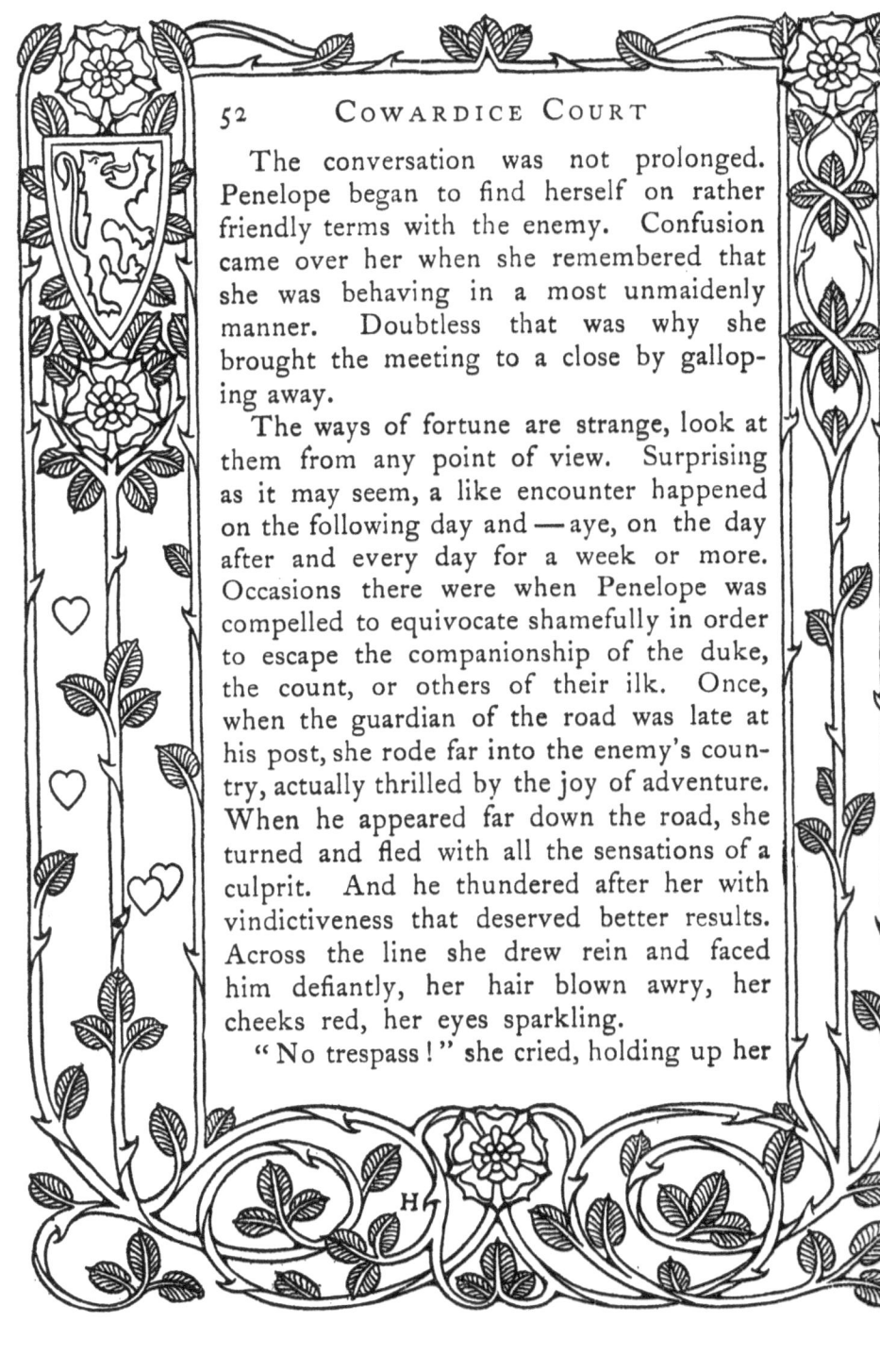

The conversation was not prolonged. Penelope began to find herself on rather friendly terms with the enemy. Confusion came over her when she remembered that she was behaving in a most unmaidenly manner. Doubtless that was why she brought the meeting to a close by galloping away.

The ways of fortune are strange, look at them from any point of view. Surprising as it may seem, a like encounter happened on the following day and — aye, on the day after and every day for a week or more. Occasions there were when Penelope was compelled to equivocate shamefully in order to escape the companionship of the duke, the count, or others of their ilk. Once, when the guardian of the road was late at his post, she rode far into the enemy's country, actually thrilled by the joy of adventure. When he appeared far down the road, she turned and fled with all the sensations of a culprit. And he thundered after her with vindictiveness that deserved better results. Across the line she drew rein and faced him defiantly, her hair blown awry, her cheeks red, her eyes sparkling.

"No trespass!" she cried, holding up her

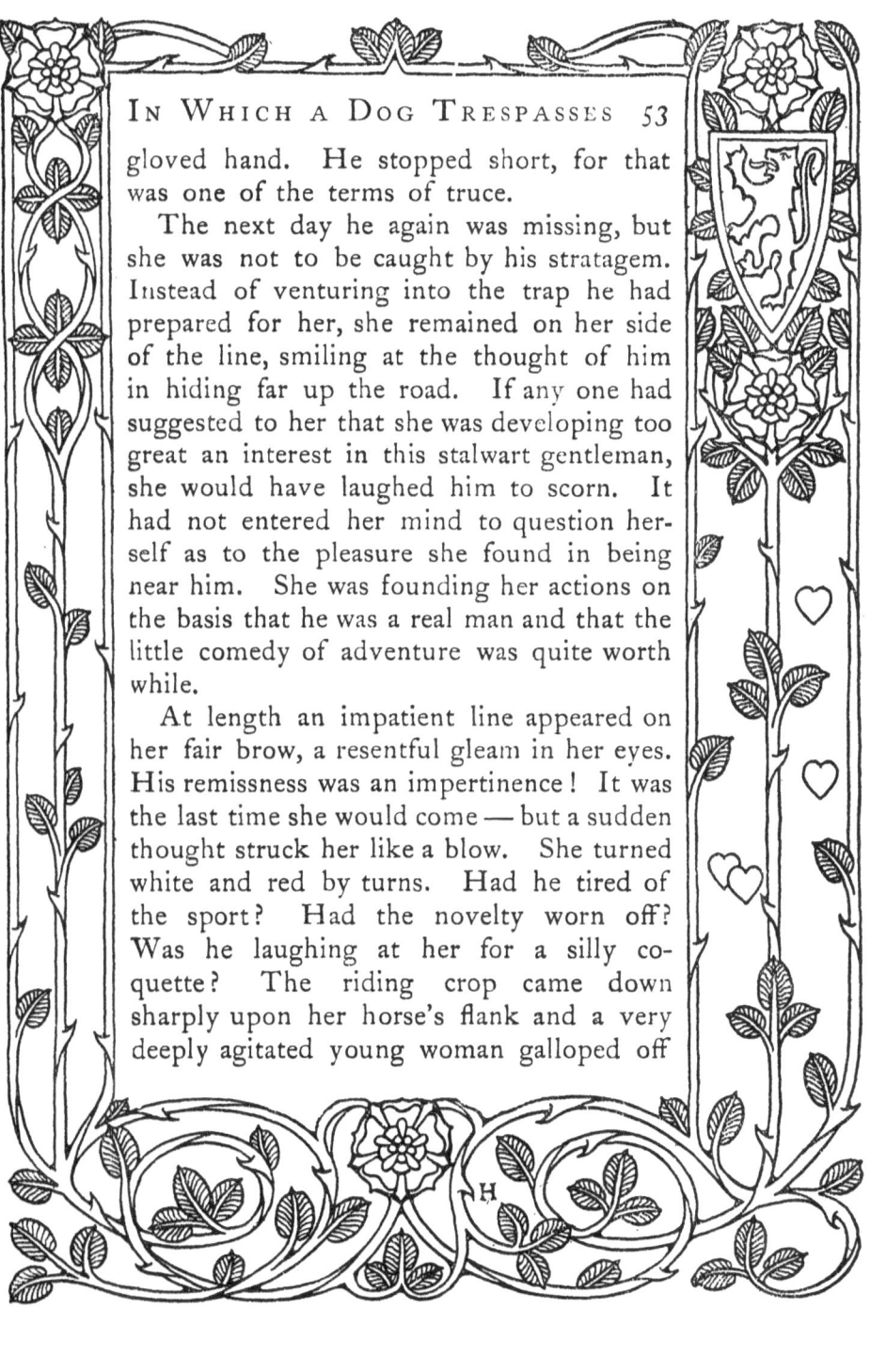

gloved hand. He stopped short, for that was one of the terms of truce.

The next day he again was missing, but she was not to be caught by his stratagem. Instead of venturing into the trap he had prepared for her, she remained on her side of the line, smiling at the thought of him in hiding far up the road. If any one had suggested to her that she was developing too great an interest in this stalwart gentleman, she would have laughed him to scorn. It had not entered her mind to question herself as to the pleasure she found in being near him. She was founding her actions on the basis that he was a real man and that the little comedy of adventure was quite worth while.

At length an impatient line appeared on her fair brow, a resentful gleam in her eyes. His remissness was an impertinence! It was the last time she would come — but a sudden thought struck her like a blow. She turned white and red by turns. Had he tired of the sport? Had the novelty worn off? Was he laughing at her for a silly co-quette? The riding crop came down sharply upon her horse's flank and a very deeply agitated young woman galloped off

toward Bazelhurst Villa, hurrying as though afraid he might catch sight of her in flight.

A quarter of a mile brought a change in her emotions. British stubbornness arose to combat an utter rout. After all, why should she run away from him? With whimsical bravado, she turned off suddenly into the trail that led to the river, her colour deepening with the consciousness that, after all, she was vaguely hoping she might see him somewhere before the morning passed. Through the leafy pathway she rode at a snail's pace, brushing the low-hanging leaves and twigs from about her head with something akin to petulance. As she neared the river the neighing of a horse hard by caused her to sit erect with burning ears. Then she relapsed into a smile, remembering that it might have come from the game warden's horse. A moment later her searching eyes caught sight of Shaw's horse tied to a sapling and on Bazelhurst ground, many hundred feet from his own domain. She drew rein sharply and looked about in considerable trepidation. Off to the right lay the log that divided the lands, but nowhere along the bank of the river could she see the trespasser. Carefully she resumed her

H

way, ever on the lookout, puzzled not a little
by the unusual state of affairs.

Near the river trail she came upon the
man, but he paid no heed to her approach.
He sat with his face in his hands and — she
could not believe her eyes and ears — he
was sobbing bitterly. For an instant her
lips curled in the smile of scornful triumph
and then something like disgust came over
her. There was mockery in her voice as
she called out to him.

"Have you stubbed your toe, little boy?"

He looked up, dazed. Then he arose,
turning his back while he dashed his hand
across his eyes. When he glanced back at
her he saw that she was smiling. But she
also saw something in his face that drove
the smile away. Absolute rage gleamed in
his eyes.

"So it is real war," he said hoarsely, his
face quivering. "Your pitiful cowards want
it to be real, do they? Well, that's what
it shall be, hang them! They shall have
all they want of it! Look! This is their
way of fighting, is it? Look!"

He pointed to his feet. Her bewildered
eyes saw that his hand was bloody and a
deathly sickness came over her. He was

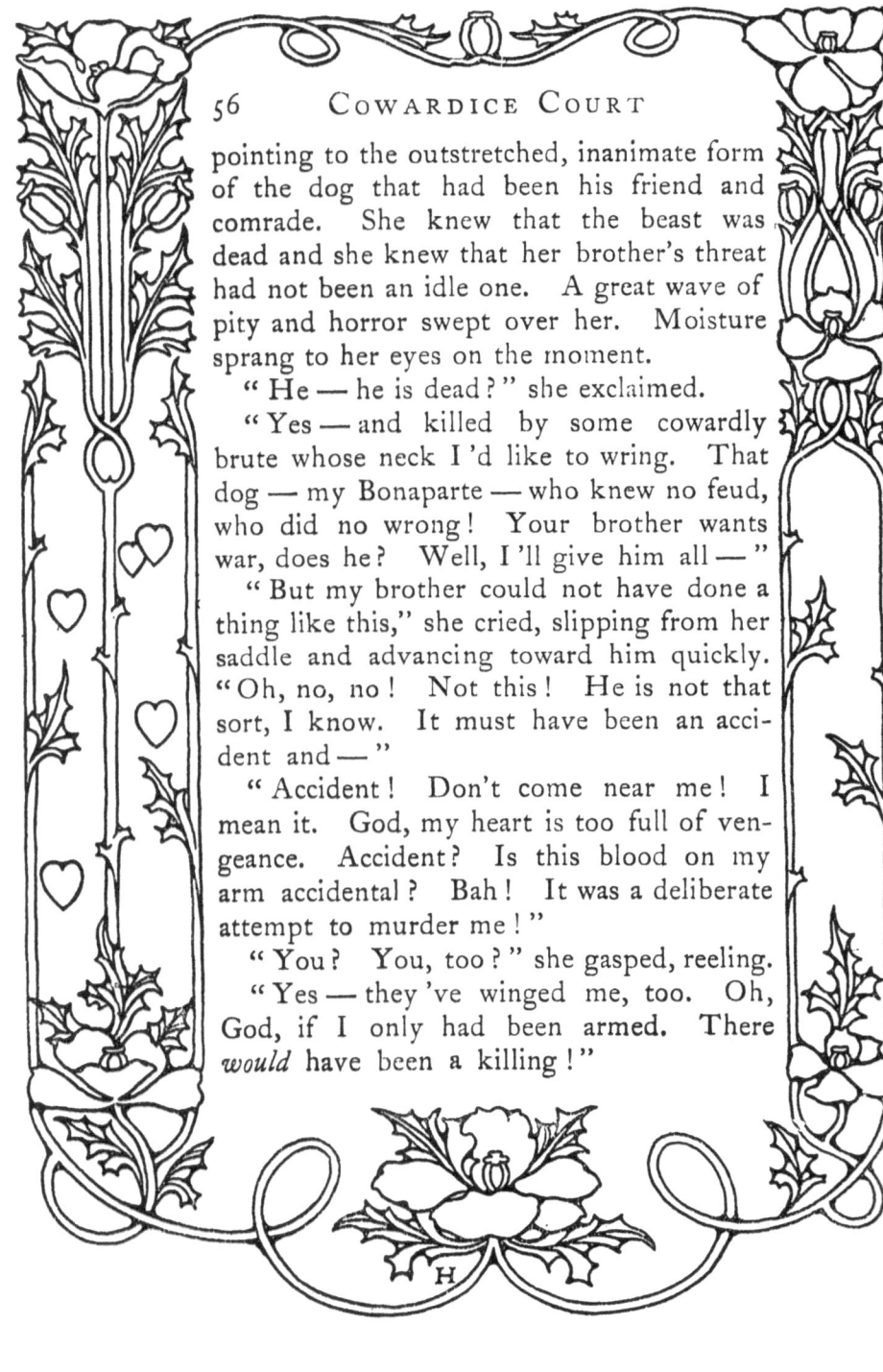

pointing to the outstretched, inanimate form of the dog that had been his friend and comrade. She knew that the beast was dead and she knew that her brother's threat had not been an idle one. A great wave of pity and horror swept over her. Moisture sprang to her eyes on the moment.

"He — he is dead?" she exclaimed.

"Yes — and killed by some cowardly brute whose neck I'd like to wring. That dog — my Bonaparte — who knew no feud, who did no wrong! Your brother wants war, does he? Well, I'll give him all —"

"But my brother could not have done a thing like this," she cried, slipping from her saddle and advancing toward him quickly. "Oh, no, no! Not this! He is not that sort, I know. It must have been an accident and —"

"Accident! Don't come near me! I mean it. God, my heart is too full of vengeance. Accident? Is this blood on my arm accidental? Bah! It was a deliberate attempt to murder me!"

"You? You, too?" she gasped, reeling.

"Yes — they've winged me, too. Oh, God, if I only had been armed. There *would* have been a killing!"

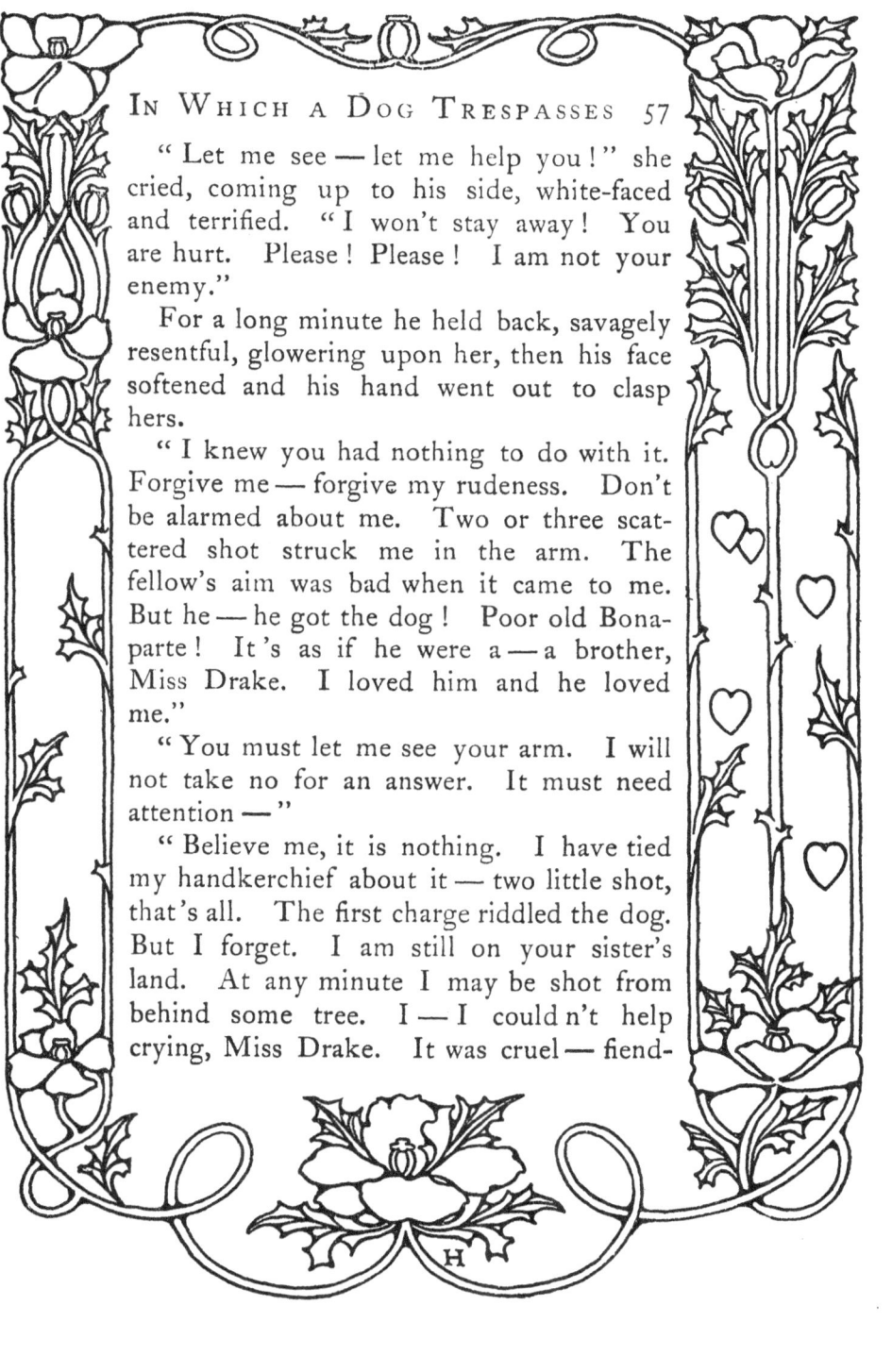

"Let me see — let me help you!" she cried, coming up to his side, white-faced and terrified. "I won't stay away! You are hurt. Please! Please! I am not your enemy."

For a long minute he held back, savagely resentful, glowering upon her, then his face softened and his hand went out to clasp hers.

"I knew you had nothing to do with it. Forgive me — forgive my rudeness. Don't be alarmed about me. Two or three scattered shot struck me in the arm. The fellow's aim was bad when it came to me. But he — he got the dog! Poor old Bonaparte! It's as if he were a — a brother, Miss Drake. I loved him and he loved me."

"You must let me see your arm. I will not take no for an answer. It must need attention — "

"Believe me, it is nothing. I have tied my handkerchief about it — two little shot, that's all. The first charge riddled the dog. But I forget. I am still on your sister's land. At any minute I may be shot from behind some tree. I — I couldn't help crying, Miss Drake. It was cruel — fiend-

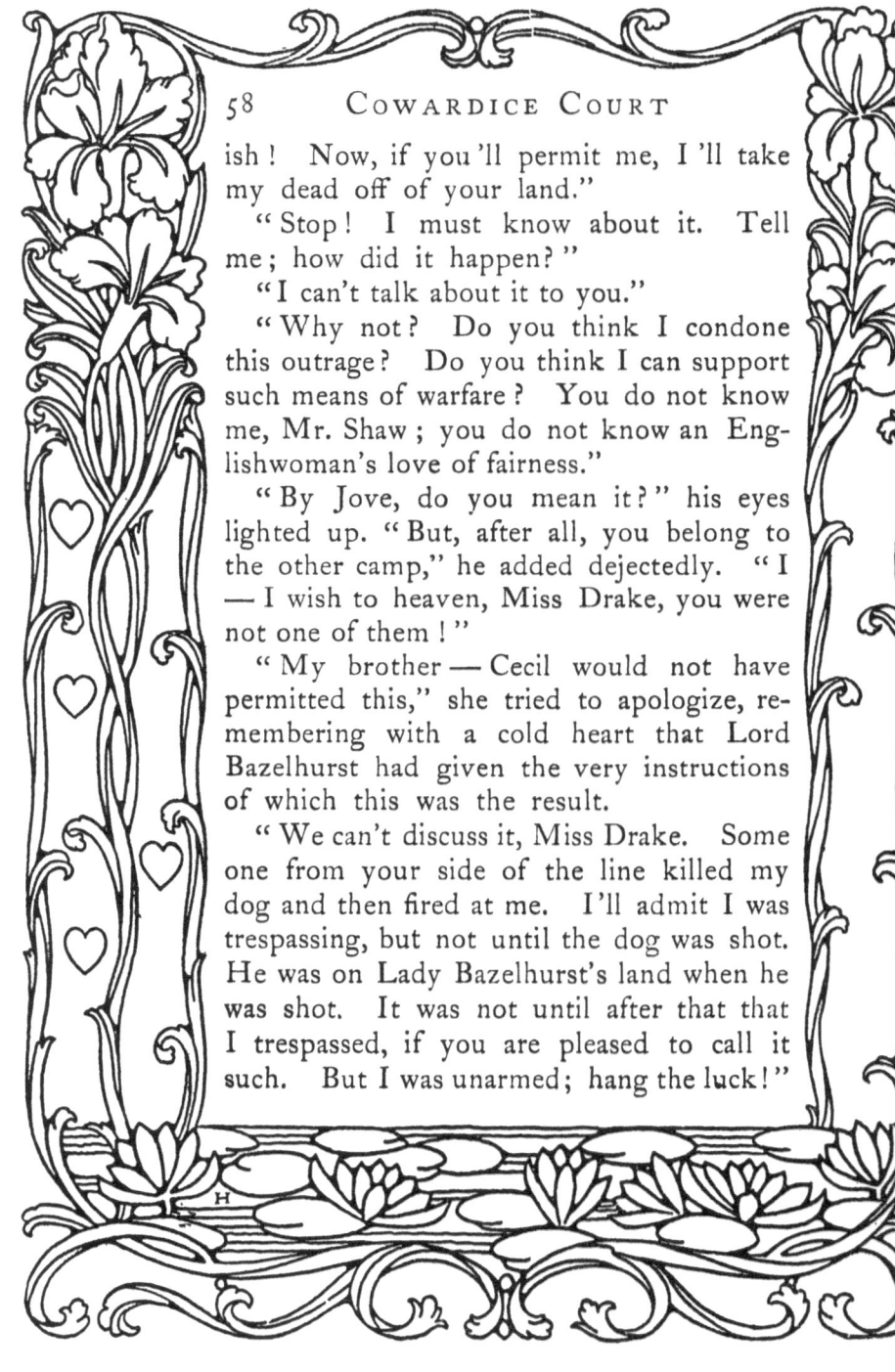

ish! Now, if you'll permit me, I'll take my dead off of your land."

"Stop! I must know about it. Tell me; how did it happen?"

"I can't talk about it to you."

"Why not? Do you think I condone this outrage? Do you think I can support such means of warfare? You do not know me, Mr. Shaw; you do not know an Englishwoman's love of fairness."

"By Jove, do you mean it?" his eyes lighted up. "But, after all, you belong to the other camp," he added dejectedly. "I — I wish to heaven, Miss Drake, you were not one of them!"

"My brother — Cecil would not have permitted this," she tried to apologize, remembering with a cold heart that Lord Bazelhurst had given the very instructions of which this was the result.

"We can't discuss it, Miss Drake. Some one from your side of the line killed my dog and then fired at me. I'll admit I was trespassing, but not until the dog was shot. He was on Lady Bazelhurst's land when he was shot. It was not until after that that I trespassed, if you are pleased to call it such. But I was unarmed; hang the luck!"

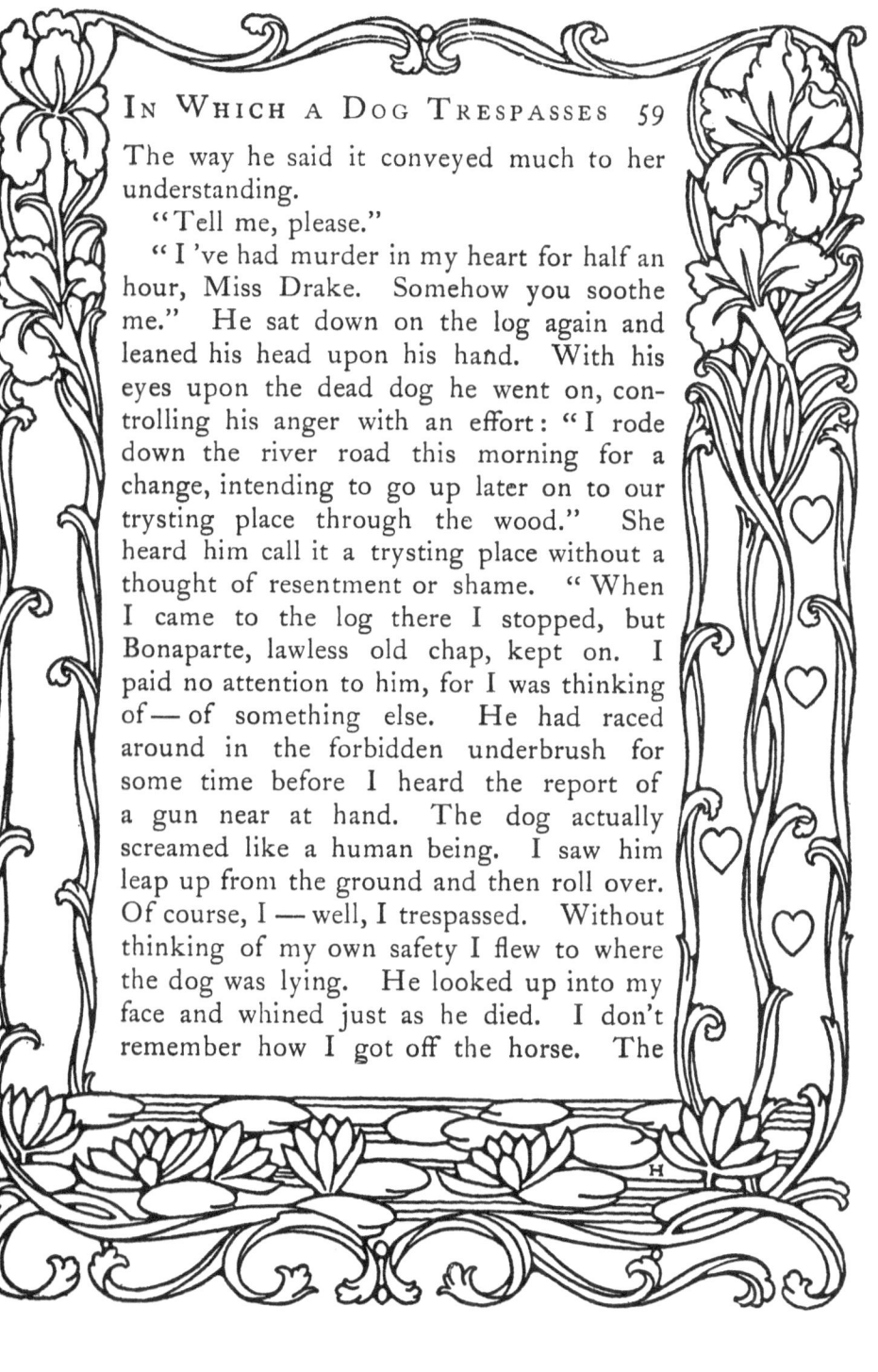

The way he said it conveyed much to her understanding.

"Tell me, please."

"I've had murder in my heart for half an hour, Miss Drake. Somehow you soothe me." He sat down on the log again and leaned his head upon his hand. With his eyes upon the dead dog he went on, controlling his anger with an effort: "I rode down the river road this morning for a change, intending to go up later on to our trysting place through the wood." She heard him call it a trysting place without a thought of resentment or shame. "When I came to the log there I stopped, but Bonaparte, lawless old chap, kept on. I paid no attention to him, for I was thinking of — of something else. He had raced around in the forbidden underbrush for some time before I heard the report of a gun near at hand. The dog actually screamed like a human being. I saw him leap up from the ground and then roll over. Of course, I — well, I trespassed. Without thinking of my own safety I flew to where the dog was lying. He looked up into my face and whined just as he died. I don't remember how I got off the horse. The

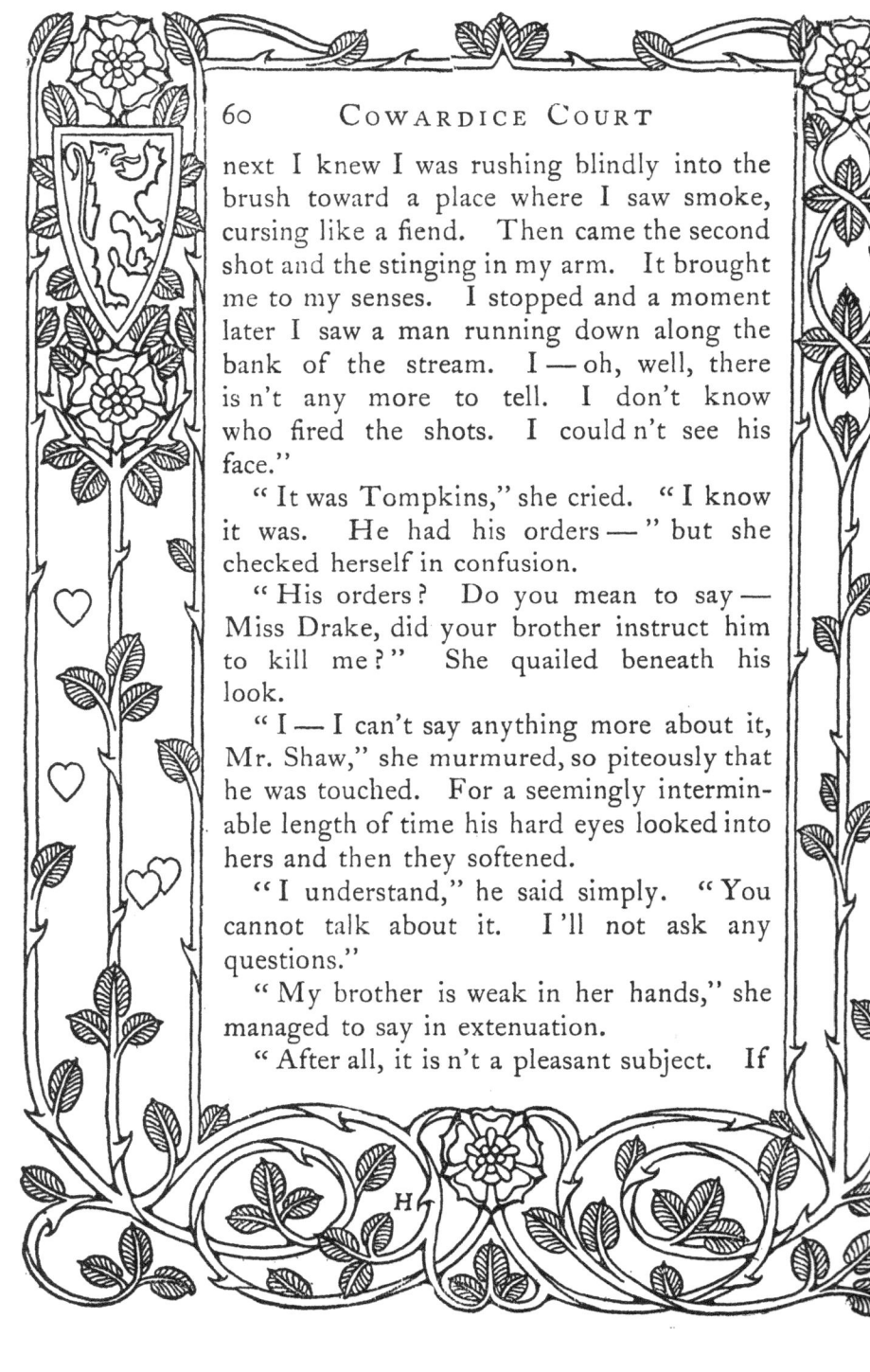

next I knew I was rushing blindly into the brush toward a place where I saw smoke, cursing like a fiend. Then came the second shot and the stinging in my arm. It brought me to my senses. I stopped and a moment later I saw a man running down along the bank of the stream. I — oh, well, there isn't any more to tell. I don't know who fired the shots. I couldn't see his face."

"It was Tompkins," she cried. "I know it was. He had his orders — " but she checked herself in confusion.

"His orders? Do you mean to say — Miss Drake, did your brother instruct him to kill me?" She quailed beneath his look.

"I — I can't say anything more about it, Mr. Shaw," she murmured, so piteously that he was touched. For a seemingly interminable length of time his hard eyes looked into hers and then they softened.

"I understand," he said simply. "You cannot talk about it. I'll not ask any questions."

"My brother is weak in her hands," she managed to say in extenuation.

"After all, it isn't a pleasant subject. If

you don't mind, we'll let it drop — that is,
between you and me, Miss Drake. I hope
the war won't break off our — "

"Don't suggest it, please! I'd rather
you would n't. We are friends, after all.
I thought it was playing at war — and I
can't tell you how shocked I am."

"Poor old Bonaparte!" was all he said in
reply. She stooped and laid her hand on
the fast-chilling coat of the dog. There were
tears in her eyes as she arose and turned
away, moving toward her horse. Shaw
deliberately lifted the dead animal into his
arms and strode off toward his own land.
She followed after a moment of indecision,
leading the horse. Across the line he went
and up the side of the knoll to his right.
At the foot of a great tree he tenderly
deposited his burden. Then he turned to
find her almost beside him.

"You won't mind my coming over here,
will you?" she asked softly. He reached
out and clasped her hand, thoughtlessly, with
his blood-covered fingers. It was not until
long afterward that she discovered his blood
upon the hand from which she had drawn
her riding glove.

"*You* are always welcome," he said. "I

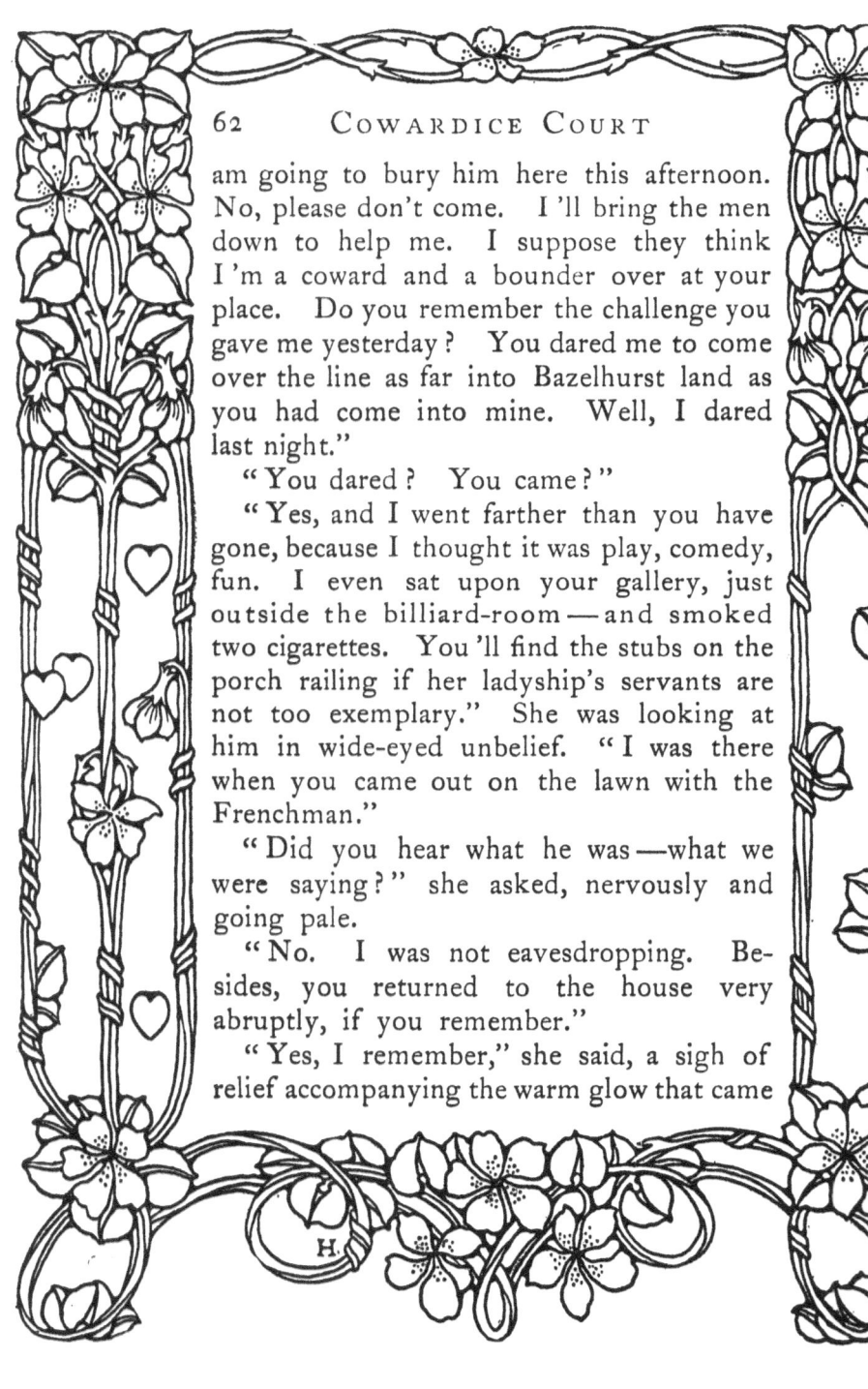

am going to bury him here this afternoon.
No, please don't come. I'll bring the men
down to help me. I suppose they think
I'm a coward and a bounder over at your
place. Do you remember the challenge you
gave me yesterday? You dared me to come
over the line as far into Bazelhurst land as
you had come into mine. Well, I dared
last night."

"You dared? You came?"

"Yes, and I went farther than you have
gone, because I thought it was play, comedy,
fun. I even sat upon your gallery, just
outside the billiard-room — and smoked
two cigarettes. You'll find the stubs on the
porch railing if her ladyship's servants are
not too exemplary." She was looking at
him in wide-eyed unbelief. "I was there
when you came out on the lawn with the
Frenchman."

"Did you hear what he was — what we
were saying?" she asked, nervously and
going pale.

"No. I was not eavesdropping. Besides, you returned to the house very
abruptly, if you remember."

"Yes, I remember," she said, a sigh of
relief accompanying the warm glow that came

to her cheek. "But were you not afraid of being discovered? How imprudent of you!"

"It was a bit risky, but I rather enjoyed it. The count spoke to me as I left the place. It was dark and he mistook me for one of your party. I could n't wait to see if you returned to renew the tête-à-tête — "

"I did not return," she said. It was his turn to be relieved.

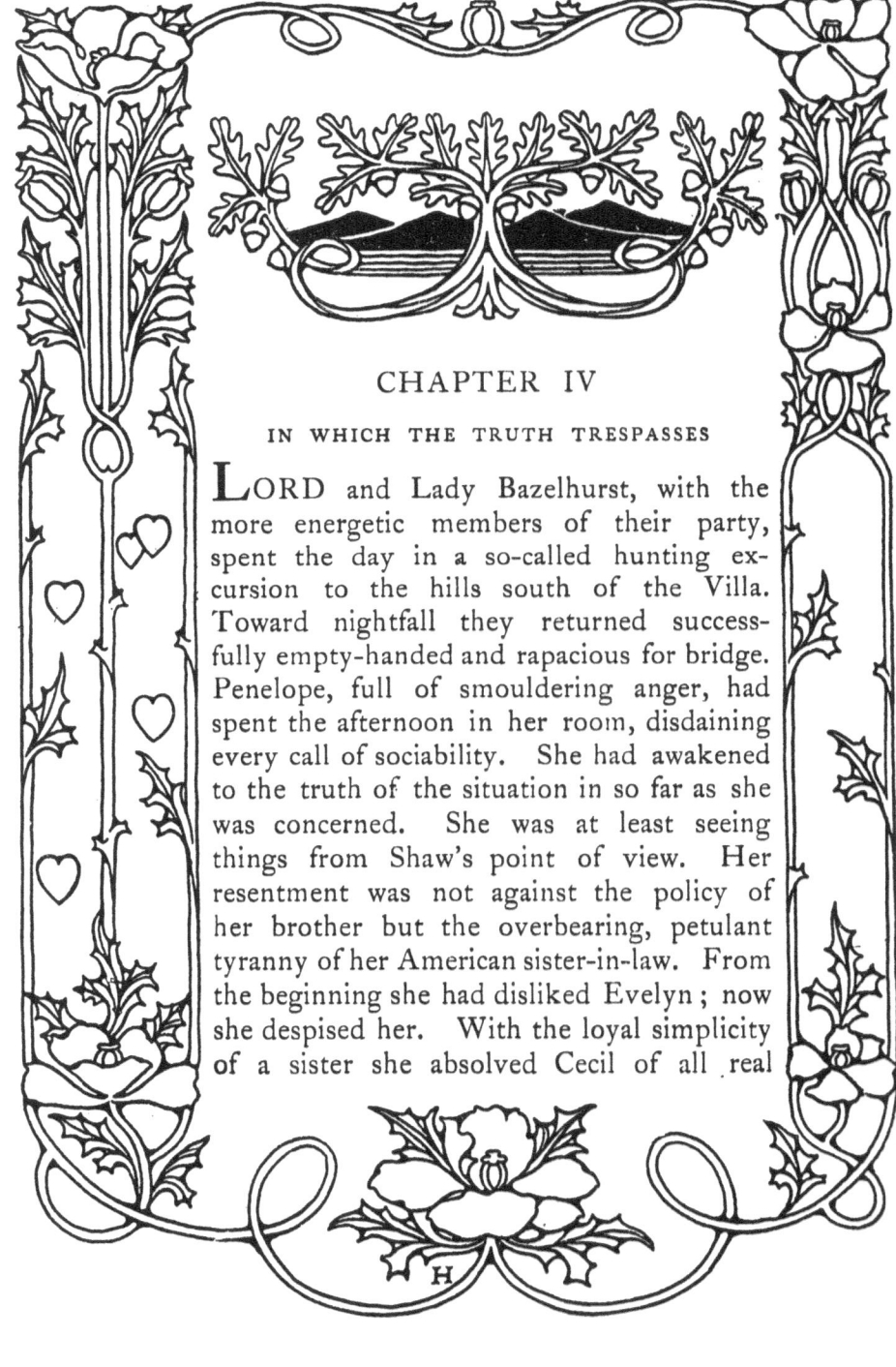

CHAPTER IV

IN WHICH THE TRUTH TRESPASSES

LORD and Lady Bazelhurst, with the more energetic members of their party, spent the day in a so-called hunting excursion to the hills south of the Villa. Toward nightfall they returned successfully empty-handed and rapacious for bridge. Penelope, full of smouldering anger, had spent the afternoon in her room, disdaining every call of sociability. She had awakened to the truth of the situation in so far as she was concerned. She was at least seeing things from Shaw's point of view. Her resentment was not against the policy of her brother but the overbearing, petulant tyranny of her American sister-in-law. From the beginning she had disliked Evelyn; now she despised her. With the loyal simplicity of a sister she absolved Cecil of all real

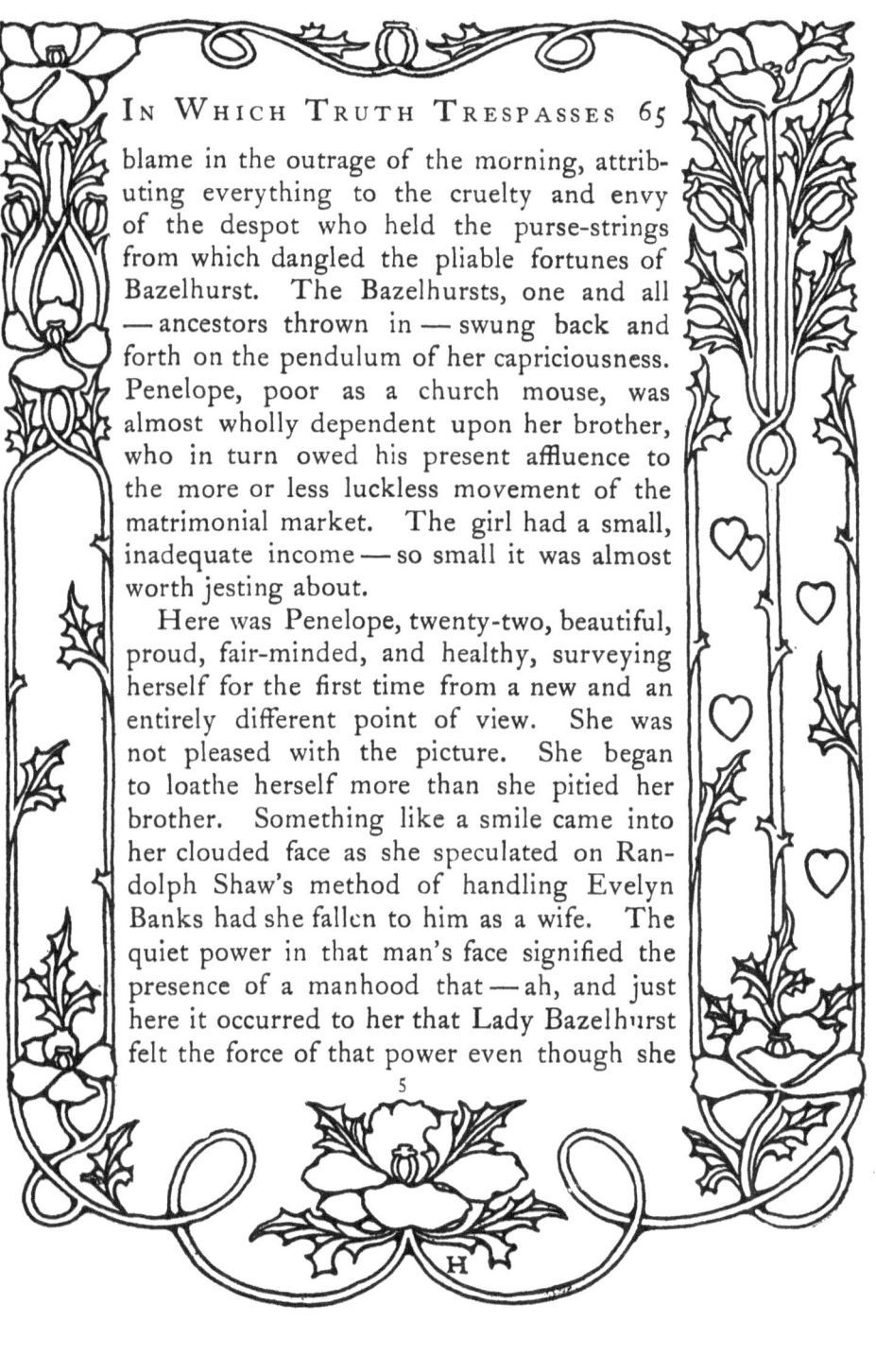

blame in the outrage of the morning, attrib-
uting everything to the cruelty and envy
of the despot who held the purse-strings
from which dangled the pliable fortunes of
Bazelhurst. The Bazelhursts, one and all
— ancestors thrown in — swung back and
forth on the pendulum of her capriciousness.
Penelope, poor as a church mouse, was
almost wholly dependent upon her brother,
who in turn owed his present affluence to
the more or less luckless movement of the
matrimonial market. The girl had a small,
inadequate income — so small it was almost
worth jesting about.

Here was Penelope, twenty-two, beautiful,
proud, fair-minded, and healthy, surveying
herself for the first time from a new and an
entirely different point of view. She was
not pleased with the picture. She began
to loathe herself more than she pitied her
brother. Something like a smile came into
her clouded face as she speculated on Randolph Shaw's method of handling Evelyn
Banks had she fallen to him as a wife. The
quiet power in that man's face signified the
presence of a manhood that — ah, and just
here it occurred to her that Lady Bazelhurst
felt the force of that power even though she

5

H

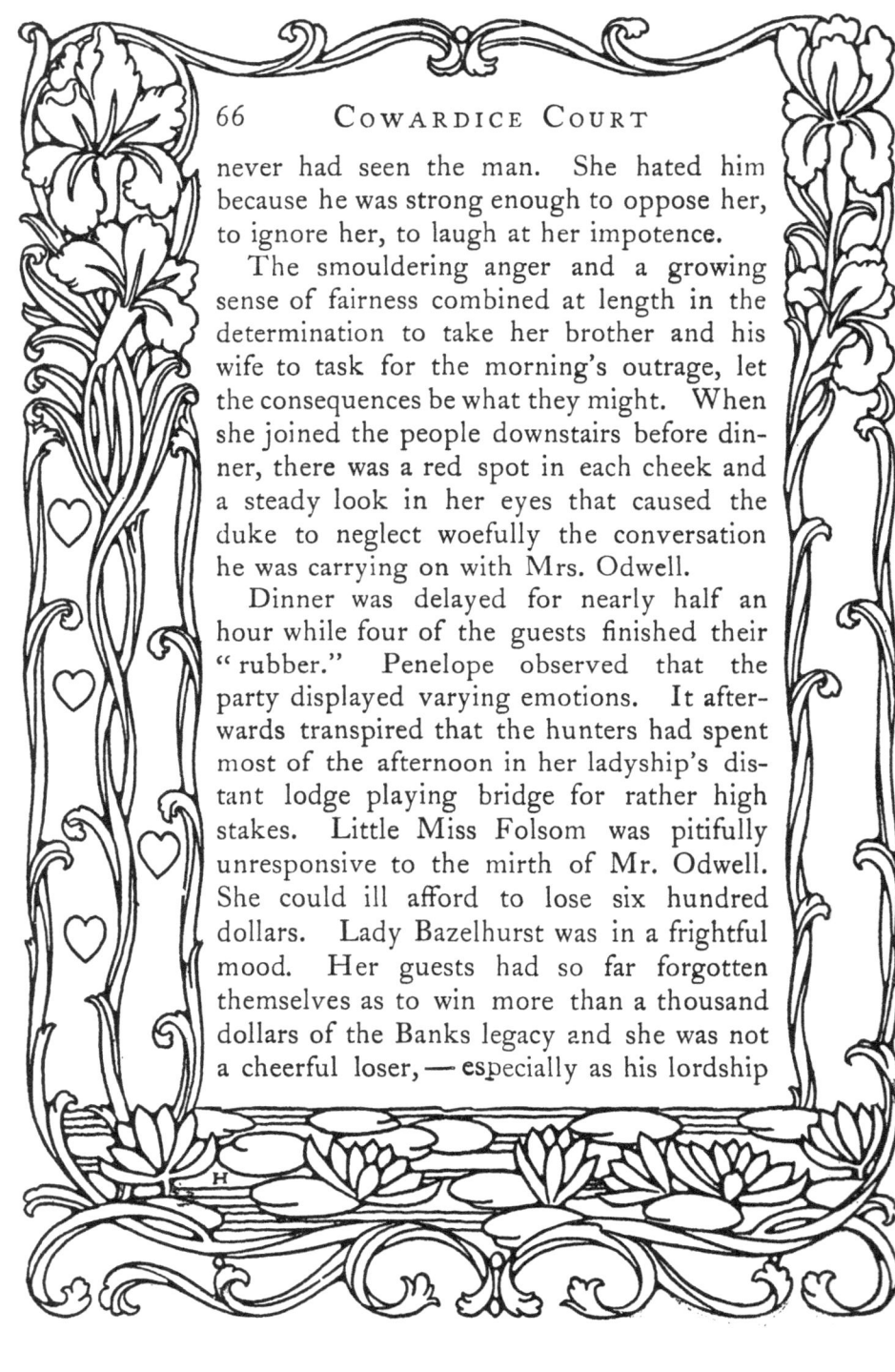

never had seen the man. She hated him because he was strong enough to oppose her, to ignore her, to laugh at her impotence.

The smouldering anger and a growing sense of fairness combined at length in the determination to take her brother and his wife to task for the morning's outrage, let the consequences be what they might. When she joined the people downstairs before dinner, there was a red spot in each cheek and a steady look in her eyes that caused the duke to neglect woefully the conversation he was carrying on with Mrs. Odwell.

Dinner was delayed for nearly half an hour while four of the guests finished their "rubber." Penelope observed that the party displayed varying emotions. It afterwards transpired that the hunters had spent most of the afternoon in her ladyship's distant lodge playing bridge for rather high stakes. Little Miss Folsom was pitifully unresponsive to the mirth of Mr. Odwell. She could ill afford to lose six hundred dollars. Lady Bazelhurst was in a frightful mood. Her guests had so far forgotten themselves as to win more than a thousand dollars of the Banks legacy and she was not a cheerful loser, — especially as his lordship

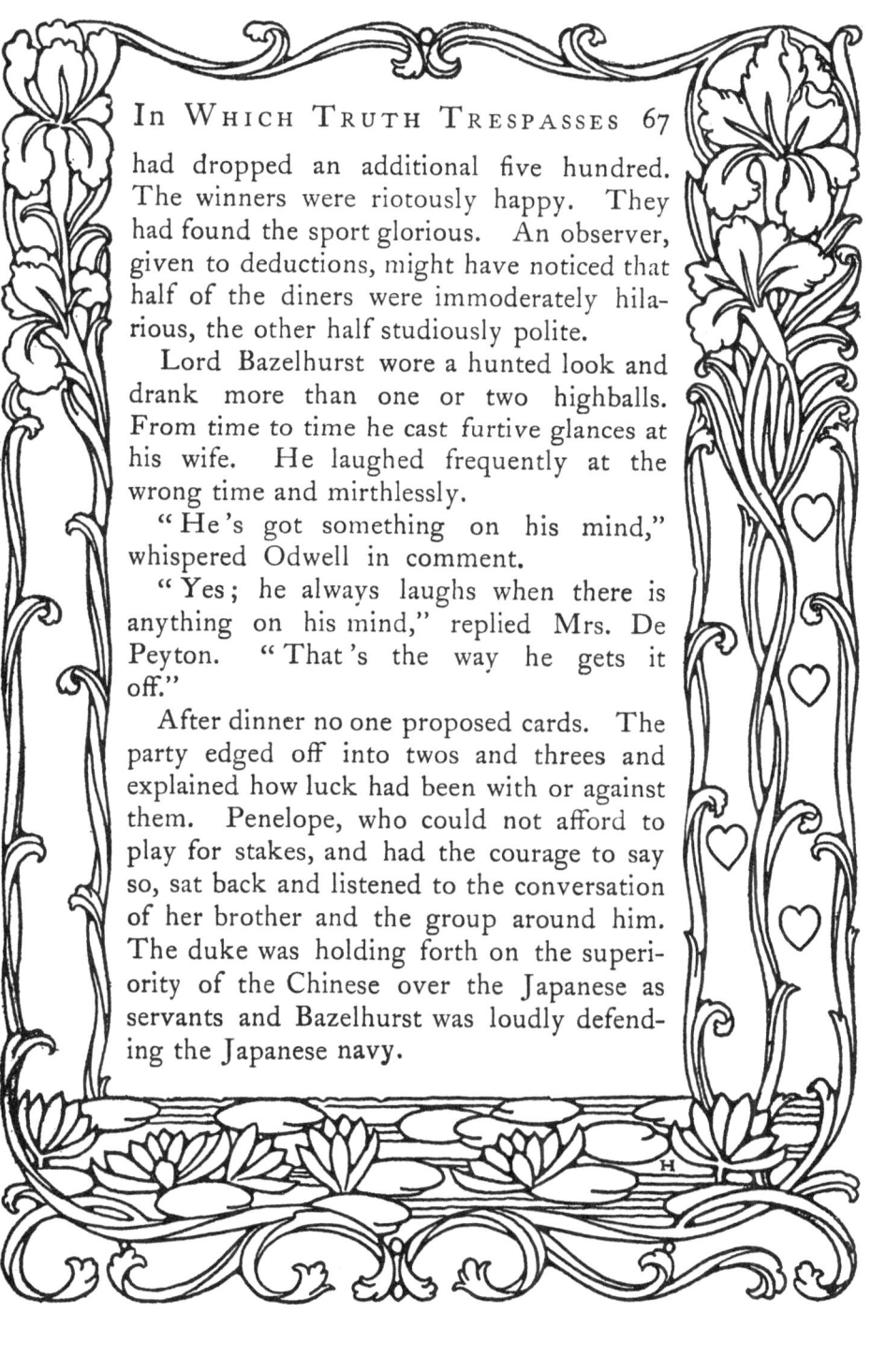

had dropped an additional five hundred.
The winners were riotously happy. They
had found the sport glorious. An observer,
given to deductions, might have noticed that
half of the diners were immoderately hila-
rious, the other half studiously polite.

Lord Bazelhurst wore a hunted look and
drank more than one or two highballs.
From time to time he cast furtive glances at
his wife. He laughed frequently at the
wrong time and mirthlessly.

"He's got something on his mind,"
whispered Odwell in comment.

"Yes; he always laughs when there is
anything on his mind," replied Mrs. De
Peyton. "That's the way he gets it
off."

After dinner no one proposed cards. The
party edged off into twos and threes and
explained how luck had been with or against
them. Penelope, who could not afford to
play for stakes, and had the courage to say
so, sat back and listened to the conversation
of her brother and the group around him.
The duke was holding forth on the superiority of the Chinese over the Japanese as
servants and Bazelhurst was loudly defend-
ing the Japanese navy.

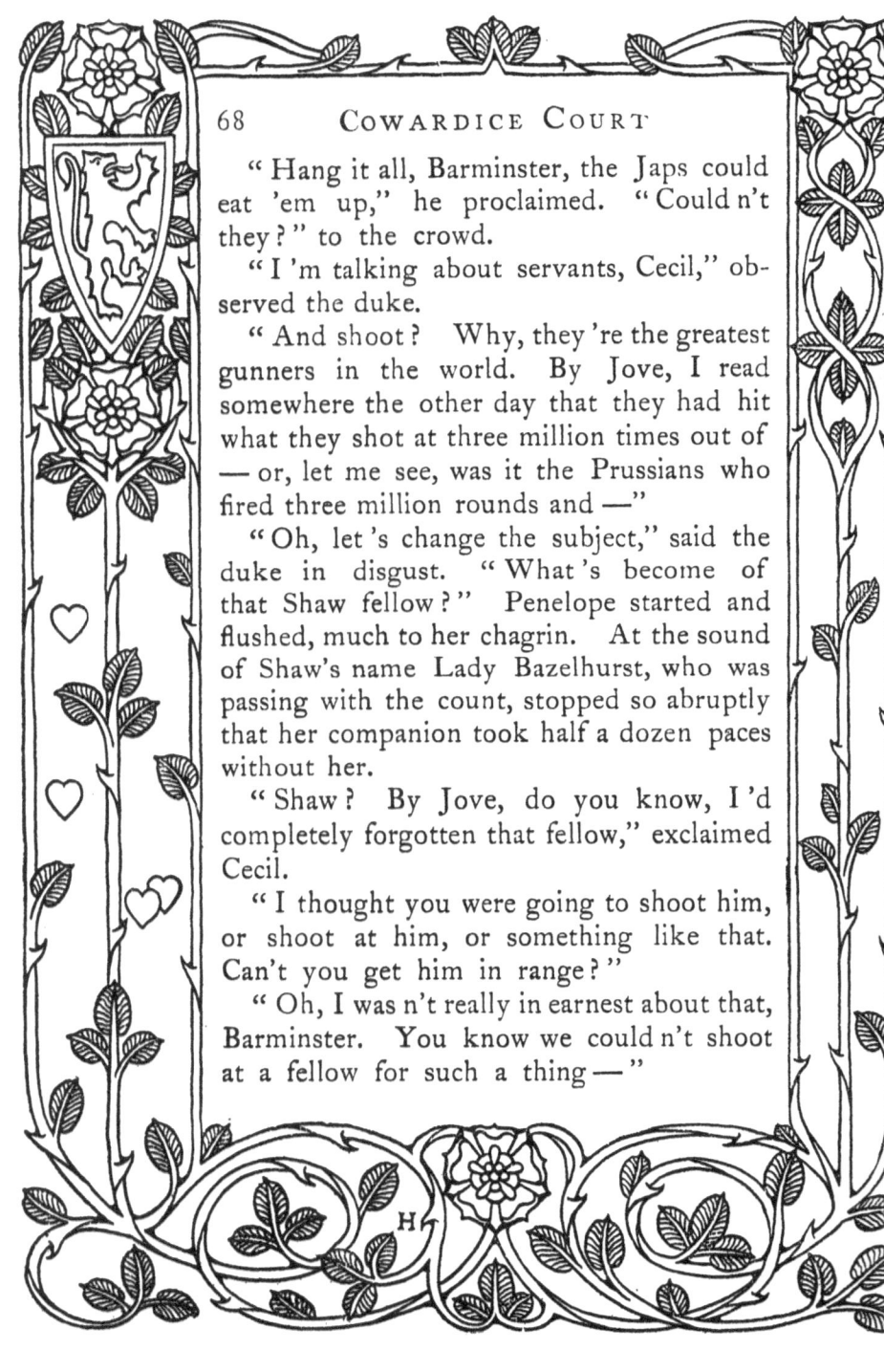

"Hang it all, Barminster, the Japs could eat 'em up," he proclaimed. "Couldn't they?" to the crowd.

"I'm talking about servants, Cecil," observed the duke.

"And shoot? Why, they're the greatest gunners in the world. By Jove, I read somewhere the other day that they had hit what they shot at three million times out of — or, let me see, was it the Prussians who fired three million rounds and —"

"Oh, let's change the subject," said the duke in disgust. "What's become of that Shaw fellow?" Penelope started and flushed, much to her chagrin. At the sound of Shaw's name Lady Bazelhurst, who was passing with the count, stopped so abruptly that her companion took half a dozen paces without her.

"Shaw? By Jove, do you know, I'd completely forgotten that fellow," exclaimed Cecil.

"I thought you were going to shoot him, or shoot at him, or something like that. Can't you get him in range?"

"Oh, I wasn't really in earnest about that, Barminster. You know we couldn't shoot at a fellow for such a thing —"

"She was her own mistress and privileged to ride as often
as she pleased"

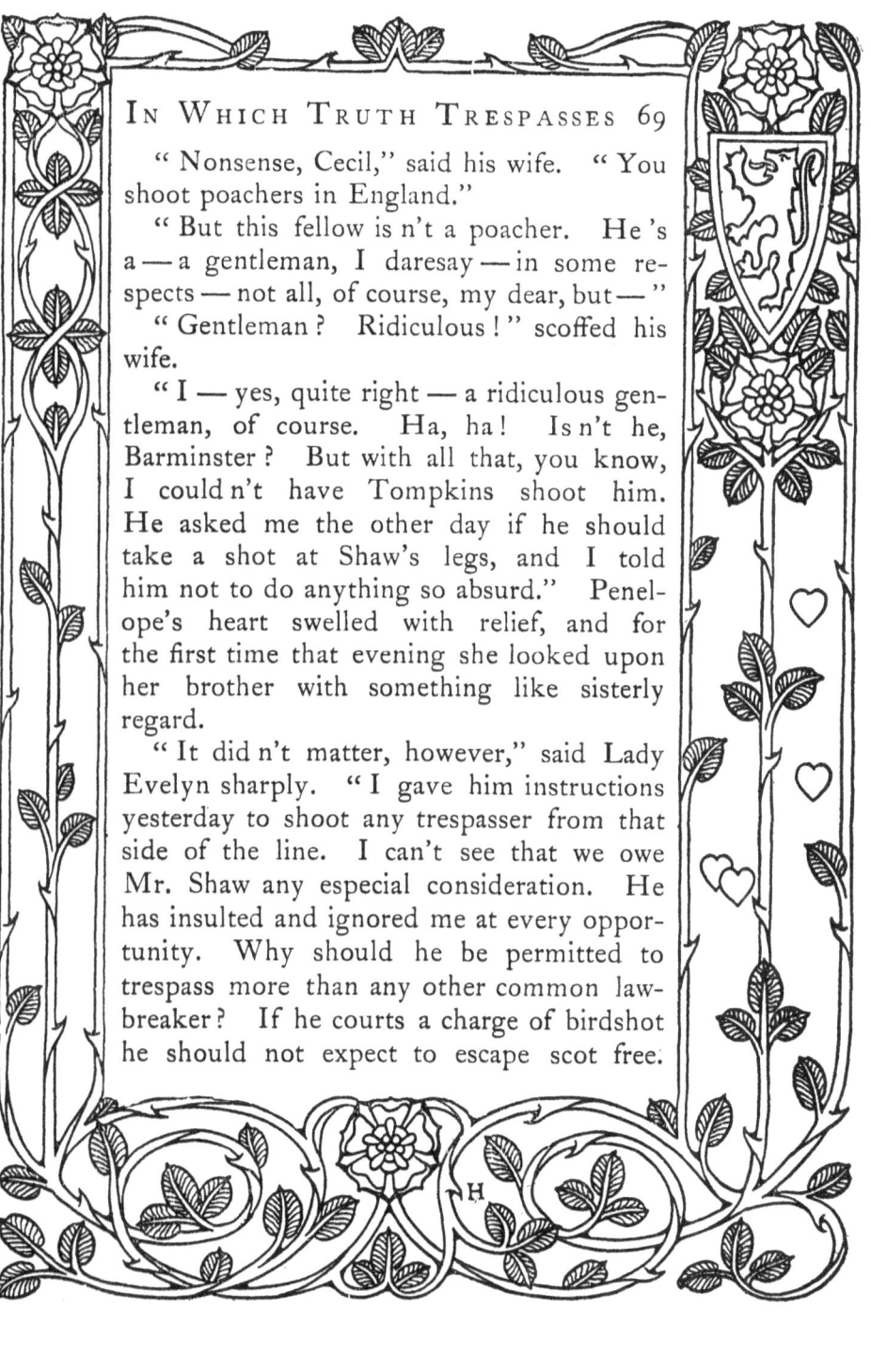

" Nonsense, Cecil," said his wife. " You shoot poachers in England."

" But this fellow is n't a poacher. He 's a — a gentleman, I daresay — in some respects — not all, of course, my dear, but — "

" Gentleman ? Ridiculous ! " scoffed his wife.

" I — yes, quite right — a ridiculous gentleman, of course. Ha, ha ! Is n't he, Barminster ? But with all that, you know, I could n't have Tompkins shoot him. He asked me the other day if he should take a shot at Shaw's legs, and I told him not to do anything so absurd." Penelope's heart swelled with relief, and for the first time that evening she looked upon her brother with something like sisterly regard.

" It did n't matter, however," said Lady Evelyn sharply. " I gave him instructions yesterday to shoot any trespasser from that side of the line. I can't see that we owe Mr. Shaw any especial consideration. He has insulted and ignored me at every opportunity. Why should he be permitted to trespass more than any other common lawbreaker ? If he courts a charge of birdshot he should not expect to escape scot free.

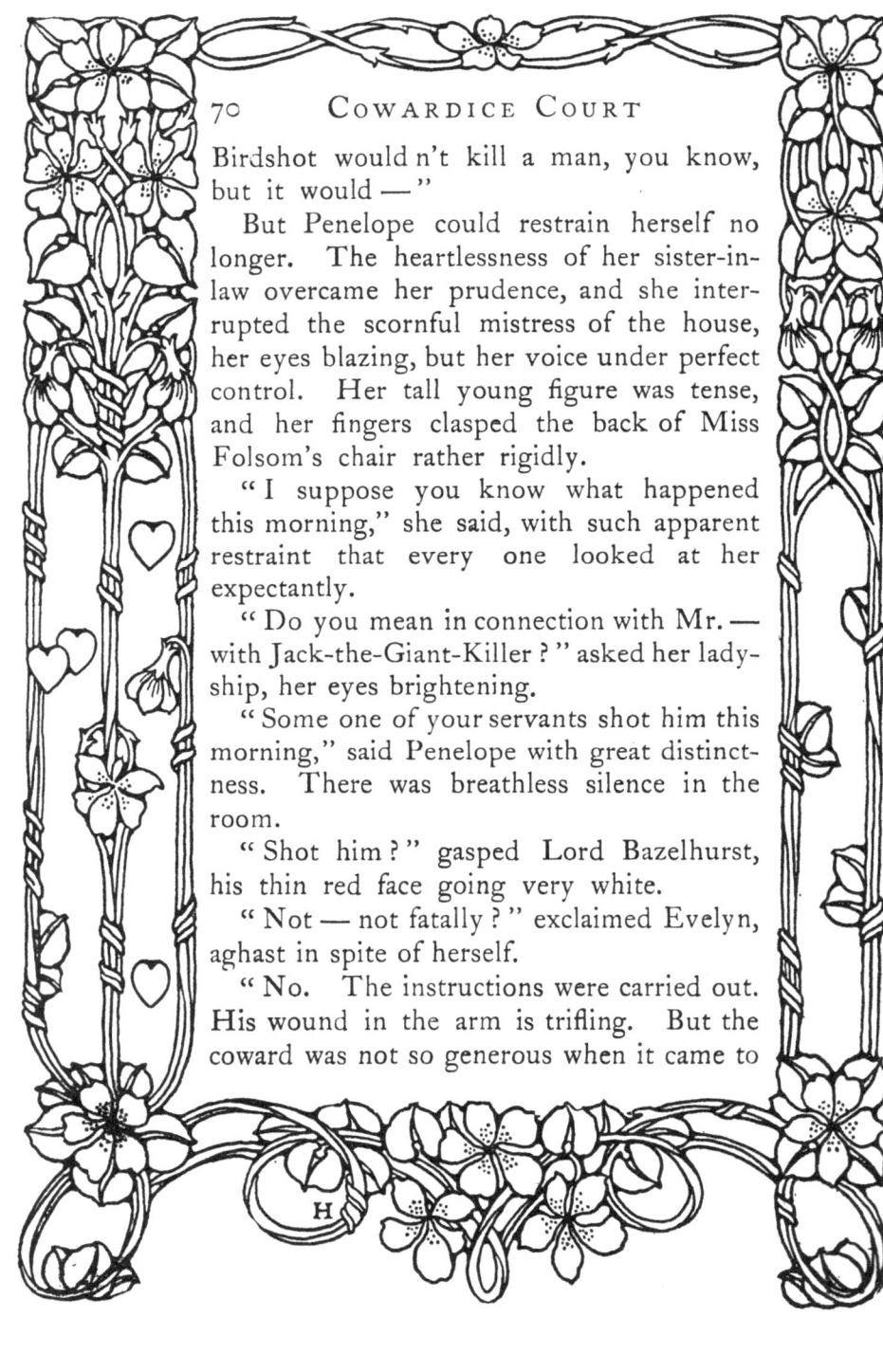

Birdshot would n't kill a man, you know, but it would — "

But Penelope could restrain herself no longer. The heartlessness of her sister-in-law overcame her prudence, and she interrupted the scornful mistress of the house, her eyes blazing, but her voice under perfect control. Her tall young figure was tense, and her fingers clasped the back of Miss Folsom's chair rather rigidly.

" I suppose you know what happened this morning," she said, with such apparent restraint that every one looked at her expectantly.

" Do you mean in connection with Mr. — with Jack-the-Giant-Killer ? " asked her ladyship, her eyes brightening.

" Some one of your servants shot him this morning," said Penelope with great distinctness. There was breathless silence in the room.

" Shot him ? " gasped Lord Bazelhurst, his thin red face going very white.

" Not — not fatally ? " exclaimed Evelyn, aghast in spite of herself.

" No. The instructions were carried out. His wound in the arm is trifling. But the coward was not so generous when it came to the life of his innocent, harmless dog. He killed the poor thing. Evelyn, it's — it's like murder."

"Oh," cried her ladyship, relieved. "He killed the dog. I daresay Mr. Shaw has come to realize at last that we are earnest in this. Of course I am glad that the man is not badly hurt. Still, a few shot in the arm will hardly keep him in bounds. His legs were intended," she laughed lightly. "What miserable aim Tompkins must take."

"He's a bit off in his physiology, my dear," said Cecil, with a nervous attempt at humour. He did not like the expression in his sister's face. Somehow, he was ashamed.

"Oh, it's bad enough," said Penelope. "It was his left arm — the upper arm, too. I think the aim was rather good."

"Pray, how do you know all of this, Penelope?" asked her ladyship, lifting her eyebrows. "I've heard that you see Mr. Shaw occasionally, but you can't be his physician, I'm sure."

Penelope flushed to the roots of her hair, but suppressed the retort which would have been in keeping with the provocation.

"Oh, dear, no!" she replied. "I'm too

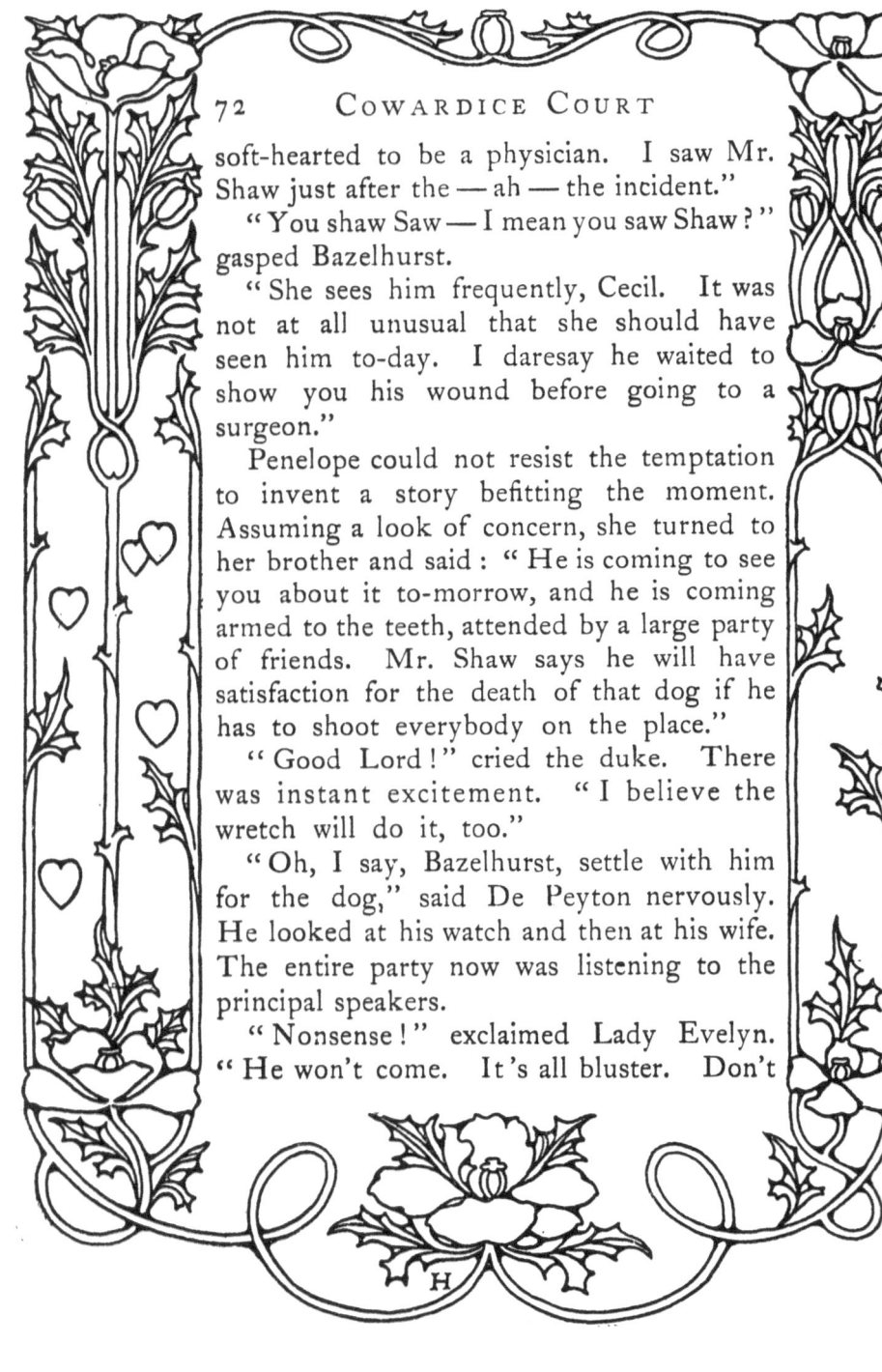

soft-hearted to be a physician.   I saw Mr.
Shaw just after the — ah — the incident."

"You shaw Saw — I mean you saw Shaw?"
gasped Bazelhurst.

"She sees him frequently, Cecil.   It was
not at all unusual that she should have
seen him to-day.   I daresay he waited to
show you his wound before going to a
surgeon."

Penelope could not resist the temptation
to invent a story befitting the moment.
Assuming a look of concern, she turned to
her brother and said : " He is coming to see
you about it to-morrow, and he is coming
armed to the teeth, attended by a large party
of friends.   Mr. Shaw says he will have
satisfaction for the death of that dog if he
has to shoot everybody on the place."

" Good Lord !" cried the duke.   There
was instant excitement.   " I believe the
wretch will do it, too."

"Oh, I say, Bazelhurst, settle with him
for the dog," said De Peyton nervously.
He looked at his watch and then at his wife.
The entire party now was listening to the
principal speakers.

" Nonsense !" exclaimed Lady Evelyn.
" He won't come.   It's all bluster.   Don't

H

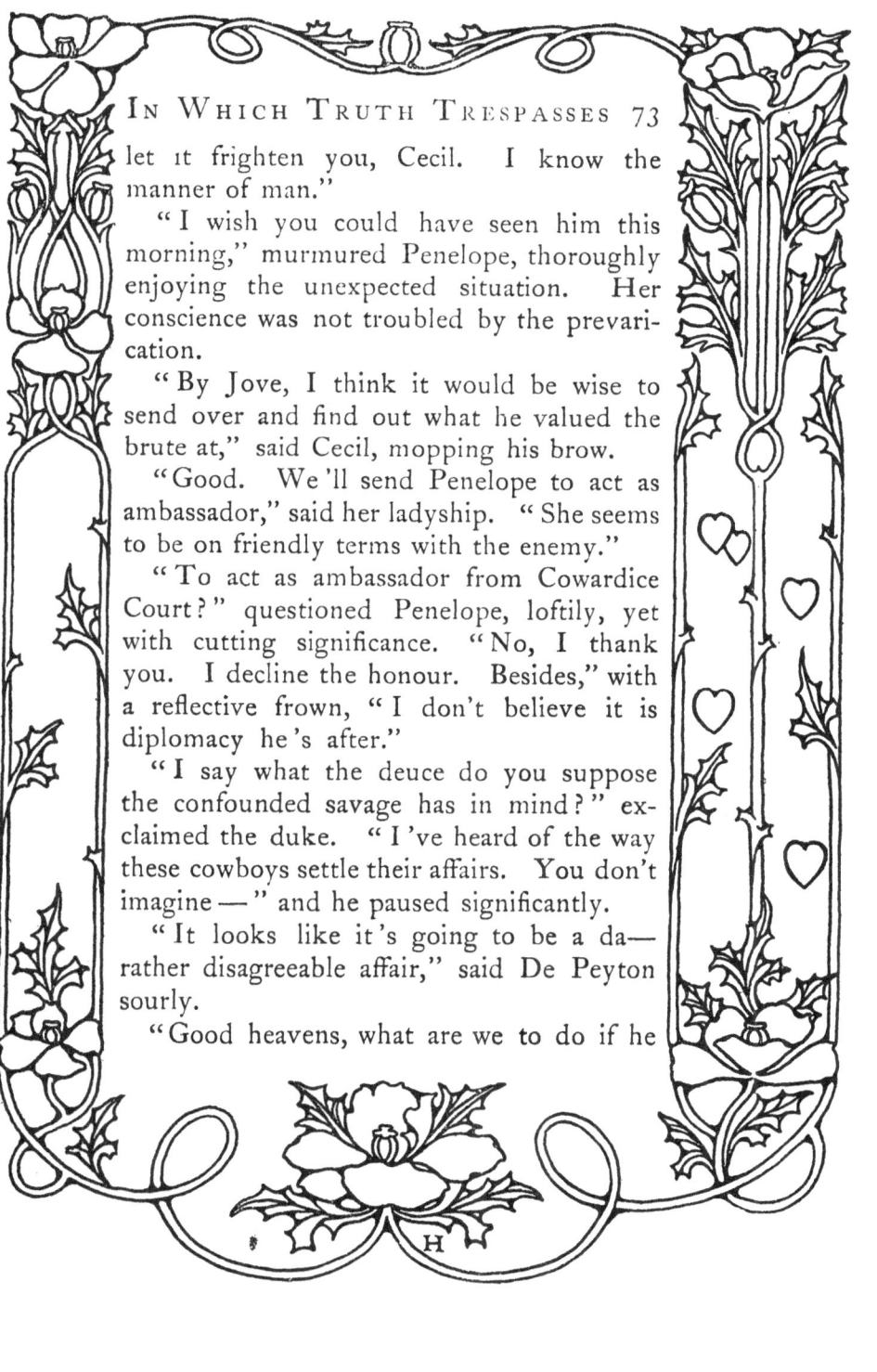

let it frighten you, Cecil. I know the manner of man."

"I wish you could have seen him this morning," murmured Penelope, thoroughly enjoying the unexpected situation. Her conscience was not troubled by the prevarication.

"By Jove, I think it would be wise to send over and find out what he valued the brute at," said Cecil, mopping his brow.

"Good. We'll send Penelope to act as ambassador," said her ladyship. "She seems to be on friendly terms with the enemy."

"To act as ambassador from Cowardice Court?" questioned Penelope, loftily, yet with cutting significance. "No, I thank you. I decline the honour. Besides," with a reflective frown, "I don't believe it is diplomacy he's after."

"I say what the deuce do you suppose the confounded savage has in mind?" exclaimed the duke. "I've heard of the way these cowboys settle their affairs. You don't imagine —" and he paused significantly.

"It looks like it's going to be a da— rather disagreeable affair," said De Peyton sourly.

"Good heavens, what are we to do if he

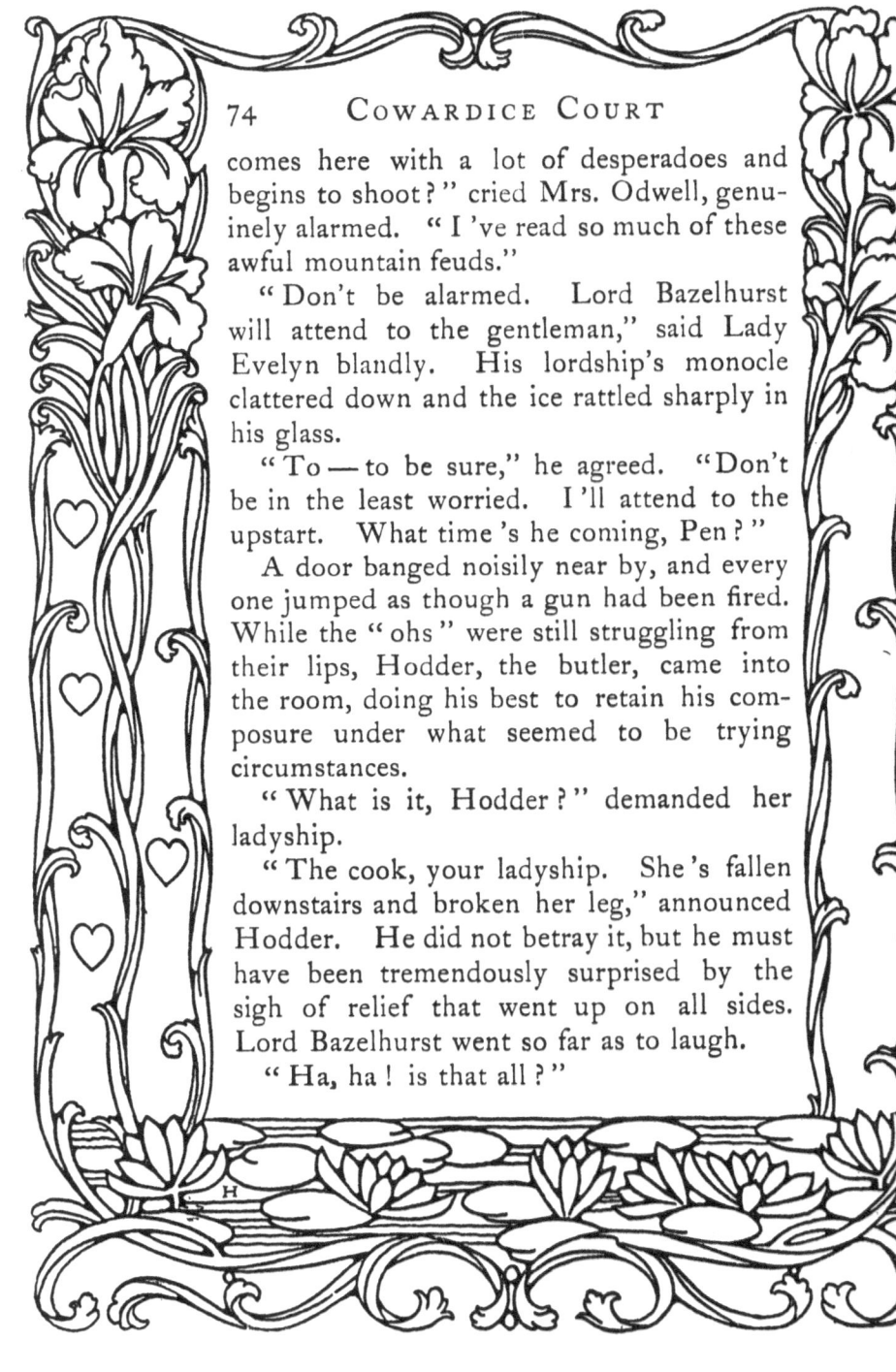

comes here with a lot of desperadoes and begins to shoot?" cried Mrs. Odwell, genuinely alarmed. "I've read so much of these awful mountain feuds."

"Don't be alarmed. Lord Bazelhurst will attend to the gentleman," said Lady Evelyn blandly. His lordship's monocle clattered down and the ice rattled sharply in his glass.

"To — to be sure," he agreed. "Don't be in the least worried. I'll attend to the upstart. What time's he coming, Pen?"

A door banged noisily near by, and every one jumped as though a gun had been fired. While the "ohs" were still struggling from their lips, Hodder, the butler, came into the room, doing his best to retain his composure under what seemed to be trying circumstances.

"What is it, Hodder?" demanded her ladyship.

"The cook, your ladyship. She's fallen downstairs and broken her leg," announced Hodder. He did not betray it, but he must have been tremendously surprised by the sigh of relief that went up on all sides. Lord Bazelhurst went so far as to laugh.

"Ha, ha! is that all?"

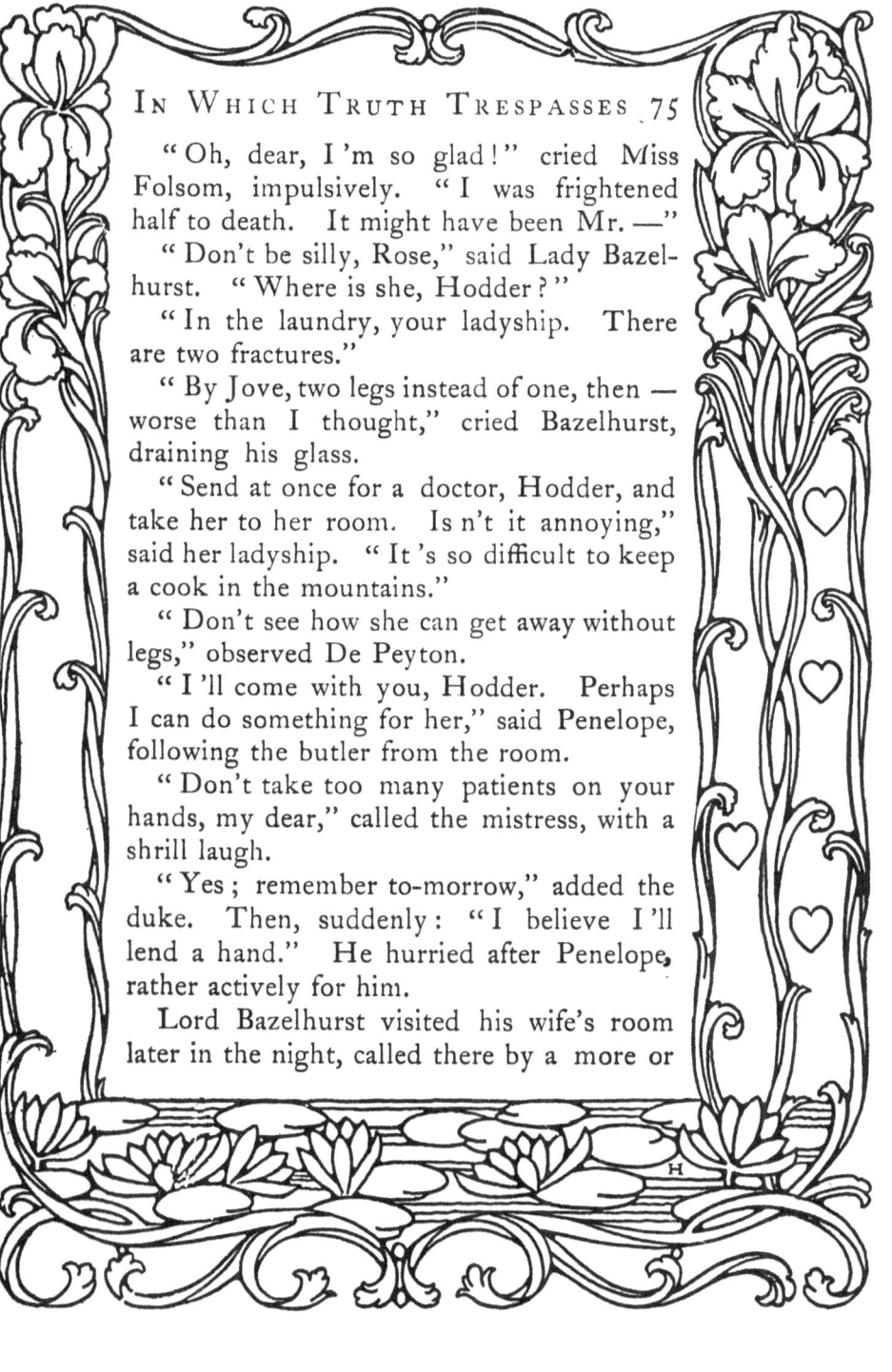

"Oh, dear, I 'm so glad!" cried Miss Folsom, impulsively. "I was frightened half to death. It might have been Mr. —"

"Don't be silly, Rose," said Lady Bazelhurst. "Where is she, Hodder?"

"In the laundry, your ladyship. There are two fractures."

"By Jove, two legs instead of one, then — worse than I thought," cried Bazelhurst, draining his glass.

"Send at once for a doctor, Hodder, and take her to her room. Is n't it annoying," said her ladyship. "It 's so difficult to keep a cook in the mountains."

"Don't see how she can get away without legs," observed De Peyton.

"I 'll come with you, Hodder. Perhaps I can do something for her," said Penelope, following the butler from the room.

"Don't take too many patients on your hands, my dear," called the mistress, with a shrill laugh.

"Yes; remember to-morrow," added the duke. Then, suddenly: "I believe I 'll lend a hand." He hurried after Penelope, rather actively for him.

Lord Bazelhurst visited his wife's room later in the night, called there by a more or less peremptory summons. Cecil had been taking time by the forelock in anticipation of Shaw's descent in the morning and was inclined to jocundity.

"Cecil, what do you think of Penelope's attitude toward Mr. Shaw?" she asked, turning away from the window which looked out over the night in the direction of Shaw's place.

"I did n't know she had an attitude," replied he, trying to focus his wavering gaze upon her.

"She meets him clandestinely and she supports him openly. Is n't that an attitude, or are you too drunk to see it?"

"My dear, remember you are speaking of my sister," he said with fine dignity but little discrimination. "Besides, I am not too drunk. I *do* see it. It 's a demmed annoying attitude. She 's a traitor, un 'stand me? A traito-tor. I intend to speak to her about it."

"It is better that you should do it," said his wife. "I am afraid I could not control my temper."

"Penelope 's a disgrace — a nabsolute disgrace. How many legs did Hodder say she 'd — she 'd broken?"

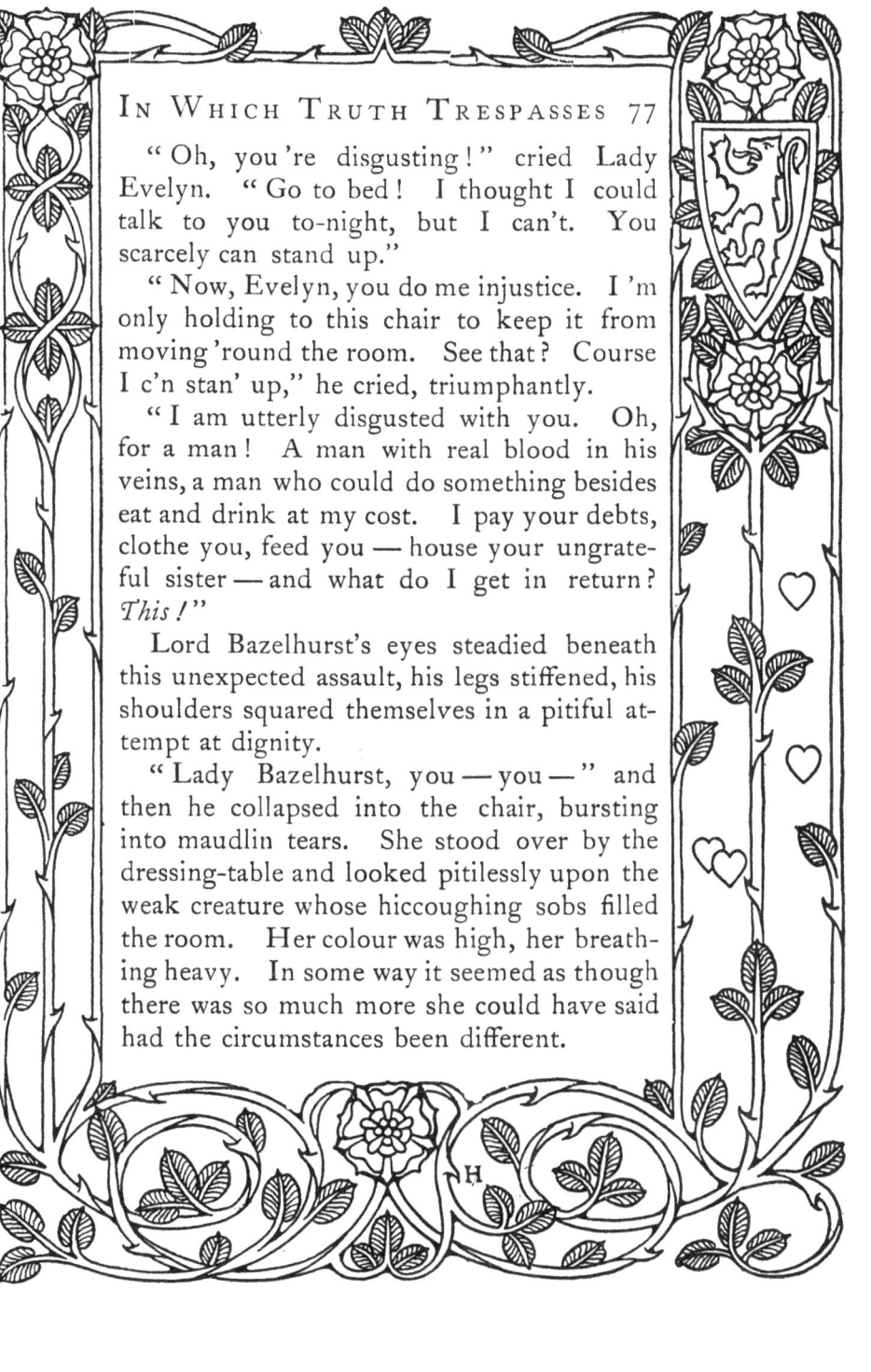

"Oh, you're disgusting!" cried Lady Evelyn. "Go to bed! I thought I could talk to you to-night, but I can't. You scarcely can stand up."

"Now, Evelyn, you do me injustice. I'm only holding to this chair to keep it from moving 'round the room. See that? Course I c'n stan' up," he cried, triumphantly.

"I am utterly disgusted with you. Oh, for a man! A man with real blood in his veins, a man who could do something besides eat and drink at my cost. I pay your debts, clothe you, feed you — house your ungrateful sister — and what do I get in return? *This!*"

Lord Bazelhurst's eyes steadied beneath this unexpected assault, his legs stiffened, his shoulders squared themselves in a pitiful attempt at dignity.

"Lady Bazelhurst, you — you —" and then he collapsed into the chair, bursting into maudlin tears. She stood over by the dressing-table and looked pitilessly upon the weak creature whose hiccoughing sobs filled the room. Her colour was high, her breathing heavy. In some way it seemed as though there was so much more she could have said had the circumstances been different.

There came a knock at the door, but she did not respond. Then the door opened quietly and Penelope entered the room, resolutely, fearlessly. Evelyn turned her eyes upon the intruder and stared for a moment.

"Did you knock?" she asked at last.

"Yes. You did not answer."

"Was n't that sufficient?"

"Not to-night, Evelyn. I came to have it out with you and Cecil. Where is he?"

"There!"

"Asleep?" with a look of amazement.

"I hope not. I should dislike having to call the servants to carry him to his room."

"I see. Poor old chap!" She went over and shook him by the shoulder. He sat up and stared at her blankly through his drenched eyes. Then, as if the occasion called for a supreme effort, he tried to rise, ashamed that his sister should have found him in his present condition. "Don't get up, Cecil. Wait a bit and I'll go to your room with you."

"What have you to say to me, Penelope?" demanded Evelyn, a green light in her eyes.

"I can wait. I prefer to have Cecil — understand," she said, bitterly.

"If it's about our affair with Shaw, it won't make any difference whether Cecil understands or not. Has your friend asked you to plead for him? Does he expect me to take him up on your account and have him here?"

"I was jesting when I said he would come to-morrow," said Penelope, ignoring the thrust and hurrying to her subject. "I could n't go to sleep to-night if I neglected to tell you what I think of the outrage this morning. You and Cecil had no right to order Tompkins to shoot at Mr. Shaw. He is not a trespasser. Some one killed his dog to-day. When he pursued the coward, a second shot was fired at him. He was wounded. Do you call that fair fighting? Ambushed, shot from behind a tree. I don't care what you and Cecil think about it, I consider it despicable. Thank God, Cecil was not really to blame. It is about the only thing I can say to my brother's credit."

Lady Bazelhurst was staring at her young sister-in-law with wide eyes. It was the first time in all her petted, vain life that any one had called her to account. She was,

at first, too deeply amazed to resent the sharp attack.

"Penelope Drake!" was all she could say. Then the fury in her soul began to search for an outlet. "How dare you? How dare you?"

"I don't mean to hurt you. I am only telling you that your way of treating this affair is a mistake. It can be rectified. You don't want to be lawless; you don't understand what a narrow escape from murder you have had. Evelyn, you owe reparation to Mr. Shaw. He is —"

"I understand why you take his side. You cheapen and degrade yourself and you bring shame upon your brother and me by your disgraceful affair with this ruffian. Don't look shocked! You meet him secretly, I know — how much farther you have gone with him I don't know. It is enough that you —"

"Stop! You shall not say such things to me!"

"You came in here to have it out with me. Well, we'll have it out. You think because you're English, and all that, that you are better than I. You show it in your every action; you turn up your nose at me because I am an American. Well, what if I am? Where would you be if it were not for me? And where would *he* be? You'd starve if it were not for me. You hang to me like a leech — you sponge on me, you gorge yourself — "

"That is enough, Evelyn. You have said all that is necessary. I deserve it, too, for meddling in your affairs. It may satisfy you to know that I have always despised you. Having confessed, I can only add that we cannot live another hour under the same roof. You need not order me to go. I shall do so of my own accord — gladly." Penelope turned to the door. She was as cold as ice.

"It is the first time you have ever done anything to please me. You may go in the morning."

"I shall go to-night!"

"As you like. It is near morning. Where do you expect to go at this hour of night?"

"I am not afraid of the night. To-morrow I shall send over from the village for my trunks." She paused near the door and then came back to Cecil's side. "Good-bye, Cecil. I'll write. Good-bye." He looked up with a hazy smile.

6

H

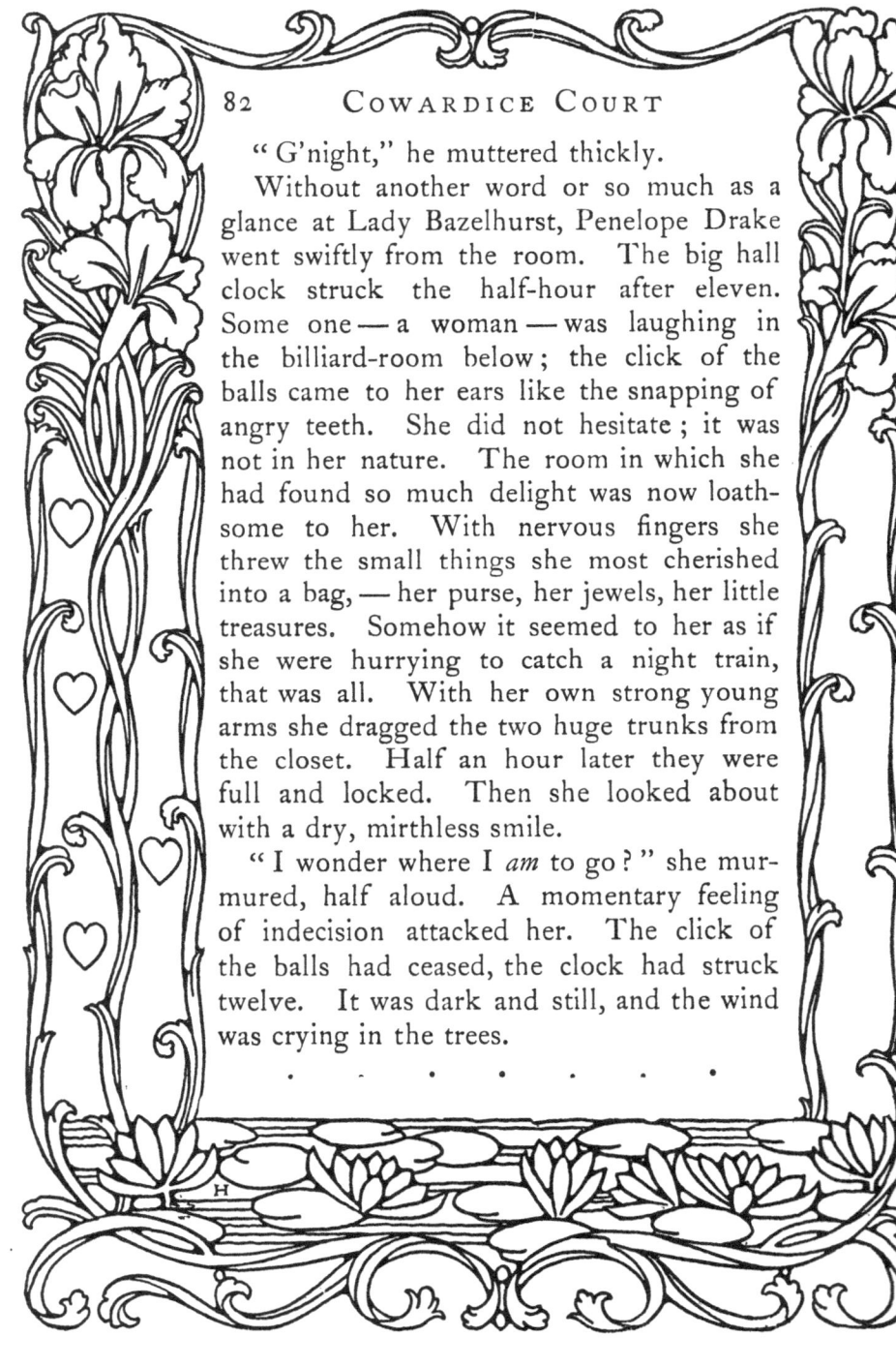

"G'night," he muttered thickly.

Without another word or so much as a glance at Lady Bazelhurst, Penelope Drake went swiftly from the room. The big hall clock struck the half-hour after eleven. Some one — a woman — was laughing in the billiard-room below; the click of the balls came to her ears like the snapping of angry teeth. She did not hesitate; it was not in her nature. The room in which she had found so much delight was now loathsome to her. With nervous fingers she threw the small things she most cherished into a bag, — her purse, her jewels, her little treasures. Somehow it seemed to her as if she were hurrying to catch a night train, that was all. With her own strong young arms she dragged the two huge trunks from the closet. Half an hour later they were full and locked. Then she looked about with a dry, mirthless smile.

"I wonder where I *am* to go?" she murmured, half aloud. A momentary feeling of indecision attacked her. The click of the balls had ceased, the clock had struck twelve. It was dark and still, and the wind was crying in the trees.

.   -   .   .   .   .   .

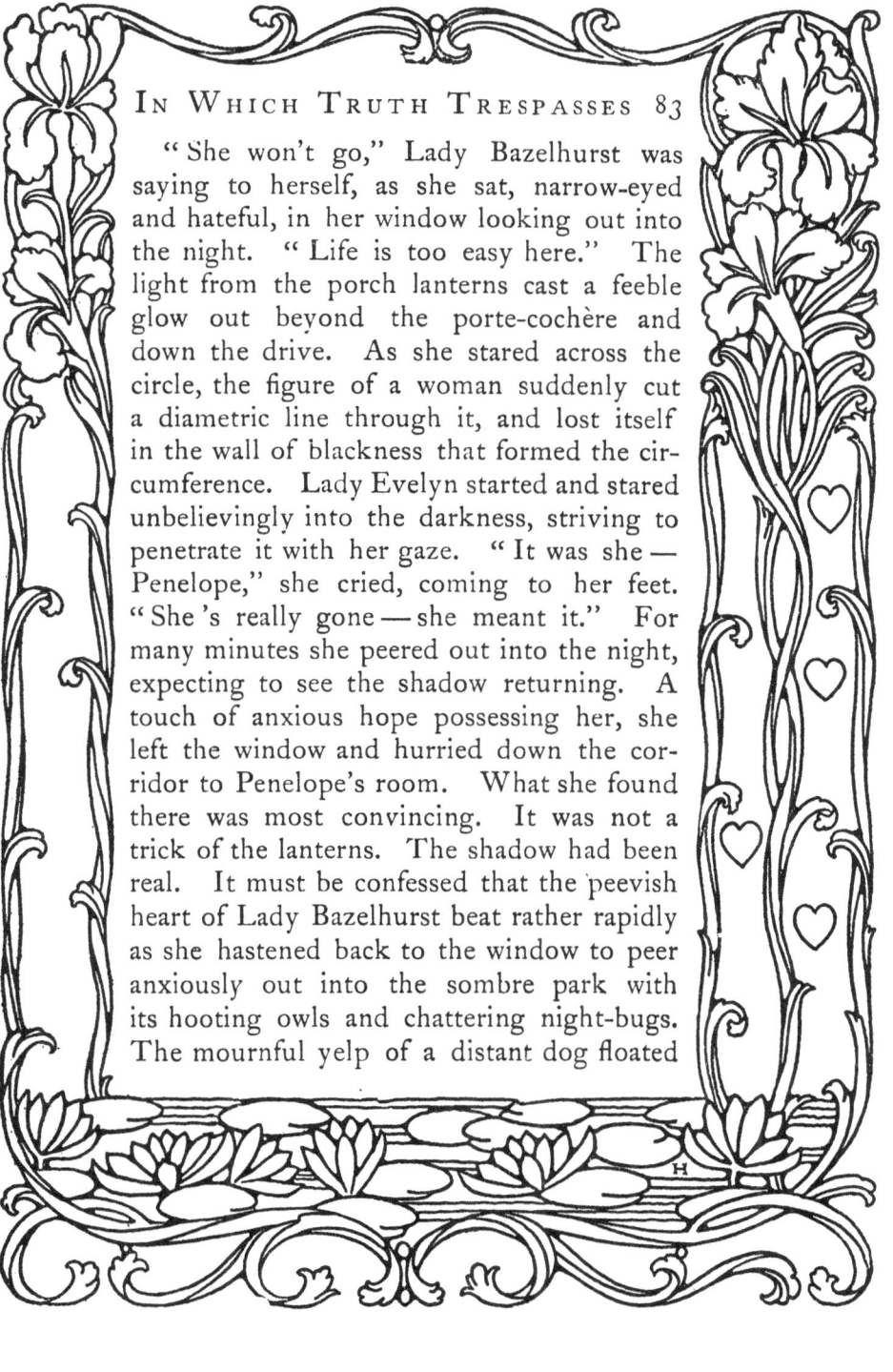

"She won't go," Lady Bazelhurst was saying to herself, as she sat, narrow-eyed and hateful, in her window looking out into the night. "Life is too easy here." The light from the porch lanterns cast a feeble glow out beyond the porte-cochère and down the drive. As she stared across the circle, the figure of a woman suddenly cut a diametric line through it, and lost itself in the wall of blackness that formed the circumference. Lady Evelyn started and stared unbelievingly into the darkness, striving to penetrate it with her gaze. "It was she — Penelope," she cried, coming to her feet. "She's really gone — she meant it." For many minutes she peered out into the night, expecting to see the shadow returning. A touch of anxious hope possessing her, she left the window and hurried down the corridor to Penelope's room. What she found there was most convincing. It was not a trick of the lanterns. The shadow had been real. It must be confessed that the peevish heart of Lady Bazelhurst beat rather rapidly as she hastened back to the window to peer anxiously out into the sombre park with its hooting owls and chattering night-bugs. The mournful yelp of a distant dog floated across the black valley. The watcher shuddered as she recalled stories of panthers that had infested the great hills. A small feeling of shame and regret began to develop with annoying insistence.

An hour dragged itself by before she arose petulantly, half terrified, half annoyed in spite of herself. Her husband still was sitting in the big chair, his face in his hands. His small, dejected figure appealed to her pity for the first time in the two years of their association. She realized what her temper had compelled her to say to him and to his sister; she saw the insults that at least one of them had come to resent.

" I hope that foolish girl will come back," she found herself saying, with a troubled look from the window. " Where can the poor thing go ? What will become of her ? What will everyone say when this becomes known ? " she cried, with fresh selfishness. "I — I should not have let her go like this."

Even as she reproached herself, a light broke in upon her understanding ; a thought whirled into her brain and a moment later a shrill, angry, hysterical laugh came from her lips.

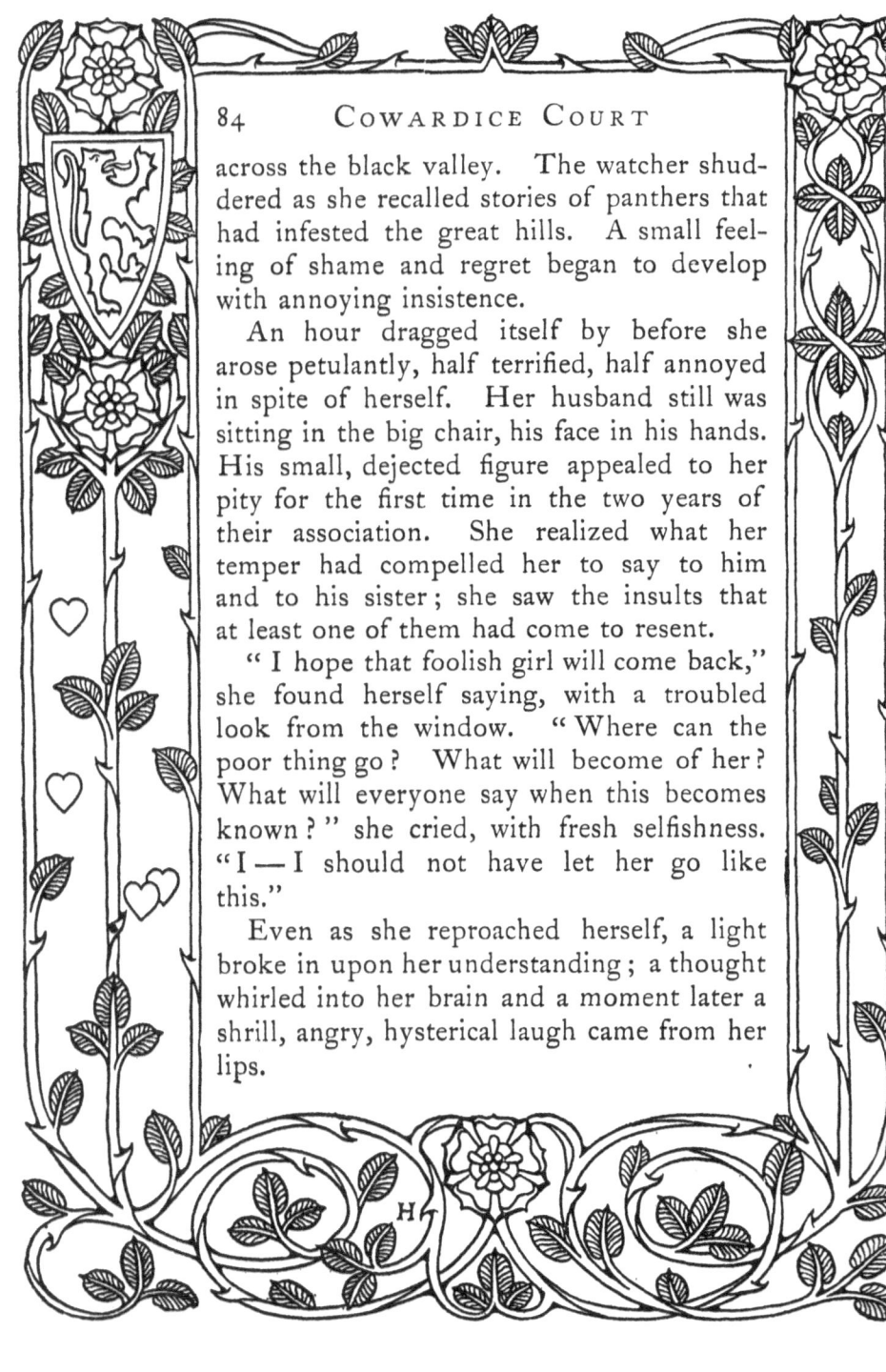

"She knew where she could go! How simple I am. Shaw will welcome her gladly. She's with him by this time — his doors have opened to her. The little wretch! And I've been trying so hard to pity her!" She laughed again so shrilly that his lordship stirred and then looked up at her stupefied, uncertain.

"Hullo," he grunted. "What time is it?"

"Oh, you're awake, are you?" scornfully.

"Certainly. Have I been dozing? What's there to laugh at, my dear?" he mumbled, arising very unsteadily. "Where's Pen?"

"She's gone. She's left the house," she said, recurring dread and anxiety in her voice. A glance at the darkness outside brought back the growing shudders.

"What — what d' ye mean?" demanded he, bracing up with a splendid effort.

"She's left the house, that's all. We quarrelled. I don't know where she's gone. Yes, I do know. She's gone to Shaw's for the night. She's with him. I saw her going," she cried, striving between fear and anger.

"You've — you've turned her out?" gasped Lord Bazelhurst, numbly. "In the

night ? Good Lord, why — why did you let her go ? " He turned and rushed toward the door, tears springing to his eyes. He was sobering now and the tears were wrenched from his hurt pride. " How long ago ? "

"An hour or more. She went of her own accord. You 'll find her at Shaw's," said her ladyship harshly. She hated to admit that she was to blame. But as her husband left the room, banging the door after him, she caught her breath several times in a futile effort to stay the sobs, and then broke down and cried, a very much abused young woman. She hated everybody and everything.

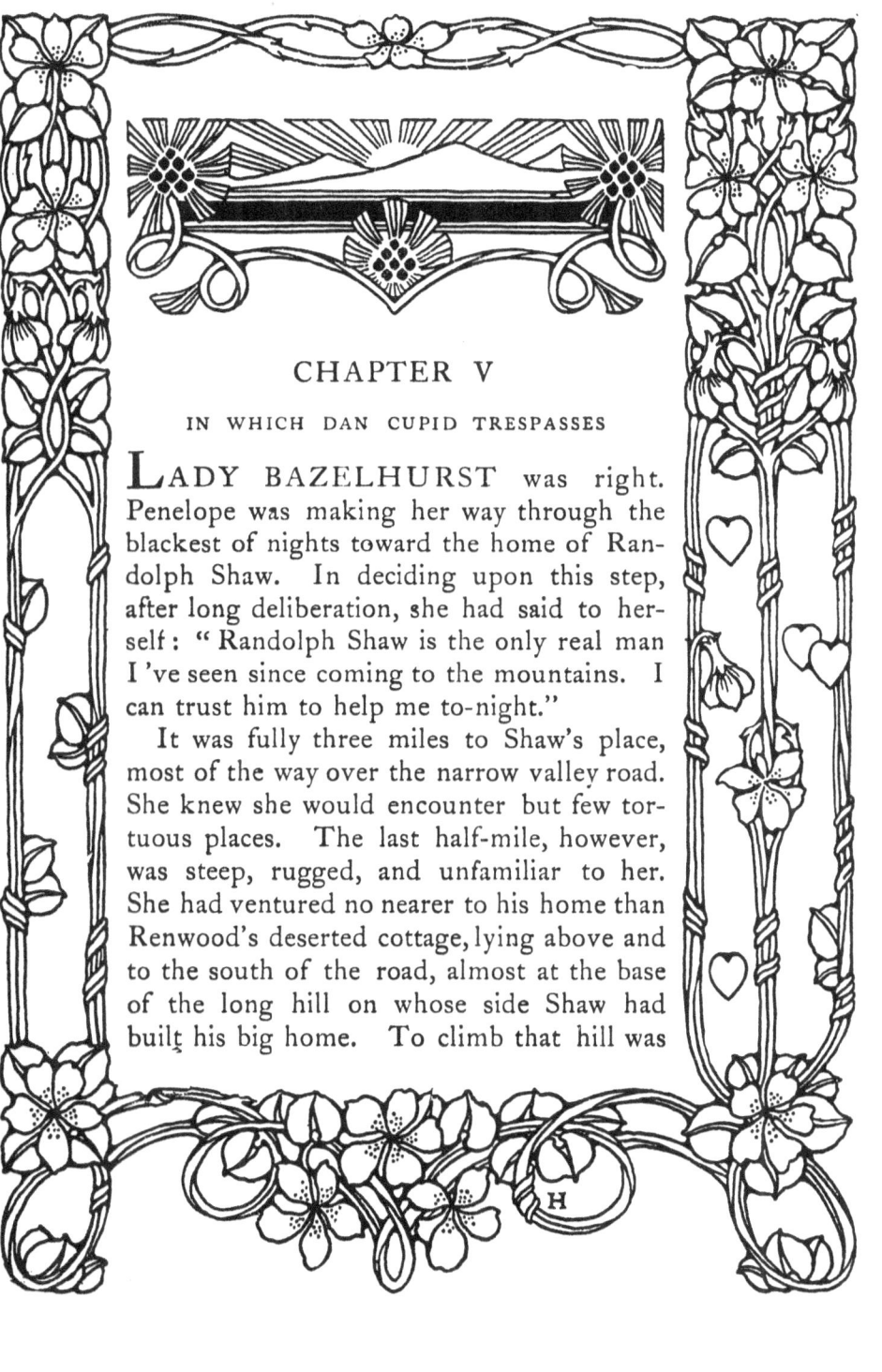

CHAPTER V

IN WHICH DAN CUPID TRESPASSES

LADY BAZELHURST was right. Penelope was making her way through the blackest of nights toward the home of Randolph Shaw. In deciding upon this step, after long deliberation, she had said to herself: " Randolph Shaw is the only real man I 've seen since coming to the mountains. I can trust him to help me to-night."

It was fully three miles to Shaw's place, most of the way over the narrow valley road. She knew she would encounter but few tortuous places. The last half-mile, however, was steep, rugged, and unfamiliar to her. She had ventured no nearer to his home than Renwood's deserted cottage, lying above and to the south of the road, almost at the base of the long hill on whose side Shaw had built his big home. To climb that hill was

no easy task in daylight; at midnight, with
the stars obscured by clouds and tree-tops,
there was something perilously uncertain in
the prospect.

Only the knowledge that patience and
courage eventually would bring her to the
end made the journey possible. Time would
lead her to the haven; care would make the
road a friend; a stout heart was her best
ally. Strength of limb and strength of purpose she had, in use and in reserve. No
power could have made her turn back will-
ingly. Her anxious eyes were set ahead in
the blackness; her runaway feet were eager
in obedience to her will.

"Why couldn't I have put it off until
morning?" she was saying to herself as she
passed down the gravelled drive and advanced
to meet the wall of trees that frowned blackly
in her face. "What will he think? What
will he say? Oh, he'll think I'm such a
silly, romantic fool. No, he won't. He'll
understand. He'll help me on to Plattsburg to-morrow. But will he think I've
done this for effect? Won't he think I'm
actually throwing myself at his head? No,
I can't turn back. I'd rather die than go
back to that house. It won't matter what

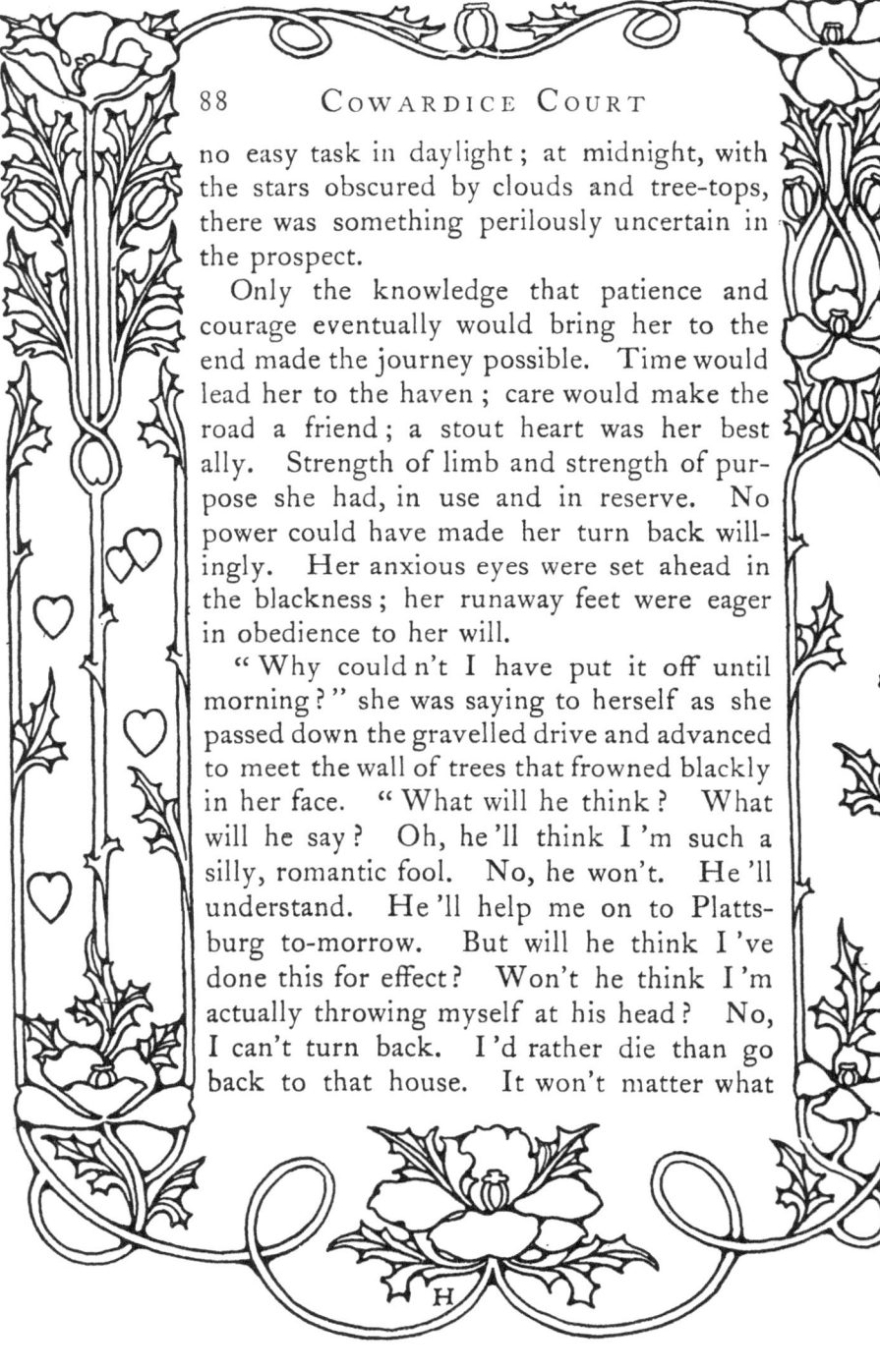

he thinks; I'll be away from all of it to-morrow.   I'll be out of his life and I won't care what he thinks.   England!   Goodness, what's that?"   She had turned a bend in the drive and just ahead there was a light.   A sigh of relief followed the question.   It came from the lantern which hung to a stake in the road where the new stone gate-posts were being built by workmen from town.   Bazel-hurst Villa was a quarter of a mile, through the park, behind her; the forest was ahead.

At the gate she stopped between the half-finished stone posts and looked ahead with the first shiver of dismay.   Her limbs seemed ready to collapse.   The flush of anger and excitement left her face; a white, desolate look came in its stead.   Her eyes grew wide and she blinked her lashes with an awed uncertainty that boded ill for the stability of her adventure.   An owl hooted in mournful cadence close by and she felt that her hair was going straight on end.   The tense fingers of one hand gripped the handle of the travelling-bag while the other went spasmodically to her heart.

"Oh!" she gasped, moving over quickly to the stake on which the lantern hung.   The wind was rushing through the tree-tops with

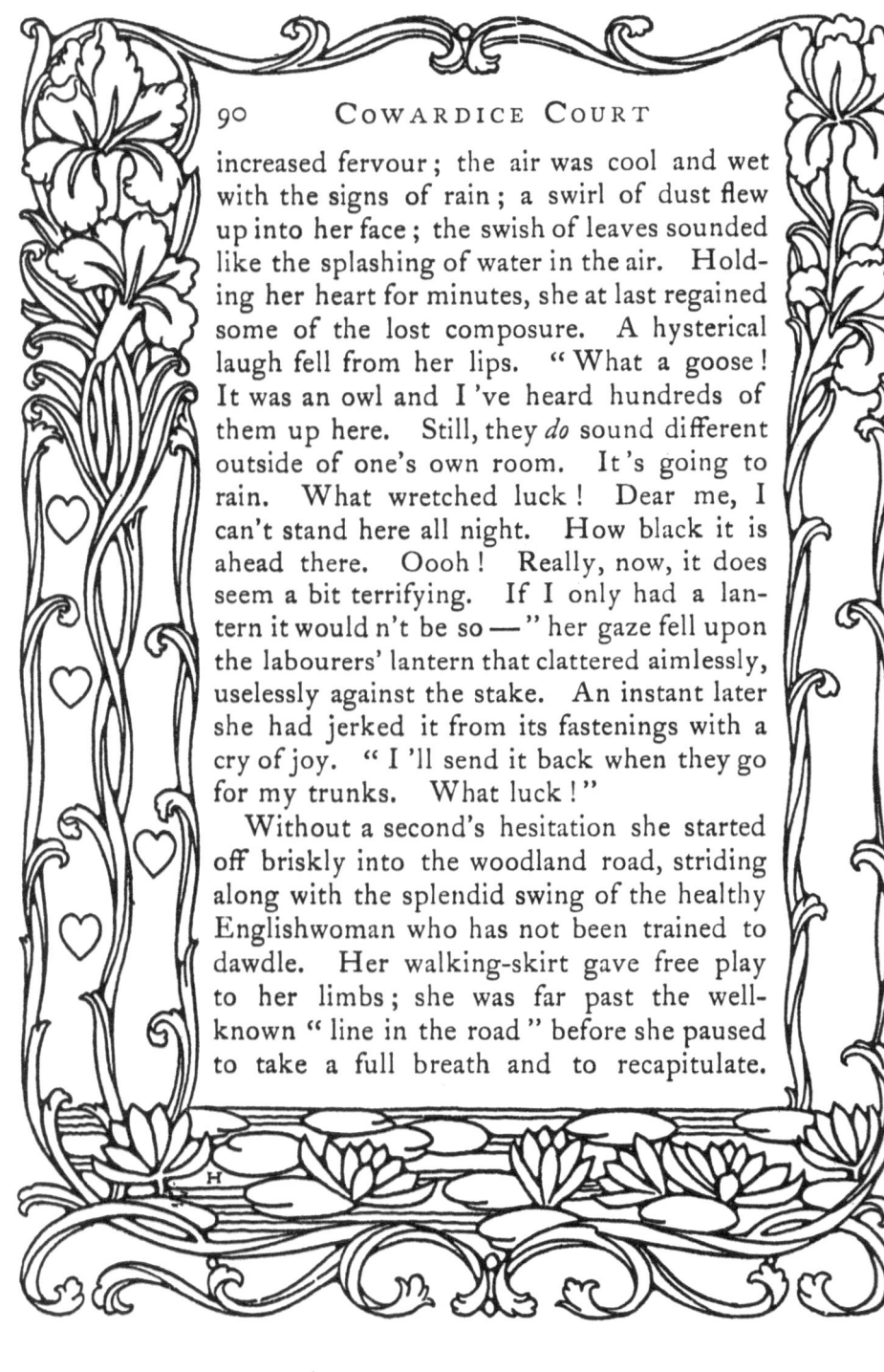

increased fervour; the air was cool and wet
with the signs of rain; a swirl of dust flew
up into her face; the swish of leaves sounded
like the splashing of water in the air.   Holding her heart for minutes, she at last regained
some of the lost composure.   A hysterical
laugh fell from her lips.   "What a goose!
It was an owl and I've heard hundreds of
them up here.   Still, they *do* sound different
outside of one's own room.   It's going to
rain.   What wretched luck!   Dear me, I
can't stand here all night.   How black it is
ahead there.   Oooh!   Really, now, it does
seem a bit terrifying.   If I only had a lantern it wouldn't be so — " her gaze fell upon
the labourers' lantern that clattered aimlessly,
uselessly against the stake.   An instant later
she had jerked it from its fastenings with a
cry of joy.   "I'll send it back when they go
for my trunks.   What luck!"

Without a second's hesitation she started
off briskly into the woodland road, striding
along with the splendid swing of the healthy
Englishwoman who has not been trained to
dawdle.   Her walking-skirt gave free play
to her limbs; she was far past the well-
known "line in the road" before she paused
to take a full breath and to recapitulate.

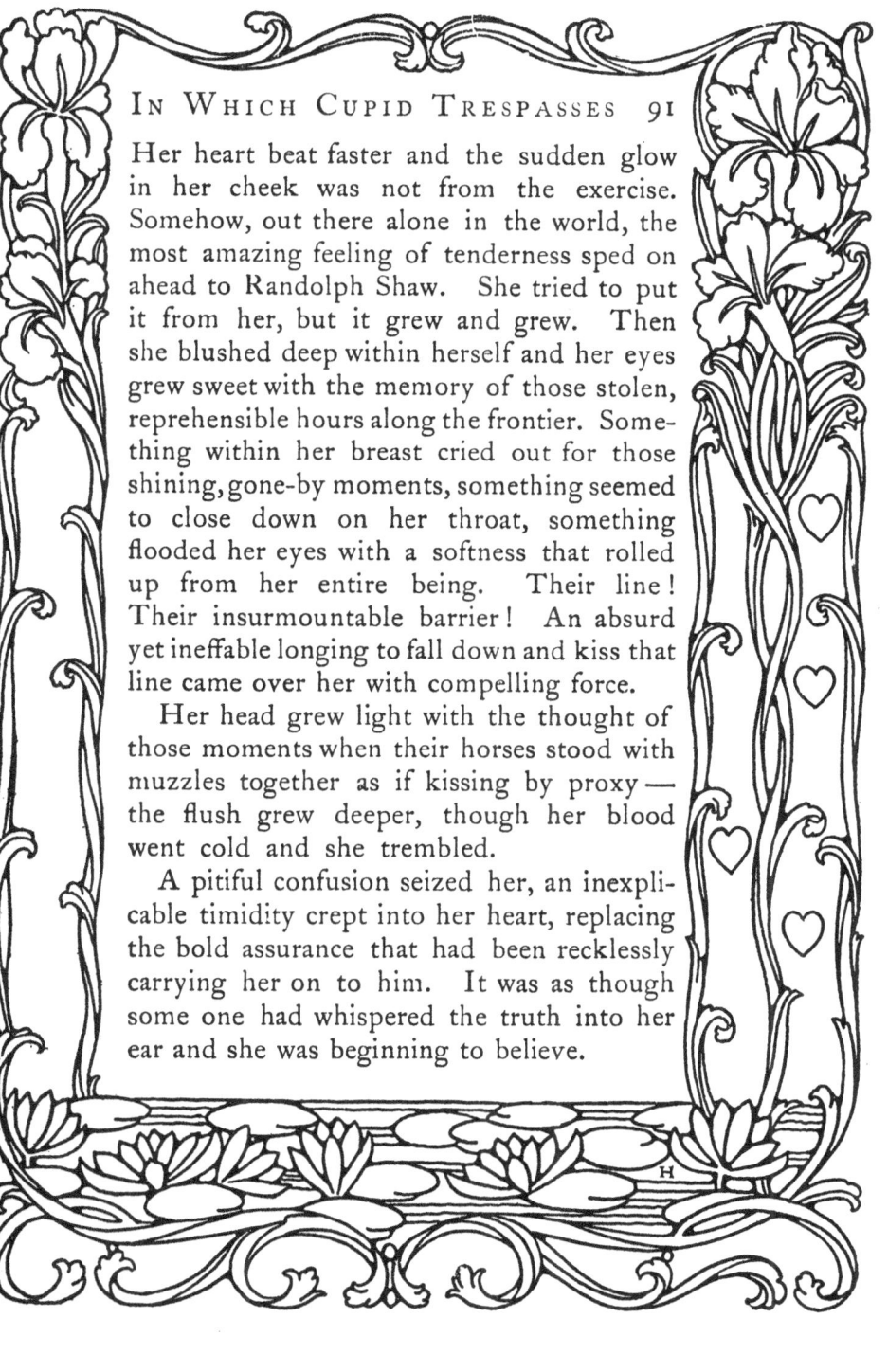

Her heart beat faster and the sudden glow in her cheek was not from the exercise. Somehow, out there alone in the world, the most amazing feeling of tenderness sped on ahead to Randolph Shaw. She tried to put it from her, but it grew and grew. Then she blushed deep within herself and her eyes grew sweet with the memory of those stolen, reprehensible hours along the frontier. Something within her breast cried out for those shining, gone-by moments, something seemed to close down on her throat, something flooded her eyes with a softness that rolled up from her entire being. Their line! Their insurmountable barrier! An absurd yet ineffable longing to fall down and kiss that line came over her with compelling force.

Her head grew light with the thought of those moments when their horses stood with muzzles together as if kissing by proxy — the flush grew deeper, though her blood went cold and she trembled.

A pitiful confusion seized her, an inexplicable timidity crept into her heart, replacing the bold assurance that had been recklessly carrying her on to him. It was as though some one had whispered the truth into her ear and she was beginning to believe.

From that moment her courage began to fail. The glow from her lantern was a menace instead of a help. A sweet timorousness enveloped her and something tingled — she knew not what.

Spattering raindrops whizzed in her face, ominous forerunners from the inky sky. The wind was whistling with shrill glee in the tree-tops and the tree-tops tried to flee before it. A mile and a half lay between her and the big cottage on the hillside — the most arduous part of the journey by far. She walked and ran as though pursued, scudding over the road with a swiftness that would have amazed another, but which seemed the essence of slowness to her. Thoughts of robbers, tramps, wild beasts, assailed her with intermittent terrors, but all served to diminish the feeling of shyness that had been interfering with her determination.

Past Renwood's cottage she sped, shuddering as she recognized the stone steps and path that ran up the hillside to the haunted house. Ghosts, witches, hobgoblins fell into the procession of pursuers, cheered on by the shrieking wind that grew more noisome as her feet carried her higher up the mountain. Now she was on new ground. She had never

before explored so far as this. The hill was
steep and the road had black abysses out
beyond its edges. . . .

She was breathless, half dead from fatigue
and terror when at last her feet stumbled up
the broad steps leading to his porch. Trem-
bling, she sank into the rustic bench that
stood against the wall. The lantern clattered
to her feet, and the bag with her jewels, her
letter of credit, and her curling irons slid to
the floor behind the bench. Here was his
home! What cared she for the storm?

Even as she lay there gasping for breath,
her eyes on the shadowy moon that was
breaking its way through the clouds, three
men raced from the stables at Bazelhurst
Villa bent on finding the mad young person
who had fled the place. Scarcely knowing
what direction he took, Lord Bazelhurst led
the way, followed by the duke and the count,
all of them supplied with carriage lamps,
which, at any other time, would have been
sickening in their obtrusiveness. Except
for Lady Evelyn, the rest of the house slept
the sleep of ease.

Gradually Penelope recovered from the
effects of the mad race up the hill. The
sputtering flame in the lantern called her

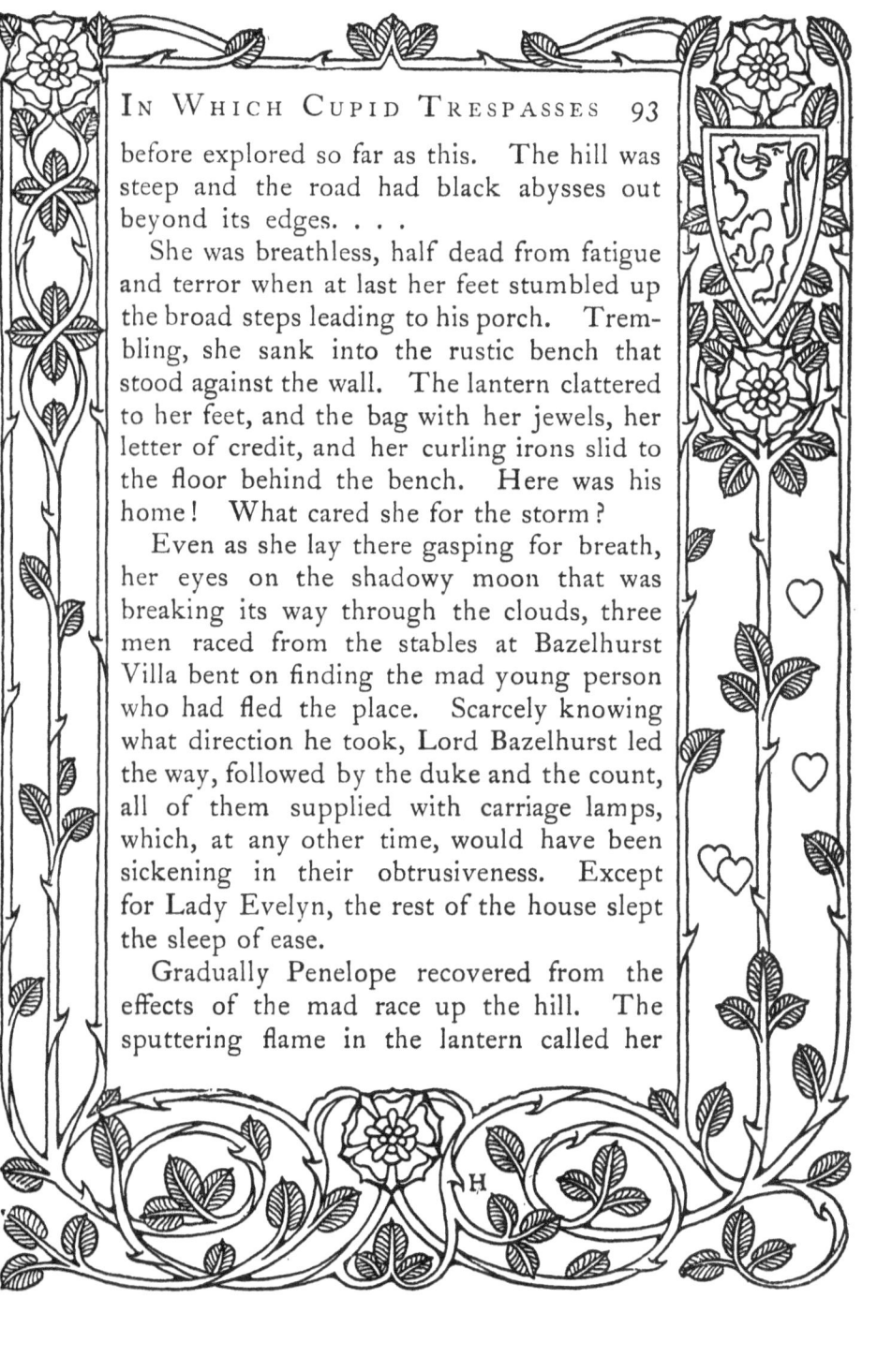

into action. Clutching it from the floor
of the porch, she softly began a tour of
inspection, first looking at her watch to
find that it was the unholy hour of two!
Had some one yelled boo! she would have
swooned, so tense was every nerve. Now
that she was here, what was she to do? Her
heart came to her mouth, her hand shook,
but not with fear; a nervous smile tried to
wreak disaster to the concern in her eyes.

The house was dark and still. No one
was stirring. The porch was littered with
rugs and cushions, while on a small table
near the end stood a decanter, a siphon, and
two glasses. Two? He had said he was
alone except for the housekeeper and the
servants. A visitor, then. This was not
what she had expected. Her heart sank.
It would be hard to face the master of the
house, but — a stranger? Cigarette stubs
met her bewildered, troubled gaze — many
of them. Deduction was easy out there in the
lonely night. It was easy to see that Shaw
and his companion sat up so late that the
servants had gone to bed.

Distractedly she looked about for means
of shelter on the porch until daylight could
abet her in the flight to the village beyond.

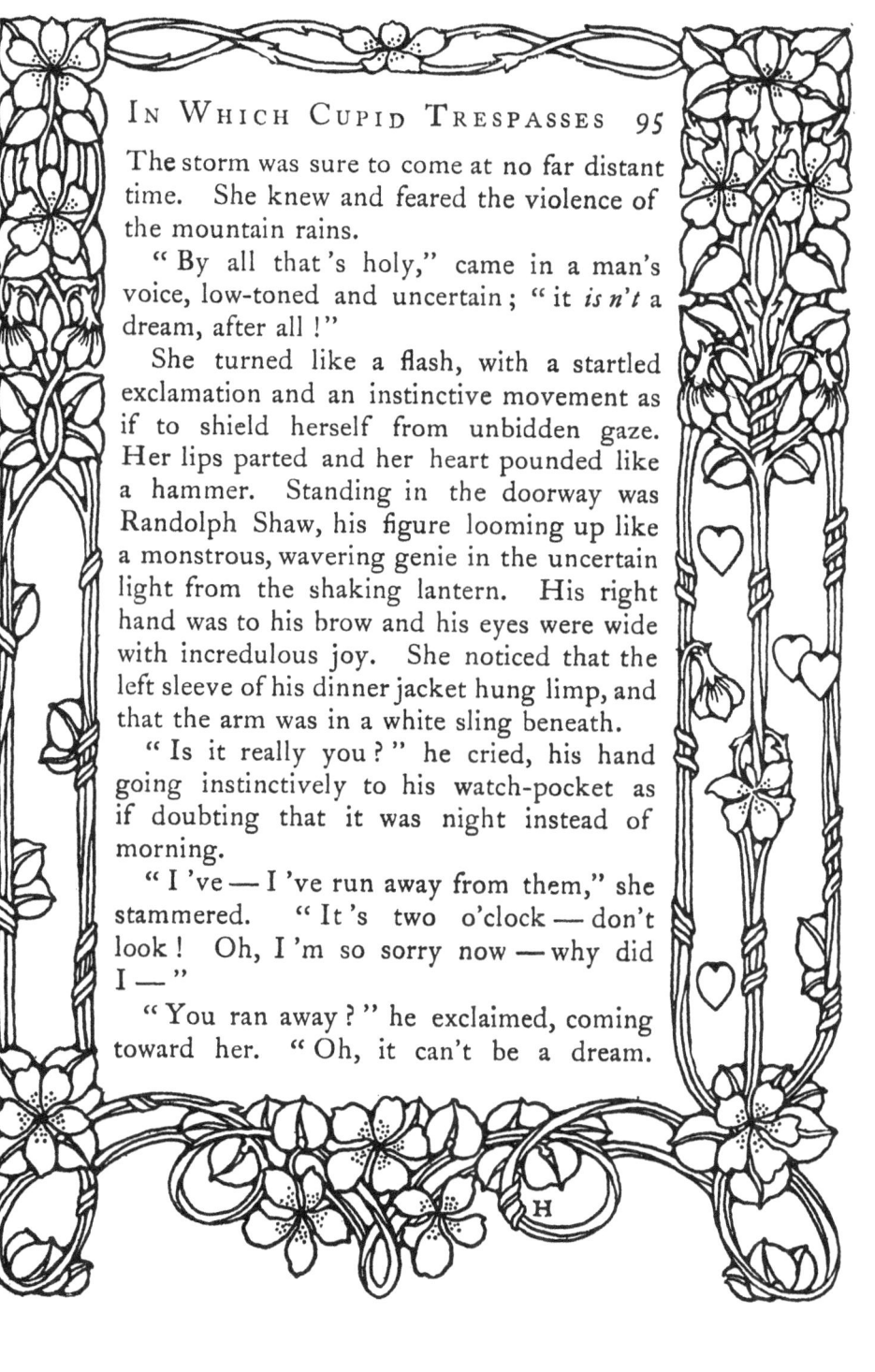

The storm was sure to come at no far distant time. She knew and feared the violence of the mountain rains.

"By all that's holy," came in a man's voice, low-toned and uncertain; "it *isn't* a dream, after all!"

She turned like a flash, with a startled exclamation and an instinctive movement as if to shield herself from unbidden gaze. Her lips parted and her heart pounded like a hammer. Standing in the doorway was Randolph Shaw, his figure looming up like a monstrous, wavering genie in the uncertain light from the shaking lantern. His right hand was to his brow and his eyes were wide with incredulous joy. She noticed that the left sleeve of his dinner jacket hung limp, and that the arm was in a white sling beneath.

"Is it really you?" he cried, his hand going instinctively to his watch-pocket as if doubting that it was night instead of morning.

"I've — I've run away from them," she stammered. "It's two o'clock — don't look! Oh, I'm so sorry now — why did I —"

"You ran away?" he exclaimed, coming toward her. "Oh, it can't be a dream.

H

You are there, are n't you?" She was a
pitiable object as she stood there, powerless
to retreat, shaking like a leaf. He took her
by the shoulder. "Yes — it is *you*. Good
Lord, what does it mean? What has happened? How did you come here? Are
you alone?"

"Utterly, miserably alone. Oh, Mr.
Shaw!" she cried despairingly. "You *will*
understand, won't you?"

"Never! Never as long as I live. It
is beyond comprehension. The wonderful
part of it all is that I was sitting in there
dreaming of you — yes, I was. I heard
some one out here, investigated and found
you — *you*, of all people in the world. And
I was dreaming that I held you in my arms.
Yes, I was! I was dreaming it —"

"Mr. Shaw! You should n't —"

"And I awoke to find you — not in my
arms, not in Bazelhurst Villa, but here —
here on my porch."

"Like a thief in the night," she murmured. "What *do* you think of me?"

"Shall I tell you — really?" he cried.
The light in his eyes drove her back a step
or two, panic in her heart.

"N—no, no — not now!" she gasped,

but a great wave of exaltation swept through
her being. He turned and walked away,
too dazed to speak. Without knowing it,
she followed with hesitating steps. At the
edge of the porch he paused and looked into
the darkness.

"By Jove, I *must* be dreaming," she heard
him mutter.

"No, you are not," she declared desper-
ately. "I *am* here. I ask your protection
for the night. I am going away — to England — to-morrow. I could n't stay there
— I just could n't. I 'm sorry I came
here — I 'm —"

"Thank heaven, you *did* come," he exclaimed, turning to her joyously. "You
are like a fairy — the fairy princess come
true. It 's unbelievable ! But — but what
was it you said about England?" he con-
cluded, suddenly sober.

"I am go— going home. There 's no
place else. I can't live with her," she said,
a bit tremulously.

"To England? At once? Your father
— will he —"

"My father? I have no father. Oh !"
with a sudden start. Her eyes met his in
a helpless stare. "I never thought. My

7

H

home was at Bazelhurst Castle — their home. I can't go there. Good heavens, what am I to do?"

A long time afterward she recalled his exultant exclamation, checked at its outset, — recalled it with a perfect sense of understanding. With rare good taste he subdued whatever it was that might have struggled for expression and simply extended his right hand to relieve her of the lantern.

"We never have been enemies, Miss Drake," he said, controlling his voice admirably. " But had we been so up to this very instant, I am sure I'd surrender now. I don't know what has happened at the Villa. It does n't matter. You are here to ask my protection and my help. I am at your service, my home is yours, my right hand also. You are tired and wet and — nervous. Won't you come inside? I'll get a light in a jiffy and Mrs. Ulrich, my housekeeper, shall be with you as soon as I can rout her out. Come in, please." She held back doubtfully, a troubled, uncertain look in her eyes.

"You *will* understand, won't you?" she asked simply.

" And no questions asked," he said from

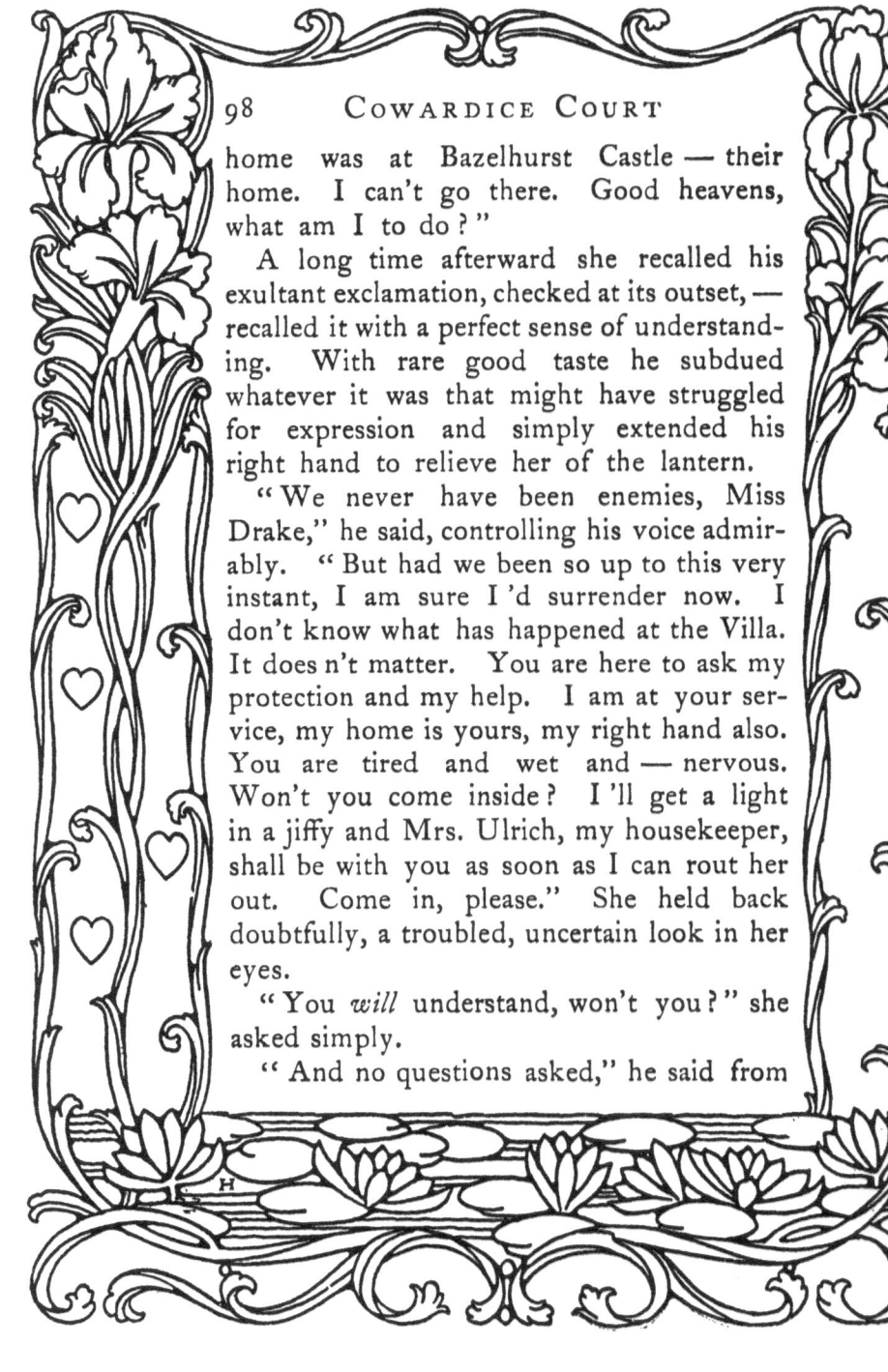

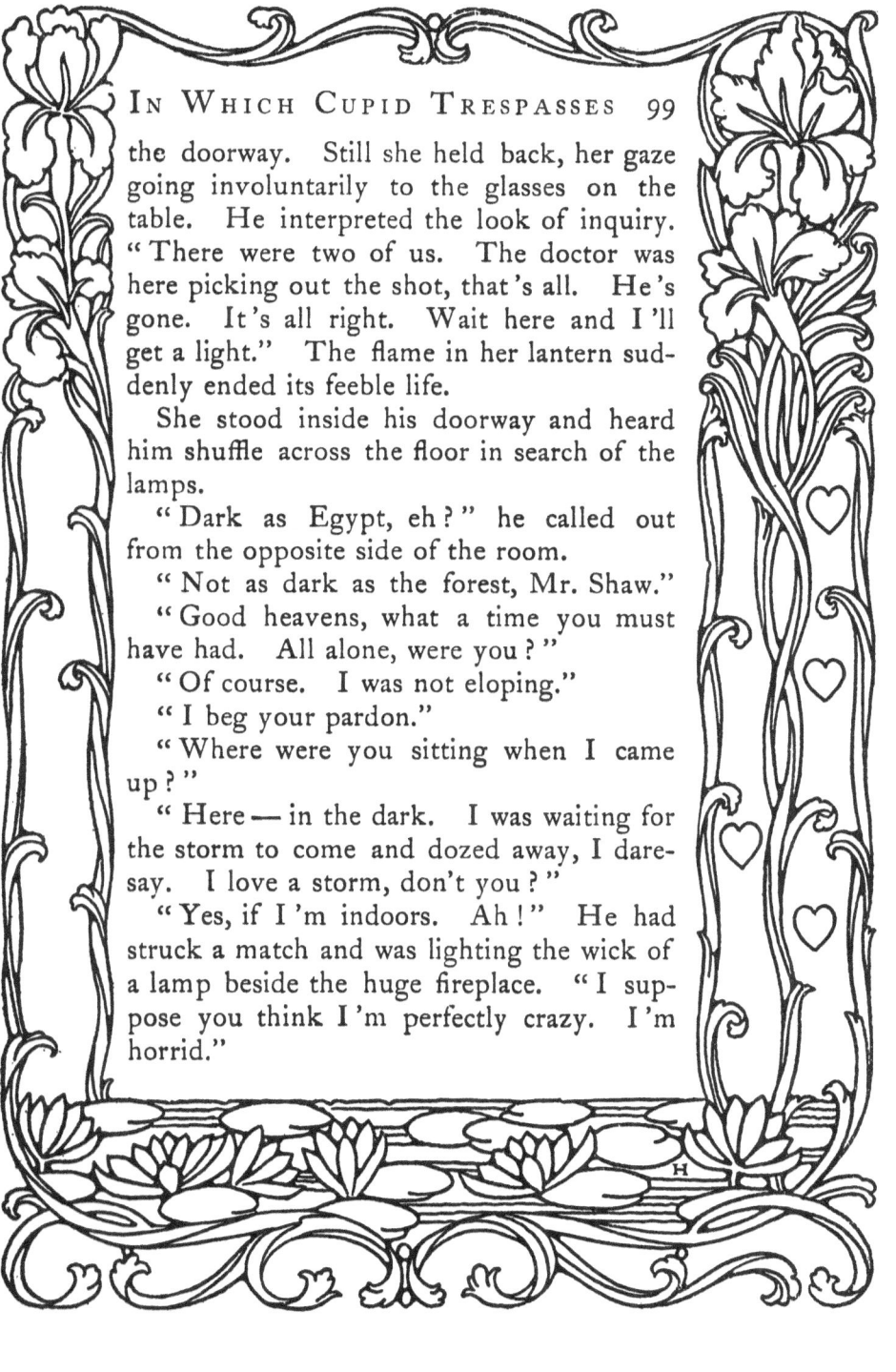

the doorway. Still she held back, her gaze
going involuntarily to the glasses on the
table. He interpreted the look of inquiry.
"There were two of us. The doctor was
here picking out the shot, that's all. He's
gone. It's all right. Wait here and I'll
get a light." The flame in her lantern suddenly ended its feeble life.

She stood inside his doorway and heard
him shuffle across the floor in search of the
lamps.

"Dark as Egypt, eh?" he called out
from the opposite side of the room.

"Not as dark as the forest, Mr. Shaw."

"Good heavens, what a time you must
have had. All alone, were you?"

"Of course. I was not eloping."

"I beg your pardon."

"Where were you sitting when I came
up?"

"Here — in the dark. I was waiting for
the storm to come and dozed away, I daresay. I love a storm, don't you?"

"Yes, if I'm indoors. Ah!" He had
struck a match and was lighting the wick of
a lamp beside the huge fireplace. "I suppose you think I'm perfectly crazy. I'm
horrid."

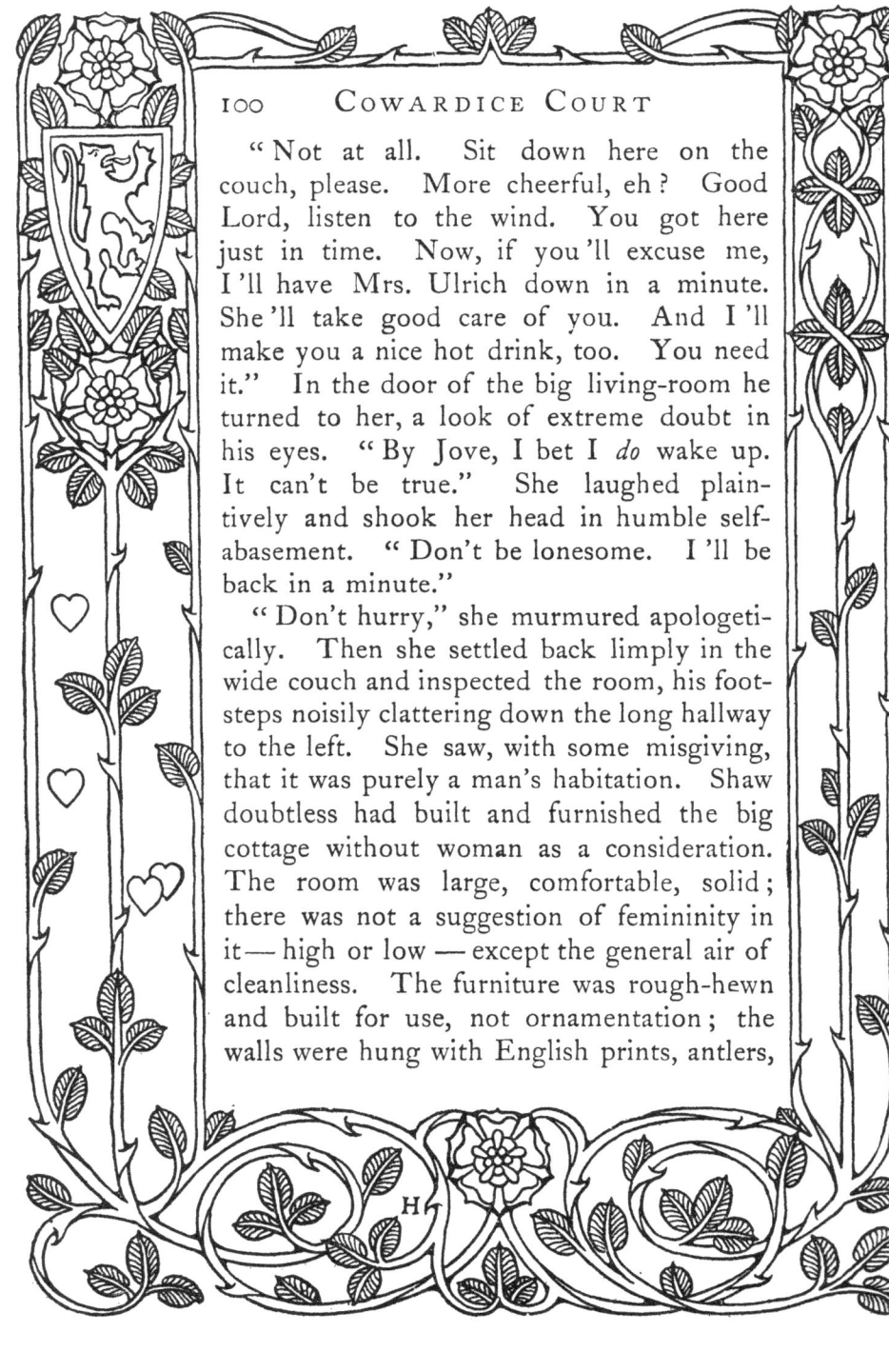

"Not at all. Sit down here on the couch, please. More cheerful, eh? Good Lord, listen to the wind. You got here just in time. Now, if you'll excuse me, I'll have Mrs. Ulrich down in a minute. She'll take good care of you. And I'll make you a nice hot drink, too. You need it." In the door of the big living-room he turned to her, a look of extreme doubt in his eyes. "By Jove, I bet I *do* wake up. It can't be true." She laughed plaintively and shook her head in humble self-abasement. "Don't be lonesome. I'll be back in a minute."

"Don't hurry," she murmured apologetically. Then she settled back limply in the wide couch and inspected the room, his footsteps noisily clattering down the long hallway to the left. She saw, with some misgiving, that it was purely a man's habitation. Shaw doubtless had built and furnished the big cottage without woman as a consideration. The room was large, comfortable, solid; there was not a suggestion of femininity in it — high or low — except the general air of cleanliness. The furniture was rough-hewn and built for use, not ornamentation; the walls were hung with English prints, antlers, mementoes of the hunt and the field of sport; the floor was covered with skins and great "carpet rag" rugs. The whole aspect was so distinctly mannish that her heart fluttered ridiculously in its loneliness. Her cogitations were running seriously toward riot when he came hurriedly down the hall and into her presence.

"She 'll be down presently. In fact, so will the cook and the housemaid. Gad, Miss Drake, they were so afraid of the storm that all of them piled into Mrs. Ulrich's room. I wonder at your courage in facing the symptoms outdoors. Now, I 'll fix you a drink. Take off your hat — be comfortable. Cigarette? Good! Here's my sideboard. See? It's a nuisance, this having only one arm in commission; affects my style as a barkeep. Don't stir; I 'll be able — "

"Let me help you. I mean, please don't go to so much trouble. Really I want nothing but a place to sleep to-night. This couch will do — honestly. And some one to call me at daybreak, so that I may be on my way." He looked at her and laughed quizzically. "Oh, I 'm in earnest, Mr. Shaw. I would n't have stopped here if it had n't been for the storm."

"Come, now, Miss Drake, you spoil the fairy tale. You *did* intend to come here. It was the only place for you to go — and I'm glad of it. My only regret is that the house is n't filled with chaperons."

"Why?" she demanded with a guilty start.

"Because I could then say to you all the things that are in my heart — aye, that are almost bursting from my lips. I — I can't say them now, you know," he said, and she understood his delicacy. For some minutes she sat in silence watching him as he clumsily mixed the drinks and put the water over the alcohol blaze. Suddenly he turned to her with something like alarm in his voice. "By George, you don't suppose they'll pursue you?"

"Oh, would n't that be jolly? It would be like the real story-book — the fairy and the ogres and all that. But," dubiously, "I'm sorely afraid they consider me rubbish. Still — " looking up encouragingly — "my brother would try to find me if he — if he knew that I was gone."

To her surprise, he whistled softly and permitted a frown of anxiety to creep over his face. "I had n't thought of that," he

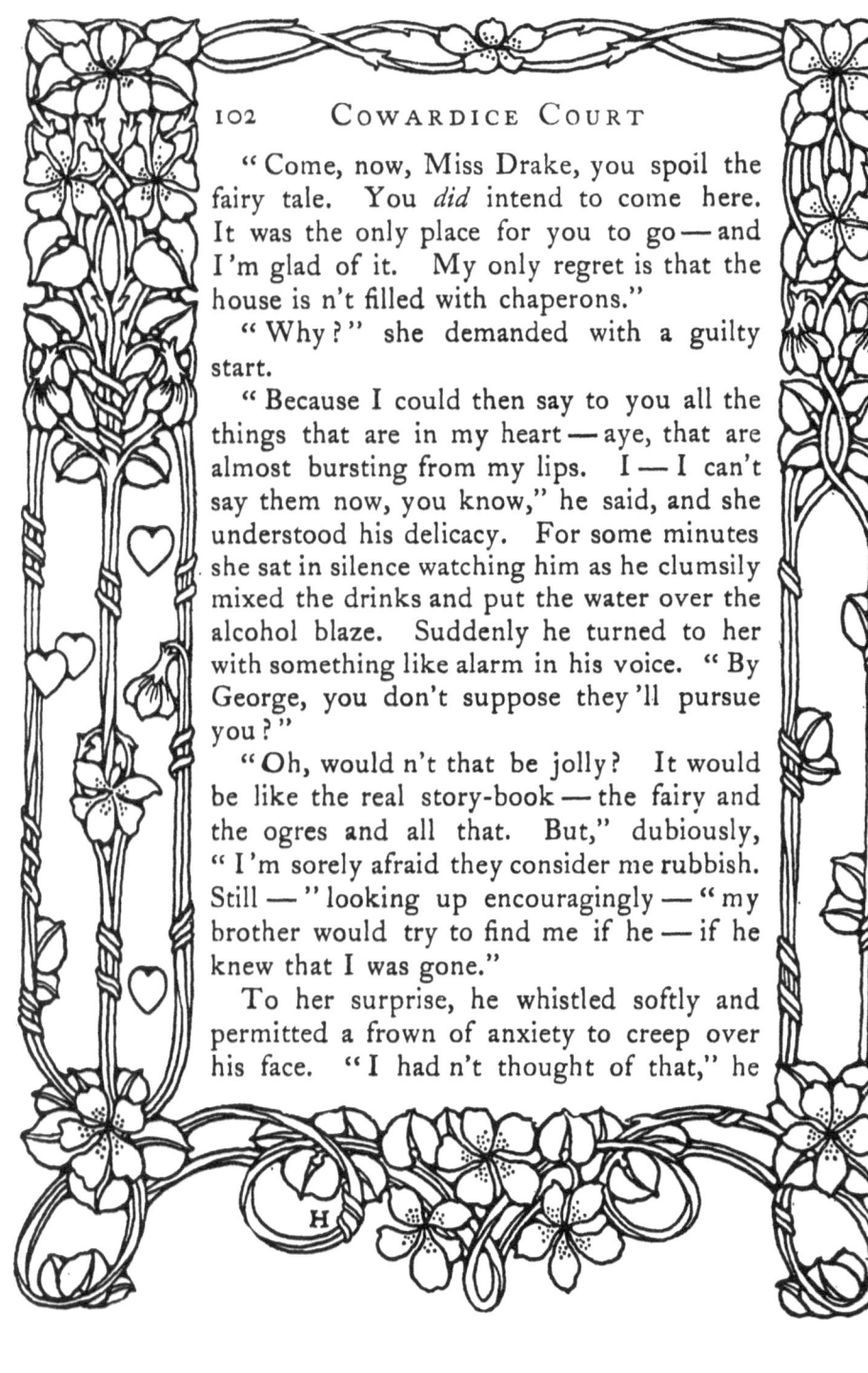

observed reflectively. Then he seemed to throw off the momentary symptoms of uneasiness, adding, with a laugh: "I daresay nothing will happen. The storm would put a stop to all idea of pursuit."

"Let them pursue," she said, a stubborn light in her eyes. "I am my own mistress, Mr. Shaw. They can't take me, willy nilly, as if I were a child, you know."

"That's quite true. You don't understand," he said slowly, his back to her.

"You mean the law? Is it different from ours?"

"Not that. The — er — situation. You see, they might think it a trifle odd if they found you here — with me. Don't you understand?" He turned to her with a very serious expression. She started and sat bolt upright to stare at him comprehensively.

"You mean — it — it is n't quite — er —"

"Regular, perhaps," he supplied. "Please keep your seat! I'm not the censor; I'm not even an opinion. Believe me, Miss Drake, my only thought was and is for your good."

"I see. They would believe evil of me

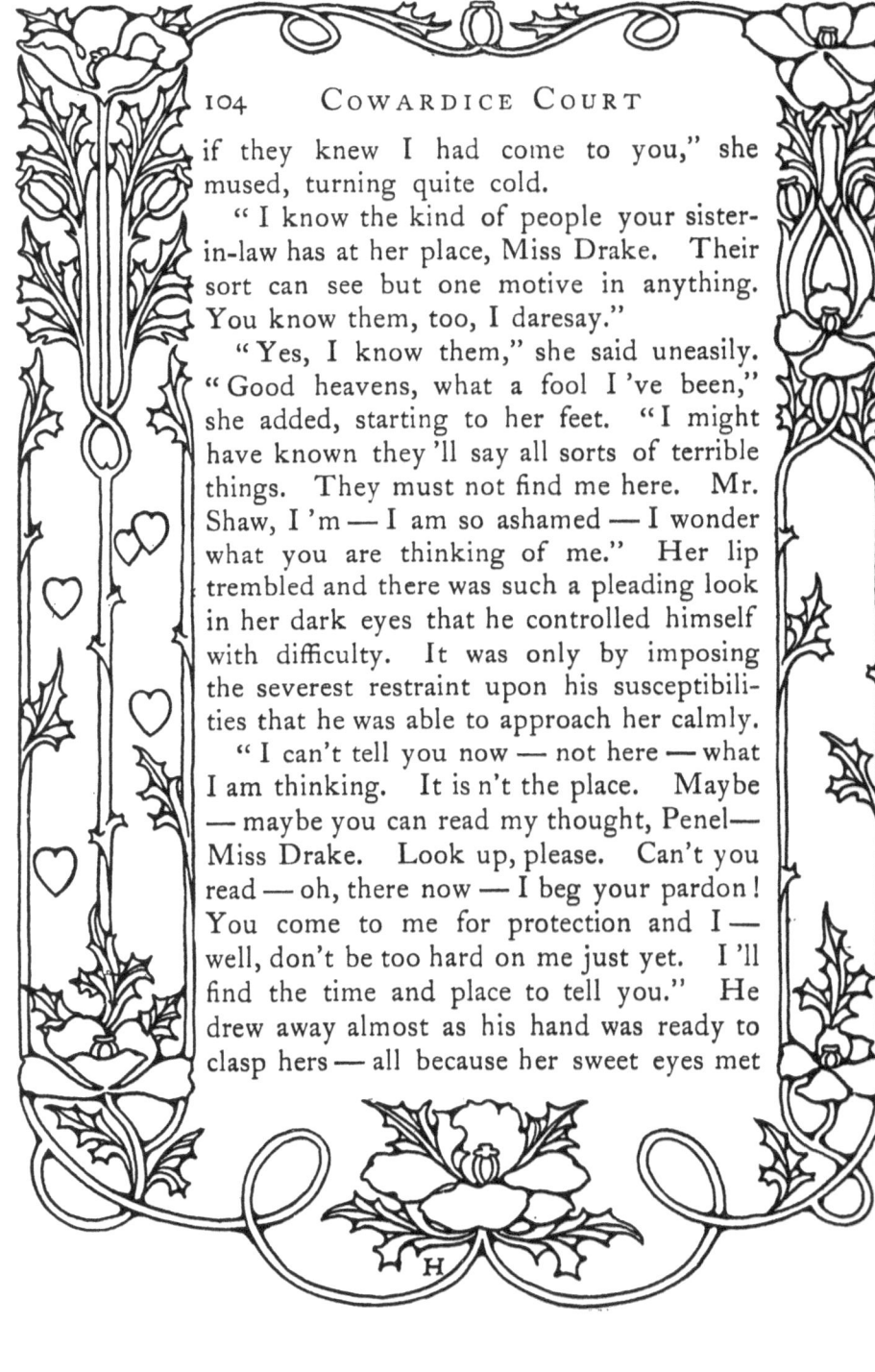

if they knew I had come to you," she
mused, turning quite cold.

"I know the kind of people your sister-
in-law has at her place, Miss Drake. Their
sort can see but one motive in anything.
You know them, too, I daresay."

"Yes, I know them," she said uneasily.
"Good heavens, what a fool I've been,"
she added, starting to her feet. "I might
have known they'll say all sorts of terrible
things. They must not find me here. Mr.
Shaw, I'm — I am so ashamed — I wonder
what you are thinking of me." Her lip
trembled and there was such a pleading look
in her dark eyes that he controlled himself
with difficulty. It was only by imposing
the severest restraint upon his susceptibili-
ties that he was able to approach her calmly.

"I can't tell you now — not here — what
I am thinking. It isn't the place. Maybe
— maybe you can read my thought, Penel—
Miss Drake. Look up, please. Can't you
read — oh, there now — I beg your pardon!
You come to me for protection and I —
well, don't be too hard on me just yet. I'll
find the time and place to tell you." He
drew away almost as his hand was ready to
clasp hers — all because her sweet eyes met

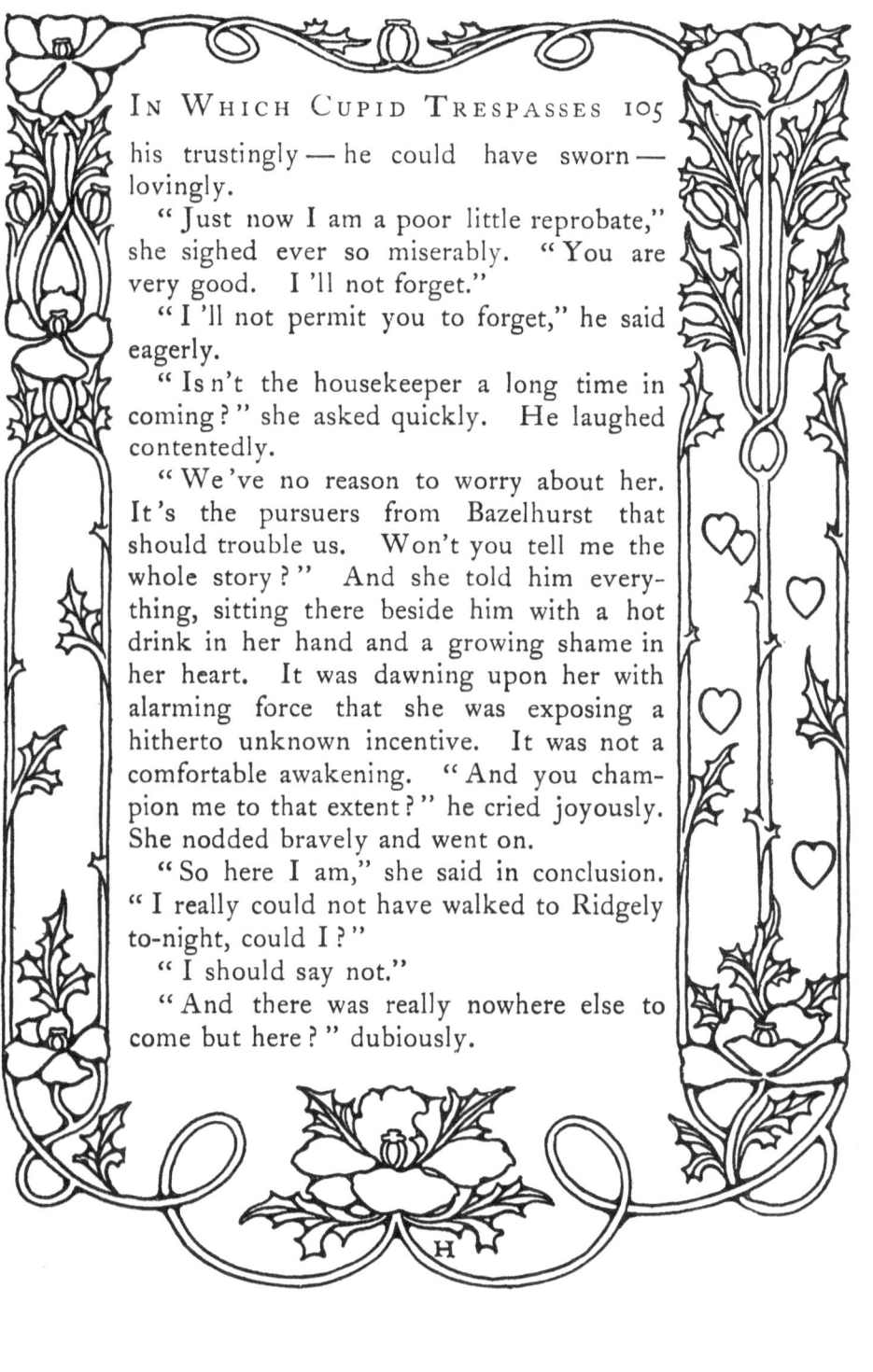

his trustingly — he could have sworn —
lovingly.

"Just now I am a poor little reprobate,"
she sighed ever so miserably. "You are
very good. I 'll not forget."

"I 'll not permit you to forget," he said
eagerly.

"Isn't the housekeeper a long time in
coming?" she asked quickly. He laughed
contentedly.

"We've no reason to worry about her.
It's the pursuers from Bazelhurst that
should trouble us. Won't you tell me the
whole story?" And she told him everything, sitting there beside him with a hot
drink in her hand and a growing shame in
her heart. It was dawning upon her with
alarming force that she was exposing a
hitherto unknown incentive. It was not a
comfortable awakening. "And you cham-
pion me to that extent?" he cried joyously.
She nodded bravely and went on.

"So here I am," she said in conclusion.
"I really could not have walked to Ridgely
to-night, could I?"

"I should say not."

"And there was really nowhere else to
come but here?" dubiously.

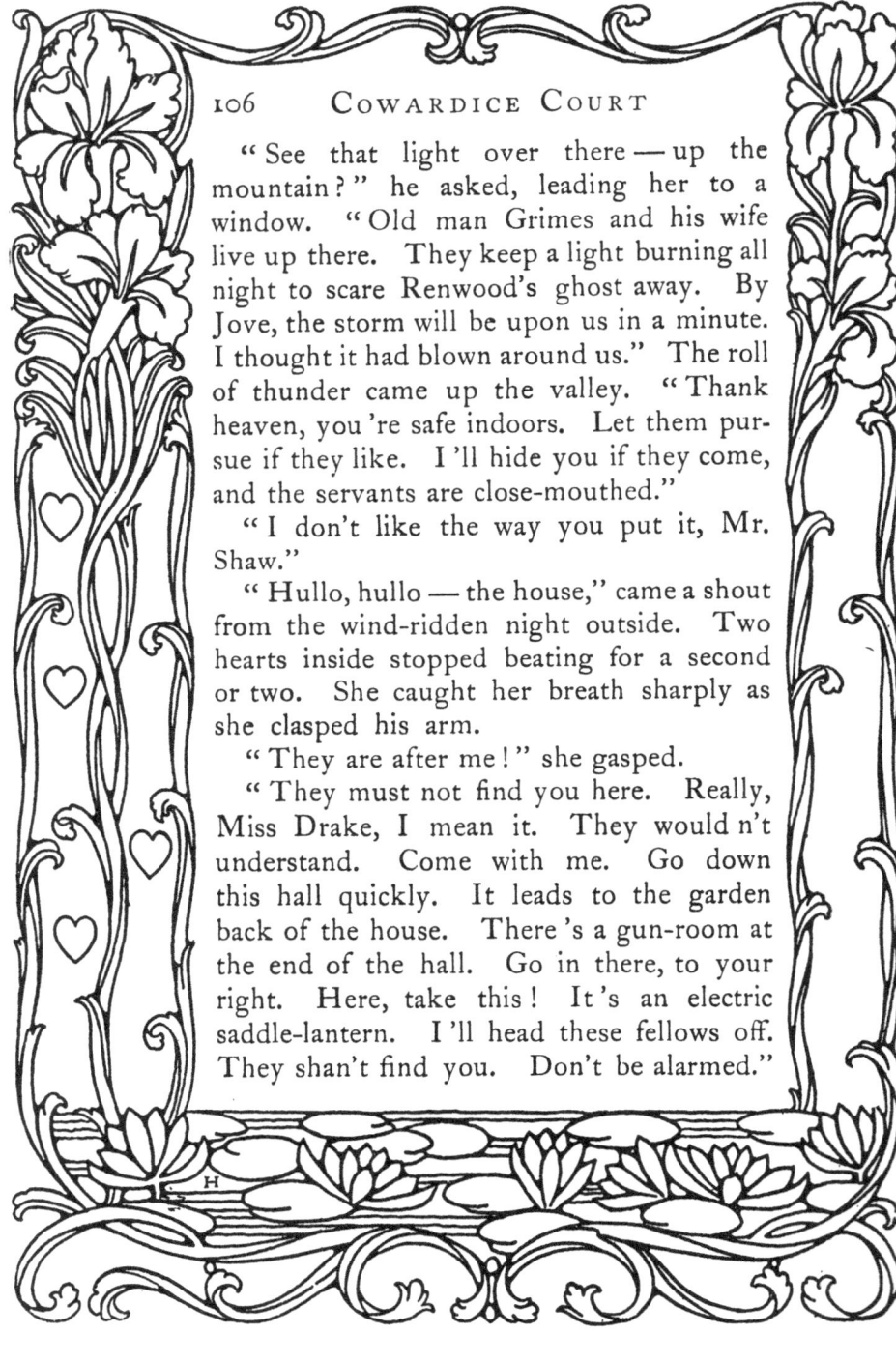

"See that light over there — up the mountain?" he asked, leading her to a window. "Old man Grimes and his wife live up there. They keep a light burning all night to scare Renwood's ghost away. By Jove, the storm will be upon us in a minute. I thought it had blown around us." The roll of thunder came up the valley. "Thank heaven, you're safe indoors. Let them pursue if they like. I'll hide you if they come, and the servants are close-mouthed."

"I don't like the way you put it, Mr. Shaw."

"Hullo, hullo — the house," came a shout from the wind-ridden night outside. Two hearts inside stopped beating for a second or two. She caught her breath sharply as she clasped his arm.

"They are after me!" she gasped.

"They must not find you here. Really, Miss Drake, I mean it. They wouldn't understand. Come with me. Go down this hall quickly. It leads to the garden back of the house. There's a gun-room at the end of the hall. Go in there, to your right. Here, take this! It's an electric saddle-lantern. I'll head these fellows off. They shan't find you. Don't be alarmed."

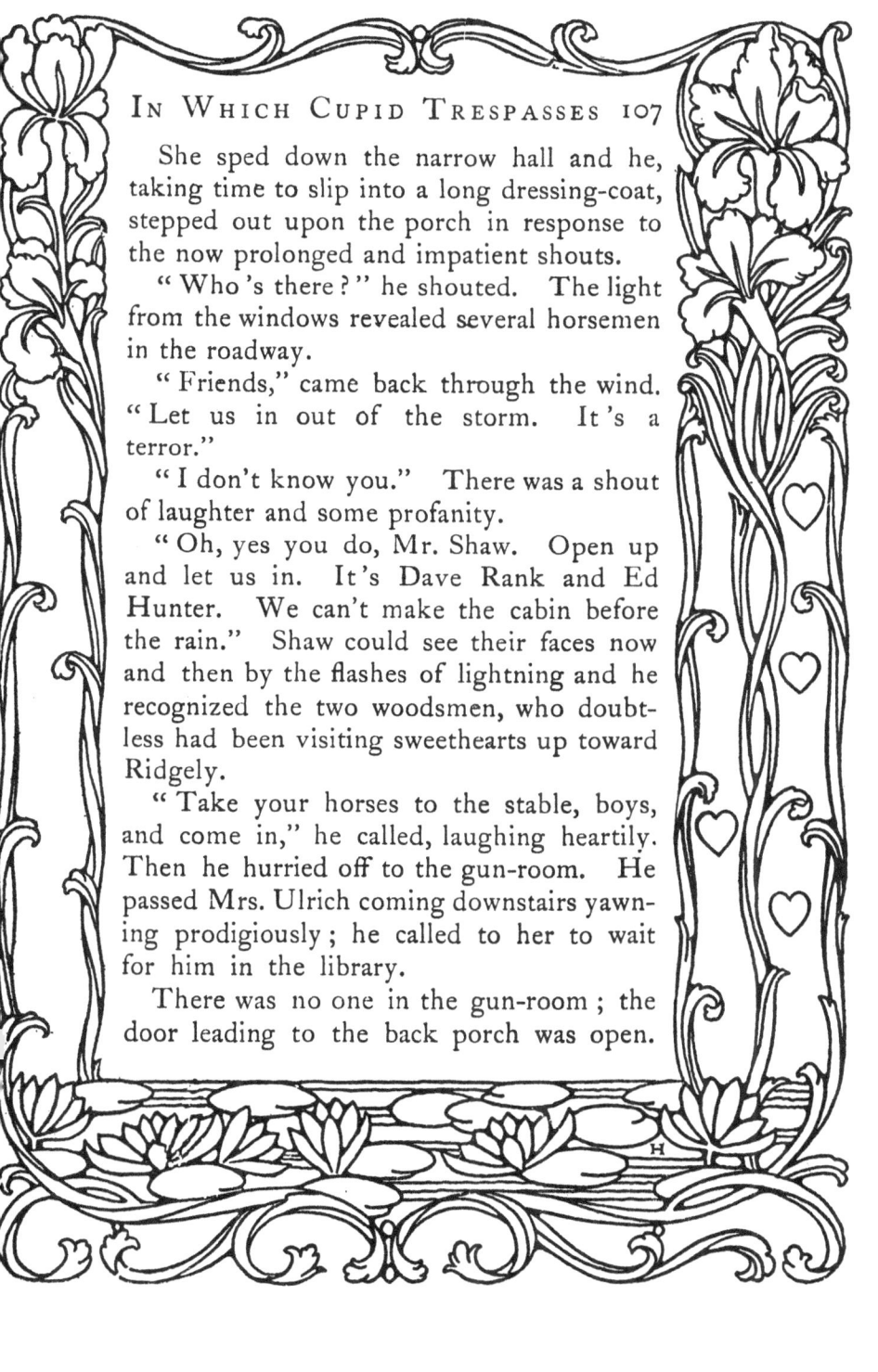

She sped down the narrow hall and he, taking time to slip into a long dressing-coat, stepped out upon the porch in response to the now prolonged and impatient shouts.

"Who's there?" he shouted. The light from the windows revealed several horsemen in the roadway.

"Friends," came back through the wind. "Let us in out of the storm. It's a terror."

"I don't know you." There was a shout of laughter and some profanity.

"Oh, yes you do, Mr. Shaw. Open up and let us in. It's Dave Rank and Ed Hunter. We can't make the cabin before the rain." Shaw could see their faces now and then by the flashes of lightning and he recognized the two woodsmen, who doubtless had been visiting sweethearts up toward Ridgely.

"Take your horses to the stable, boys, and come in," he called, laughing heartily. Then he hurried off to the gun-room. He passed Mrs. Ulrich coming downstairs yawning prodigiously; he called to her to wait for him in the library.

There was no one in the gun-room; the door leading to the back porch was open.

With an exclamation he leaped outside and looked about him.

"Good heavens!" he cried, staggering back.

Far off in the night, a hundred yards or more up the road, leading to Grimes' cabin he saw the wobbling, uncertain flicker of a light wending its way like a will-o'-the-wisp through the night. Without a moment's hesitation and with something strangely like an oath, he rushed into the house, almost upsetting the housekeeper in his haste.

"Visitors outside. Make 'em comfortable. Back soon," he jerked out as he changed his coat with small respect for his injured arm. Then he clutched a couple of rain-coats from the rack and flew out of the back door like a man suddenly gone mad.

CHAPTER VI

IN WHICH A GHOST TRESPASSES

THE impulse which drove Penelope out for the second time that night may be readily appreciated. Its foundation was fear; its subordinate emotions were shame, self-pity and consciousness of her real feeling toward the man of the house. The true spirit of womanhood revolted with its usual waywardness.

She was flying down the stony road, some distance from the cottage, in the very face of the coming tornado, her heart beating like a trip-hammer, her eyes bent on the little light up the mountain-side, before it occurred to her that this last flight was not only senseless but perilous. She even laughed at herself for a fool as she recalled the tell-tale handbag on the porch and the damning presence of a Bazelhurst lantern in the hallway.

The storm which had been raging farther

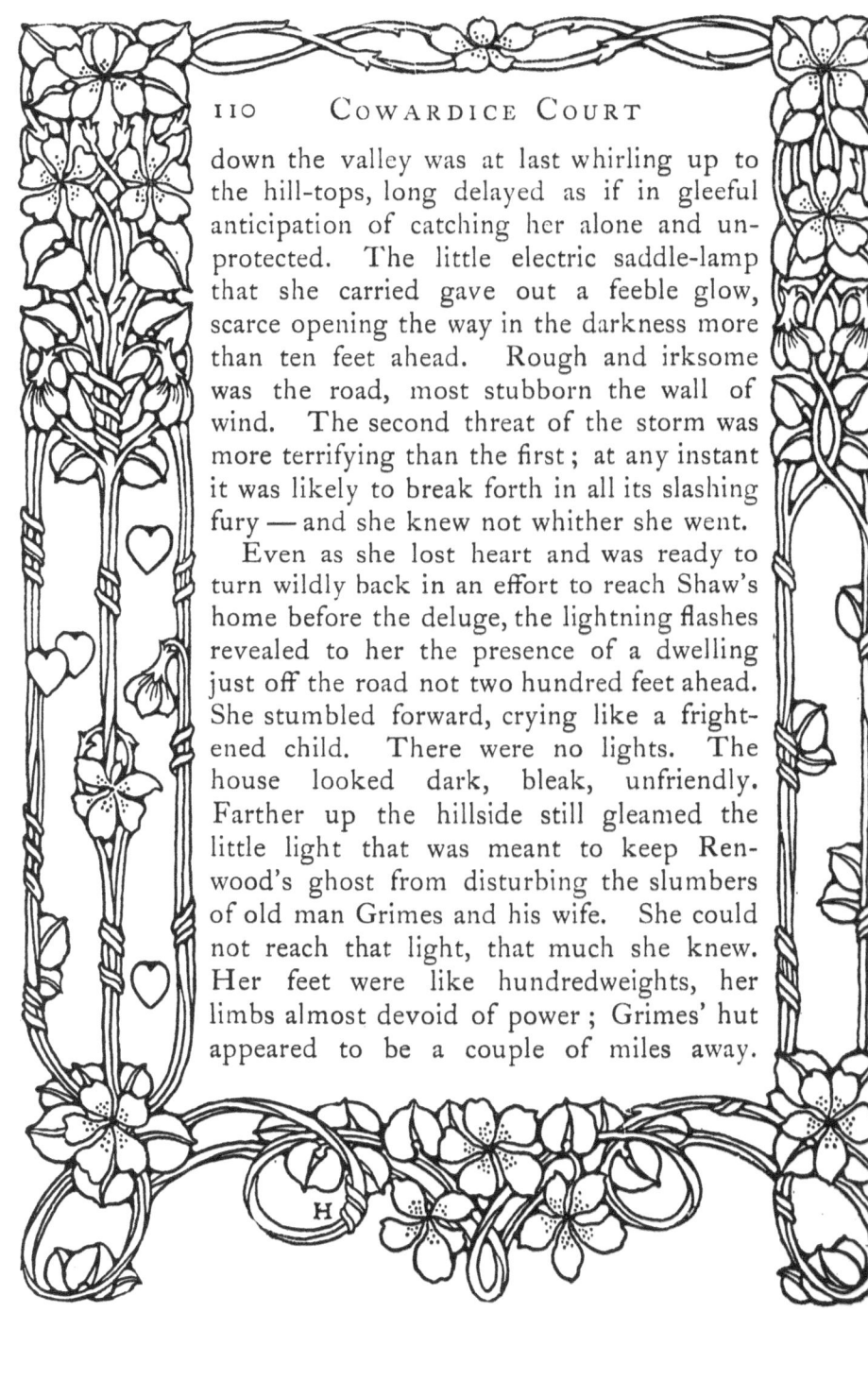

down the valley was at last whirling up to
the hill-tops, long delayed as if in gleeful
anticipation of catching her alone and un-
protected. The little electric saddle-lamp
that she carried gave out a feeble glow,
scarce opening the way in the darkness more
than ten feet ahead. Rough and irksome
was the road, most stubborn the wall of
wind. The second threat of the storm was
more terrifying than the first; at any instant
it was likely to break forth in all its slashing
fury — and she knew not whither she went.

Even as she lost heart and was ready to
turn wildly back in an effort to reach Shaw's
home before the deluge, the lightning flashes
revealed to her the presence of a dwelling
just off the road not two hundred feet ahead.
She stumbled forward, crying like a frightened child. There were no lights. The
house looked dark, bleak, unfriendly.
Farther up the hillside still gleamed the
little light that was meant to keep Renwood's ghost from disturbing the slumbers
of old man Grimes and his wife. She could
not reach that light, that much she knew.
Her feet were like hundredweights, her
limbs almost devoid of power; Grimes' hut
appeared to be a couple of miles away.

With a last, breathless effort, she turned off the road and floundered through weeds and brush until she came to what proved to be the rear of the darkened house. Long, low, rangy it reached off into the shadows, chilling in its loneliness. There was no time left for her to climb the flight of steps and pound on the back door. The rain was swishing in the trees with a hiss that forbade delay.

She threw herself, panting and terror-stricken, into the cave-like opening under the porch, her knees giving way after the supreme effort. The great storm broke as she crouched far back against the wall; her hands over her ears, her eyes tightly closed. She was safe from wind and rain, but not from the sounds of that awful conflict. The lantern lay at her feet, sending its ray out into the storm with the senseless fidelity of a beacon light.

"Penelope!" came a voice through the storm, and a second later a man plunged into the recess, crashing against the wall beside her. Something told her who it was, even before he dropped beside her and threw his strong arm about her shoulders. The sound of the storm died away as she buried her face on his shoulder and shivered so mightily that he was alarmed. With her

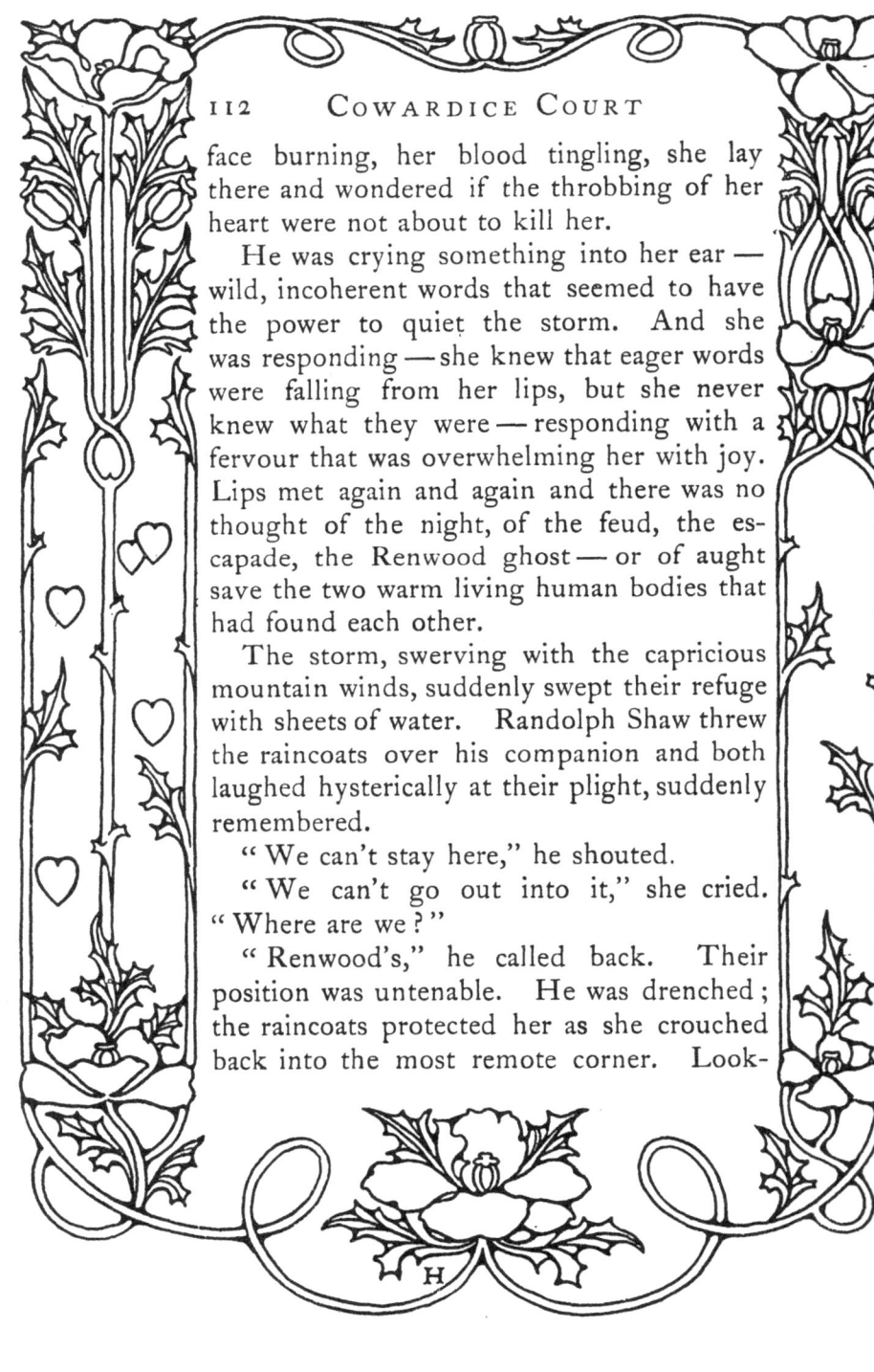

face burning, her blood tingling, she lay there and wondered if the throbbing of her heart were not about to kill her.

He was crying something into her ear — wild, incoherent words that seemed to have the power to quiet the storm. And she was responding — she knew that eager words were falling from her lips, but she never knew what they were — responding with a fervour that was overwhelming her with joy. Lips met again and again and there was no thought of the night, of the feud, the escapade, the Renwood ghost — or of aught save the two warm living human bodies that had found each other.

The storm, swerving with the capricious mountain winds, suddenly swept their refuge with sheets of water. Randolph Shaw threw the raincoats over his companion and both laughed hysterically at their plight, suddenly remembered.

"We can't stay here," he shouted.

"We can't go out into it," she cried. "Where are we?"

"Renwood's," he called back. Their position was untenable. He was drenched; the raincoats protected her as she crouched back into the most remote corner. Look-

ing about, he discovered a small door leading to the cellar. It opened the instant
he touched the latch. "Come, quick," he
cried, lifting her to her feet. "In here —
stoop! I have the light. This is the cellar.
I'll have to break down a door leading to
the upper part of the house, but that will
not be difficult. Here's an axe or two.
Good Lord, I'm soaked!"

"Whe— where are we going?" she
gasped, as he drew her across the earthern
floor.

"Upstairs. It's comfortable up there."
They were at the foot of the narrow stairway. She held back.

"Never! It's the — the haunted house!
I can't — Randolph."

"Pooh! Don't be afraid. I'm with
you, dearest."

"I know," she gulped. "But you have
only one arm. Oh, I can't!"

"It's all nonsense about ghosts. I've
slept here twenty times, Penelope. People
have seen my light and my shadow, that's
all. I'm a pretty substantial ghost."

"Oh, dear! What a disappointment.
And there are no spooks? Not even Mrs.
Renwood?"

H

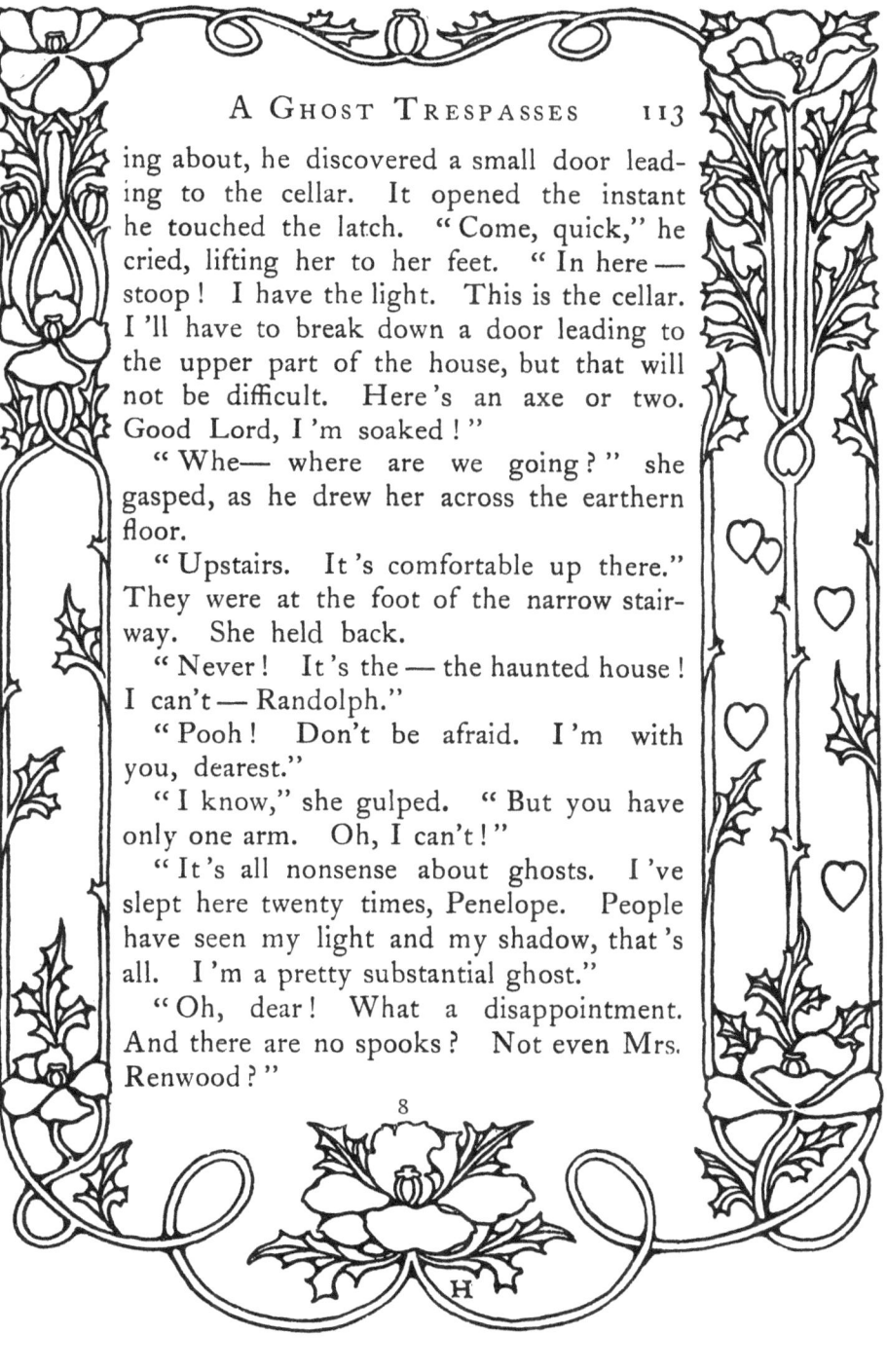

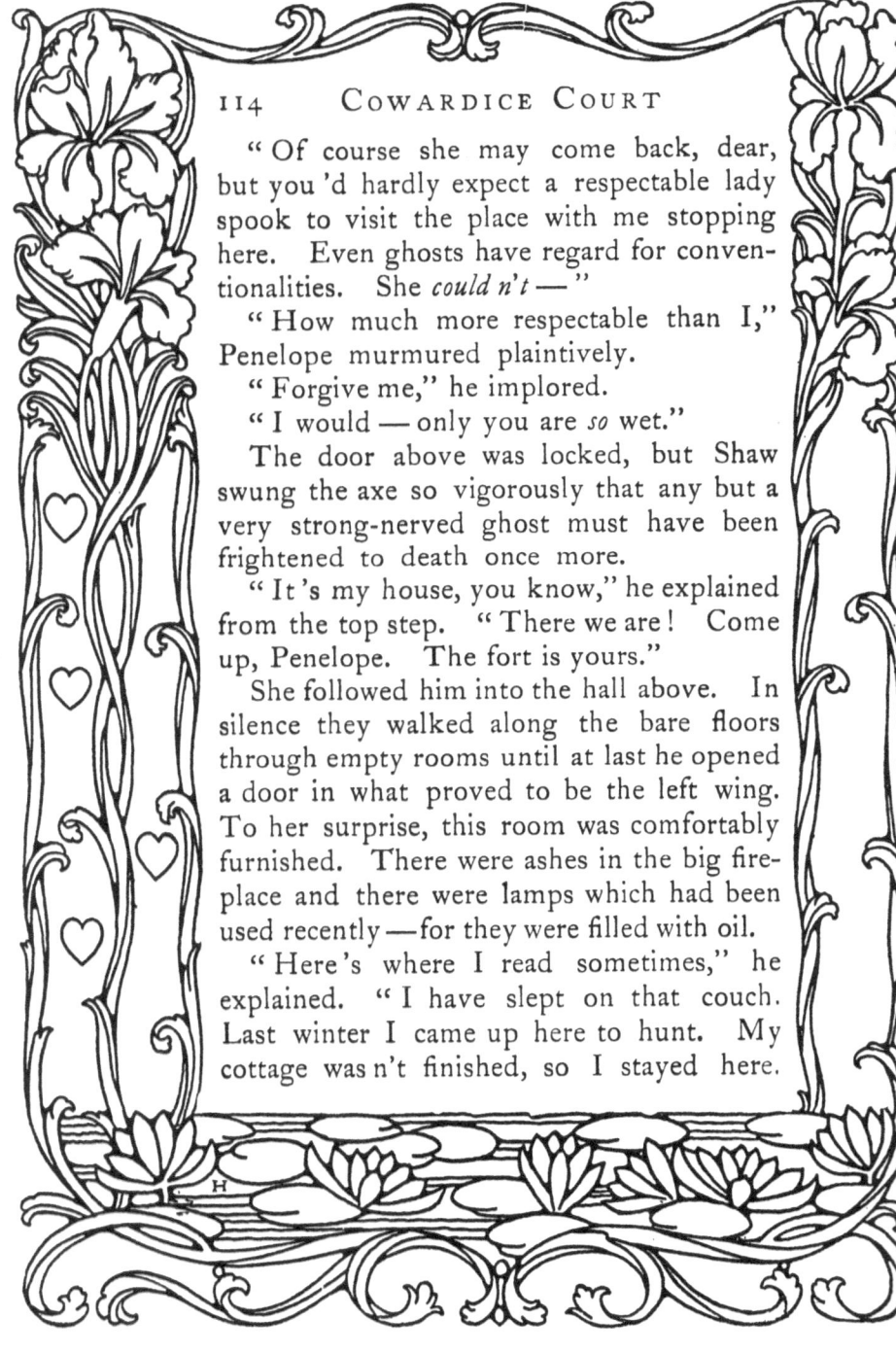

"Of course she may come back, dear, but you'd hardly expect a respectable lady spook to visit the place with me stopping here. Even ghosts have regard for conventionalities. She *could n't* —"

"How much more respectable than I," Penelope murmured plaintively.

"Forgive me," he implored.

"I would — only you are *so* wet."

The door above was locked, but Shaw swung the axe so vigorously that any but a very strong-nerved ghost must have been frightened to death once more.

"It's my house, you know," he explained from the top step. "There we are! Come up, Penelope. The fort is yours."

She followed him into the hall above. In silence they walked along the bare floors through empty rooms until at last he opened a door in what proved to be the left wing. To her surprise, this room was comfortably furnished. There were ashes in the big fireplace and there were lamps which had been used recently — for they were filled with oil.

"Here's where I read sometimes," he explained. "I have slept on that couch. Last winter I came up here to hunt. My cottage was n't finished, so I stayed here.

I'll confess I've heard strange sounds — now, don't shiver! Once or twice I've been a bit nervous, but I'm still alive, you see." He lighted the wicks in the two big lamps while she looked on with the chills creeping up and down her back. "I'll have a bully fire in the fireplace in just a minute."

"Let me help you," she suggested, coming quite close to him with uneasy glances over her shoulders.

Ten minutes later they were sitting before a roaring fire, quite content even though there was a suggestion of amazed ghosts lurking in the hallway behind them. No doubt old man Grimes and his wife, if they awoke in the course of the night, groaned deep prayers in response to the bright light from the windows of the haunted house. Shaw and Penelope smiled securely as they listened to the howling storm outside.

"Well, this *is* trespassing," she said, beaming a happy smile upon him.

"I shall be obliged to drive you out, alas," he said reflectively. "Do you recall my vow? As long as you are a Bazelhurst, I must perforce eject you."

"Not to-night!" she cried in mock dismay.

"But, as an alternative, you'll not be a Bazelhurst long," he went on eagerly, suddenly taking her hands into his, forgetful of the wounded left. "I'm going to try trespassing myself. To-morrow I'm going to see your brother. It's regular, you know. I'm going to tell the head of your clan that you are coming over to Shaw, heart and hand."

"Oh!" she exclaimed. "You — you — no, no! You must not do that!"

"But, my dear, you *are* going to marry me."

"Yes — I — suppose so," she murmured helplessly. "That isn't what I meant. I mean, it isn't necessary to ask Cecil. Ask me; I'll consent for him."

Half an hour passed. Then he went to the window and looked out into the storm.

"You *must* lie down and get some sleep," he insisted, coming back to her. "The storm's letting up, but we can't leave here for quite a while. I'll sit up and watch. I'm too happy to sleep." She protested, but her heavy eyes were his allies. Soon he sat alone before the fire; she slept sound on the broad couch in the corner, a steamer rug across her knees. A contented smile curved

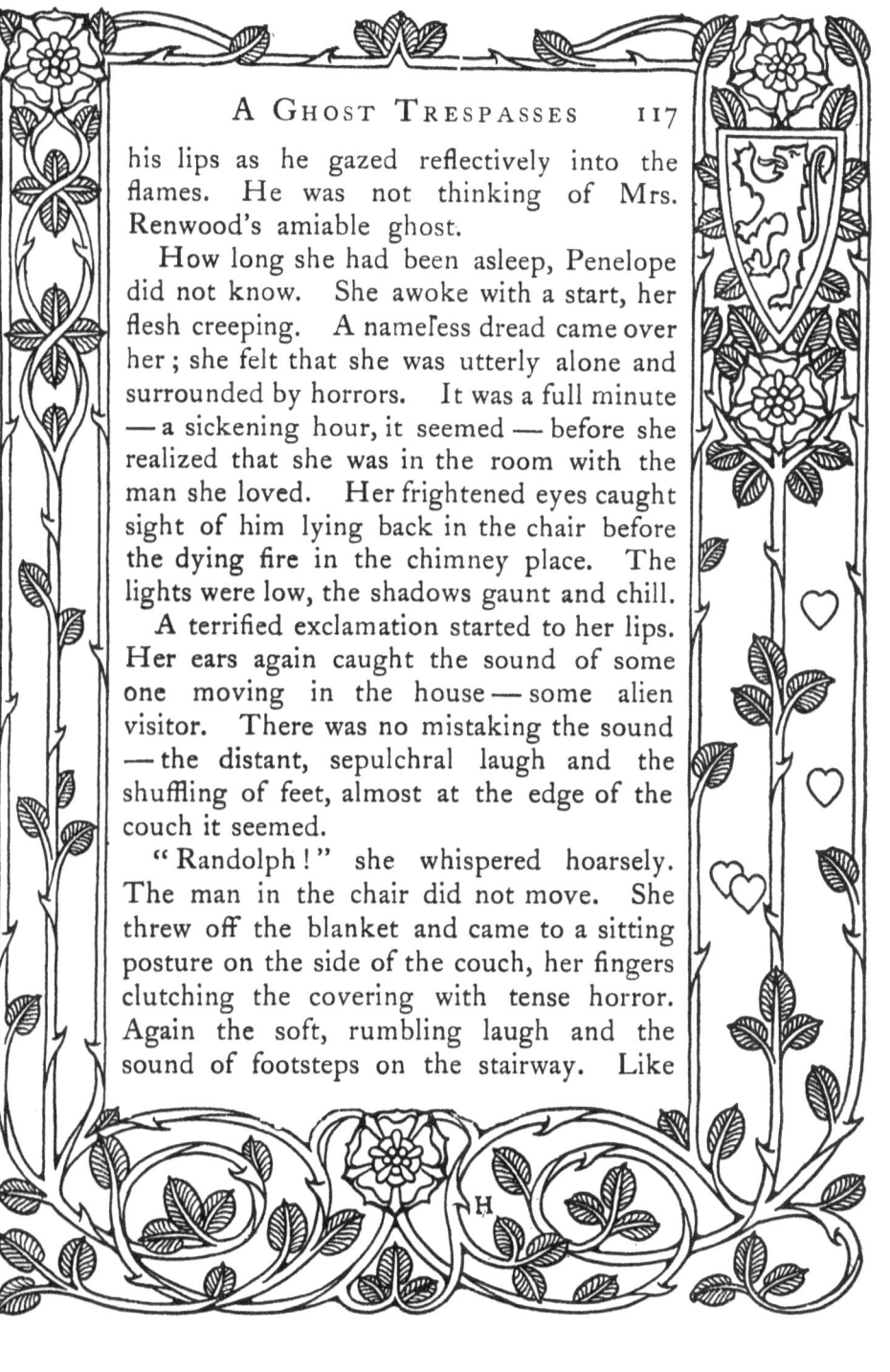

his lips as he gazed reflectively into the flames. He was not thinking of Mrs. Renwood's amiable ghost.

How long she had been asleep, Penelope did not know. She awoke with a start, her flesh creeping. A nameless dread came over her; she felt that she was utterly alone and surrounded by horrors. It was a full minute —a sickening hour, it seemed — before she realized that she was in the room with the man she loved. Her frightened eyes caught sight of him lying back in the chair before the dying fire in the chimney place. The lights were low, the shadows gaunt and chill.

A terrified exclamation started to her lips. Her ears again caught the sound of some one moving in the house — some alien visitor. There was no mistaking the sound — the distant, sepulchral laugh and the shuffling of feet, almost at the edge of the couch it seemed.

"Randolph!" she whispered hoarsely. The man in the chair did not move. She threw off the blanket and came to a sitting posture on the side of the couch, her fingers clutching the covering with tense horror. Again the soft, rumbling laugh and the sound of footsteps on the stairway. Like

a flash she sped across the room and
clutched frantically at Randolph's shoulders.   He awoke with an exclamation, staring bewildered into the horrified face above.

"The — the ghost!" she gasped, her
eyes glued upon the hall door.   He leaped
to his feet and threw his arms about her.

"You've had a bad dream," he said.
"What a beast I was to fall asleep.   Lord,
you're frightened half out of your wits.
Don't tremble so, dearest.   There's no
ghost.   Every one knows — "

"Listen — listen!" she whispered.   Together they stood motionless, almost breathless before the fire, the glow from which
threw their shadows across the room to
meet the mysterious invader.

"Good Lord," he muttered, unwilling to
believe his ears.   "There *is* some one in
the house.   I've — I've heard sounds here
before, but not like these."   Distinctly to
their startled ears came the low, subdued
murmur of a human voice and then unmis-
takable moans from the very depth of the
earth — from the grave, it seemed.

"Do you hear?" she whispered.   "Oh,
this dreadful place!   Take me away, Randolph, dear, — "

H

"Don't be afraid," he said, drawing her close. "There's nothing supernatural about those sounds. They come from lips as much alive as ours. I'll investigate." He grabbed the heavy poker from the chimney corner, and started toward the door. She followed close behind, his assurance restoring in a measure the courage that had temporarily deserted her.

In the hallway they paused to look out over the broad porch. The storm had died away, sighing its own requiem in the misty tree-tops. Dawn was not far away. A thick fog was rising to meet the first glance of day. In surprise Shaw looked at his watch, her face at his shoulder. It was after five o'clock.

"Ghosts turn in at midnight, dear," he said with a cheerful smile. "They don't keep such hours as these."

"But who can it be? There are no tramps in the mountains," she protested, glancing over her shoulder apprehensively.

"Listen! By Jove, that voice came from the cellar."

"And the lock is broken," she exclaimed. "But how silly of me! Ghosts don't stop for locks."

"I'll drop the bolts just the same," he

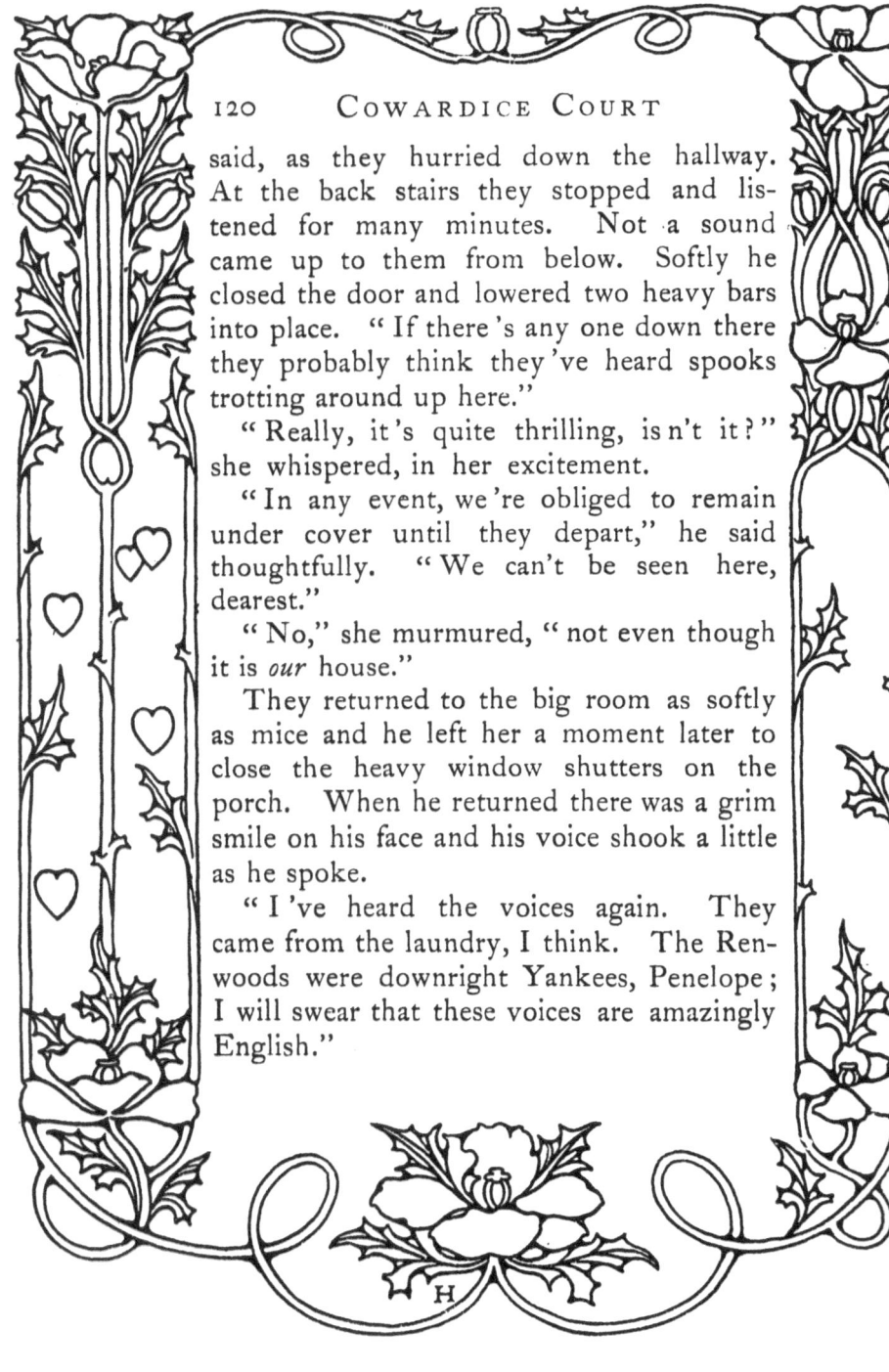

said, as they hurried down the hallway. At the back stairs they stopped and listened for many minutes. Not a sound came up to them from below. Softly he closed the door and lowered two heavy bars into place. " If there 's any one down there they probably think they 've heard spooks trotting around up here."

" Really, it 's quite thrilling, is n't it ? " she whispered, in her excitement.

" In any event, we 're obliged to remain under cover until they depart," he said thoughtfully. " We can't be seen here, dearest."

" No," she murmured, " not even though it is *our* house."

They returned to the big room as softly as mice and he left her a moment later to close the heavy window shutters on the porch. When he returned there was a grim smile on his face and his voice shook a little as he spoke.

" I 've heard the voices again. They came from the laundry, I think. The Renwoods were downright Yankees, Penelope ; I will swear that these voices are amazingly English."

CHAPTER VII

IN WHICH THE AUTHOR TRESPASSES

THIS narrative has quite as much to do with the Bazelhurst side of the controversy as it has with Shaw's. It is therefore but fair that the heroic invasion by Lord Cecil should receive equal consideration from the historian. Shaw's conquest of one member of the force opposing him was scarcely the result of bravery; on the other hand Lord Cecil's dash into the enemy's country was the very acme of intrepidity. Shaw had victory fairly thrust upon him; Lord Bazelhurst had a thousand obstacles to overcome before he could even so much as stand face to face with the enemy. Hence the expedition that started off in the wake of the deserter deserves more than passing mention.

Down the drive and out into the mountain road clattered the three horsemen. Lady

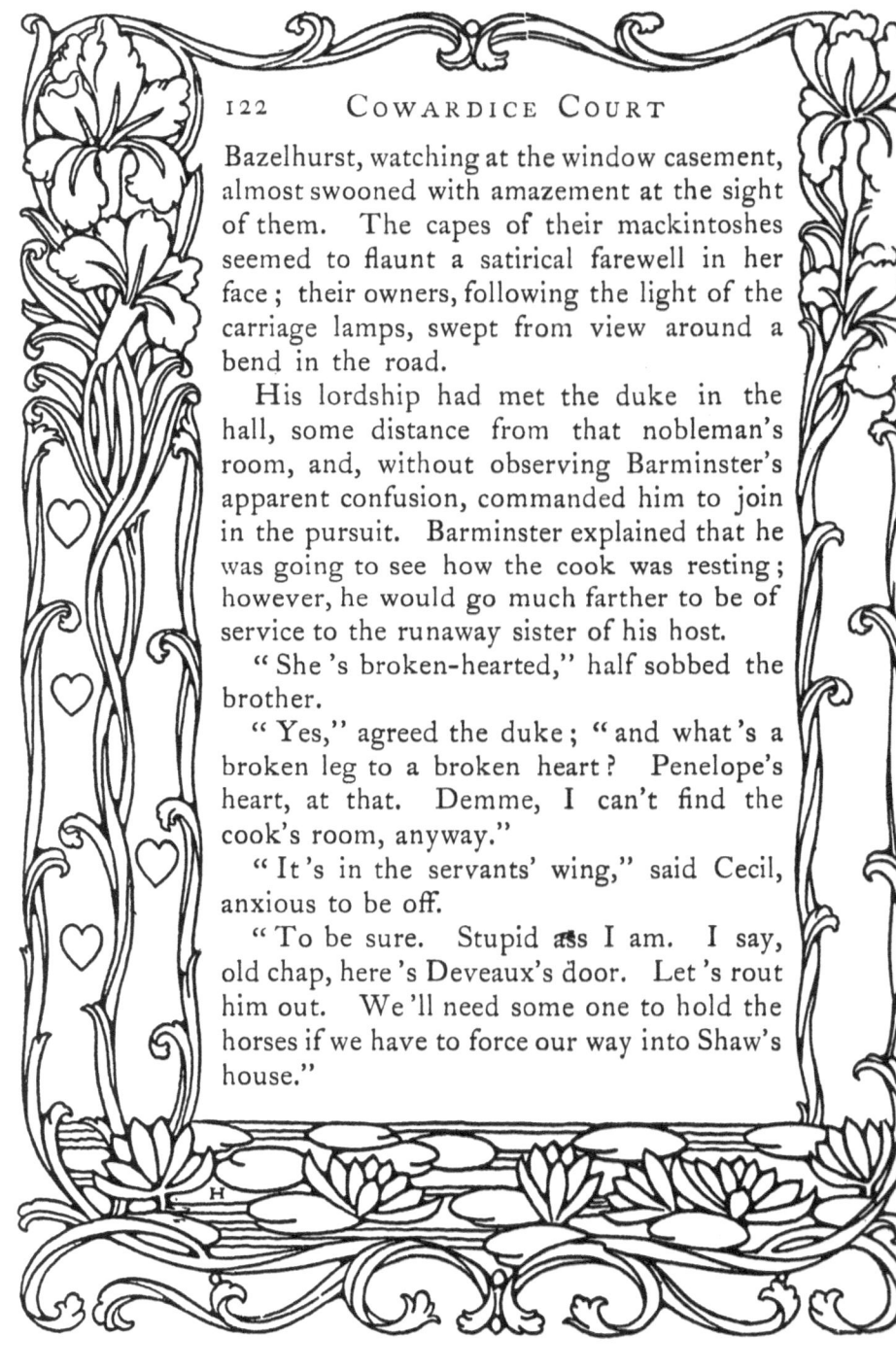

Bazelhurst, watching at the window casement, almost swooned with amazement at the sight of them. The capes of their mackintoshes seemed to flaunt a satirical farewell in her face; their owners, following the light of the carriage lamps, swept from view around a bend in the road.

His lordship had met the duke in the hall, some distance from that nobleman's room, and, without observing Barminster's apparent confusion, commanded him to join in the pursuit. Barminster explained that he was going to see how the cook was resting; however, he would go much farther to be of service to the runaway sister of his host.

"She's broken-hearted," half sobbed the brother.

"Yes," agreed the duke; "and what's a broken leg to a broken heart? Penelope's heart, at that. Demme, I can't find the cook's room, anyway."

"It's in the servants' wing," said Cecil, anxious to be off.

"To be sure. Stupid ass I am. I say, old chap, here's Deveaux's door. Let's rout him out. We'll need some one to hold the horses if we have to force our way into Shaw's house."

"'Good heaven, Randolph, go to him! He is hurt'"

The count was not thoroughly awake until he found himself in the saddle some time later; it is certain that he did not know until long afterward why they were riding off into the storm. He fell so far behind his companions in the run down the road that he could ask no questions. Right bravely the trio plunged into the dark territory over which the enemy ruled. It was the duke who finally brought the cavalcade to a halt by propounding a most sensible question.

"Are you sure she came this way, Cecil?"

"Certainly. This is Shaw's way, isn't it?"

"Did she say she was going to Shaw's?"

"Don't know. Evelyn told me. Hang it all, Barminster, come along. We'll never catch up to her."

"Is she riding?"

"No — horses all in."

"Do you know, we may have passed her. Deuce take it, Bazelhurst, if she's running away from us, you don't imagine she'd be such a silly fool as to stand in the road and wait for us. If she heard us she'd hide among the trees."

"But she's had an hour's start of us."

"Where ees she coming to?" asked the

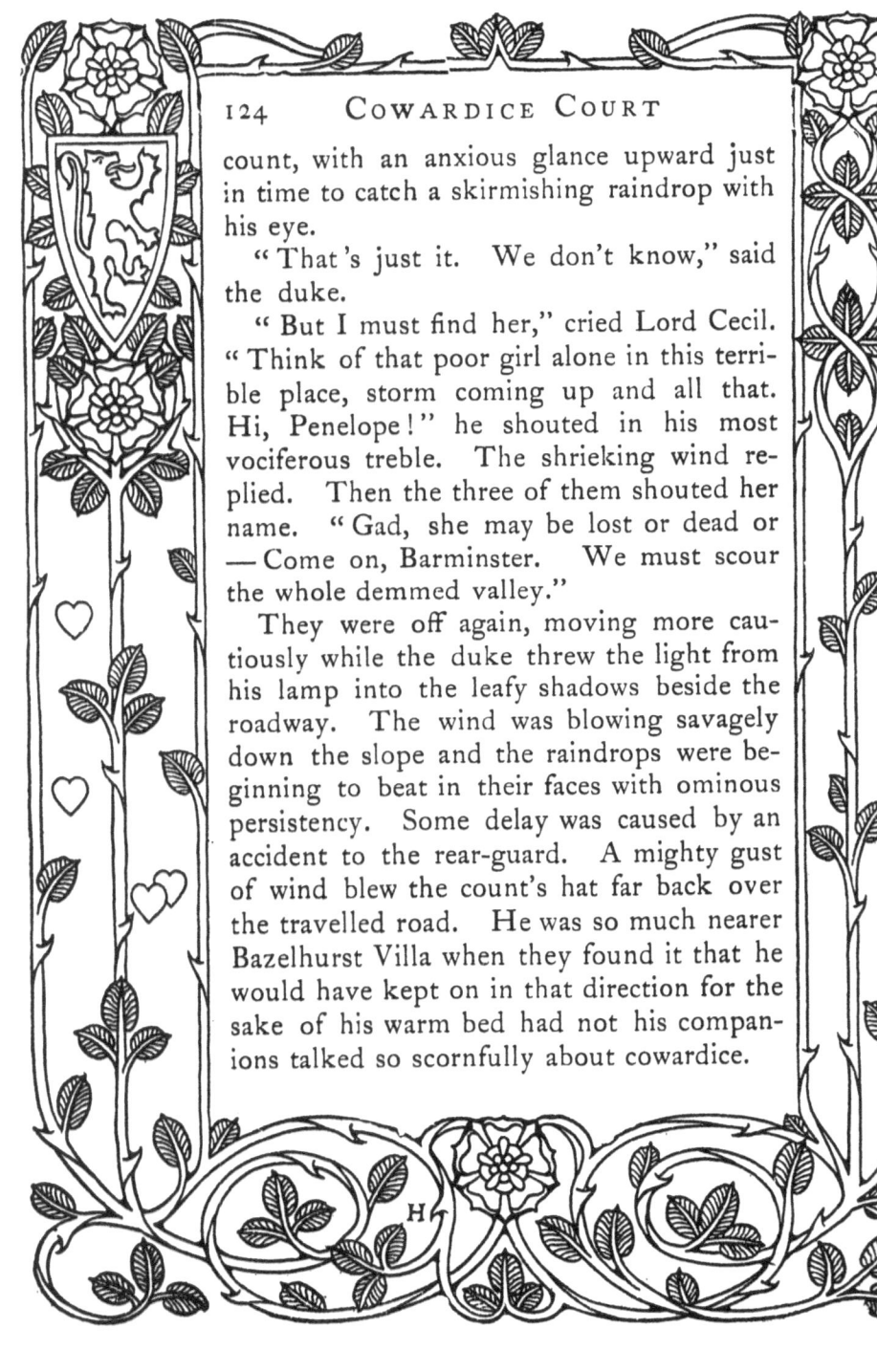

count, with an anxious glance upward just in time to catch a skirmishing raindrop with his eye.

"That's just it. We don't know," said the duke.

"But I must find her," cried Lord Cecil. "Think of that poor girl alone in this terrible place, storm coming up and all that. Hi, Penelope!" he shouted in his most vociferous treble. The shrieking wind replied. Then the three of them shouted her name. "Gad, she may be lost or dead or — Come on, Barminster. We must scour the whole demmed valley."

They were off again, moving more cautiously while the duke threw the light from his lamp into the leafy shadows beside the roadway. The wind was blowing savagely down the slope and the raindrops were beginning to beat in their faces with ominous persistency. Some delay was caused by an accident to the rear-guard. A mighty gust of wind blew the count's hat far back over the travelled road. He was so much nearer Bazelhurst Villa when they found it that he would have kept on in that direction for the sake of his warm bed had not his companions talked so scornfully about cowardice.

"He's like a wildcat to-night," said the duke in an aside to the little Frenchman, referring to his lordship. "Demme, I'd rather not cross him. You seem to forget that his sister is out in all this fury."

"Mon Dieu, but I do not forget. I would gif half my life to hold her in my arms thees eenstan'."

"Dem you, sir, I'd give her the other half if you dared try such a thing. We did n't fetch you along to hold her. You've got to hold the horses, that's all."

"Diable! How dare you to speak to—"

"What are you two rowing about?" demanded his lordship. "Come along! We're losing time. Sit on your hat, Deveaux."

Away they swept, Penelope's two admirers wrathfully barking at one another about satisfaction at some future hour.

The storm burst upon them in all its fury — the maddest, wildest storm they had known in all their lives. Terrified, half drowned, blown almost from the saddles, the trio finally found shelter in the lee of a shelving cliff just off the road. While they stood there shivering, clutching the bits of their well-nigh frantic horses, the glimmer

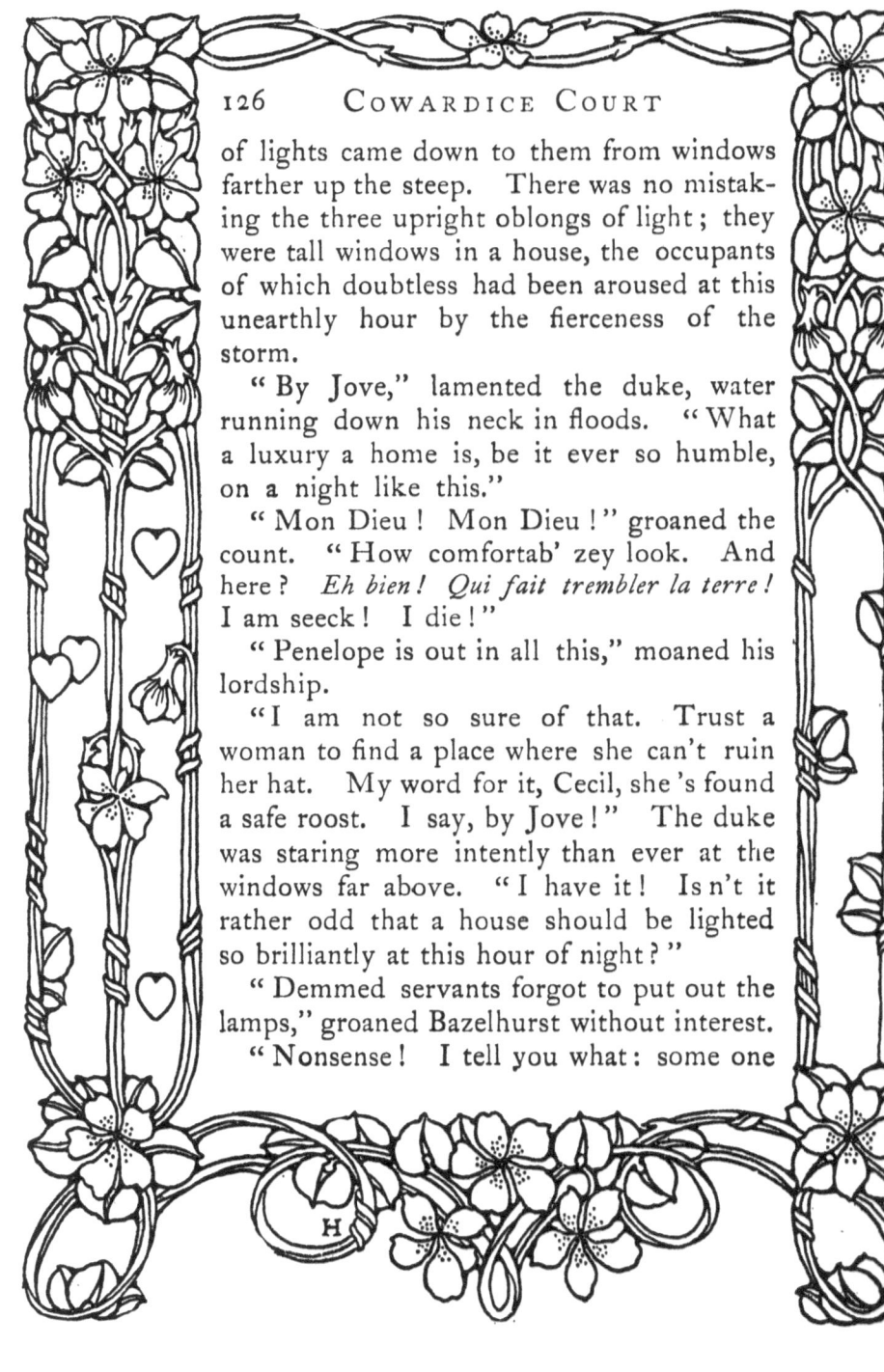

of lights came down to them from windows
farther up the steep.   There was no mistaking the three upright oblongs of light; they
were tall windows in a house, the occupants
of which doubtless had been aroused at this
unearthly hour by the fierceness of the
storm.

"By Jove," lamented the duke, water
running down his neck in floods.   "What
a luxury a home is, be it ever so humble,
on a night like this."

"Mon Dieu! Mon Dieu!" groaned the
count.   "How comfortab' zey look.   And
here?   *Eh bien! Qui fait trembler la terre!*
I am seeck!   I die!"

"Penelope is out in all this," moaned his
lordship.

"I am not so sure of that.   Trust a
woman to find a place where she can't ruin
her hat.   My word for it, Cecil, she's found
a safe roost.   I say, by Jove!"   The duke
was staring more intently than ever at the
windows far above.   "I have it!   Isn't it
rather odd that a house should be lighted
so brilliantly at this hour of night?"

"Demmed servants forgot to put out the
lamps," groaned Bazelhurst without interest.

"Nonsense!   I tell you what: some one

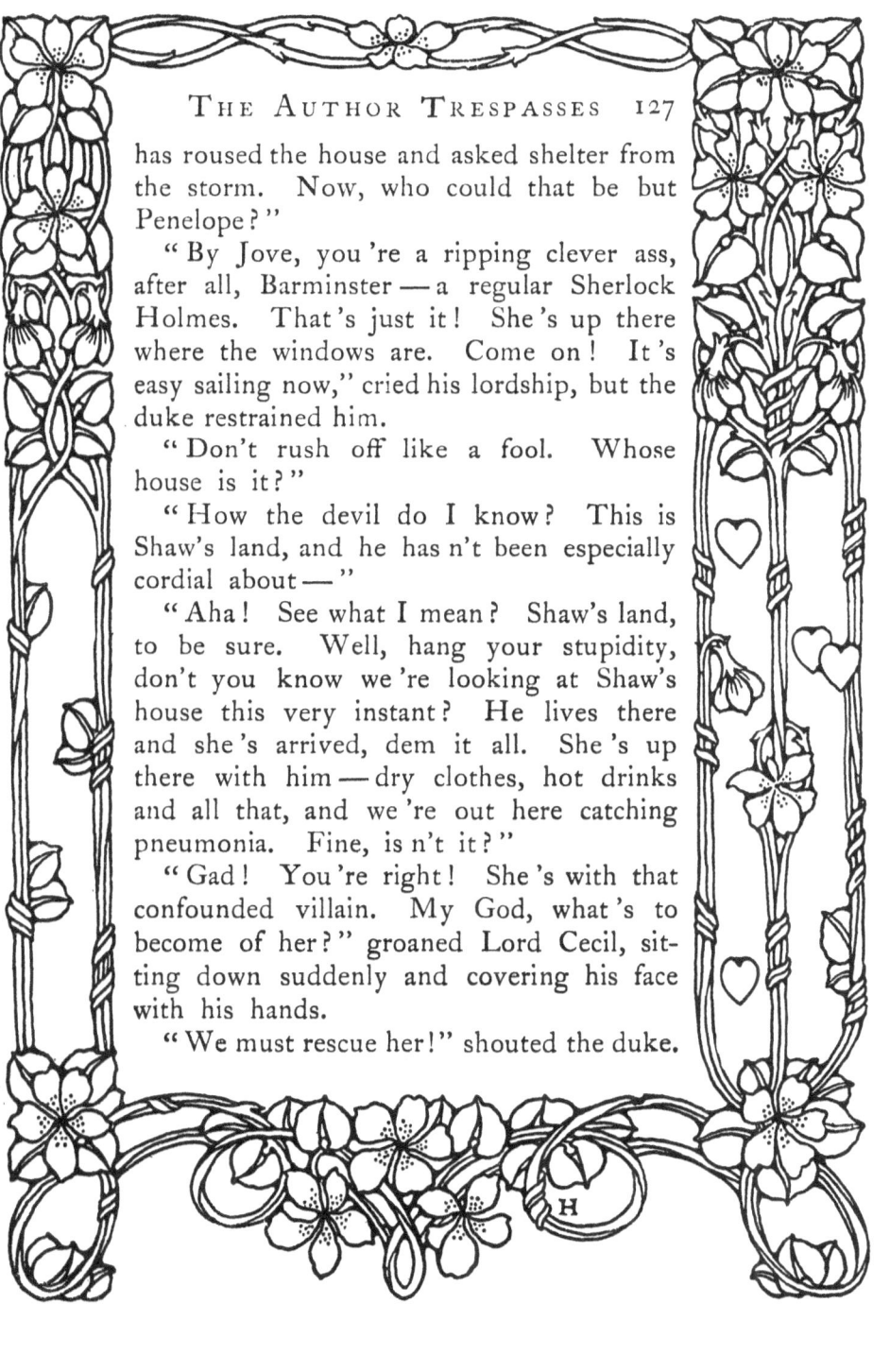

has roused the house and asked shelter from the storm. Now, who could that be but Penelope?"

"By Jove, you're a ripping clever ass, after all, Barminster — a regular Sherlock Holmes. That's just it! She's up there where the windows are. Come on! It's easy sailing now," cried his lordship, but the duke restrained him.

"Don't rush off like a fool. Whose house is it?"

"How the devil do I know? This is Shaw's land, and he has n't been especially cordial about — "

"Aha! See what I mean? Shaw's land, to be sure. Well, hang your stupidity, don't you know we're looking at Shaw's house this very instant? He lives there and she's arrived, dem it all. She's up there with him — dry clothes, hot drinks and all that, and we're out here catching pneumonia. Fine, is n't it?"

"Gad! You're right! She's with that confounded villain. My God, what's to become of her?" groaned Lord Cecil, sitting down suddenly and covering his face with his hands.

"We must rescue her!" shouted the duke.

H

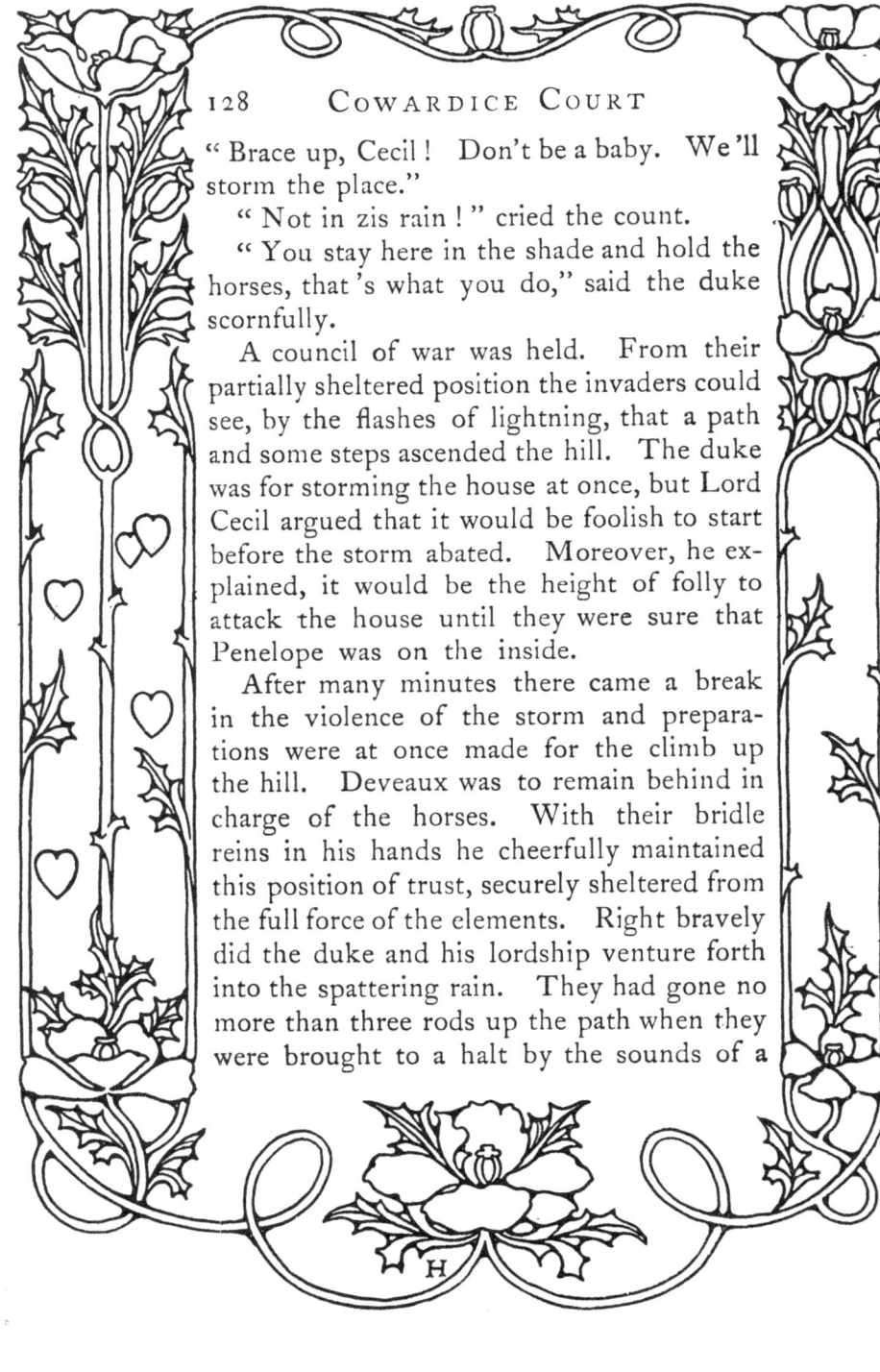

"Brace up, Cecil! Don't be a baby. We'll storm the place."

"Not in zis rain!" cried the count.

"You stay here in the shade and hold the horses, that's what you do," said the duke scornfully.

A council of war was held. From their partially sheltered position the invaders could see, by the flashes of lightning, that a path and some steps ascended the hill. The duke was for storming the house at once, but Lord Cecil argued that it would be foolish to start before the storm abated. Moreover, he explained, it would be the height of folly to attack the house until they were sure that Penelope was on the inside.

After many minutes there came a break in the violence of the storm and preparations were at once made for the climb up the hill. Deveaux was to remain behind in charge of the horses. With their bridle reins in his hands he cheerfully maintained this position of trust, securely sheltered from the full force of the elements. Right bravely did the duke and his lordship venture forth into the spattering rain. They had gone no more than three rods up the path when they were brought to a halt by the sounds of a

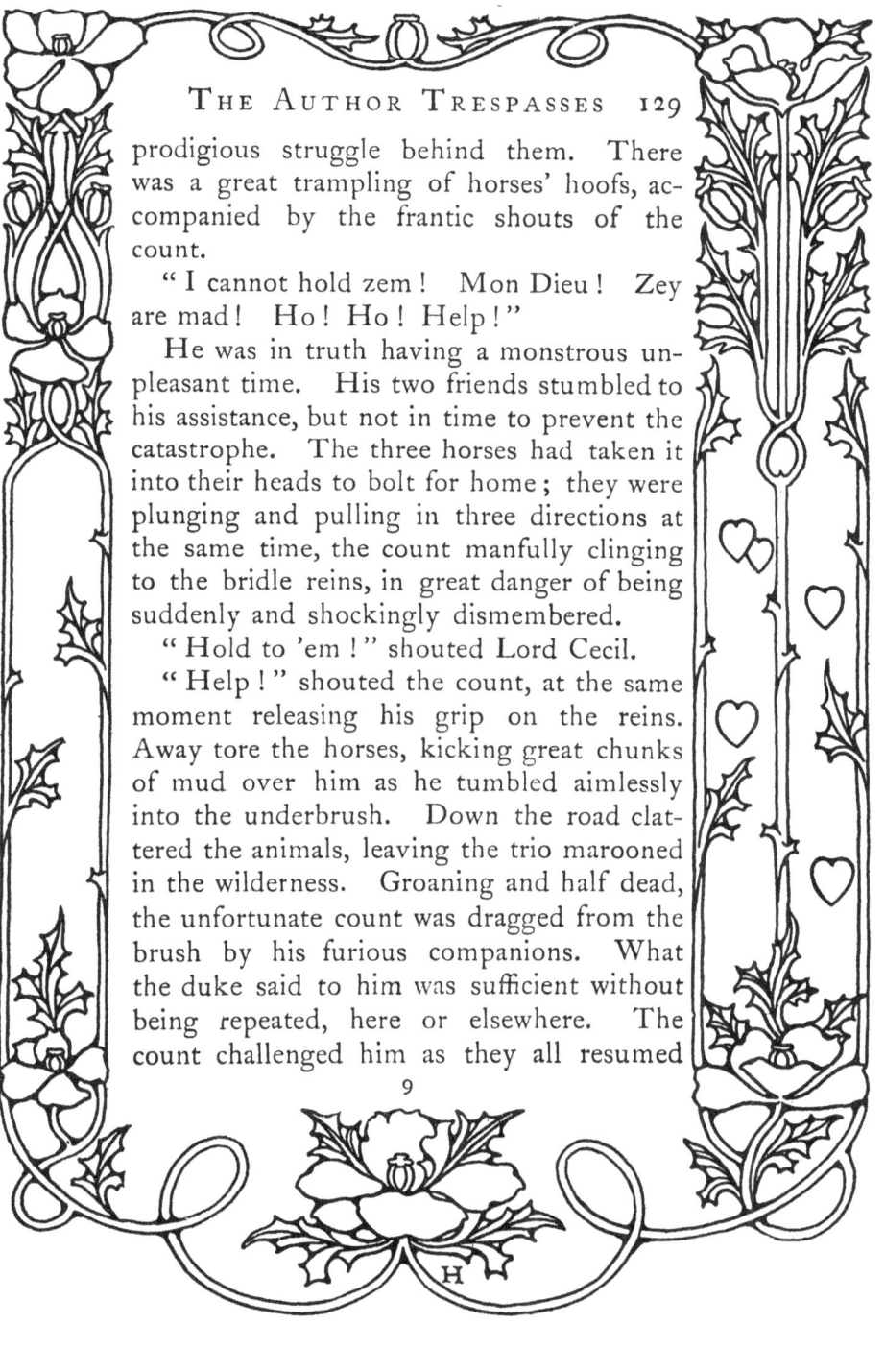

prodigious struggle behind them. There was a great trampling of horses' hoofs, accompanied by the frantic shouts of the count.

"I cannot hold zem! Mon Dieu! Zey are mad! Ho! Ho! Help!"

He was in truth having a monstrous unpleasant time. His two friends stumbled to his assistance, but not in time to prevent the catastrophe. The three horses had taken it into their heads to bolt for home; they were plunging and pulling in three directions at the same time, the count manfully clinging to the bridle reins, in great danger of being suddenly and shockingly dismembered.

"Hold to 'em!" shouted Lord Cecil.

"Help!" shouted the count, at the same moment releasing his grip on the reins. Away tore the horses, kicking great chunks of mud over him as he tumbled aimlessly into the underbrush. Down the road clattered the animals, leaving the trio marooned in the wilderness. Groaning and half dead, the unfortunate count was dragged from the brush by his furious companions. What the duke said to him was sufficient without being repeated, here or elsewhere. The count challenged him as they all resumed

9

H

the march up the hill to visit the house with the lighted windows.

"Here is my card, m'sieur," he grated furiously.

"Demme, I know you!" roared the duke. "Keep your card and we'll send it in to announce our arrival to Shaw."

In due course of time, after many slips and falls, they reached the front yard of the house on the hillside. It was still raining lightly; the thunder and lightning were crashing away noisily farther up the valley. Cautiously they approached through the weeds and brush.

"By Jove!" exclaimed his lordship, coming to a standstill. He turned the light of his lantern toward the front elevation of the house. "Every door and window, except these three, are boarded up. It can't be Shaw's home."

"That's right, old chap. Deuced queer, eh? I say, Deveaux, step up and pound on the door. You've got a card, you know."

"Que diable!" exclaimed the count, sinking into the background.

"We might reconnoitre a bit," said Bazelhurst. "Have a look at the rear, you know."

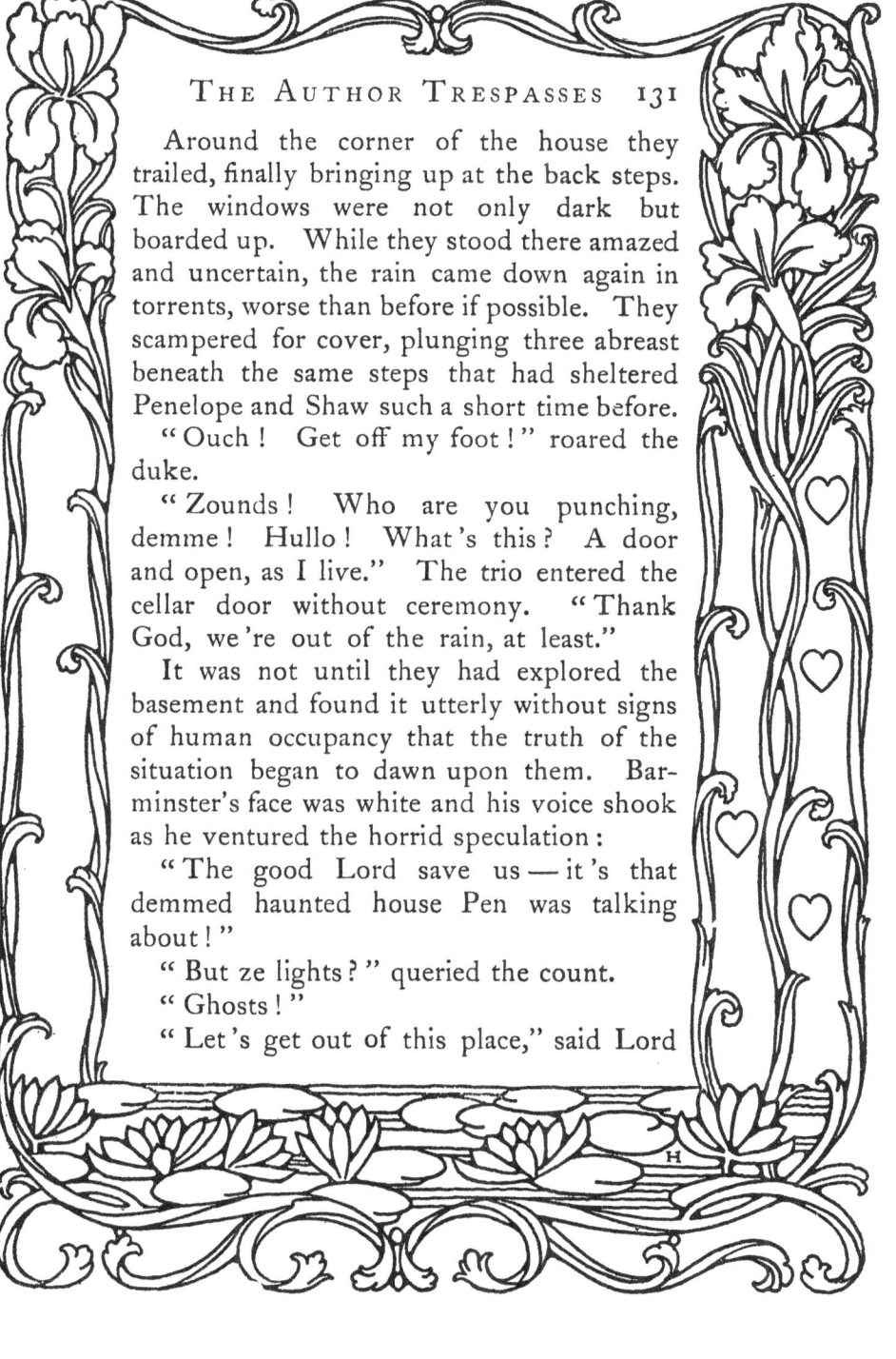

Around the corner of the house they trailed, finally bringing up at the back steps. The windows were not only dark but boarded up. While they stood there amazed and uncertain, the rain came down again in torrents, worse than before if possible. They scampered for cover, plunging three abreast beneath the same steps that had sheltered Penelope and Shaw such a short time before.

"Ouch! Get off my foot!" roared the duke.

"Zounds! Who are you punching, demme! Hullo! What's this? A door and open, as I live." The trio entered the cellar door without ceremony. "Thank God, we're out of the rain, at least."

It was not until they had explored the basement and found it utterly without signs of human occupancy that the truth of the situation began to dawn upon them. Barminster's face was white and his voice shook as he ventured the horrid speculation:

"The good Lord save us — it's that demmed haunted house Pen was talking about!"

"But ze lights?" queried the count.

"Ghosts!"

"Let's get out of this place," said Lord

Bazelhurst, moving toward the door. "It's
that beastly Renwood house. They say he
comes back and murders her every night
or so."

"Mon Dieu!"

"Penelope is n't here. Let's move on,"
agreed the duke readily. But even fear of
the supernatural was not strong enough to
drive them out into the blinding storm.
"I say! Look ahead there. By Harry,
there's Shaw's place."

Peering through the door they saw for
the first time the many lights in Shaw's
windows, scarce a quarter of a mile away.
For a long time they stood and gazed at
the distant windows. Dejectedly they sat
down, backs to the wall, and waited for the
storm to spend its fury. Wet, cold, and
tired, they finally dozed. It was Lord
Cecil who first saw the signs of dawn. The
rain storm had come to a mysterious end,
but a heavy fog in its stead loomed up.
He aroused his companions and with many
groans of anguish they prepared to venture
forth into the white wall beyond.

Just as they were taking a last look about
the wretched cellar something happened that
would have brought terror to the stoutest

heart.   A wild, appalling shriek came from somewhere above, the cry of a mortal soul in agony.

The next instant three human forms shot through the narrow door and out into the fog, hair on end, eyes bulging but sightless, legs travelling like the wind and as purposeless.   It mattered not that the way was hidden ; it mattered less that weeds, brush, and stumps lurked in ambush for unwary feet.   They fled into the foggy dangers without a thought of what lay before them — only of what stalked behind them.

Upstairs Randolph Shaw lay back against the wall and shook with laughter.   Penelope's convulsed face was glued to the kitchen window, her eyes peering into the fog beyond.   Shadowy figures leaped into the white mantle ; the crash of brush came back to her ears, and then, like the barking of a dog, there arose from the mystic gray the fast diminishing cry :

" Help ! Help ! Help ! "   Growing fainter and sharper the cry at last was lost in the phantom desert.

They stood at the window and watched the fog lift, gray and forbidding, until the trees and road were discernible.   Then, arm

in arm, they set forth across the wet way
toward Shaw's cottage.   The mists cleared
as they walked along, the sun peeped through
the hills as if afraid to look upon the devas-
tation of the night; all the world seemed at
peace once more.

"Poor Cecil!" she sighed.   "It was cruel
of you."   In the roadway they found a hat
which she at once identified as the count's.
Farther on there was a carriage lamp, and
later a mackintosh which had been cast aside
as an impediment.   "Oh, it *was* cruel!"
She smiled, however, in retrospection.

An hour later they stood together on the
broad porch, looking out over the green,
glistening hills.   The warm fresh air filled
their lungs and happiness was overcrowding
their hearts.   In every direction were signs
of the storm's fury.   Great trees lay blasted,
limbs and branches were scattered over the
ground, wide fissures split the roadway
across which the deluge had rushed on its
way down the slope.

But Penelope was warm and dry and safe
after her thrilling night.   A hot breakfast was
being prepared for them; trouble seemed to
have gone its way with the elements.

"If I were only sure that nothing serious

had happened to Cecil," she murmured anxiously.

"I'm sorry, dear, for that screech of mine," he apologized.

Suddenly he started and gazed intently in the direction of the haunted house. A man —a sorry figure—was slowly, painfully approaching from the edge of the wood scarce a hundred yards away. In his hand he carried a stick to which was attached a white cloth — doubtless a handkerchief. He was hatless and limped perceptibly. The two on the porch watched his approach in amazed silence.

"It's Cecil!" whispered Penelope in horror-struck tones. "Good heaven, Randolph, go to him! He is hurt."

It was Lord Bazelhurst. As Shaw hurried down the drive to meet him, no thought of the feud in mind, two beings even more hopelessly dilapidated ventured from the wood and hobbled up behind the truce-bearer, who had now paused to lift his shoulders into a position of dignity and defiance. Shaw's heart was touched. The spectacle was enough to melt the prejudice of any adversary. Lord Cecil's knees trembled; his hand shook as if in a chill. Mud-

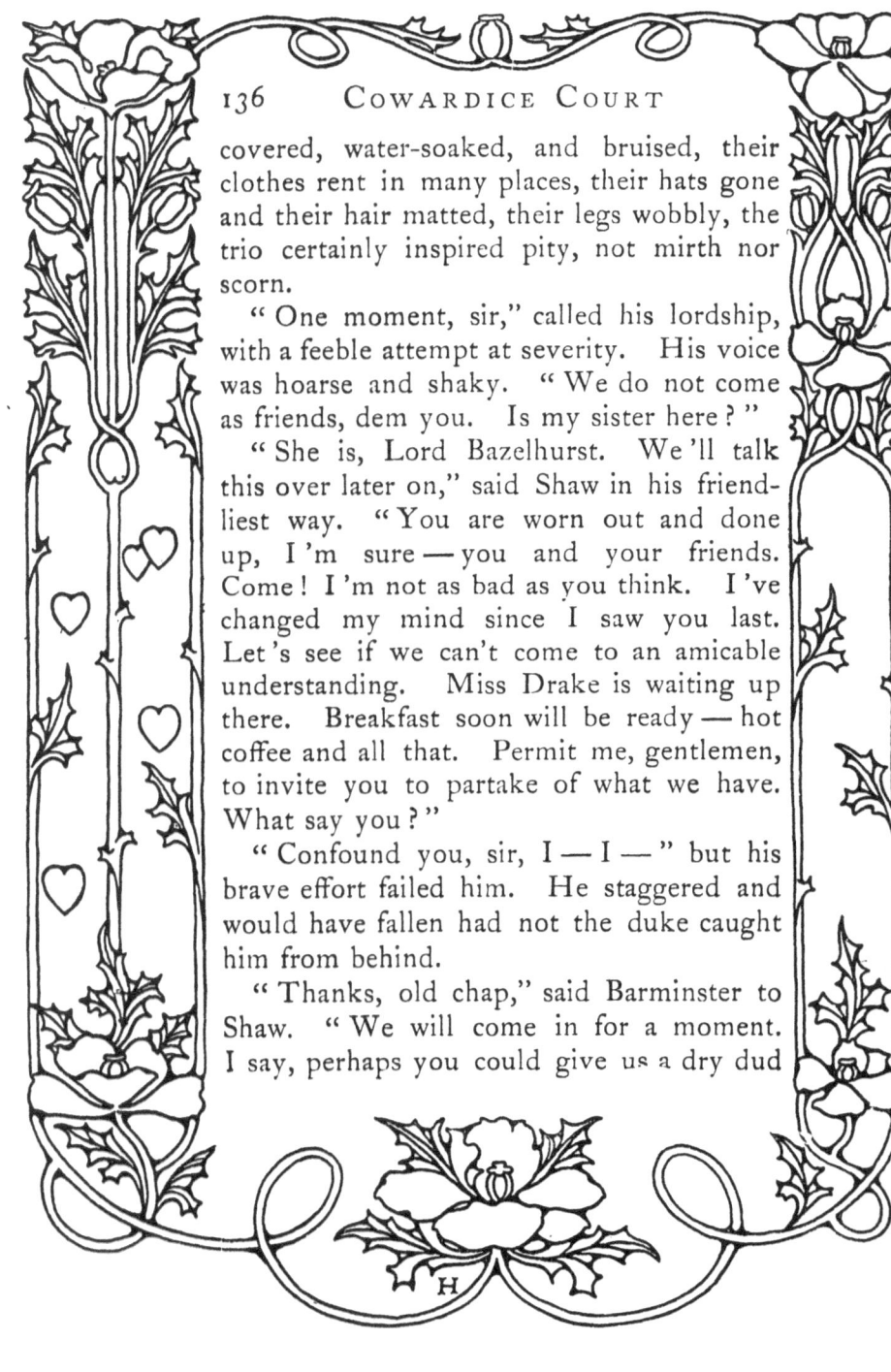

covered, water-soaked, and bruised, their
clothes rent in many places, their hats gone
and their hair matted, their legs wobbly, the
trio certainly inspired pity, not mirth nor
scorn.

"One moment, sir," called his lordship,
with a feeble attempt at severity. His voice
was hoarse and shaky. "We do not come
as friends, dem you. Is my sister here?"

"She is, Lord Bazelhurst. We'll talk
this over later on," said Shaw in his friend-
liest way. "You are worn out and done
up, I'm sure — you and your friends.
Come! I'm not as bad as you think. I've
changed my mind since I saw you last.
Let's see if we can't come to an amicable
understanding. Miss Drake is waiting up
there. Breakfast soon will be ready — hot
coffee and all that. Permit me, gentlemen,
to invite you to partake of what we have.
What say you?"

"Confound you, sir, I — I — " but his
brave effort failed him. He staggered and
would have fallen had not the duke caught
him from behind.

"Thanks, old chap," said Barminster to
Shaw. "We will come in for a moment.
I say, perhaps you could give us a dry dud

or two.   Bazelhurst is in a bad way and so is the count.   It was a devil of a storm."

"*Mon Dieu! c'était épouvantable!*" groaned the count.

Penelope came down from the porch to meet them.   Without a word she took her brother's arm.   He stared at her with growing resentment.

"Dem it all, Pen," he chattered, "you're not at all wet, are you?   Look at me!   All on your account, too."

"Dear old Cecil!   All on Evelyn's account, you mean," she said softly, wistfully.

"I shall have an understanding with her when we get home," he said earnestly. "She shan't treat my sister like this again."

"No," said Shaw from the other side; "she shan't."

"By Jove, Shaw, are you *with* me?" demanded his lordship in surprise.

"Depends on whether you are with me," said the other.   Penelope flushed warmly.

Later on, three chastened but ludicrous objects shuffled into the breakfast-room, where Shaw and Penelope awaited them. In passing, it is only necessary to say that Randolph Shaw's clothes did not fit the gentlemen to whom they were loaned.

H

Bazelhurst was utterly lost in the folds of a gray tweed, while the count was obliged to roll up the sleeves and legs of a frock suit which fitted Shaw rather too snugly. The duke, larger than the others, was passably fair in an old swallow-tail coat and brown trousers. They were clean, but there was a strong odour of arnica about them. Each wore, besides, an uncertain, sheepish smile.

Hot coffee, chops, griddle cakes, and maple syrup soon put the contending forces at their ease. Bazelhurst so far forgot himself as to laugh amiably at his host's jokes. The count responded in his most piquant dialect, and the duke swore by an ever-useful Lord Harry that he had never tasted such a breakfast.

"By Jove, Pen," exclaimed her brother, in rare good humour, "it's almost a sin to take you away from such good cooking as this."

"You're not going to take her away, however," said Shaw. "She has come to stay."

There was a stony silence. Coffee-cups hung suspended in the journey to mouths, and three pairs of eyes stared blankly at the smiling speaker.

"What — what the devil do you mean,

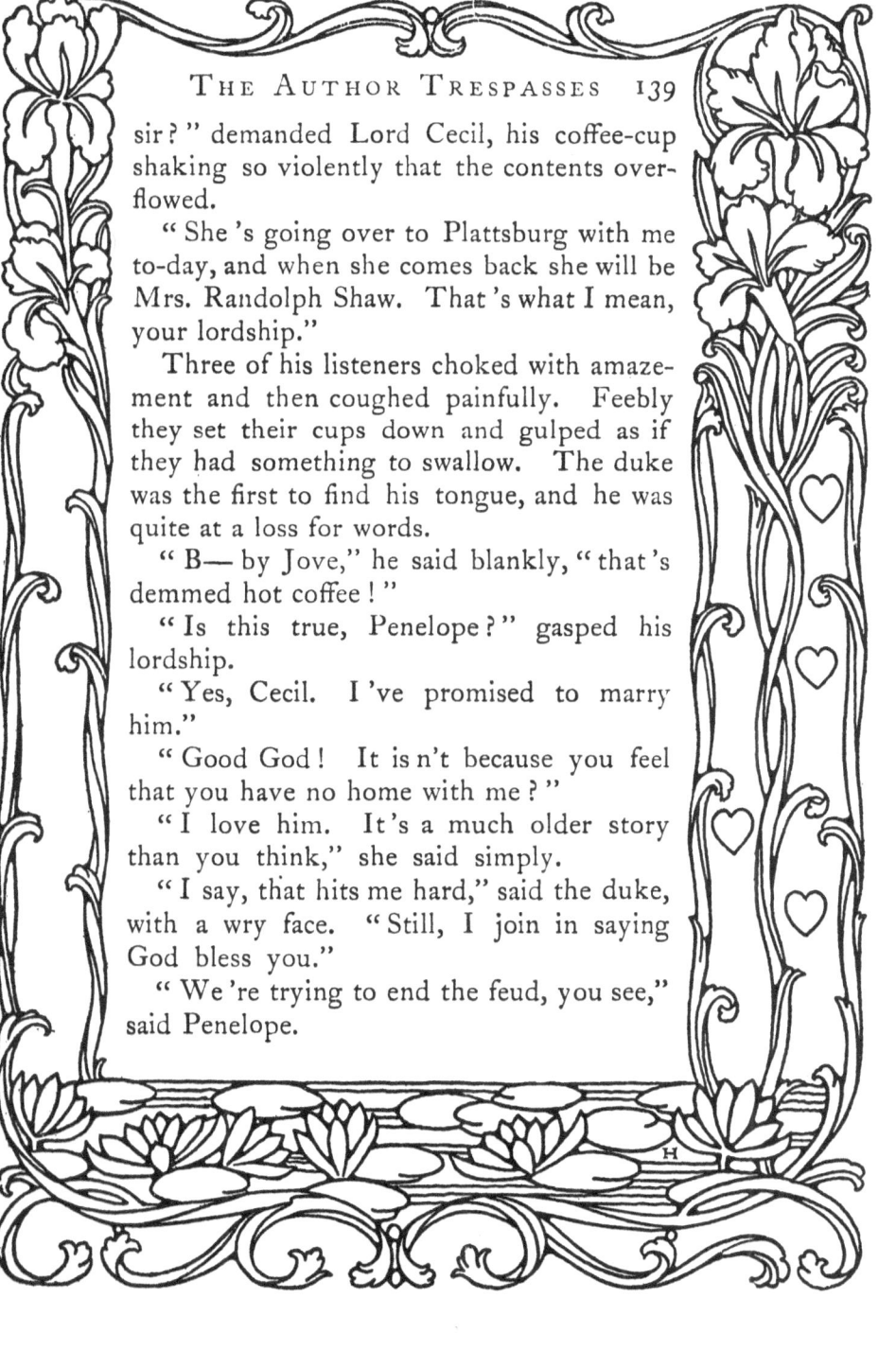

sir ? " demanded Lord Cecil, his coffee-cup
shaking so violently that the contents over-
flowed.

"She 's going over to Plattsburg with me
to-day, and when she comes back she will be
Mrs. Randolph Shaw. That 's what I mean,
your lordship."

Three of his listeners choked with amazement and then coughed painfully. Feebly
they set their cups down and gulped as if
they had something to swallow. The duke
was the first to find his tongue, and he was
quite at a loss for words.

"B— by Jove," he said blankly, "that 's
demmed hot coffee ! "

"Is this true, Penelope?" gasped his
lordship.

"Yes, Cecil. I 've promised to marry
him."

"Good God ! It is n't because you feel
that you have no home with me ? "

"I love him. It 's a much older story
than you think," she said simply.

"I say, that hits me hard," said the duke,
with a wry face. "Still, I join in saying
God bless you."

"We 're trying to end the feud, you see,"
said Penelope.

Tears came into his lordship's pale eyes. He looked first at one and then at the other, and then silently extended his hand to Randolph Shaw. He wrung it vigorously for a long time before speaking. Then, as if throwing a weight off his mind, he remarked:

"I say, Shaw, I'm sorry about that dog. I've got an English bull-terrier down there that's taken a ribbon or so. If you don't mind, I'll send him up to you. He — he knows Penelope."

www.ingramcontent.com/pod-product-compliance
Lightning Source LLC
Chambersburg PA
CBHW020649180626
46816CB00003B/1196